Ninety Day Wonder

NINETY DAY WONDER

Lynn Ellen Doxon

Artemesia
Publishing

ISBN: 978-1-951122-38-6 (paperback)
ISBN: 978-1-951122-47-8 (ebook)
LCCN: 2022939432
Copyright © 2022 by Lynn Ellen Doxon
Cover Illustration © 2022 by Elisa Pinizzotto
Front cover photo from the author's family photo collection, taken in 1942.
Back cover photo of a 3" antiaircraft gun is from Kevin Nolan's collection on coastartilleryimages.com and is used with permission.
Cover Design: Geoff Habiger

Artemesia Publishing
9 Mockingbird Hill Rd
Tijeras, New Mexico 87059
www.apbooks.net
info@artemesiapublishing.com

Content Notice: This book contains descriptions of war and trauma that may be disturbing to some people. The book also uses racial slurs that were in use at the time that this book is set. We have kept this language to reflect its usage at the time, but the author and the publisher condemn the usage of such language whether it was used in the past or today.

Dedicated to
Lieutenant Colonel Kermit Lynn Doxon, U.S. Army Retired
1914 - 1995

CHAPTER 1
ST CLAIR

I sat down on the step and puffed on the hand-rolled cigarette Brasseux passed around. I sniffed the loose leaves in the bag next to me and recognized the distinctive aroma of marijuana. It grew wild on the ditch banks at home, and Granny used it for headaches and added it to her cough medicine.

The cigarette came around to me again.

"I really shouldn't," I said.

"Aw, come on, Sinclair. Don't be such a fuddy-duddy. Take another drag."

I did and passed it on to Carson, next to me.

My eyes dropped to the letters in my hand, the one from Morris, my best pre-Pearl Harbor buddy, sitting on top. I became mesmerized with the letter as it sat unopened in my hands, thinking of Morris, now attending flight school, until Brasseux nudged me and handed me the cigarette stub.

I started to feel light-headed after drawing in the smoke. The porch lights faded. I found myself sitting with several other men around a campfire in a clearing in the woods.

A cloud of smoke surrounded me. In my hands, I now held a long-necked, hand-carved pipe. I took a short puff on the pipe. Tobacco. I handed it to Brasseux. Or was it Brasseux? He looked like Brasseux, but he smelled like he hadn't taken a bath in a year. His long, unkempt hair and tunic and trousers of animal skins gave off a distinctly sweaty, smoky scent.

"The chief of the Shawnee, Delaware, Mingo, Seneca, Wyandot, Potawatomi, and Ottawa," Brasseux said in French, indicating the men on the other side of the fire. "I'm translating for the Ottawa Chief. He's a nephew of Pontiac."

I understood French. How?

I looked at the men on my right. Closest to me sat Morris. He had gained some weight. No, I realized. This man was Lewis Morris, the New Yorker whose family had governed Colonial politics for the last hundred years. He sat on a worn leather and wood camp stool. The 1775 New York General Assembly had sent him to the Continental Congress, now meeting in Philadelphia, and the Congress had selected him as their chief negotiator of this treaty. Next to him sat Thomas Walker, a physician, explorer, and breeder of superior foxhounds from Virginia. He'd recently negotiated the peace when that scoundrel Dunsmore and his crony Andrew Lewis had attacked the Indians at Point Pleasant. The youngest of the group was James Wilson, a Scotsman like me, in his early thirties. He represented Pennsylvania in the Continental Congress. He was a thoughtful young man, and I felt he would go far.

None of this made sense. I didn't know these men, yet I did. And how had I arrived in the middle of the American Revolution?

"You have come a long way and doubtless suffered many hardships along the way." Lewis Morris spoke, sitting straight and speaking formally. I recorded the words in English on parchment with a quill pen and then translated them to French for Brasseux. Brasseux translated them to Odawa. Morris continued. "It gives me great joy to see you now meeting together at the invitation of your English brothers. We wish to renew and further establish the great friendship that has long existed between our people. With this wampum, we dry up your tears for the loss of your friends who have died since we last assembled. We remove all grief from your hearts so that your minds may be at ease as we deliver the message from the Great Council of Wise Men, now assembled in Philadelphia. Collect the bones of your deceased friends and bury them deep in the ground, then transplant the tree of peace over them so our friendship will not be interrupted or our minds disturbed."

He rose and gave a string of wampum to each of the Chiefs, pretty worthless beads and trinkets from my perspective. And what did he mean by 'our great friendship?'

Morris returned to his camp stool and spoke formally again, welcoming the chiefs to the edge of the forest and thanking them for making the long journey. He gave them more wampum and invited them to begin negotiating a treaty.

The Indians spoke among themselves for a little bit, then their spokesperson said, "We will keep the path open so friend-ship and cooperation will continue between our people. We will meet with you on the day you call Monday and tell you who will negotiate with you."

The Indian Chiefs and their followers filed out of the council area. I stood with the others, realizing I towered over everyone else. This wasn't my body. I was me, but another awareness occu-pied this body. What had happened?"

"Gentlemen," a Black man in buckskin approached from be-hind. "Cook has dinner waiting."

"Thank you, Josiah," Morris said.

Josiah led the way to a rough wooden house a little way from the council circle. He had set the table for the evening meal with China and crystal of good quality, chipped but serviceable. That surprised me here on the western frontier. A large venison roast, surrounded by small roasted potatoes, sat on a platter in the table's center. Walker passed me a pan of coarse cornbread, the only other dish. Josiah filled my glass with a full-bodied red wine.

"We have Arthur St. Clair to thank for this fine wine, straight from his Pennsylvania vineyard," Morris announced. The men all raised their glasses to me. I raised mine in response, realizing that Arthur St. Clair was me. Or I was Arthur St. Clair, although I still felt like Eugene Sinclair.

We dug into the roast and slathered freshly made butter on the cornbread. Then, for a while, we ate in silence.

"I'm afraid we didn't make much progress today," sighed Wilson at last.

"Progress is always slow with treaties," Dr. Walker said. "And very frustrating with all the protocol, speeches, and arguments. It will be at least a month before we've settled the terms. And by that time, it will be almost winter. You know, in my younger years, I had no problem riding out through the worst weather, but I'm getting old. I long to go home and sit by the fire."

"You would be bored to death sitting by the fire even now," teased Wilson.

I rejoined, "You have always been a man of action. Your mind is still going strong even if the body is a bit worn."

"Yes, and I believe there will be much for me to do what with the trouble these fellows are stirring up." He indicated Wilson and Morris.

"What is the news on that account?" I asked.

"Washington has taken command of the Continental Army in Boston," Morris answered. "He sent Schuyler to invade Quebec, but Schuyler became ill, so Richard Montgomery led the expedition. You know Montgomery, don't you, St. Clair? What do you think of him?"

"I served with him during the Siege of Louisburg," I responded. "He's a man of integrity, although he has that Irish temper. He served longer than I did but eventually got frustrated by his inability to gain promotion after North came into power."

"North has cost the Empire many a good man," Morris said. "I think the self-declared Lord has done more to set this Revolution in motion than any man in America."

"It's a courtesy title, not a self-declared title." I replied, "I wouldn't go so far as to say he is responsible for the revolution, but he has cost King George dearly."

"Always the aristocrat," Morris shot back.

"No title for me. I'm just a Pennsylvania farmer." I said.

"Hardly. You own more land than anyone in Western Pennsylvania," Wilson said. "I don't know why you didn't campaign to be a delegate to the Continental Congress."

"I didn't want to miss the birth of my new baby daughter. "

"You mean Phoebe wouldn't let you. Those Bayard girls have always been hard-headed." Morris said. "How about it, Arthur. Do you intend to get involved in this little rebellion we have going on?"

"I hold that no man has a right to withhold his services when his country needs him. I'll serve if called." I replied.

"That is good," Wilson said, "Because John Hancock has

charged me, as a representative of Pennsylvania, to commission you as a Colonel of the Continental army and compel you to raise a regiment from Pennsylvania to join Montgomery in Quebec."

"Consider it done," I replied.

I retired to the room they had provided for me. A rough wooden platform held a lumpy featherbed, covered with three threadbare quilts. A couple of candles stood on the little antique washstand brought over from England. I lit the candles from the fire on the hearth. As I poured water into the bowl on the washstand, I glanced in the cloudy mirror above the basin. I couldn't believe it. I looked like my Dad. I was my Dad. Or maybe not. They had called me Arthur St. Clair. Wasn't that the name of the general Dad had spoken about on the porch back home? I had said things I didn't realize I knew and had expressed some of them in a foreign language. Even my body was not my own. It made no sense at all.

But I was bone tired and hungry as hell despite the cook's excellent dinner. Too tired to figure anything out. I lay down to sleep.

***

I woke sprawled out on the barracks' hard pinewood porch, the early morning sun glaring down at me. I sat up and looked around carefully. Yes, Fort Bliss. I wore my 1942 army uniform. I sat there, trying to figure out what had happened.

My mind kept returning to the statement, "I hold that no man has a right to withhold his services when his country needs him. I'll serve if called."

That was a far cry from how I'd reacted to the current war. My mind went back to the week the army drafted me.

CHAPTER 2
THE ARMY CALLS

I swooped into the prime parking spot under the arching elm tree, whose shade provided significant relief from the glaring Kansas sun. I felt a sense of victory as I always did whenever I beat the traveling salesman, who had recently moved into the room next to me, to the spot. I hopped out of my 1936 Buick Sports Coupe. Although five years old, it was still the newest vehicle I had ever owned. Pulling my pasteboard suitcase and scuffed old briefcase out of the back, I headed across the lawn, still wet from the afternoon thunderstorm. Judy Garland's recent hit 'It's a Great Day for the Irish' blasted out of the radio through the kitchen's open window. *Oops. Forgot Mom's cookies. I'll want those for my midnight snack.*

I had a dream and a plan. If Dr. Ingersoll, our hometown doctor, was right, that plan finally unfolded perfectly. I leaped over the flowerbed, landing in the mud. The deep footprint in the wet soil might disturb Mrs. Brennan, but to track mud onto the pristine floors of her immaculate boarding house would undoubtedly lead to retribution. I stomped the mud off my shoe and scraped it on the cement walkway leading to the front steps of the old Victorian house, then tried to kick the clumps of mud off the walk. Still, after years of blowing dust, the rain and its accompanying mud were welcome here. I bounded up the six steps to the broad porch two at a time. Tucking the briefcase under my arm, I threw open the door.

"Is that you, Gene?" my landlady called as the screen door slammed behind me.

I hadn't thought she could hear me over the radio.

Mrs. Brennan appeared at the door to the dining room, flour

covering her arms to the elbows, a white smudge on her cheek, and one on her forehead. "How was your weekend? I trust your mother's well?"

"Just fine, Ma'am. She sends her regards." Mrs. Brennan and Mom went to high school together and had remained devoted friends through the years. Besides my rent, and perhaps more important to Mrs. Brennan, I provided a conduit for gossip between the two old friends. I could be caught up in a long conversation if I didn't get my mail—full of good news, I hoped—and run. I stepped sideways toward the mailboxes.

"Have you made up your mind about next year? I have to tell you I need to advertise the room now if you aren't staying." She tilted her head, frowning, to emphasize the urgency and lifted it again to express hope. If I stayed, she wouldn't have to find another boarder, and I could continue to bring the hometown news.

Having made my way to the mailboxes, I reached into the pigeonhole where she put my mail. "This may tell me."

"Oh, yes. That came for you Friday. I thought it looked important, so I put it up top."

My heart beat faster. I ripped open the envelope and read frantically. "All right!" I shouted.

I leaped into the air, throwing my arms over my head. Just then, the sun came out from behind the clouds and shone through the leaded stained-glass window on the landing. Shimmering patches of color danced on the walls like bright confetti; the old house was celebrating with me, and the sun as well, its light as bright as my heart.

"Good news, Gene?"

I blurted, "I was accepted into medical school! Wow! Since we were boys, Don Ingersoll and I have planned to open a practice together. He's already in his second year 'cause his father could afford to send him. I've saved everything I could from my teaching salary so I could go."

She seemed a bit surprised, like she expected something different. "Well," she said, a bit disgruntled, "might have been sooner if you hadn't bought that fancy car from your brother."

"Albert bought it right before his daughter came along, and

Nancy quit teaching. She was furious with him for buying a sports car without a decent back seat for the kids, and they needed the money, so he sold it to me cheap."

I started toward the stairs to my room to write to Don.

Stopping me, she said, "Don't forget the rest of your mail." She handed me the newspaper. Another letter fell out of the box. She picked up the letter and gave it to me. "It's from the Selective Service. Did you forget to register for the draft?"

"I registered the first day. I don't know what they would want now." I ripped the envelope open, my hands shaking at the thought of what might be in it.

"Damn." I kicked the wastebasket. It bounced off the wall and rolled into the living room.

"Eugene! Watch your tongue! And your foot!"

"Sorry, Mrs. Brennan. I... It's just... this is a draft notice. They drafted me. Right when I got into medical school."

"Don't they know how bad you want to go to medical school?"

"The draft board doesn't know anything about it. Why should they? The medical school doesn't communicate with the draft board when they accept a student."

"You need to tell them then."

Just when I had finally made it, everything fell apart again— the lesson of my life.

"I hope to goodness we won't get into this war. You know the Great War was how I lost Mr. Brennan; God rest his soul." Her hand fluttered over her heart. Her chin trembled, as it did whenever she mentioned her "dear departed husband," generally several times a day. "War is a terrible waste. Believe you me, if there is any way we can avoid it, I think we should."

"What's the big idea!" Herman Hazelton, the traveling salesman, burst through the door. "I go to the druggist to get something for my piles, and I come back to find that you've stolen my parking place."

"There really aren't designated parking places," Mrs. Brennan said.

"Now I have to park out back under the tree where the owl roosts. Do you have any idea how disgusting that owl mess is?"

"You could park in front," I said, absently stuffing the draft notice into my pocket.

"Then people would see my car and know I'm here."

I shrugged my shoulders, and he stomped up the stairs.

"He left his wife," Mrs. Brennan said. "She comes by every once in a while to try to collect money. Always on weekends when you're gone."

I turned to go up the stairs, then turned back. "By the way, I agree with you about the war. You know that William Allen White formed a committee to try to keep us out of the war. They pushed through the lend-lease program to help the allies win without dragging us in. If I know anything about Mr. White, he'll do everything in his power to keep America out of it."

She nodded sagely. "Mr. White practically runs the country from his little newspaper in Emporia." She paused for a moment, squinting as though to remember something. "Didn't you say you worked your way through college as his houseboy? I bet you saw everything that went on in that house."

"I did. Worked for him for three years. I wouldn't say he runs the country, but he has a lot of influence on important people. And some fascinating visitors, from Douglas Fairbanks to Albert Einstein. They all visited that big house in that little Kansas town."

"You don't know what I would have given to have met Douglas Fairbanks," Mrs. Brennan interrupted me. "I saw every movie he ever made!" Her voice trembled with passion. "Some of them several times. Who's Albert Einstein? I don't think I've ever seen any of his movies."

"Einstein is a university professor. He's one of the most brilliant physicists alive. He lectured on his theory of relativity at my college. Fascinating." I replied, confused that she hadn't heard of Albert Einstein. I smiled, recalling the lecture and our meeting.

The scent of burning pie filling drifted from the kitchen. Mrs. Brennan spun around. "I had better rescue those pies if we're going to have any dessert tonight.

I sprinted up the stairs, grateful for my reprieve and thankful for the pies. As I entered my room, the bright pink swans swimming in the wallpaper's deep navy background slapped me in the face as they always did after a weekend surrounded by the pale rose and cream patterns Mom preferred. I had no idea where Mrs. Brennan had found that design and did not wish to know, anyway. Three and a half years ago, when I replaced science teacher Gerald Carlson, who had suffered a stroke midyear, I planned to spend a few months in the boarding house, then find a decent apartment at a lower rate. That had never happened. Still, the place had become comfortable—nice bed, interesting, if competitive boarders, and reasonable enough price for meals and a room. Mrs. Brennan treated me like the son she never had. My time here has been the best of my life so far.

Dropping the mail and bag of cookies on the bedside table, I tossed the suitcase on the bed. Its age and cheap construction meant it popped open, spilling some of my clothes onto the floor. I had been using it since I began college. I hadn't expected it to last this long. I picked up the clothes and threw them on the bed.

What to do now? Just when life was moving forward as I had dreamed, I had been drafted. The first thing was to tell Don what had happened. I pulled some stationery from the drawer of the flimsy desk Mrs. Brennan had placed in my room and decided to write the letter on the porch. It was a lovely day, and the last time I tried to use the desk, it had tipped over, and Mrs. Brennan admonished me not to destroy her furniture. I dropped my pipe and tobacco into my pocket. As I pulled a book from the shelf for a writing surface, I noticed a stack of clean towels on the overstuffed chair in the corner next to the bookcase. On my way out, I made the mistake of sticking my head into the kitchen.

"Thank you for washing the sheets and towels, Mrs. Brennan."

"My pleasure, Gene. Did you see Mary Jane Howland while you were home?"

"Yes," I said, trying to turn away

"Did she set up her business?" Mrs. Brennan persisted.

"Yes. She bought Letha's beauty shop equipment and set up the business in her house." I took a step toward the dining room.

"Your mother is always telling me how talented Mary Jane is with her hair."

Usually, I would spend an hour or so catching Mrs. Brennan

up on all the gossip from home, but I needed to be alone with my thoughts right now. "Yes, mom's been going there." I tried to take another step toward the dining room.

"Has anyone done anything about the Legion Hall? It really needs to be taken care of." Her questions were like a fishhook.

"Mr. Walters got Cook's to donate some paint and repainted it. Looks better than I ever remember it." I stepped into the dining room on my way out to the porch.

"He's running the Corner Café now, isn't he?"

"Yes, Ma'am," I called back.

"How about Longacre Café? Do they still have dances every Saturday night?"

"Not since Rose Gugleman took over managing it." I moved a bit farther into the dining room.

"How are the new elm trees doing in the park?"

"Growing fast," I said over my shoulder.

"Well, Gene, I would love to talk with you some more, but I have to finish making dinner. Maybe we can continue the conversation when I'm not so busy."

"Yes, Ma'am." I shook my head and finally headed out the door.

I settled into the porch swing. Lighting my pipe, I puffed a few times to gather my thoughts. Don and I had always felt we would be perfect medical partners. He was interested in the complexities of surgery and the intellectual analysis of diseases and syndromes. As for me, I wanted to be the general practitioner who cared for everyone in town. I would treat the mind, body, and soul. Now, thanks to the draft board, it might never happen. We weren't even in the war, and they were pulling me away from my plan.

"Gene, oh, Gene." I jerked my head up. The slim, prim school district superintendent's wife came up the walk waving her handkerchief. "Gene, my niece Gertrude is coming for a visit next weekend. Will you be staying in town? I would love to have you join us for dinner to meet her."

Madeline Glass had been trying to get me to marry one niece or another for the past three years. She never caught on that I was not interested in marriage right now. I couldn't afford a wife and family while in medical school. After establishing my practice, I planned to marry, a plan crafted and honed over the years in many conversations with Mom, Don, and Granny. As the world changed and I grew, we revised and refined the plan. I would become a doctor, join Don in practice, then start a family.

"I'm so sorry, Mrs. Glass. I'll be working on some new lesson plans."

She frowned. "With only five weeks left in the school year? What kind of new lessons are you coming up with at this late date?"

"Um... Einstein. I'm going to teach my senior students about the theory of relativity."

"Oh, Mr. Glass follows all the new advances in science. He didn't think anybody else in this dusty little town knew anything about it. He'll be so excited. Where did you learn about Dr. Einstein's work?"

"I went to a lecture by Einstein in college. Then served him breakfast the next morning and had a personal conversation with him."

"You talked with him? What did he say?"

"I told him I didn't completely understand his theory of relativity. He said, 'neither do I, son.'"

"I must go home and tell Mr. Glass." She waggled her upright hand as she hurried down the sidewalk.

Why had I said that? Now I would have to teach the theory of relativity. In my first year, Mr. Samuels, my principal, warned me when I introduced the theory of evolution that I should teach strictly by the book. Nevertheless, I had kept subtly inserting evolution into my lesson plans. Thankfully, my students knew better than to tell their parents and kept quiet. Their tacit approval kept me employed without having to compromise my principles. I believed they deserved to know current scientific concepts, even if their parents might not have thought so.

I pulled out the draft notice I'd stuffed in my pocket and stared at it. Now, keeping my job didn't matter. By the fall, I would be in the army. I could openly teach evolution. I could even teach relativity. None of it would matter. I quickly dashed off the letter to Don and went upstairs to plan my new physics lessons.

***

I usually entered school hallways filled with the cheerful sounds of friends greeting each other with all the exuberance a building full of teenagers could embody. The noise could be deafening, even in this small high school. Today I was early, needing to prepare new material for my physics class. From the echoing halls, I walked through the workroom, filled with the busy clack and hum of the mimeograph machine and the sweet scent of duplicating fluid, into the cigarette smoke dimness of the teacher's lounge.

"I've been drafted," I announced to the small crowd that usually gathered there before school.

"Oh, Gene," cried both Dorothy Bucks and Dianne Hammond. They had both attempted to be wife-worthy, which I had effectively staved off. Dorothy had been incredibly persistent, and I had been sorely tempted, but in the end, Mom convinced me to stick to the plan. A plan that was now ruined.

"Gene, how dare you leave! I've been training you for three years to be senior class sponsor. You're the only one who knows how to organize the senior trip and plan commencement, and now you're leaving as I'm planning to retire," exclaimed Miss Burkhardt. "I've waited so long. If both you and I go now, who will sponsor the senior class?"

"Emma, I hope you won't reconsider your retirement because Gene is leaving," said Henry Martin, the history teacher. Henry would be happy to see both of us leave. When Miss Burkhardt retired, he would be the senior teacher in the school. He and his brother Billy, the Baptist preacher, were behind the uproar when I taught evolution theory to my biology class. I had been furious with their interference. Neither of them knew a thing about science, yet they saw fit to dictate what went on in my class. I told them they were ignorant fools stuck in the last century, and I was glad I was raised in the Methodist church, where we don't have to check our brains at the door. I nearly got myself fired after only

13

two months of teaching. I knew they would pressure the school board to get a more traditional, somewhat backward science teacher.

"I'm sure someone will be able to take on the seniors," I told Miss Burkhardt. "If you leave all your notes and lists, everything should be fine."

She looked doubtful.

I returned to the workroom and prepared a few handouts for my physics lessons. When I introduced natural selection to these same students three years earlier, Mr. Samuels and the Martins shut me down. I couldn't cover it completely. Now I would introduce them to the theory of relativity point-blank.

Even though I hadn't been teaching long, some groups of students stood out, and this senior class was one of them. Two of the most brilliant and multitalented students I had ever taught, Betty Sanders and Jimmy Hanson, led the class. She was a boy-crazy cheerleader who deliberately underplayed her intelligence. We had an understanding. I wouldn't brag about her physics expertise if she kept me posted on what was happening with the students. She was a fantastic source of information on her peers. Jimmy was just as brilliant but naive. His importance to me was that he was the star pitcher on the baseball team. He helped me demonstrate real-world physics applications, like the path of a trajectory, many times.

The warning bell rang. I dashed down the stairs to my classroom in the basement of the three-story schoolhouse. I should have been there ten minutes ago. A loud, rowdy knot of students clustered in the middle of the hallway. The students encircled three boys. I sprinted toward them, realizing it wasn't a fight only when I noticed that the three senior boys at the center of the group were grinning, arms locked around each other's shoulders. I unlocked the classroom door.

"Everybody in your seats," I said as the class filed into the room.

Betty turned to me. "Mr. Sinclair, Junior, Bobby, and Jimmy joined the army. Isn't it exciting? They are going off to fight the Krauts."

"Them Krauts don't stand a chance against us," Bobby declared.

"We may not even get involved in the war," I responded. "For now, let's leave the Germans to the British and French and learn some physics."

I walked to the board, took a deep breath, and wrote $E=mc^2$.

***

Herman's car was already parked under the tree when I got home. He ambushed me on the porch.

"I got it," he gloated.

"You're never home this early. Is something wrong?"

"No. I quit early, so I didn't have to get owl shit all over my car."

"Do you notice where my car is parked?" I asked. "No owl shit. Just a lot of sunshine. Are you truly willing to sacrifice sales to park under the tree?"

He nodded. "I lose much more than I would have made on those sales if my wife sees me here. She's constantly after me for money for those two brats of hers, and I'm not even sure one of them is mine."

"But if she's your wife, aren't you obligated to support her?"

"Not if she's gonna sleep around whenever I'm on a sales trip."

I nodded and went into the house, wondering how much sleeping around he did on those sales trips. He seemed the type. I sat in my overstuffed chair to consider my options.

Don and I had come up with The Plan in sixth grade. Then, during my junior year in high school, the stock market crashed, the rain stopped, and the Great Depression hit. I worked and scrimped throughout college and three and a half years of teaching to save enough money. Now, just when I had the money and acceptance into med school, the army drafted me. It was as though the Goddess Fortuna had frowned on my plans from the beginning. What could I do to make Fortune smile?

***

I ducked into the school office to make a quick telephone call to the County Selective Service before classes started the following day. I asked Cici, the school secretary, if I could use the phone on her desk. When she nodded, I picked up the handset and gave the operator the number. A woman answered. I could hear a dog barking in the background. I picked up the base of the phone and turned my back to Cici, trying to keep the conversation private.

"Hello, Eugene Sinclair speaking. I'm calling to request a deferment."

"A deferment? Oh, for the selective service? You're a conscientious objector?"

"No. I got accepted into medical school." How stupid of me. I realized I should have said I was a conscientious objector. After all, I had been President of Students for Peace in College. But they probably would have sent me to one of those new Public Service camps, and I still wouldn't get to medical school anyway. Too late now. I had been so proud of the medical school acceptance that I had to blurt it out.

"I have to find my husband. I think he went out to the garage to work on his car. Please hold on." A muffled shout came through the receiver. "Pete. Pete, get in here. You have some Selective Service business." The first warning bell rang, sending students to class. I was late again for my own class. I continued to hold. Finally, someone came back on the line.

"Hello. Pete Fleming here. You say you want a draft deferment to attend medical school?"

"Yes"

"But you didn't register as a medical student?"

"I won't be a medical student until the fall."

"What do you currently do?"

"I'm a high school science teacher." I paced back and forth at the end of the phone cord. Students would be gathering outside my locked classroom.

"So, are you in good health and physical condition? You can read and write?"

"Of course I can read and write. I'm a high school teacher." The final bell rang.

"I'm sorry we cannot offer you any deferment at this point. Please report as ordered."

"You don't understand. I got accepted into medical school. The army will need doctors if we go to war." Pete Fleming must be denser than lead.

"Report as ordered. Do you understand?"

"Yes, I understand. Thank you, sir."

What was wrong with these people? They must be as noodled as the Nazis. If we did end up in this war, they would be desperate for doctors.

I slammed the handset back onto the phone.

"Mr. Sinclair!" Cici exclaimed.

"I got drafted," I said. "And they won't give me a deferment."

"If they gave you a deferment, the war would end before you got out of medical school. If we send our boys over there, the war is as good as over."

"Well, I don't want to be one of those boys," I stomped out of the office and slammed the door behind me.

***

That afternoon Cici knocked on the classroom door as I struggled to quiet the unruly freshman general science class. They were a handful. This class made me glad I was leaving, whether to the army or medical school.

"Pastor Billy Martin is in Mr. Samuels' office. Mr. Samuels wants you there immediately. I'm to watch your class and tell you that you better watch your tongue." As I pushed past her, she whispered, "Why don't you ask for a deferment from the medical school?"

Cici! That was it! I would ask the medical school to defer my acceptance until my one year enlistment was over. I climbed the stairs with a lighter step even though Billy Martin and Bruce Samuels waited for me with loaded guns, so to speak.

I wasn't surprised Pastor Martin was here. Science had made many advances in the early years of the twentieth century, but many people in small town Kansas were not interested in scientific progress. On the other hand, several of the students in my classes were the first of their families to go to high school, which was progress enough for them.

Through the windows from the outer office, I could see Mr. Samuels tapping his fingers on his massive mahogany desk. I paused, then knocked on the door before I opened it. "You wanted to see me?"

Pastor Martin jumped out of the straight-backed chair in front of the desk. "What are you teaching these children?" he shouted.

"What do you mean? I'm teaching them science."

He paused, then accused me. "You are teaching them blasphemy!"

"I am teaching science. What is blasphemous about that?"

"I heard that you are teaching about the lies and fabrications spouted by Mr. Albert Einstein. That man is German, and he spreads seditious German lies." He took a step toward me.

I took a deep breath to calm myself. "Dr. Einstein is an American citizen, and his new theories might have huge consequences for these students. It could change their lives in ways we don't even understand yet. Just because we live in a small town doesn't mean our children need to have an inferior education."

"You should teach facts, not theories," Mr. Samuels interjected. "I thought we cleared that up with that evolution thing."

"Facts? Science is theory. In science, we prove things wrong, but we can't definitively prove them right. We follow the theory that fits the data best until we discover something that doesn't fit. Then we develop a new theory that does fit the data. That is the scientific process, and it leads to more and more knowledge and discoveries. But I have to teach the theories so that the students have the background to make those discoveries."

Pastor Martin stepped closer and pulled himself up to his full five-foot-four. "In my day, we learned the truth, not some feeble theory we might throw away next year. And we did not espouse the ideas of the enemy. What are you thinking, presenting these ideas to impressionable young students? They need to learn factual information that will be useful if they have to go to war."

I stood a bit straighter myself. "These concepts are essential to the war effort. The country that best understands these principles might even win the war."

Mr. Glass walked into the office.

"Oh, excuse me, Bruce. I didn't realize you were in a meeting." He turned to me. "Hello, Gene. My wife told me you're teaching the theory of relativity. I find it fascinating."

Pastor Martin gasped.

Mr. Glass turned back to Mr. Samuels. "Bruce, aren't you impressed with this young man? Unfortunately, you know he hasn't signed his contract for the coming year. We need to get that corrected right away."

I interposed. "I'm afraid I won't be signing a contract for next year. I've been drafted."

Mr. Glass frowned, and the frown on Pastor Martin's face faded away.

"I'm sorry to hear that. Our loss is the army's gain. I wish you the best of luck. Now Bruce, unless this meeting is crucial, we need to discuss some issues with next year's basketball schedule."

"I should go back down and rescue Cici from the freshman science class. James Williams started a fire in the sink last week. I wouldn't want them to burn down the building on Cici's watch."

I slipped out and hurried back to my classroom, silently praising Mr. Glass for his timing and intervention. Cici winked at me when I told her he had arrived.

***

I acted on Cici's suggestion. At noon, I got a plate from the lunchroom, some paper from the workroom, and, using my favorite fountain pen, sat in the teacher's lounge and wrote a letter to the medical school's dean.

Dear Dr. Graham,

I recently received my acceptance letter from the Washington University School of Medicine. Unfortunately, yesterday I received a draft notice. I'm currently obligated *to serve our country in the United States Army for a year. Therefore, I'm writing to request that my acceptance to the School of Medicine be deferred until after completing my service. I will return to the school immediately on my discharge from the army if you can be so kind as to allow this deferred admission.*

Yours respectfully,
Eugene W. Sinclair

I took a stamp from the school supply, dropped three pennies into the drawer, and placed the letter in the outgoing mailbox on Cici's desk as I returned to the classroom. She nodded and continued her typing.

***

I checked the mail every afternoon, but there was no letter from Dr. Graham.

In physics class, Betty and Jimmy asked questions that challenged my limited knowledge of the theory of relativity, so we all made it through those last five weeks with a better understanding of recent advances in physics. Commencement day finally arrived.

The students marched into the auditorium with all the pomp and grandeur possible for a small town graduation with twenty students. Betty, the valedictorian, gave an emotional speech—how wherever they went, they would recall these years as the best time of their lives, thanking their parents for the long hours and teachers for teaching them math and English, responsibility, and work ethic. When she finished, there wasn't a dry eye in the place.

Jimmy's dry humor soon had everyone laughing at his Salutatorian speech. I had let him read my high school graduation speech, an amusing juxtaposition of lines plagiarized from Shakespeare, Thomas Jefferson, Plato, and Anonymous, names changed to those of students in my school and our teachers. He had borrowed the concept but had been even more clever in his choice of quotes.

Mr. Perry, the music teacher, led the band in several selections from Miss Burkhardt's approved Commencement list—Pomp and Circumstances, of course, but she let me slip in one new one—God Bless America, my new favorite.

The diplomas were all in order and handed to the correct student. Everything went off without a hitch. When the recessional began, Mr. Samuels stood and held up his hand. The music stopped. Sitting beside me, Miss Burkhardt patted my knee, smiling, as I looked around for the problem. Was he going to fire me in front of the whole town for teaching relativity? I had already resigned.

"Will Jimmy Hanson, Bobby Kuhn, William Daniels, Jr., and Eugene Sinclair please come to the front of the stage?" I tried to duck out, but Miss Burkhardt glared at me, grabbed my hand to make me stop, and pointed toward Mr. Samuels. I acquiesced.

"These young men will be joining the army in a few short days. We want to let them know how proud we are that they will be defending our nation and providing for our safety. Please show them how grateful you are."

After the townsfolk's standing ovation, Mr. Samuels asked the faculty and staff to lead the graduates out of the auditorium. At the reception on the lawn, it seemed everyone wanted to shake my hand.

"Mr. Sinclair, if we get into the war, I bet we can beat them in nothing flat," Jimmy Hanson said. "Aren't you excited about going?"

"I'm hoping we don't have to fight. I hope the war will be over before we're forced into it."

"I agree," Jimmy's father said. "But we need to be prepared. We weren't ready for the Great War, which cost us more than it should have. If it does come to war, at least you'll be trained."

"Most of the country agrees with you, Mr. Hanson," I said. "Particularly in the Midwest. The argument is whether we should support the Allies with arms and equipment or stay out of it completely. There are very few Americans who are pushing for war."

"Unfortunately, Roosevelt is one of those who are, and he may get us into it yet."

The war dominated conversations around the lawn. On this day of celebration of our graduates, our thoughts turned to the war they might have to fight.

I slipped away at the first opportunity.

CHAPTER 3
AT HOME

I checked my room one more time. When I anticipated the medical school acceptance, I had joyously started packing my things, two boxes to go with me to St. Louis and two boxes to be stored in my parents' attic. Now all destined for the attic and stacked on Mrs. Brennan's front porch. My future had been stolen; my life put on hold. The grubby little suitcase, carefully taped up, sat on the bed, packed with a few clothes, my shaving kit, and the letter from the selective service, the only things the army allowed us to bring. I carried it downstairs.

Mrs. Brennan came out on the porch as I slammed the trunk on the last box.

"You be careful now," she said. She hugged me and patted my back.

"I will. It's only for a year."

Frank Harvey, the mailman, came through the front gate.

"Gene, I'm glad I caught you. I have a letter from the Washington School of Medicine."

I turned and grabbed the letter. At last! It had arrived in the nick of time. I ripped the envelope and pulled out the letter from Dean Graham. I read it, crumpled it up, and angrily threw it behind the rose bushes.

Mrs. Brennan retrieved the letter. "Gene, what did you do that for? What is it??"

"They won't defer my medical school acceptance. I have to reapply when I am out of the army. Why can no one see how ridiculous this all is. I'll still have the same qualifications next year. Why can't they keep it all on file?"

"Don't worry. They accepted you once. They'll accept you

again. All things happen for a reason." Her cheerful face angered me even more.

"Let's say a proper goodbye then so I can get a move on." I squeezed her in a big bear hug, climbed into the Coupe, and punched the starter. As I left, Herman pulled into the parking space under the tree, jumped out of his car, and held up his hand in the V for Victory sign. I waved. The great parking spot battle ended, and he had won.

I waved at Mr. Carlton, the science teacher I had replaced midyear in '38. He had recovered sufficiently from his stroke to be mowing his lawn with a new-fangled gasoline-powered lawn-mower. Mike topped off my tank at the filling station and washed the windshield. He had been in one of my first science classes. With nightly tutoring and lots of encouragement, I had helped him graduate. He was already the best mechanic in town and might someday own the business. Betty waved to me on her way to her summer job at the swimming pool. Tommy Kuhn saluted when I passed him on his tractor. This was now home as much as Formoso, one-hundred-thirty miles to the north, where I grew up. I became more despondent with each friend I passed. Maybe it would have been different if I had been off to medical school but leaving this friendly little town to join the army left me feeling cold, even on this bright June day.

Mom burst out the front door of the little white farmhouse the moment I pulled up, wiping her hands on her apron.

"Gene, come in, sit down, and have some cookies," she pushed me through the front room.

She had set up the house for a special occasion. The lace curtains were closed on Mom's sewing nook in the bay window. Extra leaves stretched the dining table, covered by the best lace tablecloth. The clutter on the passthrough of the built-in china cabinet had been tamed somewhat, with Dad's work gloves and Doris's books picked up. The kitchen smelled of herbs and cinnamon—Mom's motto: anything for a party.

"Robert, get his things out of the car. Doris, get him some coffee," she called out to my younger brother and sister. Doris had gotten an elementary teaching certificate through a program at our high school and started teaching immediately after graduation. She still lived at home. After completing his first year at Kansas State Teacher's College, Robert was home for a few weeks.

"Mom, I was just here three weeks ago."

"But after this week, we may not see you again for a whole year. Here, let me have your hat. Eat some cookies." She straightened the red floral oilcloth on the kitchen table and set a plate of cookies in front of me.

Doris plunked a cup of coffee beside it. She and Robert sat down and helped themselves to cookies. "So, did you iron things out with the medical school?" Doris asked.

"I wrote Dr. Graham asking if they could hold my place 'till next year. His answer came right before I left Burns. He said I have to start all over again."

"What the heck?" John asked

Doris's face looked like a lost puppy as she took a sip of her coffee. "They can't do that to you, can they? You were accepted, and it isn't your fault the army won't let you off."

"Don't worry," Mom said too brightly. "Things will work out for you. You have been planning on this all your life. You might even be able to save up some money while you are in the army to help pay for it."

This was as much Mom's plan as mine. I knew the news disappointed Mom, maybe even more than me, but she always tried to put the best outlook on things. When we lost the farm, she said, "at least there will be fewer chores now." She had encouraged all of us to go to college. Only Ken, the second of her five children, had not been interested. He loved horses. His farm enabled him to buy and raise horses.

"Well, my pay will be okay, I guess. And I probably won't have too much opportunity to spend it. Anyway, I already saved up fifteen hundred dollars. I want to invest it so I'll have more by the time I start medical school. I can probably invest a little bit of my army pay too."

"Where will you invest it?" asked Robert, whose main ambition, even at twenty years old, was to be rich someday.

"I thought I'd buy stock. I was thinking either General Electric or Boeing. Both should produce good returns, what with the lend-lease program expanding by the day."

"Are you out of your mind, boy?" roared my father, arriving home from his job at the creamery. "Never gamble on stocks. Invest your money in land."

I shuddered. Dad and I always seemed at odds. I had never been able to please him when I worked with him in the field. He'd send me back to the house to chop wood, milk cows, and help Mom in the garden while he did the fieldwork with my brothers. I began helping Mom around the house and learned to bake. I thrived under Mom's gentler instruction and let my brothers work in the field with Dad.

"You put that money in the bank here in town where I can keep an eye on it."

I had learned long ago not to talk back to him, so I kept my mouth shut and let the matter drop.

"Gene, could you go pick up Granny?" asked Mom. "Your Aunt Kate has to get the paper out and can't come tonight."

"Hmph," Dad grunted. He had disapproved of his sister's wild ways and suffragette stance when they were younger. Now, he had a dim view of her editing the little weekly rag that passed for a newspaper in town. It held more gossip than news, but Kate dedicated a lot of time to it. She had a witty and sometimes cutting writing style that helped make the paper very interesting to read. I liked it.

"Sure. Be right back." I told Mom.

Granny and I had always had a special bond. Before Dr. Ingersoll came to town, Granny, with her herbs and compounds, was the only source of medical help for miles around. She and the doctor competed to see whose cures worked better ever since he arrived. Granny's came with much more love and attention. Even now, nobody thought to call Dr. Ingersoll to deliver a baby. Granny had birthed so many of the babies in the area that everyone called her Granny. Thanks to her teaching and encouragement, I wanted to be a doctor. As a boy, I spent many hours in her kitchen, helping her prepare tinctures and tisanes. Most importantly, she helped people. I wanted to be the kind of M.D. who made a lasting difference in my patients' lives. Would I ever have that opportunity now?

I pulled the car close to Aunt Kate's front door as Granny stepped out. A tiny woman, never over four foot eight and even smaller now, she was still spry and witty and beat my assistance off with a flapping hand. Then, smiling broadly, she approached the car leaning more heavily on her cane than before.

"Off to the army, just like my Johnny," she said. My grandfather was hailed as the last Civil War hero of northern Kansas when he died a few years ago. I grew up listening to his many stories of marching through Georgia with General William Tecumseh Sherman. I learned from him to push for peace to avoid the horrors of war. The so-called glories of war were not so glorious but rather atrocities on the grandest scale. Grandad's stories led all his descendants to avoid going to war.

"Yes, Granny. I hope I can serve as bravely as he did."

"You'll do every bit as good." She laughed. "His stories got bigger and bigger as time went on. You only heard the twentieth century version." Her eyes sparkled like she knew something, which I'm sure she did, having been married to Granddad for 63 years.

I helped her into the car. "How's Don doing these days?"

I walked around the car, climbing into the driver's seat before answering. Her good ear was on the left.

"Don's fine. In his second year of medical school. I'm still hoping to join him after I get out of the army." I pushed the starter, and we rolled up the dirt road. Sometimes, it became impassable after a rain, in stark contrast to the drought days when great plumes of yellow dust rose as cars passed, swirling and eddying like a moving explosion.

"You remember the time the two of you tried to smoke a cigarette?"

I laughed. "I sure do. Don had an awful reaction. When his dad heard his cough later that evening, Dr. Ingersoll put him to bed and treated him for bronchitis. I sneaked into the house to take him some eucalyptus oil and your lemon horehound drops. Cleared it right up! Oh, he hated the taste."

"I'm glad you confessed. No telling what poison Dr. Ingersoll would of given him."

"Don said he would never do what I told him to again. But he always did."

"Everybody wants to follow you. Have since you were a youngster and built that fort in the tallgrass pasture."

"I don't know about that. Sure, a bunch of kids followed the secret trails we made, and everybody wanted a chance to blaze new trails. I made up a lot of games to play there like we were exploring the frontier or searching the prairie for lost cattle, but those were kids' games. I like people and all, but people don't follow me like they do, Dad."

"You had every kid in town out there, and they all had fun even though they worked harder chopping those trails than doing their chores at home. Your dad compels, you inspire. Different styles, same result."

I knew how much Granny doted on her youngest surviving son. But what was she saying now? Had she insulted him by saying he compelled people to follow him? Some of the stories I'd heard about him spoke of a different person. A fun-loving minor league baseball player, the most handsome guy in town who had swept the beautiful eighteen-year-old daughter of the bank's board chairman off her feet. What had hardened him into the man I knew? The only soft spot I had seen was his absolute devotion to Mom.

Albert's car sat in front of the house. Granny's great-grand-children came running out to meet us. They hugged Granny, nearly knocking her down. Three-year-old Ellen ran and jumped into my arms. I swung her around, onto my back, then said hello to her older brothers. I galloped into the house with Ellen on my back, ducking through the door to avoid a head smack, and greeted my brother and his wife.

Albert taught history and economics in the county seat high school. As the oldest son, he had a special relationship with Dad, and Dad always held him up as the shining example with whom I compared very poorly.

Ken, two years older than me, arrived with his new wife, Trish.

"Sit down, everyone," Mom called. "Supper time."

"Dick, you sit caddy-corner from your brother. I don't want you two getting into it," Nancy told her oldest son. Dick pushed his brother toward the opposite side of the table and slipped into the seat beside his grandpa

Mom served all my favorite foods, meatloaf, fried potatoes, pickled beets, and cinnamon fried apples. As we passed the food, Granny asked Albert. "What're you doing this summer?

"I need some continuing education to keep my teaching certificate. I'll be going to Washington, DC, for the summer to participate in a committee that will develop a new high school civics program."

Granny said effusively, "That's a good learning experience for the children." A look passed between Albert and Nancy.

"Nancy and the children won't come with. The stipend isn't enough to rent a place for the whole family, and Dick got a spot on a new baseball team."

Dad gave Dick a thumbs up and a smile. "Good for you." Though Dad had not played in over thirty years, he was still an avid fan of any baseball game he could watch and encouraged Dick every chance he got. His games would give him a summer full of pleasure.

"He's only ten years old," Granny said. "He'll get a chance to play baseball later, but who knows if he'll get another chance to summer in Washington, DC." Albert shifted in his seat but said nothing. Something must be up because Granny had just subtly rebuked both Albert and Dad.

The women were trying to decide when they should come out to help Trish put up apricots. This crop would be her first canning season as a married woman. Ken farmed a place owned by Trish's great uncle, which had two big apricot trees in the front yard. Those trees would provide enough fruit for the entire extended family.

Dad turned to Ken. "How's that new horse of yours doing?"

"She's a magnificent mare. When I get her with Colton's stallion, she'll produce some of the finest quarter horses in the county, maybe the state."

"Please, not in front of the children," Mom said.

"We know how foals get made," Dick replied.

Mom's eyes widened, and her mouth dropped open.

"'Scuse me. Could I have more apples?" Ellen asked.

I passed her the apples, and Mom went to get the Bundt cake she had made for dessert. No one spoke as we shoveled down big mouthfuls of the moist delicacy.

As Mom and the women began clearing the table, the children ran into the yard to catch fireflies. Albert and I excused ourselves and retired to the front porch for a smoke.

"It's quite an honor to be on that federal committee," I said.

"I used you a bit to get in. Got a recommendation from Mr. White. I was surprised he remembered me, considering I only met him once when I went down to pick you up."

"He got where he is, in part, because of his prodigious ability to remember names and people," I replied.

Albert wasn't above using any advantage he had to get ahead. He started college in 1928. Got married in 1929, just before the crash. Getting through school with a wife and young children during the depression taught him a thing or two.

We sat, contemplating the last remnants of a brilliant sunset. Then, because he taught economics and because, as my oldest brother, he had always been one of my most trusted advisors, I asked, "What do you think of the idea of putting my savings in the stock market? I thought maybe one of the companies that make war materiel for the lend-lease program."

"The stock market is set up for longer-term investments. You would have to hire a broker. By the time you recover the fee, you might not come out ahead in one year. It would be an excellent idea if you could hold onto the stocks for a while. But since you want to use it for school starting next year, I would stay away from stocks. I know $1500 seems like a lot of money, but I think you'll be better off putting it in a savings account and getting the interest."

Nancy came out on the porch and called the children. "It's time to get them home to bed," she told Albert. He went inside to say goodbye to Mom and Dad. Ken and Tricia came out with Granny.

Always the caretaker, she said, "I left a packet of my dysentery formula by your bed. It's got coriander seed, witch hazel, and cranesbill. Add a bit of lemon juice if you can get it."

"I doubt I'll get dysentery," I said.

"Every army ever formed got dysentery," she told me. "You hold onto it. You'll need it sooner or later."

"I will," I promised her, feeling a profound sense of good fortune to have a Granny like her.

When they left, I tapped the ashes out of my pipe and went inside to help Mom and Doris put the good China on the top shelf. Then I retired to the sleeping porch, where I put the dysentery medicine in my suitcase and stripped down to my skivvies. Finally, Robert and I crawled into our childhood bunks.

"You know, I'm a little jealous. You're gonna get out of this little town."

"I've been out of this little town for nine years."

"But you've only been in other small Kansas towns."

"I would've been in St. Louis now if it hadn't been for the draft."

"You might go even farther than St. Louis in the army."

"I don't know. First stop is Fort Leavenworth. Just another small Kansas town. I might spend the whole year there. We'll see."

Soon the sound of Robert's snoring rose from the lower bunk. I lay awake listening to the trains rumble along the tracks at the other end of the pasture. My anger with Dad's treating me like I didn't know what I was doing with my money played over and over in my mind. He still treated me like a little kid when I was twenty-six years old. To me, buying stock had seemed such a good idea. But like Albert said, probably not in one year. In the bank, I would get a guaranteed three percent. Albert had never steered me wrong. I would put it in the bank.

***

31

Dad left for work long before I woke up. Since we had lost the farm, he managed the creamery and had to be there as early as when we worked the farm to greet the farmers who brought in the morning milking. Dad was also the Justice of the Peace, Mayor, and the county's most popular auctioneer. I'd always thought he was just a popular guy, but Granny's words from yesterday were running around in my head.

I gobbled a bowl of corn flakes, excused myself, and walked toward Main, turning onto the limestone boulevard, a hundred feet wide and four blocks long. A car pulled up and parked in front of the bank. I waved at Joe Clark as he got out. A pickup sat in front of the creamery. Otherwise, the street was empty. I could remember when over four hundred people had lived in the thriving little town, a commercial center for several hundred surrounding farmers. Now the population numbered around half that, the devastation of the depression visible in the abandoned homesteads and businesses. I sat for a moment in the shade of the Victorian-era bandstand to reconsider my decision. I valued the control I had gained over my money. Should I put it in a joint account with Dad? My earliest memory came to mind—toddling among the legs of celebrating adults at the end of the Great War, collecting the pretty little pieces of paper that flew everywhere. There were concerts every Tuesday and Saturday night, the street crowded with farmers and townspeople, shopping, visiting, and enjoying the company. I recalled how Dad had been cheerful, confident, and hopeful in those earlier years.

Now only the High School band remained, playing about three concerts a year, and Dad seemed beaten down, stoop-shouldered, unable to thoroughly shake the losses of the depression. I rose and turned toward the creamery, stopping to wave hello to my cousin Millie through the telephone office window.

In the creamery, Dad poured milk into the separator and turned the crank while Mr. Sanford looked on. The cream flowed into the creamery vat and the skim milk back into Mr. Sanford's cans.

"Gene, heard you're on your way to serve our country."

"Yes, sir."

"Well, you're a good man for the job."

Indifferent to Mr. Sanford's comment, Dad paid him for the cream and shook his hand. I wondered what Dad really thought of me going into the army—if anything.

I picked up one milk can, and Mr. Sanford hefted the other. Once we had them in the back of his pickup, he hurried back to his wife and ten children.

"You know, I worry about those young'uns," Dad said. "Every morning, he brings in all his milk. I separate the cream, and he takes the skim milk back to feed the family. I think those poor youngsters are undernourished."

"I'm sure they still get plenty of meat and vegetables. Doris said little Russel is the strongest student in her class."

"I don't know about that. But you didn't come here to talk about the Sanford children. What's on your mind?"

"I thought it over. I'll put the money in the bank. Mr. Swisher will see to it that it gets the best possible interest. Maybe we should make it a joint account, just in case."

"That's great, son. Glad you came 'round. Do you know the price of milk is up three cents a gallon? Farm prices are going up. You're on the right track. Keep the money in the community, bring it back to life. I'll gladly put my name on the account."

We walked down the street to the bank—the big brick building dating from the peak of the railroad era's prosperity. The bank had been the richest in the county when my maternal grandfather and his friends founded it in 1885. The marble-faced counters, barred teller's windows, and pressed tin ceiling were unchanged since the eighteen-eighties. I felt a bit like a little boy again, remembering other times I had gone to the bank with Dad.

Mr. Swisher, the third-generation bank president, rose from his desk and came into the lobby when he saw Dad enter. He always made sure Dad got the best service. "Good morning, Charlie, Gene. What can we do for you today?"

"Morning, Dwight," Dad said.

"We want to put Dad's name on my savings account," I told him. "Dad will manage things while I'm in the army."

"Wise move with you going into the service and all. Keith,

help Gene with that, won't you? Charlie, come sit down in my office while they take care of the paperwork. I have the handbill for that sale this weekend." They disappeared into the office while Keith and I opened the account.

After a delay while Dad and Mr. Swisher took care of business, Keith and I took the papers to the office for Dad to sign, then he and I headed back to the creamery. "If anything happens to me, you and Mom use the money for whatever you need. I know the depression wiped out all your savings. It's all yours if I don't come back."

"You aren't going to war. It's a purely defensive army."

"I don't know. Granny thinks I'll get dysentery; Miss Burkhardt thinks Roosevelt will get us into the war one way or another. It is a very insecure world right now."

"The world's always insecure. We have to create our own safety. You can't count on anyone else to keep yourself or your family safe."

That attitude comes from my grandfather, orphaned at age four and raised by his grandmother, then off to war at seventeen. It had been cemented in place by the trials of the depression.

***

That afternoon I drove to the two-room schoolhouse where Doris taught. I had promised her at my going-away-to-the-army dinner that I would help shut down for the summer. She had already removed everything from the walls and put her books and papers in the workroom.

"Boy, you got this room all tore up."

"Yeah. I want to do something different next year, so I'm getting a head start now."

"At least you get a chance to do what you want. I have to go to the army. Don't they know that they will need doctors if we get into the war? Why couldn't they let me go to medical school."

"Gene, it's only a year."

"Right, but I'm not getting any younger."

"You're talking like Dad now. Grab hold of this desk."

I helped her move all the desks outside.

"What was going on between Albert and Nancy last night? Why isn't he taking the family to Washington?"

"It is about money and Dick's baseball. But they've had some problems, too. She wants to go to work when Ellen goes to school, but Albert doesn't want her to."

"It's a waste of a college degree if she just sits at home."

"He doesn't see it that way. He thinks she's implying that he can't support them. Mr. McCutcheon got drafted, and she wanted to apply for the high school English position."

"The way they're building up the military, more women will need to take jobs. Even married women."

"He said she could apply if they couldn't find anyone else, but I think they hired Mr. Kingsley."

"He must be eighty years old. He retired the year I graduated high school."

"He's only seventy-five, but he does tend to fall asleep in the middle of a lesson. Nancy's a better teacher. We'll see what happens."

I mopped the floor while she scrubbed the desks. Then we moved all twenty-five of them back inside. I wondered if this presaged the work I would do in the army. Move in, move out, dig a hole, refill a hole. Doris, of course, hoped to do something different to make a difference for her students. But what difference would I be making in the army?

She looked around the tiny classroom. "I guess that about does it for this year. Shall we go home and see what's for supper?"

Doris went in to help Mom with supper while I parked my coupe in the corner of the hay shed Dad had cleared out. He and Doris had promised to drive it once in a while to keep the battery charged and the tires pumped up. I covered it with canvas, shaking my head with regret that I had spent almost half a year's salary on the car when I could have used that for medical school. I sauntered to the house.

Mom had spent the day washing the laundry, so supper was cold, leftover fried chicken and canned three-bean salad. Doris and I pulled the kitchen table away from the wall and helped Mom get everything ready. Robert wandered in from a visit with friends. We sat down as soon as Dad got home. After saying grace, we all waited for Dad to lead the conversation.

As he helped himself to three pieces of chicken, he asked, "Doris, will you help me at the sale on Saturday?"

"I planned on it."

Mom, who always had permission to interrupt Dad, asked," What time will you leave tomorrow, Robert."

"I have to be at work by ten, so we need to leave early. Can you be up by five-thirty, Gene, or do you keep bankers' hours now?"

"I can be ready if that old jalopy of yours can get us there."

"It isn't a fancy coupe with six cylinders like you got, but it'll get us there."

"Let's make ice cream in honor of your last night here," Doris suggested.

"Great idea."

Dad seemed disgruntled and ate the rest of his dinner in silence.

After dinner, Dad helped Mom clear the dishes. I pulled out the ice cream maker and began chipping ice off the block in the icebox. Doris mixed up the recipe while Robert picked strawberries from the garden out back., As the sun sank low in the west, we took turns at the crank. Albert and Nancy showed up with their brood as we pulled the paddles from the ice cream. Ken and Trish came in after they finished their chores and dinner. We sat on the porch, eating our ice cream.

"You know, we've had a lot of army men in the family," Dad said, moving into one of his reminiscing lectures. "Someone from the family fought in every war, from the French and Indian War to the Civil War. There was even one general way back in the Revolution. Arthur St. Clair. He came to the colonies to fight in the French-Indian War. He decided to stay, got married, owned a lot of land, then joined Continental Army and became a Major General. They said he was a good friend of George Washington. The name came to be Sinclair within two generations, but he was a direct ancestor of ours..."

"Gene and Robert have to be up early, and Gene hasn't even packed yet." Mom said, "We had better call it a night."

"I'm packed," I said. "They only allow us to bring three days' clothes and a shaving kit." Mom brought some cookies to tuck into the suitcase, and I was ready to go off to the army instead of medical school.

***

I heard Mom banging around in the kitchen before my alarm went off the next morning. She had a full breakfast of fried eggs, bacon, toast, and jam on the table by the time Robert and I got our clothes on.

"Mom, you didn't have to," I said.

"But, we're glad you did." Robert loaded his plate with double portions of everything.

"Still eating like a teenager," I teased.

"I was a teenager until three months ago. Are you ready?" He gobbled the last bite of toast.

"I've barely started eating, you glutton. We still have at least fifteen minutes."

By the time I finished eating, he sat behind the wheel of his old Ford, honking the horn. I grabbed my suitcase, shook hands with Dad, hugged Mom and Doris, and rushed out the door before Mom burst into tears. Dad seemed on the verge of tears, too. He walked out after me.

"Be careful, son," he said, patting me on the back. I realized that his mood was caused by his concern for me. Then he turned and walked around the house to his sheep pen, escaping before becoming more emotional.

CHAPTER 4
IN THE ARMY NOW

No one stirred on the streets of Marion as we pulled up in front of the courthouse at eight a.m. Like most small Kansas towns, it would be hopping by Saturday afternoon, but the action wouldn't start until the farmers had done their chores.

"I guess this is it, big brother," Robert said. "Good luck in the army."

We leaned close and clapped each other on the shoulder, as emotional as it got for the men in my family. As we separated, he looked at his watch. "Gotta go. I told Laura I would stop by and see her before work."

"Always the ladies' man," I said. I climbed out of the car, reached through the open window for my fedora on the back seat, and said, "Take care,"

"Sure."

I pulled my suitcase out of the trunk and slammed it shut as he sped off to meet Laura.

Crossing the expansive lawn, I brushed off a spot on the courthouse steps to avoid getting my suit pants too dirty and contemplated my situation. What did it all mean: anger, fear, love, duty, security, menace? Thoughts sailed across my mind as quickly as the clouds moved across the sky. The puffy little clouds built and boiled, folding in on themselves, growing and expanding until they were giant thunderheads that the high winds aloft blew to the east. I concentrated on the grass of the courthouse lawn, the stone of the building, things grounded to the earth that would not boil and roil and get carried away.

"An eager recruit, here so early!"

Startled out of my reverie, I looked up to see a tall man striding across the courthouse lawn, balancing a stack of papers on top of a flat cardboard box.

"My brother had to get to work, so he dropped me off early. I'm not that eager."

The man didn't seem to believe me, probably because of my round, babyish face. People always thought I was eager or cheerful. That generally worked in my favor. It was easy for me to strike up a conversation with strangers who naturally assumed I would be friendly. It also made me look younger than my twenty-six years, which more often irritated me. The man shifted the box and held out his hand. "Peter Fleming."

"Eugene Sinclair," I shook his hand.

"I remember you. Sorry, I couldn't defer your enlistment. If I'd rejected you, that would have raised questions whenever you applied for a job. Didn't want to stick you with that stigma."

I followed him up the courthouse steps. He indicated a row of oak chairs inside the massive doors along the paneled wall.

"Have a seat. I brought some sweet rolls my wife made. Help yourself." He opened the box, set it on a table in the hall, then disappeared with his papers behind the iced glass and varnished wood of the Marion County Health Department door.

Despite my hearty breakfast, the scent of the rolls beckoned. I selected one and bit into it. I thought my mother was the best baker in Kansas, but Mrs. Flemming made a sweet roll the likes of which I had never tasted. I wolfed it down. As I sat waiting, other draft board members arrived, snatched a sweet roll from the box, nodded in my direction, and entered the health department.

Sitting alone in the dim hallway became unbearable. I needed some water to moisten a mouth parched, both by apprehension and the sugary sweet roll. So I left the chairs and wandered through the darkened halls typical of Kansas courthouses—federalist style, lots of polished wood and marble. Around a couple of corners, I found a drinking fountain, gulped some water, and returned through the echoing hallways to the row of chairs. Jimmy, Junior, and Bobby, the three high school students who had enlisted, lounged in the chairs. Their parents stood on the opposite side of the hallway.

Junior's mother saw me coming. "I'm so glad you're going, too, Mr. Sinclair. You'll keep an eye on my boy, won't you?" Three years ago, this same woman told me that I couldn't possibly be old enough to teach high school students.

"I'll do my best," I promised.

The chairs gradually filled. Most of the draftees were younger than me, but three or four must have been in their thirties. Finally, at precisely ten o'clock, Mr. Fleming emerged from the room, a stack of cards in his hand.

"Each of you will receive one of these cards. Proceed through each check station. The Selective Service officer will record your results on the card. Please line up in alphabetical order when I call your name."

By the time he called Sinclair, the line stretched down the hall and around the corner. We inched forward. Finally, card in hand, I reached the oak door. The board member at the entrance took my card and looked at me.

"Eyes blue. Hair sandy." He said as he recorded the information on my card.

At least ten people, four desks, one scale, and two extra chairs in the small office made it difficult to move. A stout draftee in front of me stepped backward off the scale, right onto my toes.

"Hey, watch it there. That hurt."

"Complexion ruddy."

"Ruddy? My complexion is not ruddy."

"I just write what I see. Seems to be getting ruddier by the second." He handed me back the card. "Move along now. You're holding up the line.

"But..."

"Step on the scale." The next man took the card from my hand. "One hundred forty pounds. Five feet six inches. Next."

The local dentist pronounced my teeth sound. I quickly read the 20/20 line on the eye chart. The draftee who had stepped on my toes stumbled through the paragraph Mr. Fleming asked him to read.

"Unfit," Fleming announced, stamping a big, red 'Rejected' on his card.

I read. Fleming stamped my card 'Accepted' and sent me out to wait on the lawn. The thunderheads had piled up on the eastern horizon. Above us, only the pale cyan sky and furious sunlight. Boys wrestled on the grass, shouting mock insults and slapping each other on the back as parents and well-wishers stood in the shade. I wandered among them. A few fathers murmured about the lend-lease program, others the likelihood of war. A gaggle of mothers praised the bravery and strength of their sons. I leaned against a tree out of hearing of the war talk. Too restless to stand still for long, I ambled over to the roped-off area where the bus would stop. When I started to sweat in the glaring sun, I headed back to the shade. Bobby's father stopped me as I passed.

"I imagine you're the only one who has a reasonable idea of what you're getting into."

"I'm not sure I do, but at least I don't think it will be all glory and triumph. I'm not at all excited about going."

"No. In France during the Great War, we didn't experience much triumph or glory. Mostly boredom, terror, trench foot, and dysentery. I hope it doesn't come to war for these boys. They're so young and inexperienced. I'm glad you're going. Maybe you can help them deal with what's coming."

"I'll try," I promised, knowing I would be out of my element just like the boys.

A rattletrap army green bus rolled up; the mood changed. Fathers shook hands with their sons; mothers hugged them and wiped their eyes.

A Corporal stepped off the bus. "Everybody load up!"

The boys climbed aboard, stuffing their suitcase or duffel bag into the overhead net. Several other boys were already on the bus. Pushing and shoving, everyone managed to find a seat. I climbed the steps last, stowed my pasteboard suitcase, and settled into a seat near the front of the bus, next to a boy dressed in homespun pants and shirt.

"You the chaperone or something?" he asked. No one else wore a suit.

"I was drafted like everyone else."

"Not me. I volunteered."

The Marion County boys waved out the window, then settled in for the five-hour trip to Fort Leavenworth.

"Gene Sinclair," I said, extending my hand.

"Joseph Zook," he said, smiling shyly. "Call me Joe."

"Where you from, Joe?"

"Newton."

His badly cut light brown hair framed a face deeply tanned across the middle but pale above the hat line. His cheeks and chin, scratched and nicked by a poor job of shaving, were pale too.

"Are you Mennonite?" I asked, examining his work-roughened hands and innocent eyes.

"Ya, until my father found out I enlisted. So I'm pretty much on my own now."

"Why didn't you register as a conscientious objector?"

"Bad things are happening. We're gonna have to fight sooner or later. I wanna be part of it."

"I'm not so certain. I don't want to fight, but I respect your convictions. How did you learn about what's happening in Europe?"

"I like to read. Our school only goes to eighth grade. We don't have radio or newspapers at home, so I went to the library in town. I checked out a bunch of history and philosophy books."

I raised my eyebrows.

"I read some newspapers, too."

"You're certain this is what you want to do?"

"I made up my mind. I do kinda miss my mom and sisters, though." He slumped into the seat, looking very young.

"How old are you?"

He looked down sheepishly. "Don't tell. I'll be seventeen by the time we finish boot camp. I'll be old enough when I get to the front."

"I'm sure you will be."

After that, he curled up in his corner of the seat, staring out the window. Alone at sixteen, something I understood. I graduated from high school at sixteen. My mother thought I was too young to go off to college. Dad didn't have any money to pay for it anyway. It was 1930, and we had just lost the farm. So dad got me a job on the railroad. Shoveling gravel, carrying heavy loads from the supply cars, that sort of thing. I didn't lay any rail but still worked hard. Our Irish foreman had cobbled together a crew of Irish, Chinese, and Mexican workers, along with a few of us local boys, for unskilled labor. We built branch lines to some of the smaller towns. I thought nothing could be worse than my first night there, but I found out different. My muscles ached like they never had. The experienced crew yelled at us because we didn't know what we were doing. Even the other boys didn't completely accept me because I had graduated from high school. Joe shouldn't have to feel that way. Wouldn't feel that way if I could help it.

***

The bus stopped in Emporia to pick up a third group of inductees. I grabbed one of the sandwiches the Corporal handed out. Telling him I would be right back, I sprinted across the street to the Gazette office. Even before I walked through the door, Mr. White came out of his office. He located his office behind the storefront window to watch his beloved little town.

"Gene, what brings you to Emporia on this fine summer's day?"

"On my way to Fort Leavenworth. I was drafted. Just after I received my acceptance letter from medical school. They wouldn't let me out of the draft for medical school."

"Ironic. The President of Students for Peace drafted. You're in once your name comes up, no matter what plans you might have had. You might be able to get some medical training in the army, although I would recommend officer's training for you. You would be an excellent officer."

"It's only a one-year enlistment. I don't intend to stay any longer. I'm counting on you and your committee to keep the supplies flowing to Europe. Let them win the war and keep us out of it."

"Doing my best." His telephone jangled. He trotted off to answer it, calling, "Good luck, Gene. It's great seeing you."

***

The creaky bus bumped steadily northeast between wheat and cornfields, through the dusty small towns. Sweat began to bead on my face. The bus smelled ripe, crowded as it was with teen boys.

"Can anybody open a window?" I asked.

Only two windows would budge, but even those didn't open all the way—a slight breeze gave little relief from the heat and humidity of the eastern Kansas summer. Pulling off my suit jacket, I stuffed it into the netting with my suitcase. Boys grumbled and complained as we rode along inside this oven of a bus. The mood threatened to escalate. Their excitement had worn off, and some of the young men were getting surly. Joe looked back at the other boys, pulled a harmonica out of his pocket, and began playing. First, he played old hymns we all knew. A few of the boys sang along. We stopped noticing the heat. Then the boys asked for their favorite popular songs. He knew them all. Somewhere along the line he must have been listening to the radio. With music, time passed much more quickly.

***

The corporal stood as the bus rolled to a stop at Fort Leavenworth.

"Chow is in the mess to your right. You will sleep in Barracks D immediately to the north of the mess hall. Be there by 1830."

We hauled our luggage out and trudged into the mess hall.

"Look, a whole busload of hicks from the sticks," shouted one of the diners when we walked in. "We'll have to show 'em how it's done."

This group still wore civilian clothes and toted suitcases – another group of recruits. I spotted Tom Morris, the brother of Robert's former girlfriend. That wasn't hard. He stood a head taller than most of the recruits, his slick black hair gleaming with pomade. We had met in Emporia at the football game where Robert and Tom's sister broke up. Tom and I tried unsuccessfully to defuse the situation. Robert and Jenny never spoke to each other again, but Tom and I had dinner together afterward, and we hit it off. We never expected to see each other after that, but here we were in the same army mess hall.

"Tom, good to see you? You got drafted too?"

"How ya doing', Gene. I enlisted. I graduated and figured that I'd most likely be drafted if I got a job. I decided to join up before they drew me. I'll have more control over what I do and where I end up."

"Are these wise guys all from Kansas City?"

"Yeah. We've been here about 20 minutes."

"You! Get in line. We're not here to renew old friendships." The Corporal shouted, pointing at me. I got in line for my slab of spam, mashed potatoes, and overcooked peas. This, I assumed, would be our food for the duration. I carried my tray to the table where Bobby, Jimmy, Junior, and Zook were eating. Nearby some pushing and shoving started between some country boys and city boys.

"This is the army," a sergeant separated them and shouted, "Every one of you is an army recruit. There will be no more city or country. Only soldiers. Now eat your grub and get to your barracks. Morning comes early around here."

A Corporal escorted the Kansas City boys out to shouts of "See you later, swells." and "So long, City Slickers." Soon our Corporal herded us out the same way. In the barracks, we found bunks with a blanket and sheets folded on each mattress. I made my bed and headed for the bathroom to brush my teeth.

Everyone had their sheets on and tucked in by lights out, some more securely than others. I fell asleep quickly despite the heavy breathing, snoring, and one or two softly crying boys. I awakened at dawn when a Sergeant shouted for us to get up.

Breakfast consisted of blackened bacon, cold scrambled eggs, tarlike coffee, and burned toast. Next stop was the barbershop, where we parted with deep piles of pomaded hair. Then the clinic where we were ordered to disrobe. The odor of sixty sweaty, nervous, and embarrassed young men mixed with the clinic's alcohol and disinfectant. We shuffled forward to be poked, prodded, examined, and immunized by a gauntlet of doctors and nurses. I kept my eyes on the back of Bobby's head as I willed the line to move faster. From there, a sergeant herded us into a large, communal shower. Finally, two days' sweat and grime removed, we were back in line for lunch dressed in our new uniforms.

After lunch, a sergeant called out names on the parade ground and assigned us to squads. He ordered us to stand in a square. For several minutes he shouted at us about proper military behavior. I almost tuned out. Then he called, "Sinclair!"

"Yes, sir!"

"I am a Sergeant. Call me Sergeant. Are you a college boy, private?"

"Yes, Sergeant!"

"This is your squad, college boy. This is your college boy, squad. You'll see to this squad. Make sure you all get where you're going. Do you understand, college boy?"

"Yes, Sergeant!"

"Squads one through four will be shipping out at 0600 hours for training at Camp Callan in California. You'll be in the Coastal Artillery, defending this country from invasion. Board the bus where you disembarked last night.

"Now, you will take the oath of enlistment. This is a privilege. When making the oath, stand at attention. Follow the Captain word for word and speak loudly and clearly."

An officer stepped in front of us. "Raise your right hand and repeat after me.

I raised my hand and repeated, "I, Eugene Sinclair, do solemnly swear that I'll support the Constitution of the United States against all enemies, foreign and domestic, that I will bear true faith and allegiance to the same; that I take this obligation freely, without any mental reservation or purpose of evasion; and that I will well and faithfully discharge the duties of the office upon which I am about to enter; So help me God."

CHAPTER 5
WE'RE NOT IN KANSAS ANYMORE

"**M**ove it, move it, move it," shouted the exuberant young Sergeant who would supervise the squads on the trip to California. We stumbled through dim early morning light and dreary clouds into the same smelly bus that had brought us here. I had not slept well on the hard cots in the stuffy barracks, and breakfast had again been abominable—eggs made of rubber with a side of crap.

Most of the boys dropped off to sleep before the bus even left Leavenworth. I had never been able to sleep well in a vehicle. Everything got on my nerves, from Jimmy crowding me off the seat as he slumped in his sleep to the drizzle outside. The rain reflected my surly mood—constant but not overwhelming. My anger and frustration simmered for the entire hour it took to reach Kansas City's Union Station.

Only Sarge and I stayed awake, him probably basking in the authority he had been granted and me ruminating on lost possibilities, my assignment as squad leader, and my conflicted perspective on the oath I had taken.

As a man of my word, I could not go back on the oath I had sworn the previous day, but I could think of nothing I wanted to do less than spend a year in the army. I appreciated the privilege of living in the United States and our freedom and rights. No tyranny, no despotism. Maybe a year of helping protect our freedom and rights would be good for me. However, I didn't want to put my life on the line for a bunch of Europeans or Asians, no matter how bad their situation. While not quite as isolationist as the America First Committee, I felt no obligation to the continent my ancestors had left under duress three hundred years ago.

Since receiving the draft notice, I kicked myself for not getting into medical school sooner. Why had I spent my money on Albert's Coupe? Why had I become so attached to the senior class that I wanted to finish the year teaching them? I might spend the rest of my life regretting both decisions. I would have had a deferment if I had only chosen sooner—forgoing the Coupe to save money for school.

Sarge stood as the bus rolled to a stop at Union Station.

"Men, the army intends to get you to training as quickly as possible. For this reason, they are sending you on the California Limited. Pullman public sleeper cars have been reserved for you. Aside from the two cars reserved for you, the train will be filled with civilians. I will expect you to behave in a way that will make the army proud. Now, off the bus. The train should be here within the hour. Departure time is 0915."

"Why did we have to come so early if the train isn't even here?" complained Junior as he stumbled into the station rubbing his eyes. I felt the same.

"Private, keep your jabber to yourself," shouted the Sergeant. He looked at Junior as though he were an insect emerging from a pile of pond scum.

Sarge ordered us to benches to wait while he took off to "Check us in," he claimed. Some of the boys complained of being tired and sprawled out on the hard benches in the station until Sarge returned, kicked their feet off the bench, and told them to sit up and act like soldiers. When the train finally pulled alongside the loading platform, Sarge led us to our cars and yelled at us to board quickly and stay together. We all tried to squeeze through the doors at once, so a mild melee ensued. Somehow Sarge boarded before we did and waited at the front of the car as we shoved our way in. He assigned each squad a set of seats.

"These will be your seats, and they'll become your beds. Your squad leaders will hand out your meal passes. Every pass will be marked at each meal, so don't think you can get extra meals." He paused and sneered, "It's a long trip," and I wondered if he meant more than just a train ride. Sarge pressed a packet of meal passes into my hand, said "Dismissed," and walked down the aisle to yell at Tom Morris's squad at the other end of the car. The boys crowded around me, trying to get the meal passes. I shoved them in my pocket and scowled.

"Sit down and shut up," I commanded. I learned some things while teaching kids. Hall passes, for instance, should be handed out only when needed immediately. "I'll give you a pass when it's time to eat."

I sat down too and crossed my arms, frowning. As the train pulled out of the station, Zook sat beside me, bouncing in the seat before settling in. I looked at the boy and almost ripped into him out of some unconscious need to release my emotions. He grinned, settling me down, and said, "I know you didn't volunteer for this, but you can't do nothin about it right now. Look around. You ever traveled in a Pullman before? Feel how cool it is? The porter said it's air-conditioned! For heaven's sake, we're on the California Limited, and you look like a hobo who just hopped a rusty freight car."

Right. I'd taken the oath. Now I could only accept the trip to California, save some more money, and apply for medical school next year.

The train gathered speed as it rolled past stockyards and railyards. As we left Kansas City, the clouds parted; wheat fields stood shimmering in anticipation of the harvest. "For amber waves of grain" swelled in my head. Soon the combines would move slowly north, and all of Kansas would labor together to feed the nation. Watching the endless fields roll by lulled me to sleep.

I woke when the conductor walked through, announcing a stop in Topeka. My short sleep left me refreshed. Maybe it wouldn't be so bad after all. I glanced out the window. Across the river, the Capitol dome towered above the treetops.

"Look, guys, there's the Kansas State Capitol," I said

Everyone crowded to the left side of the train to get a look.

"It's taller than the grain silo at home," one of the Newton boys said.

"It's taller than the National Capitol in Washington, D.C.," I told him.

None of them had seen the State Capitol before, and they

stood marveling at the dome's size and height until we pulled out of the station. After we left Topeka, the conductor walked through again.

"Luncheon is served," he announced

"Luncheon?" laughed Bobby.

"Just come eat," Jimmy replied.

I pulled the meal passes out of my pocket and handed them to the boys as they filed past. So far, it seemed almost like an extended school field trip. I needed to keep track of my charges and make sure everyone had a meal ticket. Let them have fun but not get too rowdy. I could almost forget that I'd been inducted into the army, except for the uniforms everyone wore and the sergeant's presence.

Tom Morris's squad of city boys arrived at the dining car at the same time we did. The boys jockeyed for position, trying to get in first. The maître d' pulled four soldiers at a time from the crowd and showed them to their tables. Every table ended up with a mix of city and county boys, eying each other warily as they waited. Tom and I were seated last, at a table for two. Across the aisle from us, Bobby Kuhn and a boy from Newton sat with two Kansas City boys. The waiter stopped at their table, and Bobby said, "Bring me a chicken fried steak."

Next to him, the Kansas City boy said, "I'll have a chicken fried steak, too."

"I'm sorry, sir, this gentleman just ordered our last chicken fried steak. Perhaps you would like the breaded veal cutlets?"

"No, I don't want any breaded veal cutlets. I want chicken fried steak." He glared at Bobby. "Gimme the chicken fried steak."

Bobby stood up. The Kansas City boy stood too, and the waiter stepped back. Tom and I jumped out of our seats. Both boys drew back their fists. Sarge and the maître d' started up the aisle from opposite sides.

The other Kansas City boy stood and put his hand on his friend's arm. "Tommy lay off. You'll never get to be a pro boxer if you hurt the guy."

Bobby dropped his fists. "You wanna be a boxer? I been training since I was seven."

Tommy gestured to the chair, and they both sat. "What gym have you been going to?"

"Don't have no gyms in Burns. I worked with an old guy on a farm north of us that worked with Jess Willard. Said he taught Willard everything he knew."

"I didn't think Willard knew much of anything. He was just too big and heavy for anyone to knock down until Dempsey came in under him and hit him in the chin."

"You don't stay heavyweight champion of the world for eleven years unless you know somethin about fightin," Bobby retorted, but in a friendly way.

The mood in the dining car relaxed. The waiters continued taking orders, and the other boys gradually began to talk with each other. They all adjourned to the observation car at the end of the meal. Tom and I lingered in the dining car, enjoying the excellent meal and conversation, finally making our way to the observation car as the dining car filled up for the second seating.

Junior had a game of Blackjack going. Zook watched, and he caught on quickly. He asked to be dealt in an hour later and won his first hand. Zook continued to take hand after hand until the game folded with most of the chips in front of him. He had talent.

The conductor walked through the car in the middle of the afternoon, calling out, "Next stop, Newton, Kansas."

"Three exhausting days, and all I've done is get back home," complained one of the Newton boys.

"Yeah, but we don't get off here. Take one last look, 'cause we're on our way to California!" Zook replied.

We stared out the window after the train left Newton as the plains grew increasingly arid. Wheatfields gave way to alfalfa fields and pastures full of cattle. Soon we were in the badlands; rocky cliffs, scrubby grass, yucca, and cacti.

"You know what, sitting here watching Kansas go by is boring," declared Zook. He pulled out his harmonica and played "Home on the Range." I sang along, and people gathered to listen.

"You have a great voice," Zook said. "You ever done any professional singing?"

"No, I sang at church and in talent shows at school. I sang in one musical in college, but nothing ever came of it."

Zook began, "You are my Sunshine." Morris and I piped in, managing a few simple harmonies as we sang. Zook moved on to "When You Wish Upon a Star." Morris couldn't come close to the high notes. I struggled with them. A gorgeous auburn-haired girl with sparkly green eyes joined in, reaching the notes with ease. After that, more people joined in, and it became a sing-along for the rest of the afternoon.

When the conductor announced the evening meal, Morris disappeared with the red-haired beauty. The rest of us waited in our usual mob for the second seating.

***

"This is more like it," Jimmy said, breathing the cooler air at La Junta, Colorado stopover. "You ever been out of Kansas?"

"I've been to Nebraska several times, but that's fourteen miles from my hometown," I said. "And I went to Missouri with a friend to visit his grandmother. But never to Colorado." I didn't add that I had traveled worldwide in books and newsreels because of my interest in history.

None of the other boys standing around us had been out of Kansas, let alone their hometowns.

"Where're the mountains?" Zook asked.

Morris appeared out of the dusk. "They're farther west. If it weren't dark, we might see them from here. In the morning, we'll be in New Mexico. We'll miss seeing most of the mountains because we'll be going through the passes in the dark."

"How do you know?"

"My grandparents live in Arizona. I've traveled this route every summer." His standing with the boys immediately rose to new heights based on this worldly experience.

Back on board after the quick stop in La Junta, the porters had pulled down our berths for the night.

"Two men in the lower berth and one in the upper," Sarge yelled down the aisle.

I assigned berths to my squad, then climbed into a berth above Joe and Jimmy as the train jerked out of the station. I couldn't sit up without banging my head on the ceiling, but at least I had the berth to myself. I slipped out of my uniform, folded it, and placed it in the net pocket near my head. Sleep eluded me. The cars jostled back and forth along the tracks. My mind churned over and over my regret at buying the Coupe and delaying my admission into medical school.

I have no idea how long I lay awake. After a while, the train slowed to a crawl. I slipped out of my berth, put on my trousers and undershirt, and headed to the observation car. Unfortunately, I barely caught a glimpse of the mountain pass except for a few rocks immediately outside the windows. A steward came through, wiping tables and picking up trash.

"I bet this would be beautiful if we could see it," I said. The steward jumped and dropped the trash bin he carried. I picked up the container and tossed bits of trash back in.

"Oh, sir. 'Scuse me. I've got it. You don't need to help."

"I worked my way through college as a houseboy. I know how frustrating it can be to do something twice."

"I've never seen a white houseboy."

"Well, my boss pretty much didn't see skin color."

"Never met a man of that sort either," he said.

I put the last of the trash back in the bin.

"Gene Sinclair." I held out my hand. He shook it hesitantly.

"You can call me George."

"That's what the Porter in my sleeper car said. You can't all be named George."

"No. Mr. Pullman is named George, so they call all us Pullman porters George. That way, they don't have to remember our names."

"So, what is your name?"

"Samuel." He looked at me keenly, then said, "You're right. It is pretty through here. The other night, the full moon made it all so eerie. I spotted a bear standing on its hind legs ripping apart a dead tree next to the tracks."

I visited with him a bit more, then realized how tired he looked. He needed to finish cleaning up and get to sleep, so I said goodbye and went back to my berth, where I finally managed to fall asleep.

As we stood in line for breakfast, Sarge came through the cars blowing a bugle loudly, claiming he played "Reveille". Outside, layer upon layer of rugged mountains appeared out of the darkness. The sun came up, turning the rocks, the grass, the sky, everything a bright red-orange. I almost didn't hear the maître d' when he called for me to be seated as I stared at the sight. Morris joined me at the table a few minutes later, and I asked him about the girl.

"Her name is Ava Gardner. She said she's on her way to Hollywood because she has a contract with MGM. I don't know whether to believe her or not. She's from the South, but she said she'd spent some time in New York with her sister, where she was discovered. Her sister's traveling with her from New York."

"She's certainly pretty enough to be in the movies."

"She is. We'll have to be on the lookout for her when we go to the cinema."

***

A few hours later, we stepped off the train in Albuquerque and stared at the long line of brightly dressed Indian women sitting on the platform. Each woman had spread a blanket on the concrete where she'd laid out pottery, jewelry, and other trinkets for sale.

As I wandered along the platform, I almost ran into Samuel, who carried a small valise, his jacket slung over his shoulder.

"Are you leaving us?" I asked.

"Shift change," he replied. "Soon as the eastbound train comes, I'll head back the other way.

"Thanks for taking care of us," He moved off, waving an arm without looking back.

Several guys bargained with the Indian women, buying jewelry for their girlfriends. I wandered to a modest food stand near the station. I didn't recognize many of the things on the painted menu.

"What is a ta-mail?" I asked, not sure how to pronounce it.

"It is a tah-mah-lay," the girl told me. "We take a cornhusk, spread masa—cornmeal—on it, put a spicy meat in the center, roll it up, and steam it."

"I'll take one. And what is Ah-gooah Fresha dee San-diei a?"

"Cold watermelon drink,"

"Give me one of those, too," I said.

I unfolded the cornhusk. Inside I found soft cornmeal mush. I bit into it. Spicy was right. My mouth burned. The watermelon drink did a lot to cool off my mouth, but I paid for it with heartburn all the next day. I vowed to myself to be more careful about trying strange new foods.

We headed west again, and the land became dry and rocky, punctuated by tall cliffs of red rock and flat-topped mountains.

"Nothing worth farming here," said Zook.

"Mostly Indian land," Morris told us. "Unless it's a Spanish land grant or government land."

"What would anybody want with this land?" asked Zook.

"Grazing cattle, mining, and farming along the rivers," Morris said.

I realized that what at first appeared to be a uniform brown landscape held a kaleidoscope of color. Muted green and purple sage, red rocks, stripes of chalky white, and greasy browns with reds and blacks on the bluffs rising out of the flat yellow-green desert—all very subtle and complex. What had first appeared bleak and barren became a tapestry of understated beauty as I studied it. Maybe my future wasn't as grim as I thought, either. So far, things hadn't been too bad. I could spend a year learning about the rest of the country, helping the other guys adjust, and maybe becoming better for it. A year in the army might even make me a better doctor.

By sunset, we were somewhere in Arizona, a mix of mountains near Flagstaff and desert further west; I hadn't realized that Arizona had mountains. I had expected only saguaro dotted desert. We didn't see any saguaro at all along this route.

We woke up in California. As we emerged from the last mountain pass, a sea of houses came into view below us. We traveled through one town after another for miles until, at last, we pulled into the busy Los Angeles train station. I had never been to a city of over a million people before. I couldn't get over the miles and miles of people living right next door to each other as we passed through the vast city to the station.

"Listen up, men. You are not to leave the station." Sarge ordered. "We need to get some grub. There's a six-hour layover here. Follow me!"

Sarge, who rebuffed all my attempts to get better acquainted, ordered sandwiches for all of us in a modest coffee shop in the station. While we waited for the cook to slap the sandwiches together, I spotted the headline on the Sunday edition of the L.A. Times "Hitler Begins War With Russia." I bought a copy and sat in the station's unreal artificial daylight to read it. The paper was huge—44 pages of solid type. It would take hours to read thoroughly, unlike the Burns paper that would take maybe half an hour if I dawdled, or Aunt Kate's little rag that I could finish before I polished off Mom's breakfast. I took the sandwich Jimmy brought me and continued reading as I devoured it.

The benches around us began to fill up with young recruits emerging off other trains. Soon inert bodies of young soldiers were scattered everywhere like a battlefield, the enemy fatigue and boredom. When our train arrived around midnight, buddies roused buddies, and we all stumbled onto the train—no sleeper cars for this stretch of the trip. Recruits filled every seat. As we left the terminal, the lights went out except for dim little pinpoints on the floor along the aisle. I did doze a bit until Zook elbowed me in the ribs. Then he slumped onto my shoulder, so I elbowed him. The hard seat made my rear end ache. My shoulders ached. I crossed and uncrossed my legs, trying to find a comfortable position. When light began to show on the eastern horizon, I fished my shaving kit out of the duffel bag at my feet and went to the lavatory. Even if I couldn't sleep, I figured, I could shave and splash some cold water on my face in an attempt to appear well-rested. I would find out that attempting to appear well-rested would be my fate for the next few months.

CHAPTER 6
THE BASICS

The sun broke over the mountains to the east as we staggered off the train into one of the most beautiful spots I had ever seen. Neat rows of green-roofed white barracks glistened in the slanting light, surrounded by emerald grass. Between us and distant cliffs stretched grassland dotted with small pines. Beyond the grassland, the Pacific Ocean extended to the horizon. My chemistry teacher's nose sniffed an unusual scent—a bit of sulfur, some chlorine, or maybe bromine, a touch of methyl alcohol. Somehow all of that combined to create a bright, fresh scent.

The drill sergeant strode up and yelled in my face, "Stop sniffing the ocean, Private. Get in line!" I shook off my fatigue and awe and fell in with the squad. I was glad the drill sergeant didn't spit when he yelled.

"Welcome to Camp Callan," the drill sergeant yelled. "I'm Sergeant Henry. You will call me Drill Sergeant. Your life as you knew it is over. You belong to the army. Everything you do, say and think belongs to the army. We will make soldiers out of you."

My thinking will never belong to the army, I vowed silently, no matter what this guy dished out.

"Over the next few weeks, in addition to the skills you need to become a competent soldier, you'll develop the character you need to be a dedicated soldier. Once you develop the character of a soldier, you'll live it for the rest of your lives, on duty and off."

No way I would live the character of a soldier for the rest of my life. I would live the character of a doctor. I had every intention of completing the duty I had pledged. Then I would get my life back on track and go to medical school. During my year in the army, I would follow orders, uphold the Constitution, and all that, but not let go of my goal in life.

"Graham, Hanson, Montgomery, Ortiz, Puccio, Sinclair, Small, Washington, Zook!" the Sergeant shouted. "Line up, squad one!"

He called out three other squads who lined up behind us. When we were all assembled, he shouted, "This is Platoon A. Follow Corporal Miller!"

We picked up our duffel bags and ambled toward the Corporal.

"Halt!" Corporal Miller yelled. "When I call your name, come forward to get your housing paperwork. This barracks and bunk assignment will be your home for the next three months."

As soon as everyone had their paperwork, he shouted, "Duffel bags over your left shoulder. Form two straight lines, side by side."

Most of us swung our duffel bags to the left shoulder and got in line. A couple had to try twice to find their left shoulders.

"Forward march!" At the barracks, he called for us to halt.

"You'll be on the second floor. Find your assigned cot."

Fueled by hormones on overdrive and excitement at having arrived at a place with beds, the younger men charged up the stairs with a victory cry. Jimmy tripped and sprawled across the steps as other boys leaped over him to be the first upstairs.

"Everybody back out here! Bring your gear!" ordered Corporal Miller.

Thankfully, I hadn't started up the stairs yet.

"You will enter quickly! Quietly! Efficiently! Into The Barracks." Corporal Miller enunciated, glaring at us.

We tried again, but some boys seemed unable to figure out how to merge the two lines into one and get up the stairs.

"Everybody out!"

Platoon B had arrived and attempted to enter the first floor as we exited the second. That doubled the confusion. I sighed as the corporal ordered us in one more time.

This nineteen-year-old corporal got an excessive amount of pleasure from this episode. I could see no purpose to this other than that the corporal wanted to prove he was in charge. The other platoon didn't get this kind of folderol.

"Go up the right side," I said to the guys in front of me.

Before anyone had placed their duffels on the bunks, the corporal demanded, "Everybody out!"

We clambered downstairs and, for the third time, outside. Once more, Corporal Miller ordered us into the barracks. We quickly climbed the steps single file; miraculously, no one tripped or pushed. We had finally done it to the Corporal's satisfaction.

Now maybe we could sleep.

"Time for breakfast!" the Corporal yelled before we even dropped our duffel bags. "Outside! Line up for mess."

I was fed up! I threw my duffel bag on the cot with all my strength.

"Sinclair, KP duty for two days."

I glared at the Corporal but held back the curse on the tip of my tongue.

We scurried down the stairs and followed Corporal Miller to the mess hall in our two parallel lines. Sergeant Henry met us there with a cartload of books.

"Basic Training Manuals are to be placed in your right pocket. Go through the line, get your food and a drink. Don't forget to pick up silverware. Sit together at the third and fourth tables from the front. No talking during the meal. Eat quickly. You have fifteen minutes. When you have finished eating, remove the manual from your pocket and study it until you are told to stand. Return your tray to the dishwashing area and leave the chow hall through the opposite door."

The Corporal spoke quietly with Sergeant Henry.

"Sinclair, out of line," the drill sergeant ordered.

I got out of the line and stood in front of the sergeant.

"Wipe down the first and second tables from the front and their benches, then mop under them. You may join your squad at the table when you complete that task. You will perform this KP duty at every meal today and tomorrow."

I didn't see how I could wipe down the tables, mop the floor, and still have time to eat. I rushed to a pan of soapy water by the dishwashing station the corporal pointed out and grabbed a rag. Wringing it out, I wiped down the tables and benches. A mop and wheeled bucket sat in a corner near the dishwashing station, the bucket half full of cold, greasy water with food bits floating in it. I asked a dishwasher where to dump it, filled it with warm soapy water at a huge sink where I could place the bucket, and mopped the floorboards. Finally, I could get food.

The privates serving the squads in the chow line plopped scrambled eggs, sausage, and potatoes on my tray. My mood brightened at my first bite; the food tasted delicious. We wouldn't have to eat the barely edible chow served at Fort Leavenworth.

I did finish my breakfast but didn't have time to read anything in the manual. At Drill Sergeant's orders, we stood, returned our trays, and marched to the barracks to make our beds and stow our gear. I had tight sheets with hospital corners that would do Granny proud three times, but Sergeant Henry tore them off, exclaiming to me, as he had to many others in the barracks, "This is crap!"

I grabbed the sheets from the sergeant and jerked them tight across the mattress. I creased the folds of the corners with my fingers, thinking of where I would like to tell Sarge to shove it. I pulled everything so tight I feared the sheets might rip in two. Sergeant Henry came to inspect. I forced myself to concentrate on the distant sound of the ocean to avoid blowing up if he ripped the sheets off again.

"Excellent," he said.

The Sergeant wasted the rest of the morning teaching us how to fold our clothes. Did he think we were children?

As I mopped behind him at lunch, Zook softly asked me, "Why're they always yelling at us?"

"They are trying to break us; see how much we can take." I suddenly realized how senseless I had been, almost blowing up over making my bed. I grasped that the sergeant wanted to see how much I could take without losing it. He knew I could make a bed. "Somehow, they think we'll get tougher if they yell at us enough."

A lot of basic training is pretending, I thought to myself. I should act the way they want me to, and I will get through it much more comfortably. Regardless of my opinions concerning what they were doing, I decided to join the act—basic training basics.

"Everything about this is harder than I expected," Jimmy whined as he slid into his seat.

Graham dropped his tray next to Jimmy's and climbed over the bench. "My uncle always used to say, 'What doesn't kill you builds character.' I think we'll be building a lot of character in the next few weeks."

I finished the mopping and got my food.

"Where you from, Graham?" I asked as I sat down.

"We've got a ranch up in Wyoming. My mom runs it. Dad ran off early in the depression years and never came back."

"I imagine that built some character," I said.

"Cut the chatter!" the Sergeant yelled. "This is chow, not a high school social."

We finished the meal in silence.

When it looked like most of us had shoveled their grub into their pie holes, the Sergeant ordered us up. "On your feet." We stood at almost the same time, grabbing our trays. "Forward march."

After shoving our trays into the rack for the dishwasher, we followed Sergeant Henry to the parade ground.

We lined up according to directions, then Henry said, "In the army, you move as a unit, every soldier performing the same movement simultaneously. You need to obey an officer's command immediately and automatically."

First, we had to learn to stand, heels together, feet at a forty-five-degree angle, back straight, arms at our sides. Drill Sergeant Henry inspected us from every angle. I never knew there were so many wrong ways to stand. Graham didn't have his toes far enough apart, Jimmy slouched, Morris's hands were in the wrong position, and so on all through the platoon. Eventually, everyone's posture satisfied Sarge. Next, he taught us to march.

"Listen up! If this platoon is going to march together, you have to adjust your steps. Everyone must take the same size step to avoid walking on their buddies. I will set the pace and cadence. You make sure your lines are straight and your steps even."

We marched until our feet were sore. Finally, Sarge taught us to make right turns. Then left turns. When he decided we were ready, we marched around the edge of the field, then about-faced and marched around again. As the afternoon wore on, I became light-headed from lack of sleep and the physical effort of repeating the movements. I hadn't worked this hard since my brief stint as a railroad man, and I had been ten years younger then. My calves began to ache, my shoulders started creaking, and my feet felt numb in my new army issued boots. Some of the boys looked ready to drop. Just as I felt sure some of us would faint right there on the field, Sarge dismissed us for dinner. "Now you know why you call me Drill Sergeant!" he shouted at our backs.

After KP duty and a silent five minutes of dinner, I hoped to go back to the barracks and finally get some sleep. Instead, we assembled in a classroom where we watched a film strip on personal hygiene and venereal disease. Sergeant Henry walked among us, prodding anyone who looked like they might be dozing. I recognized another test, taking us into a dark room to watch a boring filmstrip after having almost no sleep in the last thirty-six hours. I determined to pass the test, but I did doze off once, luckily waking before the sergeant had a chance to poke me with his billystick. I wondered why we saw this filmstrip first. We were so exhausted we could barely comprehend it. Surely, they wanted us to remember all this.

As the lights came up at the end of the filmstrip, Sergeant Henry stepped to the front of the room. His presence immediately caused us to become more alert.

"You are in the army now! You will honor the uniform! You will behave with integrity! No clap! No crabs! Keep yourself in your pants. Now, to the barracks! Prepare for lights out."

On the way to the barracks, Washington asked me, "Why did Sarge warn us about crabs? Are we going swimming in the ocean? Wouldn't we have to take our pants off the go swimming? To put on a swimming suit?

I rolled my eyes. "Maybe," was all the answer I could muster. I was too keen on following the order for lights out.

***

The sound blaring over the loudspeaker jolted me out of deep sleep. Sergeant Henry walked up the aisle, yelling, "Calisthenics on the parade ground. Shorts and T-shirts. Run!"

I forced my sore muscles to move, dragging myself out of bed and finding my shorts and undershirt. Then ran with the others to the parade ground. Sarge stood over us as we did the exercises: jumping jacks, pushups, sit-ups, planks.

"Come on, ladies. You're breathing hard, and we haven't even started. I want to see some real man pushups. Get your butt out of the air, private." He screamed at Pucci. "Straighten your back!" All the marching yesterday hurt my feet; the calisthenics today stretched muscles that had lain dormant for years and caused much more pain.

After the workout, the boys ran to the barracks to shave and shower. My calves and thighs hurt so bad I could barely walk. I reached the barracks behind the rest of the platoon and limped up the stairs. Since men circled the sinks, I decided to shower first and shave simultaneously. I hung my little mirror from the pipes and shaved as I rinsed my body. It worked perfectly. I didn't have to compete with anyone for space or water and stood at my bunk, dressed in my uniform, putting my things away before anyone else. I spent the extra time reorganizing my footlocker.

Sergeant Henry strutted down the space between our beds, finding fault with every recruit. He came to my bunk and investigated the open footlocker. He looked at me first, apparently suspicious that I might have cheated, but his face settled into a look of acceptance.

"This is how to arrange a footlocker," he shouted through the bunkhouse floor. "Boys, look at this. Tomorrow, I want all the footlockers to look like this." I stood a little taller and allowed a slight smile on my lips.

Then he looked under my bed. "Your dress shoes should shine like a mirror, private. Tomorrow I'll expect to see a regulation spit shine on those shoes." I had not put those shoes on yet. They were as shiny as when they were issued.

Nobody passed inspection that morning. We corrected the most urgent problems identified by Sergeant Henry, and as a result, we were late for chow.

I wiped and mopped and got my food. As I sat down, the Sergeant yelled at all of us, "Report to classroom 101."

I stuffed some eggs in my mouth, made a sandwich with my toast and sausage, and returned my tray to the kitchen. I ate the sandwich on the way out of the mess hall.

We assembled outside the chow hall. "Fall in! " Sarge shouted. "Forward March!"

"Left face!"

"Halt!" Jimmy ran into my back.

Sarge sauntered over to Jimmy and looked him in the eye. Just looked. He didn't yell. "Do you boys remember a damn thing I taught you yesterday? When I say left, your left foot moves. When I say right, your right foot moves. Arms are the opposite."

Sarge stepped to Jimmy's left, still an inch from his ear, and yelled, "Forward march!"

As we marched, my mind went back to a time when my brothers and I were very young. Doris wasn't tagging along begging to be included, so I must have been less than five years old. We each had tin bowls on our heads and marched with sticks as guns, taking orders from Albert. As we strutted down the dirt road in front of our old farmhouse, we sang "Over There." In the middle of the song, Albert and Ken, the second oldest, jumped into the ditches on either side of the road, firing their stick guns at each other. The sudden action scared me, and I began to cry.

Albert exclaimed, "Aw. The baby is too little for big boy games. Go home to Mama, Genie." He sounded like my father.

I ran toward the house, tripped, and fell, badly scraping both knees and an elbow. I limped home with gravel embedded in my bloody knees. Mom cleaned me up and scolded the older boys, but Dad laughed. I think my problems with Dad began with that incident.

"Halt" This time, I almost ran into Ortiz

We covered the first two chapters of the manual in the classroom, which dealt with military life in general. At 1210 the Sergeant ended the lessons. "You are dismissed for chow. Reassemble on the parade field at 1230."

We marched double file to the chow hall. By the time I did KP duty and got my food, I had less than a minute to eat

"On your feet." I wolfed down the hot beef sandwich and potatoes on the way to return my tray. My stomach grumbled at the half-chewed food.

"Fall in. Sinclair, return that tray and get in line now!"

We picked up where we had left off the day before. We marched all over the camp for hours, turning right, then left, then about-faced, and marched back. At dinner, despite my exhaustion, I had KP duty one more time. At least I got to finish my meal at the table afterward.

In the hour and a half before lights out, I decided to help the squad study. Always the teacher, I couldn't help it. "Everybody, get out your manuals. What are the highlights of chapter one?"

We reviewed the chapters for the day and read the following two sections. Except for Zook, all the boys had recently graduated from high school, so the study session went well. We polished boots while studying, then rinsed our underwear and brushed our teeth, finishing up precisely at lights out.

After another day of studying and marching, I thought we were doing quite well marching. We could turn in either direction without breaking rank, we stayed in step, and our lines were straight. Just when I thought we had mastered marching and were ready to move on, Sarge threw in different drills. We had to learn to mark time, half step, double-time, march with a load, march double-time with a load. It was unbelievable how many ways the army could come up with to march.

That evening Morris walked back from the mess hall beside me. "Sinclair, what do you think you are doing? You're not their Daddy. Cut the study hall."

"But I'm their squad leader."

"Which means to lead, not teach. Sarge will be on them all the time if they always have the right answers. They came in as boys, but they have to leave here as men. Let them do their own studying." Morris stalked off.

His remarks concerned me. They violated what I knew about teaching and the army. No one learned without help, and in the army, we were brothers, comrades in arms. I could lead these guys to the goal of becoming competent soldiers. Teaching meant leading from my point of view, and it came naturally to me.

A few minutes later, Graham asked me, "What are we going to study tonight?"

I was admonished by Morris, and against my better judgment, I said, "You'll have to figure it out. The army is trying to make men out of you. It won't work if I treat you like schoolboys."

Montgomery opened the book. "The next chapter is about the care and use of arms, gas masks, and other field equipment. Want to read through it, so we know what to expect?"

"Mr. Sinclair," said Jimmy, "We've all hunted since we were little. We know how to handle a rifle."

"Don't call me Mr. Sinclair, Jimmy. I'm a private just like you."

"Then call me Hanson," he said

"All right, Hanson, the army will likely expect more with the rifle than your Dad."

"They couldn't be stricter than my Mom," said Graham. "She taught me to shoot, and you better believe I got a licking if that rifle wasn't completely taken apart, cleaned, put back together, and hung up right."

Zook pulled his harmonica out from under his pillow.

"They let you keep that?" exclaimed Hanson.

"I didn't ask," he replied. The boys gathered around him, and he played the old familiar songs until lights out.

We gradually became a unit, learning to depend on each other and work together. They still looked to me, the oldest by several years, for advice, but the boys were maturing into men, taking more responsibility, and gaining confidence. Some of it resulted from being far from home and making decisions on their own, some of it from sharing a challenging experience. We had the physical struggles of training and Sarge's punishments when we violated sometimes unknown standards to pull us together.

***

"Men, today, we will issue you your first weapons. You must learn to dismantle, clean and reassemble them and then fire them accurately."

For an hour and twenty minutes, Sarge lectured on dismantling, cleaning, and reassembling the rifle. Finally, we marched to the armory, signed for the rifles, and returned to the classroom, rifles on our shoulders. Sarge ordered us to disassemble our guns and clean them, even though they were already clean, then reassemble them.

I watched Zook closely. He knew how to handle a gun. Obviously, he had hunted before. He didn't betray any emotions he might have had about aiming that gun at a human being.

By chow time, we knew how to care for our rifles. We didn't know where to put the rifle while we ate. At home, we had never taken our guns to the dinner table. My squad looked at me.

I nodded and stepped out of line. "Permission to ask a question, Sergeant."

"Permission granted."

"What do we do with our rifles while we eat?"

"You sling the piece across your body. It will become your constant companion until it is the most natural thing in the world to have it attached to your body day and night."

We slung our rifles and shuffled along the food line. Fifteen minutes seemed like a leisurely meal without KP duty.

We learned how to adjust a gas mask and pack a field pack in the afternoon.

"If you adjust your mask properly, you will become accustomed to wearing it," Sarge told us.

"I'll never get used to wearing this stupid thing," Puccio said.

"On the floor, private! Fifty pushups! You don't talk back."

The rest of us adjusted our gasmasks and kept quiet about the discomfort as the straps dug into our skin.

We ate dinner with our rifles across our chests, gasmasks dangling at our sides, and stuffed field packs on our backs. The rifles felt odd on our chests, with the field packs taking up space across our backs where we had grown up carrying a gun. The army did things totally in reverse.

The evening movie covered proper nutrition.

"I see why we have to eat all our vegetables if we have to walk around in all this stuff," Hansen said as we placed the rifles in the racks by the doors in our barracks. "Did you get a load of that bird in the movie? Why don't we have gals like her in our PX?"

"Cause she's a movie star, not a real PX clerk," Montgomery said.

Everyone chuckled as we got ready for bed.

***

The first aid instructor started his slide show. "Wounds," he announced. "First, determine the extent of the wound. Expose the wound by cutting the clothing as much as necessary. Don't drag the clothing over the wound. Cut it and lift it off. If a bullet, shell casing, or other object penetrates the body, look for an exit wound. The exit wound is often larger than the entrance wound." A graphic slide illustrated each wound, which made several recruits look green.

Granny hadn't taught me anything about treating gunshot wounds. I listened carefully, examining each slide for details. The trainer continued, discussing arterial bleeding, bleeding from veins, direct pressure, and tourniquets, all his comments accompanied by detailed slides, which I took in as best I could.

We learned the signs of shock and then went on to bone wounds such as fractures, dislocations, and sprains. One of the men jumped up and left the room at the sight of the compound fracture, a gory picture with a bone sticking well out of the leg. The slide of a dislocated shoulder visibly disconcerted a couple more.

We gave each other artificial respiration—pull on the arms, push on the chest. The trick was to get the compressions in the right place on the lower lungs and press strong enough but not too strong. We also practiced moving victims in various makeshift litters, and different body carries.

The trainer said blandly, "There is other information in your manuals on snake bite, heatstroke, frostbite, and jungle diseases. Please read through those sections. Keep your manuals in your field pack with your first aid kit so you can refer to it if necessary."

Snakebite! Jungle diseases! What aren't they telling us??!

At the end of the class, I approached the instructor.

"I wondered how I might be able to get training in a medical specialty."

"You can be a medic, surgical assistant, or pharmacist with on the job training," he said. "Or you could go for a specialty at one of the training centers. There's a program for male nurses, but you would have to sign up for more than twelve months to do that."

I sprinted after my platoon, formulating a plan for getting medical training. I didn't want to sign up for a more extended enlistment. Pharmacy might be the best choice since I already knew biology and chemistry.

"Private Sinclair here thinks he has special privileges," the Drill Sergeant said as I caught up. "If he cannot stay with us, we will stay with him. Everyone, join Private Sinclair running around the track."

Thanks to me, we ran three extra miles that day. Nobody seemed too angry or upset with me. I apologized to all of them in the barracks.

"No problem. Sarge was looking for an excuse to make us run. It would have been one of us if it wasn't you," Graham said.

Our feet blistered, our backs aching, we were exhausted, but we still managed to rinse our sweaty underwear, polish our boots, and sing along to Zook's harmonica. We polished his boots and cleaned his uniform so he would have more time to play for us.

Zook took to army life as though he had always been a soldier. Perhaps he had. Even though they spoke more softly than Sarge, his Mennonite father and uncles had as many rules to follow and were very strict disciplinarians. I had been a little worried about him. He was so young, yet such a deep thinker. It turned out he adapted better than I did.

***

Finally, a day came when we didn't have classroom instruction. Instead, we marched across the hills to a shooting range, where we practiced until late afternoon.

Everyone in the squad hit the target but me. Graham hit the bullseye three times out of four. Several city slickers missed the mark at first, but one hit the bullseye every shot, even as we moved back. At 500 feet, he still hit the bullseye.

We all stopped firing and gathered around to watch him.

"Where did you learn to do that?" Graham asked the sharp-shooting city slicker.

"I don't know. I've never fired a rifle before. I did pitch for my high school baseball team. Same thing with a bigger ball. I can see the bullet's path before I pull the trigger."

As we watched, I realized that the differences between city and country had disappeared completely. We were all soldiers now, training to defend our country if needed. Of course, I still had reservations about the United States' role the politicians sometimes described as defenders of the world, but I would fight to protect my country if the need arose, and I would be prepared to do it.

Sarge approached the knot of soldiers. "You aren't going to learn to hit the target by watching him. Keep shooting until you make five shots out of ten."

I didn't. As everyone else's results improved, my bullets continued to plow into the ground at the target's base. I lined the site up the best I could, held perfectly still, and fired. Again, the bullet missed the mark.

"You're gonna shoot the toes right off of them Krauts," Graham laughed. I felt the heat creeping up the back of my neck.

"Raise the rifle," Sarge barked.

I raised the gun and shot at the top of the target but still hit low. When I raised the rifle higher and shot at the sky, the bullets went wide. I had never failed so miserably at anything in my life.

"Good thing you didn't sign up for the infantry," Graham teased.

"I didn't sign up for anything," I mumbled.

Fortunately, Sarge still wore his earmuffs and didn't hear me.

Target practice continued at least part of every day. Hard as I tried, I could not hit the target. The squad started calling me Old Eagle Eye.

The practice ended in a test in which we were to shoot twenty rounds, eight from 100 feet and twelve from 200 feet, changing positions between each round. Passing required hitting the target fifteen times. I failed to qualify. It didn't seem to be too big a deal to the Sergeant.

"I wonder where they'll send us when we finish," Hansen asked on the last night of our basic training as we cleaned the barracks.

"I read they sent some US soldiers to Iceland," Zook said. "Maybe we'll go overseas."

"I hope we don't go to Iceland," Hansen said. "I kinda like this California climate."

"Get back to work," I said. "We only have four minutes before inspection. Besides, we start specialized training next week, so we won't have to worry about where we're going until that's over, sometime in the fall."

CHAPTER 7
SPECIALISTS

Basic Training completed, passes in hand, we left the base for the first time in six weeks. Windows of houses perched on the cliffs across the bay reflected the setting sun like glittering diamonds. A long line of bars, cafes, and shops catering to young soldiers' needs and desires lined the highway, their lights blinking and flashing even brighter than the diamonds across the bay. We decided to start our evening with a tour of the bars.

"I'm not having much fun," Zook confided in me a couple of hours later as we sat in a bar with mugs of beer in front of us. "I don't quite understand all the excitement of going from one bar to another. It seems so..." He hesitated. "I don't know, so dumb. We just sit here and drink, like cows chewing on their cud."

I agreed. "I have an idea," I said. "I saw a movie theater down the highway. They're playing *Gone with the Wind*. Have you seen it? Would you like to go?"

"No. I mean, yes. I mean, I would like to see a movie, and I have not seen *Gone with the Wind*."

We backtracked to the big, ornate theater. The girl in the ticket booth had a special smile for Zook, which amplified her beauty. He had grown at least an inch during training. His smoothly shaved, evenly tanned face had matured, and he looked very sophisticated in his dress uniform. He could have modeled for an Army recruitment poster. "Look how handsome and magnetic we will make you!"

"Two tickets for *Gone with the Wind*," I said.

She took my money and handed me the tickets without taking her eyes off Zook. As I took the tickets, he nodded at her and said, "Thank you very much," but stood staring at her big smile.

I grabbed his arm and unceremoniously pulled him into the theater.

I told him, "I know she's a real doll, but you've got to ease up. You don't want to look like too much of an eager beaver. Nice girls don't like that. Now let's get us some snacks."

"What do you mean about an eager beaver?"

"Look, she likes the way you look. But does she know anything about you other than that you're in the army?" I looked him up and down in his uniform. "You need to be more than some uniformed girl magnet. Women deserve better than some guy passing through town anyway."

Zook bought popcorn and orange sodas at the concession stand. We found seats much closer to the front than I was comfortable with, but Zook insisted. This theater was much bigger than the one back home, with a larger screen. I worried I might strain my neck, looking up at it from the third row.

The red velvet curtains parted, and the cartoon started— Porky Pig. Zook laughed so hard he gasped for air. He was still laughing when the newsreel came on, but he turned serious quickly when it showed footage of the European war. Several minutes of the German offensive in Russia and a German U-boat captured off Iceland put him in a pensive mood. Zook watched the excerpts of Roosevelt's latest fireside chat intently. He acted as if he had never seen a newsreel before. The popcorn sat forgotten as Zook fidgeted until he finally tipped it over and scattered it across the floor. Seeing his frustration, I was sorry for his loss.

At last, the feature started. The overture nearly blasted us out of our seats, and I had a little trouble focusing as the title scrolled across the screen. I was almost embarrassed because it seemed we were looking up the dresses of all those hoop-skirted Southern belles. When Atlanta burned, it was as though we were in the midst of the fire. We were so close to the screen I began to feel the heat, even knowing the fire was on film. I realized I watched atrocities my grandfather had witnessed when he was as young as Zook, in his time with General Sherman.

Zook came out of the theater wide-eyed.

"That was one of the most complex movies I have ever seen,"

I said. "It truly is about a way of life gone with the wind."

"I've never seen a movie before except for training films," he said, "It was all new to me."

"Your first movie? That was pretty intense for your first movie. Maybe we should have gone to something a little less..."

"Oh, no," he said. "It was unforgettable."

As we approached the door, the ticket girl, her smile still lighting up her face, ran out of the booth, pressed a piece of paper in Zook's hand, and ran back in. Outside Zook opened the paper.

"It says Charlotte and has a phone number," he said. "But why would she give me her phone number?"

Despite my earlier lecture about uniformed girl magnets, I said. "She likes you. Give her a call."

Zook smiled at Charlotte as we climbed into a cab to return to camp. As for me, I suddenly missed Mrs. Glass and her weekly invitations to meet her nieces. I had enjoyed life as the most eligible bachelor in town more than I had thought.

***

Large topographical maps marked with battery and target locations covered the classroom tables. I scrutinized them as the instructor explained methods of calculating trajectories. I taught this every year in physics class and had memorized the formulas years ago.

"Now, it is your turn." He put a little wooden boat on the map. This target is moving toward you at the rate of thirty knots. You are using a 90mm M1. Plot the trajectory and calculate the elevation to strike the target."

I measured the distance, checked the table in the book, and calculated the numbers on the slide rule.

I said quickly, "Azimuth forty-three degrees, elevation twenty-five degrees," before anyone else had started the calculations.

"Sinclair," the instructor asked me, "can you explain how you got the answers so quickly?"

"I plugged the numbers into the equation you gave us. The gun lies thirty feet above the harbor; the boat will be at this location when we fire." I said, pointing to the map. "Enter the information into the equation, do the calculations, and you've got it. Didn't you just explain this?"

"Yes, but I've never had anyone in my class who could do it on the first try."

"I taught physics before I got drafted." If class continued like this, I thought, I would be bored to death.

Despite Morris's warning, I did a little teaching after hours. Several of the men came to me and asked for help. Since they took the initiative, I decided it was not the same as holding a class on my own accord.

A few days later, the instructor complimented the whole class on how quickly it had learned to do the calculations. I was gratified, first because we could move on to something other than this boring stuff, and second because I had helped assure that everyone in the class understood the calculations. When we tested on plotting, I qualified as an expert on my first try, and the average score of the group was higher, according to the instructor, than any previous class at the base.

We began to practice our newly learned skills at the firing range. We shot guns from the Great War—old, heavily used, obsolete guns. Factories worked overtime making ammunition for British troops even as the army failed to properly equip our own troops. Each member of the four-man gun crew adjusted the gun to the coordinates they had personally calculated. When everyone had aimed, we shot the gun once. My group usually asked me to do the final trajectory. I welcomed their request because the guns were manually loaded. I did not have to load the heavy ammunition, having directed the shot.

We obliterated the dummy enemy vessels each time.

One afternoon we couldn't get the gun to move. Zook climbed onto the old frame and peered at the gear mechanism.

"One of the teeth broke off of a gear down there and jammed up the works. Reverse the gears."

We raised the gun as high as it would go. Zook flicked the bit of metal out of the gears with his knife, and we lowered it again.

"Don't go too low," Zook said. "It'll slip at about thirteen degrees."

"Fortunately, we're pretending to shoot at airplanes today," Graham said.

The instructor came by. "What do you think you're doing?" he asked.

"Fixing the gun, Sergeant," said Zook. "It has a broken gear. Better get a new one before anybody tries to shoot targets in the water."

He looked at all of us in turn, then at Zook again. He seemed amazed. Indeed, he went on to say, "Good work, private. The previous crew on this gun failed to report the issue. They also failed to come anywhere close to the target.

This sort of aiming practice lasted for three weeks. When we tested, I barely qualified as a Cannoneer. I could easily plot the trajectory, but loading and firing the gun was not my forte.

***

The last test of our specialist training involved a war game between the Army and Navy, usually hotly contested given Sarge and our captain's comments. However, I did not know anything about the Navy except that it was not the Army.

We had spent a hot, windy afternoon setting up our equipment on the tawny gold hills in the grasslands west of camp in preparation for maneuvers. A strong wind blew in our faces the entire time, scorching the energy out of us. One of the officers called it a Santa Ana. Whatever its name, we cursed it as we lolled among the Torrey Pines, finishing our evening C-Rations, waiting for the war games to commence. Sometime tomorrow, the Navy trainees from down the coast would attempt to land on the beach. We would try to repel them. All of us were on edge.

"Sinclair, Washington, do a little recon and see what you can find out. Try not to get yourselves killed," ordered the instructor.

I grabbed my rifle, heaved my body up off the ground, and led Washington over the grassy hill hiding our camp, head up to get a good view.

"What are we supposed to do?" asked Washington.

"I assume we should go to the cliffs and see if we can find any boats heading our way," I said.

We trotted toward the cliffs to the southwest, rifles at the ready.

"Wait!" whispered Washington vehemently, grabbing my shoulder to stop me. "Look back there by that radio shack. Isn't that Navy insignia on the truck?"

I peered over to where he pointed. "I believe it is." I agreed. "Let's go see if we can find out anything."

We ran back east toward the shack. I realized that we would be easy to spot with the sun low in the western sky behind us.

"Bend down," I said. "Run from tree to tree."

We waited behind some pine trees for about half an hour for it to get fully dark, then crawled forward on our bellies like mechanized insects, maybe roaches or ants, one elbow and knee at a time—the Army way. The Navy guys had cleared the ground about fifty feet around the shack. The Santa Anas had dried the soil out and stirred up dust. "Stay on your belly," I told Washington. "If I signal you to stop, bury your face in your arms, and lie perfectly still. Stay back a ways behind me. If they get me, you complete the mission." He nodded.

Just after we had crawled out into the clearing around the shack, a jeep approached, throwing up a lot of dust, its lights sweeping across us. We froze, heads lowered, hoping our bodies melded with the dirt and dust. My heart beat so loudly I believed the Navy guys would hear it over the noise of their jeep. Somehow, they missed seeing us. The headlights flashed over us, but their beams were probably so scattered by the dust that the Navy personnel in the jeep couldn't see us. Anyway, hiding in plain sight can sometimes make you invisible.

The jeep engine stopped; the headlights went dark. Three men hopped out and entered the shack. I signaled Washington to start crawling again. Hiding among a big stack of ammo boxes behind the hut, listening, it turned out to be relatively easy to hear the conversation inside.

"We'll initiate the exercise with a flight of planes in from the east. That will distract them long enough for us to approach the beach. Downes, as the planes approach, you swing wide and bring your boats in on the south section of beach. It's a more difficult landing, but that's sure to surprise them. The rest of us will make our way to the north beach. We'll divide and conquer them."

Washington gave me the thumbs up. He had heard what I heard. We crawled back across the open space and ran to our HQ.

"Sir, reporting on our recon mission," I said breathlessly. Though in good shape by now, my excitement about the news Washington and I brought exacerbated my breathing.

Washington and I told our CO everything we had overheard.

"You went to their headquarters?" he said, somewhat astonished. "By recon, I meant that you two should check the beaches and see if you could find any signs of advance parties or preparations."

"It was Washington," I said. "He noticed that the Navy was at that shack. Otherwise, we would not have had the opportunity."

He smiled. "Good work, soldiers. Good initiative! Get some sleep because we'll be up before dawn to stop these bastards."

As we left, Washington said, "Thanks, Gene. Around here, an unschooled Okie like me never gets any credit for anything."

Back at the tents, after Washington and I told them what we had discovered, the guys slapped us on our backs and congratulated us on getting the info. My knees nearly buckled when I realized we had successfully infiltrated enemy territory. Would I have done so if we were in France fighting the Germans? In my mind, I thought so.

"Let me look at your rifle," said Graham. He grabbed it and looked down the barrel. In mock horror, he charged, "What were you trying to do, dig a foxhole with your rifle?"

"Had to crawl on my belly, and the barrel hit the ground a few times," I said.

"You get some sleep. You saved our asses. I'll clean the gun."

I heard him through my drowsy fog a few minutes later, "No wonder you can't hit anything with this. The site mount is bent."

I pried open my eyes.

"See," he said, pointing at it, "just a little bit. I bet you could've hit the target with a different rifle. See if you can get a replacement. Or maybe a new site mount installed."

Why hadn't I noticed that before? I drifted back to sleep. I dreamt we were in France fighting the Germans. I crawled behind a German tent and listened. I couldn't understand a word they said. Then the sky filled with German planes, and I fired a 155 mm Long Tom antiaircraft gun at them, but as I fired, the barrel bent, and the shell burst over a field of lavender. I sat in the lavender, trying to figure out how that could have happened. Then the Captain woke us.

"Everybody up. We need to move the guns." We jumped up, pulled on our pants and shirts, and stood at attention in front of our tents. The Santa Ana still bore down on us, making the early morning seem cold.

"Platoon A, prepare to repel an aerial attack from the northeast."

We took off, running to the bluff where we had set up our guns, turning them to face inland. The other two platoons soon arrived with trucks. They used the trucks to move their guns to the north and south, facing out to sea. We watched and waited. Shortly before dawn, aircraft appeared. We fired our tracers, and the planes turned back, shot down by the rules of the games. The other platoons repelled the boats both to the north and south. According to our sergeant, it turned out to be one of the quickest maneuvers on record.

After all was clear and the Navy had surrendered, we cheered and patted each other on our backs. "Swell job!" I shouted. "We won!" I felt ready to conquer the world.

"You goddamn did it," Sarge crowed. "Teamwork, initiative, everything the Army asks of you! Damn good work, men."

At that moment, I realized my thoughts had become army thoughts. I was pleased with the victory and glad we had performed well. I hadn't thought seriously of medical school in three or four weeks. At least in the moment of the mock battle, I had entirely forgotten my resolve never to think as an army man. I had become as bloodthirsty as any of them, eager to shoot down the planes and win the game. I had discovered a naturally competitive part of myself that until now had only been expressed as anger when my older brothers beat me at almost everything. Could I integrate that in a way that would make me more successful in life without becoming vicious?

Our graduation lacked the pomp and circumstances of Miss Brukhardt's high school ceremony, but it did mark an important milestone in my life. Despite my resistance, I proudly accepted a Certificate of Achievement, pleased to have finished Basic with distinction. When the brief ceremony ended, we ripped open our orders. Most of the class called out names of east coast cities, where they would join the coastal artillery. I held mine, hoping I would be sent to pharmacy training.

Zook approached me and showed me his orders. "Look, Sarge recommended me for mechanics training."

That gave me hope. I ripped open the envelope.

"Fort Worden, on Puget Sound, Coastal Artillery," I read aloud.

"Me too," called Tom Morris. "We'll be together."

I stuffed the orders into my pocket.

"You know, Zook," I told him, "you were right about this trip to California. It has been a real eye-opener. My guess is the next duty station will be too."

"I wish I could go north with you guys instead of back to the Midwest."

"You're not going back to the farm. Aircraft mechanics school will be poles apart from milking cows and planting wheat. That I can guarantee."

"I suppose so. And you were right about something, too. Charlotte did want me to call her. We're gonna stay in touch."

"Good job," I laughed, "mister master mechanic."

CHAPTER 8
FORT WORDEN

The sixteen of us assigned to Fort Worden rolled north on the train. Outside temperatures dropped as we left LA. It almost started to feel like October at home after the perpetual summer of San Diego. Dense fog rolled in off the ocean as we changed trains in San Francisco, tinted red by the sunset. Folds and streamers of foggy air swirled around us, muted all sound, and turned the clackety-clack of the train into the sound of drumsticks hitting the rim of a snare drum, counting out the rhythm of a song. Finally, we drifted off to sleep in a world whipped into cream by the train's passage.

We woke to oppressive grey drizzle spotting the train's windows that distorted the scenery. After another chilly train change in Portland, Oregon, Morris wandered off toward the front of the train. I stayed behind, my mood as grey as the sodden sky. *What would we find at Fort Worden, our assignment on Puget Sound? Could I handle the remainder of my year in the army, where I had no control over my future, let alone my daily activities? The army didn't care at all that I had requested pharmacy training. First, they kept me out of medical school; now, they were sending me to shoot guns instead of the training I had requested. Zook hadn't even asked for mechanics training, but they sent him. Nothing about the army made sense.*

About ten minutes later, Morris returned.

"Sinclair, there's a Monopoly game in the club car. I've recruited five players so far. We can use a sixth. Want to join us?"

"No, go ahead without me."

"Oh, come on. Why sit here moping. It will be fun!"

I followed Morris to the club car.

The cutthroat game lasted all afternoon. Our arrival in Olympia, where we would disembark from the train, forced the end of the game; I led by five hundred dollars. Whether Monopoly or war games with the Navy, winning did feel good.

"Hello, I'm Mike Jarvis," said the middle-aged private who met us on the Olympia station's platform.

He led us through the driving rain to an old green bus parked outside the terminal.

Jarvis shouted through the downpour, lifting the hood of his raincoat, "Climb in and find a seat!"

After we had all settled in, he stood at the front of the bus, explaining, "The Fort's a ways from here, so you may as well relax. We'll give you a tour tomorrow if we can. The rainy season has started, so we can't count on the weather from now until spring."

The rain never let up on the four-hour drive. We left Olympia and drove through what looked like wilderness to me. The headlights lit up trees, an occasional bridge, and a few hamlets. I almost dozed off until Private Jarvis, our driver as well as our host, slammed on the brakes making all of us sleepers plunge forward. A few knocked their heads on the seat in front, cursing as they woke up.

Jarvis called back as the bus came to a full stop, "An elk, coming back down for the winter. He's a big one!"

More awake after Jarvis shouted, I peered in awe. A magnificent animal stood in the middle of the road, head turned left to gaze into the bus's headlights. Six-point antlers extended higher than the bus. He must have weighed more than a thousand pounds.

"That is a huge elk," one of the men said.

"Roosevelt is the biggest elk species in the world, and this one is big even for a Roosevelt," Jarvis said.

The elk stared at us for a couple of minutes, then sauntered across the highway and out of sight into the forest. Jarvis hit the gas, causing our heads to lurch backward, and we sped on down the narrow road. He definitely had a lead foot.

Many of us tried fitfully to sleep again. The jouncing of the bus seemed worse than before the elk. I definitely couldn't sleep, thinking about such a magnificent beast as the elk on the highway. Graham came to sit beside me.

"I'd love to bag an elk like that. Do you think they'll let us go hunting while we are here?"

"Probably not, although maybe you can get leave to hunt after you've been here a while."

We finally arrived at the fort. "Everything go all right? We expected you over an hour ago!" the sentry shouted over the rain drumming on the roof of the bus and streaming off his helmet.

Jarvis shouted back. "Everything's fine—a little slow going in the rain and all. We spotted a good size bull elk on the way in. It should be a great hunting season."

"Good news!" the sentry agreed and waved us through.

We finally stopped, and Jarvis hustled us from the bus through the downpour. A corporal, also much older than the average soldier, met us on the covered porch of a white clapboard building. We dripped from the deluge, something we weren't used to in Kansas or California.

"Welcome to the Enlisted Men's Club," he said. "I'm Corporal Brighton."

The room looked like a fine restaurant through the windows and the door. Tablecloths bleached whiter than any my grandmother owned covered the tables. The welcoming scent of chicken soup wafted from the kitchen. Turn of the century chandeliers, Metropolitans, modified to use electric bulbs, hung from the ceiling. The corporal invited us to sit in carved walnut Jacobean chairs at tables set with China bowls and silver spoons. A cheery fire burned in the fireplace.

Standing near the kitchen door, Corporal Brighton explained, "We use this as the mess and the club. If the Fort is ever fully manned, we'll have to open up the actual mess hall, but in the meantime, we can use this place so we don't have to renovate the mess hall kitchen, which would be a piece of work." He smiled. "The cooks have a bite for you to eat before you hit the sack."

We looked at each other and shrugged, wondering, without saying it aloud. Had we taken the train into a different army? Cooks staying up until 2200 hours to feed newcomers? A private brought a giant tureen and, going from table to table, ladled chicken rice soup into our bowls. All of us looked at it. Would this happen every meal? Another private brought a basket of fresh-baked sourdough bread.

"I hate to mention this," Graham said to Brighton, who had come to sit at our table, "but it seems like some of the men here are a bit more mature than the average recruit."

We all looked at Graham. He was right, but we hadn't wanted to mention it.

Corporal Brighton smiled. When did corporals smile at privates? He said to all of us as we dug into our soup. "When they first reopened the Fort, they called up reserve and National Guard units. We're getting a few more of you young guys every week. Soon we old men will be able to go home,"

After supper, we ran through the rain to our barracks. Picking up our duffel bags and footlockers from the neat row on the wide porch of the nineteenth-century building, we ducked inside. In the damp chill, the barracks smelled strongly of fresh paint. Morris pressed the light switch; the bright, bare electric bulbs hung every four feet down the center of the ceiling, showing two long rows of metal cots. At one end, on an asbestos mat to protect the polished hardwood floor, sat a woodstove. A towering wood-pile rose to the top of the wall a foot or so behind the cold stove.

I laid a fire, lighting it with one of my pipe matches. The fire dispelled the chill for at least ten feet around the stove.

"There aren't any lockers," Graham complained.

"Hang your uniforms on the hooks in the wall. Put everything else in your footlocker," I said.

We made up the cots close to the stove and dropped into them. I grabbed one closest to the fire. Probably about four of our group were out of range of the woodstove. They grabbed blankets from unused bunks to hunker down. The old metal springs creaked whenever anyone moved, and the mattresses were thin, but we all managed to stay warm under the old wool army blankets.

***

We burst out of the barracks, the rain having dissipated, startling the deer browsing on the parade ground. Lined up for roll call, shivering in our summer uniforms, we could see the steel-blue ocean under an overcast sky. By now, we had the basic army routine down—roll call, calisthenics, mess, and on to the day's business.

A lieutenant met us at the mess to show us the Fort.

"Good morning. My name is Lieutenant Armstrong Perry, Washington National Guard. Follow me, and I'll show you around."

We trudged up what Perry called Artillery Hill as he lectured.

"The army began construction of the Fort in 1898. This part of Quimper Peninsula was contoured and reworked to prepare the gun batteries. From the Sound, it looks like a grassy hill with rock outcroppings. From this side, as you can see, there are seven gun batteries. The Fort was planned in conjunction with Fort Flagler on Marrowstone Island and Fort Casey on Whidbey Island to create the Triangle of Fire. The batteries were made with continuous pours of concrete to assure proper curing and the ability to withstand bombardment. The current batteries were completed in 1920 with the placement of disappearing guns. These guns ride down on a chassis so the enemy can't see them." Perry paused. "That factor isn't important once they start firing since the guns produce quite a flash of fire and smoke."

"We fire the disappearing guns once a week. There will be targets in the sound, and we fire until we hit them."

"That's our job, fire the guns once a week?" asked Morris.

"The rest of the time, most of us are cleaning up and refurbishing the barracks and batteries not yet open for firing. Most of you will get plenty of time behind a scrub brush and paintbrush but not too much behind a big gun. If you have restaurant experience, you might get another assignment."

I thought that that statement didn't go over well, looking at the men's faces from the end of the semicircle facing Perry. All the volunteers had signed up hoping we would get into the war with the Germans and were disappointed to be here watching the West Coast. They certainly wouldn't want to become cooks and waiters.

"Down below," Perry said, pointing, "you can see the dock.

There are a few boats there for recreational use. The fishing is great in both the Sound and the rivers. You can probably still get a few salmon, but the season is winding down. Check with HQ before taking a boat out."

"When hunting season starts, will we be able to hunt those big elk?" Graham asked.

"Sure thing," Perry nodded, then turned to walk off to the left. "Let me show you the other attractions."

We walked back down the paved path toward the center of the camp.

"Our movie theater is over there." Lieutenant Perry pointed to a building beyond the barracks. "The golf course is next to the parade grounds. Only nine holes, but it provides some diversion." I almost laughed out loud. Most of us considered golf a women's game. Men played baseball, basketball, or football.

"If you're interested," continued Perry, "we have volleyball, baseball, and softball teams. There is also a little bowling alley and handball, tennis, and badminton courts. I lead the fort choir if anyone would like to try out. Auditions will be at four p.m. today, with rehearsal immediately afterward. I'll have another audition on Saturday morning for anyone on duty this afternoon."

"When will we start working?" Morris asked. After all, we had come here to do a job, not for R&R.

"Oh, yes," Perry remembered. "Report to HQ at one—err rather 1300. You'll get assigned to your duties then. In the meantime, you can finish settling in at your barracks."

"May I ask what your civilian job is?" I asked.

"I work for the Chamber of Commerce in Seattle. I've been here for almost a year. I'm really looking forward to returning home at the beginning of December. Nice meeting you, boys. See you around."

"I bet Perry is the best man they've got at the Chamber," said Graham. We laughed, and a couple of guys imitated Perry's tour guide speech as we returned to the barracks. "He certainly is up on the history and attractions here at the Fort."

We were in one of the "new" barracks, meaning 1917 construction, but recently painted and refurbished, such as adding the woodstove and the lights down the center aisle between the bunks. The thermometer in the barracks read 60 degrees, but it seemed much colder because of the dampness. I built up the fire as much as I dared.

"We need to get winter uniforms," I said. "Morris, come with me,"

We ran through the drizzle, shivering, to headquarters. A tall, thin, young woman in a thick hand-knitted sweater sat typing at a desk inside the door.

"We need to find out about getting winter uniforms and coats," I said.

"They were issued on September thirtieth. You should have them." said the young woman without looking up.

"We were in transit on September thirtieth," Morris told her. "We didn't get them."

She slowly lifted her head and stared up at him. "Oh," she said brightly. "You're the new guys. Let me check on something." She stood, straightened her pencil skirt, and walked down the hallway. Sticking her head into a room toward the back of the building, she displayed a very provocative view of her extraordinary derrière. I looked at Morris and said, "Desist!" He stood up straight and calmed his face to a neutral expression.

We moved to sit in some chairs in front of the steam radiators, trying to get warm for the first time since arriving. Finally, the young woman came back. We stood and approached her desk.

"We requested winter uniforms for the men you replaced. They weren't issued because those men left on September twenty-seventh. Sergeant Wilcox said we could issue those to you."

"What if they don't fit?" I asked.

She looked me up and down. "In your case, you can have it cut down. It might be more of a problem for Private Morris here." She seemed pleased to have found a soldier who stood taller than her in her high heels. "We'll have to see if any pants are long enough. Get your guys over here, and Sergeant Wilcox will take care of you. Come through the door around the side." She pointed left and behind her.

We rushed back to the barracks and called everyone to follow us to the HQ storage room. After we arrived, Sergeant Wilcox lined us up by height. Then he handed us each two wool uniforms and a topcoat.

"There's a tailor on Cherry Street not too far outside the entrance to the fort." Sergeant Wilcox told us. "Yu-ling Wong will be happy to hem them up or take them in if needed."

We went back to the barracks to try on the uniforms.

"Anyone have a 34 waistband?" called out one guy.

"I'm swimming in this one," I said, "See if it works."

"I can't breathe," said another. "Sinclair, this one might fit you."

The waist worked, but the pants were four inches too long. After half an hour of trading, we each had the closest thing to a decent fit we were likely to get.

"Do we have time to get to the tailor shop and back before mess?" I asked

"No," answered Morris. "We only have about 20 minutes. Put your overcoat on, and let's go!"

I folded the extra length of the pants inside each leg, pinned them, and followed the guys to mess. The meal and service were both worthy of a fine restaurant. I wondered how the officers fared if this was what we enlisted men got.

We reported to HQ at thirteen hundred hours, as ordered, for our assignments. The captain handed typed orders to each of us in turn, calling our names for us to step forward and receive them.

"You're each assigned to a different job in a different battery. Some of you were selected for your ability to lead a squad. Several replacements for us National Guard men are coming in December, and each of you will be assigned your squad at that time. You need to be familiar with your duties to help train the replacements. Report to your stations at 0800 tomorrow morning to begin learning the ropes. Dismissed!"

Back at the barracks, Morris said, "We have two hours before supper. Let's get a boat and go out on the sound."

"I planned on going to the choir auditions," I told him. "Besides, I don't know anything about sailing a boat."

"Neither do I," said Morris. "I was planning on figuring it out as we went."

"Morris, I'll give you a sailing lesson," volunteered Private Burris. "I grew up in Newport Beach and sailed all the time."

I started toward headquarters to find out where the choir practice would be, but I heard piano music coming from the theater, so I went in that direction. In the empty theater, Lieutenant Perry sat at the piano practicing. Nobody else had shown up to audition.

"What have you prepared for your audition?" asked Lieutenant Perry.

"I haven't prepared anything. I only heard about the auditions this morning."

"What can you sing?"

"'God Bless America.'"

He played an intro on the piano, then nodded to me. I sang it the way I'd heard Kate Smith on the radio. The other fifteen choir members arrived in spurts during my audition, and all applauded at the end.

"We've needed a good strong tenor," Perry said. "Welcome to the choir. We are rehearsing for a Thanksgiving concert."

"What about Christmas?" I asked.

"Most of us will be gone by Christmas. I don't know if anyone else will want to direct the choir after I'm gone? Are you interested?"

"No. I can sing, but I don't think I can direct."

"So, we prepare for Thanksgiving, hoping someone will come to lead the choir when I leave," confirmed Perry.

***

As soon as I could, I went into town to get my uniform pants hemmed. Port Townsend had been some town in its heyday. Victorian houses and commercial buildings lined the streets. A Romanesque courthouse topped a small hill on Jefferson Street with a neo-classical library farther down. Massiveness seemed more important than consistency of style in the buildings. I supposed many prominent buildings and smaller storefronts were empty, thanks to the Great Depression. I finally found the tailor shop tucked into a tiny storefront next to an ornate Victorian hotel. A bell rang as I opened the door, and a cute young Chinese girl came from the back room.

"Hello," I said. "Is your father here?"

She looked confused.

"I'm looking for Yu-Ling Wong. I need to get my uniform tailored."

"Oh, yes. I am Yu-Ling Wong. You need the uniform hemmed?"

"Yes," I smiled. When I looked closer, I realized Yu-Ling was not as young as I thought. She was probably my age. She took the pants I carried and held them up to me. She put them on the table and measured the pantlegs.

"You want to remake the pants or just hem them?" she asked while working with the pants on the table.

"How would you remake the pants?" I asked.

"Crotch will fit, waist will fit, hips will fit." She turned, revealing a persuasive smile. I read the smile to mean that I should choose to remake the pants.

Cautious, I asked, "What will it cost to remake the pants?"

"Two and a half dollars. Hemming is only seventy-five cents." She tilted her head and raised her eyebrows slightly, questioning.

"Let's remake them."

"Do you also want the jacket to fit?"

"Can you do that?"

"Oh, yes. It takes longer and costs three dollars."

I nodded.

To remake my jacket, she lifted my arms and measured their lengths. I squirmed.

"You must stand straight while I measure."

She took a few more measurements. I did my best to stand straight. The process was somewhat ticklish.

"Very good," Yu-Ling announced, ending the measuring session. "Come back the day after tomorrow."

Could she finish remaking the whole uniform in two days? I wondered. No tailor back home would guarantee such a quick completion of the job. I know because I waited several days for retailored hand me downs of my brother's Sunday suits.

I delayed my return to pick up the uniform until almost closing time to ensure Yu-Ling had enough time to finish the job. She pulled back a curtain on a little dressing room upon my arrival. My pants and jacket, altered and pressed, were hanging on a hook. I put on the uniform. It fit perfectly. I don't think I had ever had a pair of pants cut so expertly to my size, even the hand-me-downs at home that had taken two weeks to alter. No wonder so many men in town walked around in such spiffy suits.

Yu-Ling was not only a good seamstress but a very confident businesswoman. I left the uniform I had just taken off, paid her five-fifty, promising another five-fifty for the other job, and returned to the barracks. No need to measure. She still had all my measurements on an index card in her files.

"Doesn't Sinclair look spiffy," Jefferson said as I walked in. I was surprised Yu-Ling's work was so obvious. I hadn't told anyone of my trip to the tailor shop.

"You should try getting your uniform tailored, too."

"If they gave us the right size in the first place, we wouldn't have to pay to make it fit," Morris grumbled. "How much did it cost?"

"Five fifty,"

"That's ridiculous," he said. "We're only making twenty-one dollars a month. I'm not spending a week's pay to fix something the army didn't do right in the first place."

"Well, I like the fit," I said." I think it's worth it."

***

Two soldiers at a time watched from the hill for enemy boats. The rest of us, both recruits and National Guard, worked as carpenters, electricians, painters, plumbers, landscapers, servers, and cleaning crew. The contrast between refurbished and untouched buildings stood out all over the base—clean, pristine white versus yellow, peeling, flaking paint—electric lights and woodstoves versus fireplaces and kerosene lamps—indoor versus outdoor facilities.

Wednesday, as we painted a newly renovated barracks, we

heard a loud siren. My heart jumped. Everyone raced to the batteries. I leaped down the two steps into the plotting room, crossed to the slit, and peered out. On the water, a crude raft with a blue swastika painted on it approached. Damn Nazis! I quickly calculated the azimuth and elevation and gave the numbers to the gunners. The gun creaked into position. When they fired, the plotting room reverberated like the inside of a drum. I clapped my hands over my ears. I vowed to keep cotton balls in my pocket in the future to plug my ears when the cannon fired. The other guns followed. As the thunder subsided, I looked out the slit. The target still floated toward us. I hadn't estimated its speed correctly. The raft was coming to shore faster than I expected. Picking up the slide rule, I calculated a new elevation."

"Lower the guns four degrees,"

They shot again and hit the target.

"Well, that's it for this week," Private Snyder said. He had stood watching me plot, not attempting to figure it out himself. National Guard.

"Why don't we get to do our real job more often?" I asked.

"Not enough ammunition. Our factories are ramping up, but what they make is for the lend-lease program. Anyway, suppose we weren't refurbishing the barracks and other facilities. In that case, we'd be spending all our time staring out at the sound, waiting for a very unlikely invasion looking in the opposite direction from where the real action is. Working on the barracks keeps us from going crazy,"

On the way back down the hill, I remembered I had left a wet paintbrush lying across the top of my paint can in the barracks. Enough time had passed it probably would be dry and ruined by now. I complained about it to Private Snyder.

"The drill happens every Wednesday right around 1100," Private Snyder confided in me. "You get used to it. Make sure you're not in the middle of something."

"Not great preparation for a real attack," I said.

"If you hear the siren and it isn't Wednesday morning at 1100, you'll know it's a real attack."

***

When the captain found out I understood circuits, he assigned me to string electric lights down the center aisles of the barracks we were refurbishing. Up the ladder, down the ladder, move the ladder. About halfway through the second story of one building, I dropped the wire strippers. They hit one of the ladder's steps and bounced down the aisle and toward the back of the room. Private Rogers, mopping the floor nearby, noticed my frustration.

"I can get that for you," he said. He left his bucket and mop by the stairway door and went to get the wire strippers. As Rogers bent to pick up the wire strippers, Private Jarvis came up the stairs carrying a stack of boards to repair the floor in the corner where a leak in the roof had ruined it. Jarvis tripped over the bucket as he entered, which knocked over the mop, the handle of which slid between Jarvis's knees. The bucket crashed onto its side, spilling soapy water all over the floor. Jarvis fell hard onto his side as the boards flew from his arms, and he slid on the water into the ladder. The ladder flew out from under me as I jumped to the floor. I slipped on the soapy water from the bucket and tripped over the boards scattered across the floor like pickup sticks. I stumbled into Rogers, knocking him down and falling in the opposite direction; my foot caught under one of the boards. Rogers hit his head hard on one of the posts that held up the roof. Jarvis lay on the floor, moaning. Rogers appeared to be unconscious. I pulled myself up and, as I tried to stand, stabbing pain shot through my ankle.

"Help!" I cried several times, but no one heard.

Lowering myself down, I crawled to a window, opened it, and yelled at the landscape crew working below us. They rushed upstairs.

"Call the medics!" their corporal shouted, and one of his crew dashed off.

Medics arrived less than five minutes later. They put us all on stretchers and carried us downstairs. I heard one deadpan to another, "This is the most excitement we've had in a while."

There was only one ambulance for the fort. So the medics

snugged Jarvis and Rogers into it side by side, both unconscious, leaving me sitting on the stretcher on the barrack's porch until they could return. Finally, the ambulance came back about fifteen minutes later, and the medics loaded me. When I finally arrived at the Fort hospital, the doctor carefully felt my ankle.

"Let's get an X-ray of this," he ordered a medic. "Then, put some ice on it." As the orderly wheeled me into the X-ray room a few minutes later, another wheeled Jarvis out.

After the X-ray, they put me in an examination room with a bag of ice on the ankle and told me to wait. The ice slowly melted while I sat, wishing I had a magazine or something to while away the time. I read all the posters on the wall. I became very aware of how to prevent venereal disease, the posters containing more detailed information than the filmstrip from Basic Training. Finally, the doctor showed up.

"I'm Dr. Reyes. Sorry for the wait, but I'm the only doctor on duty today." His voice was calm and reassuring. "Jarvis was banged up pretty bad, and the fall seems to have caused a clot in Rogers's brain. However, we have him stabilized, using a new drug treatment, and don't expect permanent damage."

"What's the drug?"

"Dicoumarol."

"You mean that compound from moldy hay? That can help prevent brain damage? I thought the only thing it did was kill cattle."

Dr. Reyes looked keenly at me, saying, "Your ankle isn't broken, just a bad sprain." He began wrapping it. "Can you tell me what happened?"

"Didn't Jarvis?"

"He hit his head as he went down. Seems a bit confused. A concussion."

"Jarvis tripped over a bucket. How could he get hurt that bad from tripping over a bucket?"

"These things happen."

"The ladder fell on him. When he tripped, he knocked my ladder down, and it fell on top of him pretty hard. Could that have caused the injury?"

"There are some bruises on his abdomen and side we aren't sure about. That's probably where the ladder hit him."

"This is all my fault. I dropped the wire strippers, and Rogers went to pick them up. Jarvis tripped over the bucket and mop Rogers left by the door and knocked down my ladder, then I rammed into Rogers as I fell. This never would have happened if I had been more careful with the wire strippers."

"If Rogers hadn't left the bucket where someone could trip over it, it wouldn't have happened. If Jarvis had looked where he was going, it wouldn't have happened. This is one of those chain-reaction accidents that are everyone's fault and no one's fault. Fortunately, it looks like everyone will recover, and you'll all be more careful in the future." He finished wrapping my ankle. "There you go. Put ice on it for four days, about every two hours. Nurse Haines will get you some crutches. Keep the ankle elevated above your heart whenever you can. I'll tell your CO to give you two weeks for recuperation and light duty for another four. Come back and see me in two weeks, and I'll see how the healing is progressing."

"Thank you. I wasn't aware of a hospital on the Fort. It seems a bit large for the number of men stationed here."

"We serve all the military establishments in the area; the three coastal artillery forts, including Fort Worden, the airbase, and the navy base."

I took a chance and said, "I'm very interested in medicine. Washington University Medical School accepted me into their MD program before I was drafted. So here I am. But in boot camp, the training officer said I might be able to get into pharmacy work. What are the chances I could get some training here? I've taught physics and chemistry in high school for several years, so I know that side of things very well."

"I assumed you had an education in science since you knew about the medicine we gave Rogers. I'll keep you in mind."

It took me a while to hobble back to the barracks, but I whistled all the way. Finally, finally, I had a chance at a medical career.

***

I spent a lot of time sitting on my barracks' porch smoking my pipe with my foot propped up over the next two weeks. I discovered the small Fort library with its extensive collection of classics, most musty and unopened since the fort was built. When I wasn't reading, I thought about being a pharmacist. At my two week checkup, Dr. Reyes declared me ready for light duty. I decided not to press him about my request when he examined me. Patience is a virtue!

The captain assigned me to watch for an invasion every day. Private Snyder hit the nail on the head when he said it would be boring. I had never done anything as dull as sitting on a cold metal stool in the damp, enclosed concrete bunker staring out that slit. Sometimes, when it wasn't raining, I sat outside near the bunker to feel the air and see the sky, even though it was often cloud covered, and watched the Sound. No one came to check on me, so I didn't get in trouble for not being at my specific station inside the bunker.

I began to calculate azimuth and elevation for imaginary targets just to have something to do. Then I had an idea. After my shift, I went into town and got myself a Brownie camera. Only a dollar, way cheaper than my two tailored uniforms, though I think the officers were impressed with my appearance. I returned to Yu-Ling's establishment to pick up the second uniform.

"What happened to you? I was worried," she asked as I hobbled in on my crutches.

I told her about the accident, saying I still felt guilty for dropping the wire stripper that precipitated the incident.

"Sometimes bad things happen, and something good comes from it. Keep your eyes open for the good that can come."

I promised her I would and hobbled out again with my uniform.

***

I placed the Brownie on the edge of the viewing slit and snapped photos every few degrees from left to right to make a panorama of the coast and ocean from the bunker's perspective. That weekend, I took the film to the drugstore and had it developed. A week later, I picked it up. Then, until I returned to regular duty, I drew little boats on the pictures and calculated the elevations and azimuths for each target. I wrote the coordinates at the bottom of each photo below the boat drawing and duck-taped the images to the wall.

The Wednesday after my return to full duty, the siren wailed right on time. The target approached one of my precalculated locations, and I gave the gunners the azimuth and elevation.

"Wait, not yet, not yet." I directed. Then I shouted, "Now! Fire!"

The target disappeared.

The captain rushed into the bunker. "How did you do that?" he demanded, suspicious of the outcome. Even though our crew had recently done well, sinking our targets in one or two shots within three minutes, this exercise lasted only about thirty seconds.

I showed him the pictures covering much of the main plotting room walls.

"This is a waste of time." He declared. "How will anybody else know which set of coordinates to use."

"Anyone can look at the pictures and locate the marks on them. When the boat is in position relative to the marks, all he needs to do is give the gunners the predetermined coordinates and then the order to fire. Sure, some adjustments left or right might be necessary because the target would zig-zag in a real attack. But those are easy to make compared to doing the full calculation."

"We'll see. You take next Wednesday off. Go sailing or something. Your buddy Morris is off, too. Do something with him" It sounded like an order, and I was more than willing to comply.

***

The following Wednesday, Morris checked out his favorite boat at headquarters. We raised and unfurled the sails to catch the wind, then skimmed away to the north. He had become quite the sailor. Before my accident, he had been teaching me the things he learned from Burris.

"Let's check out Whidbey Island," he suggested.

We sailed straight across the channel toward Fort Casey on Whidbey, one of the Puget Sound Triangle of Fire points. We knew they had two sixteen-inch guns there, but we saw only a squat lighthouse on a rocky hill from the Sound. After passing the alleged base, we rounded a narrow neck on the island.

"Look, a pod of seals." I shouted." Can you get any closer?"

Morris tacked as I snapped pictures with my Brownie camera. As we bobbed on the waves, an eagle dove past us and pulled a fish from the water. I got a picture of it about a foot above the water, hoping the picture wouldn't be too blurry. We moved on to the north, sticking close to the island. I snapped pictures of the cliffs, some children on a narrow beach, gulls flying close above us. Morris kept consulting a chart and checking his watch as though he had a tight schedule.

After several minutes of this weird behavior, I told him, "We have the boat all day. What's the problem?"

"Oh, nothing. I always like to know where we are. Sinclair, take the rudder while I check something out."

"Wait, I'm the deckhand. I don't know how to steer the boat."

"It's easy," he joshed.

I grabbed the rudder, with some trepidation, as he walked forward and lowered the sails.

"What are you doing that for?"

"Steer toward the island there. Just pull on the tiller."

As I turned it, the boat immediately picked up speed.

"What's happening?" I shouted.

"We're running the Deception Passage," he shouted back as the waves bounced us around. "It's like running rapids."

"You didn't say anything about running rapids!" The boat tilted precariously. "I don't think this boat can run rapids."

"Hold tight to the tiller! You have to think fast."

I tried to turn the boat around. The tide pulled so fiercely I couldn't make us turn back without turning us over. My vision narrowed to focus on the channel in front of us. Time seemed to slow down. I thought of nothing other than getting us through this.

Morris grabbed an oar and stood on the bow, bracing himself

in a wide stance.

"What are you doing with that oar?" I shouted over the thumping of the waves as the boat bounced through the water.

"Fending us off rocks!" he shouted back.

The passage wound among tiny islands with a tree or a few bushes on top and smaller rock outcroppings. I saw and thought only far enough ahead to save us from disaster, continually changing course to evade one obstacle or another. The rushing tide tried to pull us toward Whidbey Island to the south. I leaned on the tiller to steer us past it. What was Morris thinking? Suddenly the current caught us, and we headed for the most prominent northern island. I pulled the tiller hard, and Morris nearly fell overboard, catching himself with the oar. The boat moved faster and faster, thrumming on the waves, pulled one way, and another in the changing currents. Morris sat in the bow, laughing, his oar at the ready.

"Watch out!" he shouted.

A bridge loomed before us, spanning the channel's narrowest point between the two big islands. I leaned on the tiller again to miss the pilings. We raced through the small opening so fast I feared the boat would fly into a rock as its prow bounced high off the water like a plane. I kept us on course by some miracle, and we stayed on the water. We emerged, heading straight for the rocky cliff of a small island in the middle of the channel. I managed to steer the boat to the north of the island, then moved into the channel's center. As we sped past the islands, the boat slowed slightly. Then just as suddenly as the current had pulled us in, it spit us out into calmer water.

After a breathless moment from both of us, Morris crowed, "You ever had more fun in all your life?"

"I can think of a time or two," I replied, gasping slightly. "Why didn't you steer?"

"I had to keep us off the rocks." He displayed the oar. "Didn't want you to break up the boat and have to pay for it." I couldn't remember him actually using the oar except to keep himself from going overboard.

"Not to mention drown us," I declared, somewhat angry.

"Next time, ask me before you try something like that, so I know when to stay behind."

"Oh, come on, you were grinning the whole time," he said. I knew I hadn't been, of course. Mostly I was grimacing from fear of dying. "I wanted you to have a little fun. You know, you're way too serious," he said more forcefully.

After a moment's thought, I admitted, "It was pretty exciting."

"And I'd already done it. I wanted to see if you could do it."

I scooped up a handful of water and tossed it in his face. He laughed, wiping it off. "Not totally serious," he observed.

Morris took the tiller. We turned south and spotted three planes from the naval air base.

"Wouldn't it be great to fly?" Morris asked, more passion in his voice than I expected.

"As long as you don't ask me to take the stick whenever the going gets rough," I told him.

He continued to dream aloud about flying as we sailed around Whidbey Island, then turned back toward Fort Worden, a stiff breeze speeding our return from the south.

Back at the barracks, I found a note asking me to report to company headquarters. I went straight to the captain's office.

He ordered me in, looking irritated. "I don't know what you did, but the Medical Director over at the hospital is demanding your transfer to the Medical Corps. He says he's going to train you to be a pharmacist. I told him I needed you in the plotting room. Those pictures you took are pushing our kill rate for the rafts through the roof. I am going to recommend it to other Coastal Artillery groups. I don't want to let you go, but he outranks me." He looked at me, an enormous frown on his face. "Pack your gear and move into the Medical Corps barracks on Friday."

That weekend I visited Yu-Ling at the tailor shop.

"Something good did come out of my accident," I told her. "As he examined my ankle, I told the doctor how interested I am in medical training. He arranged for me to be trained as a pharmacist."

"Wonderful," she said. "I told you good things can come from bad."

"Where did you get that philosophy?" I asked her.

"From my father," she said. "He had wanted to be a great scholar, but his father was disgraced before he entered university, and he could not attend. So he became a tailor, came to the United States and discovered that he could study anything he wanted here once he learned enough English. He studied science, engineering, literature, and art until his death. He was going to send me to an American university, but he died, and I had to take over the business."

"I am so sorry about that. What could your grandfather have done that disgraced the family so badly that your father couldn't go to the University?"

"They never talked about it, but China is different from the United States. Honor is significant and dishonor a grave matter."

CHAPTER 9
PHARMACIST

Hot air blasted out of the training room as I opened the door and entered. Every other place on the Fort was freezing, but the heat in this room made it hard to breathe. The chalky seafoam-colored walls and deep blue-green chalkboards added to the soporific effect. Twenty-four men sat, three each, at long wooden tables, some already dozing off thanks to the heat, and class hadn't even started. I thought twenty-four pharmacy students were too many for a small medical unit, but I didn't make the decisions around here. I introduced myself to Private Stewart on my right and Private Puckett on my left.

"Good morning," announced Major Dr. Reyes as he walked in from the back door. We all jumped to attention. "As you were! Welcome to the specialist training class. Please fill out the forms in front of you and pass them to the right." He paced anxiously for about half an hour while we filled out the forms.

Puckett turned to me. "What is physiology?" I helped Puckett answer the question, "What is your background in human anatomy and physiology?" and a few others. I worried about him based on his answers.

Finally, all the forms were passed to the right and collected by Dr. Reyes. "We train orderlies, surgical techs, and pharmacists simultaneously," Major Dr. Reyes droned. The voice that had sounded so soothing in the exam room seemed monotone in the classroom. "All of you will study anatomy and physiology together. After these classes, you'll train by specialty. There will be six weeks of classroom work. If you qualify for on-the-job training, you will get it until you can do the job independently."

He passed out mimeographed diagrams of the human skeleton and began his lecture. I took notes directly on the mimeograph, adding a few comments of my own, fighting the heat and droning of Dr. Reyes's voice. When I glanced at Private Puckett, he looked like a scared puppy. He tried to write down the names of the bones as Dr. Reyes said them but had no idea how to spell them. If this class had been my first anatomy class, I don't believe I could have kept up. Puckett had no clue what Reyes said, while Reyes assumed some basic knowledge of human anatomy, and Puckett struggled mightily. Reyes lectured so fast I couldn't pause to help Puckett. I wished I could have been teaching the class. I know I could have done better.

"I don't expect you to memorize every bone in the body," Dr. Reyes concluded, "but I'll expect you to be able to label at least the larger bones on your test on Friday." He paused and peered around the class. He seemed expectant. Did he want a question or two? Too Bad! He had pulverized our brains with his terrible lecture style. After a moment of silence, he said, "After mess, we will cover the respiratory system. Dismissed." I shook my head. The skeletal system had taken about a week in my college class, not half a day. What a sprint!

I rushed to catch up with Puckett, who lumbered toward the mess hall like a hungry bear. As I caught up with him, I patted him on his shoulder and asked, "Puckett, where do you hail from?"

"Outside Oak Ridge, Tennessee." He shook his head. "I tell you, I don't know if I'm gonna make it in this class."

"What did you expect when you signed up?"

"I put in to be a mule skinner." I rolled my eyes. How did they think someone who considered himself a mule skinner could become a medical technician?

"See," explained Puckett, "when my Pa died, I took over the farm. I've been running mules since my twelfth year, caring for them and all. But the recruiters said they don't need no muleskinners. I guess they thought since I could take care of mules, maybe I could take care of people. I don't know what to do. I need the army pay to send home to Ma, but it seems like I can't do anything they want me to. They tried me out on the guns. I can't seem to get the hang of plotting. I don't even know what a pharmacist is or an orderly. They want me to be an orderly. I only went through seventh grade before I flunked out in eighth."

I offered to go with him to talk with Dr. Reyes.

We waited forty minutes to see the doctor. Reyes groaned after we explained the situation.

"Not another one," he complained. "I ask for educated and interested personnel, but they keep sending me people who are not prepared or interested in a medical career." He seemed genuinely angry. He took a breath and settled down.

I wondered what Puckett thought of Reyes's comments. I would have taken them very poorly.

"I'm sorry, son. I'm sure you would make an excellent muleskinner, but the army has more muleskinners than it knows what to do with right now. We must try to make a medical technician or orderly out of you." He focused on me. "Sinclair, did I see you had been a high school teacher?"

"Yes, sir."

"Could you help this man? Maybe tutor him or help him somehow grow beyond his mules?"

He phrased it as a question, but I sensed it was an order. "Yes, Sir."

That evening I worked with Puckett. He had butchered animals, so he knew where the organs were and how their bones connected. Many of them had the same names as human bones. We set up in the entryway to our barracks, where it was cool, and I tried to make the lessons enjoyable. We constructed large diagrams and put them up in the barracks. Drawing the posters helped Puckett understand the way things came together, and it turned out he was quite a good artist. The next night three others joined our little study group, causing consternation for others passing through the entryway. I tried to keep it centered around Puckett. But the others didn't understand any more than Puckett did, so my focus expanded.

The entryway became so crowded that no one could get in or out. I obtained permission through Dr. Reyes to use an empty bunker. The bunker turned out to be a pleasant room with no interruptions (except on Wednesdays during our lunch breaks when a gun two bunkers away shot at a raft.) The bunker had plenty of wall space to tape drawings. Once, the captain ran over to our bunker and made me help the gunners with their aim, but he seemed otherwise pleased with my photographic approach to sinking enemy ships.

Physiology was even more difficult than anatomy, and our group grew to fourteen. I considered Reyes a great doctor but a lousy teacher. Before I was drafted, I'd seen something similar in my high school: a couple of teachers with outstanding credentials and work experience but clueless about inspiring students to learn. Too bad for their students.

"Physiology is how the body functions," I reminded them many times as stragglers joined us over a couple of days.

"What does function mean?" asked one student.

"How it works. That is, what goes on inside your body."

Occasionally I thought I might be teaching elementary students. I realized we did a pretty good job of educating our students in Kansas based on my experience here. The great majority of Kansas graduates could read and comprehend high school material. Some of these southern and western recruits couldn't even write and could barely read a simple sentence. I worried about the state of the army with so many scarcely literate soldiers. They were supposed to have passed the GI test.

When a student failed to understand a concept, Dr. Reyes repeated precisely the same explanation, only louder. And he was very nervous standing in front of a classroom. Clearly, he did not like to teach. That was the most concerning to me. Even if they didn't know the subject matter well enough to get everything right, people who liked to teach still helped their students more than teachers who didn't want to teach.

I worked hard to help my study group understand and remember the information Dr. Reyes dumped on them. Of course, I couldn't fault him since he had six weeks to teach a subject that took one or two years at university. But I enjoyed the challenge of shoring up my study group.

On Sundays, I tried to get in some R&R. Hiking became my relief valve. I loved the shady green woods and spent almost every

Sunday afternoon wandering along the trails. I wondered who made and maintained them since I didn't run into anyone else. Rainforests were a new experience for me, raised on the Kansas plains. I invited Dennis Stewart, the only other college-educated medical trainee, to join me on a hike one Sunday afternoon.

"Why do you work so hard with those hicks, Sinclair? This should be a piece of cake for you, so why make things harder on yourself?"

"I like helping people. These boys, even some of the volunteers, don't want to be here, but they're willing to put in the extra time to try to do better. It's worth it to me to help them."

Stewart snorted. "I don't want to be here either, but it's a better choice than getting shot in the infantry. I know I'm not officer material. Too lazy. But you? You should have gone to officer training school. These boys don't want to be here, but you're getting them through. That takes some leadership. And perseverance!"

"I just want to go home and go to medical school after my year is up," I said.

"Get the army to send you to medical school. They'll pay for the education; you finish up your hitch and go home a doctor."

"*What?*" I thought, amazed. Why hadn't anyone told me about that?

At the first opportunity, I went to the director of the Fort hospital, Major Radcliff, to find out more about Stewart's suggestion.

"First," he told me, "you would go to ten weeks of officers' training, then to medical school. You would have the same training as civilian medical students along with military responsibilities. After medical school, you would have to stay for at least four years as a doctor. Then you could ask for a discharge. After that, you could become a licensed private physician or join a hospital staff."

"How do I apply?"

"Get a form from the CO. You'll have to take some tests. Be sure you make it clear you are applying to be a medical officer. There are no guarantees, but it's worth a try."

I put in my application that week.

After a week of anatomy and a week of physiology, the classes split up. Pharmacy students began memorizing medications, their uses, and interactions—all new to me. I focused on memorization, but I continued to meet with the remedial group. Now I helped them with study skills and techniques to remember their lessons.

Only five members out of the original fourteen of my tutoring program completed the six week training. Puckett failed. I was very disappointed.

"I don't know what I'll do now," he told me. "They're gonna try me on equipment repair next."

After our graduation ceremony, Major Radcliff called me into his office.

"Well, Sinclair, you've done a great job here. We now have a full complement of trained personnel in the medical detail."

"A thirty-three percent success rate is somewhat dismal," I said. I was used to eighty-five percent or more of my students earning at least a C.

"You're batting three hundred. Any baseball team would be proud to have you. You play baseball, Sinclair?"

"A little schoolyard ball with the boys back home. But my father played on a minor league team from 1904 to 1908. We got our share of baseball metaphors growing up."

"We appreciate your help getting these boys trained, Sinclair. And if you want to get involved in the baseball team, we're looking for a few more players for spring training."

What is going on here, I thought. *A medical training program being compared to baseball batting averages? Somebody at the top was striking out big time.* I thanked the Major and declined the offer, shaking my head on the way out of his office.

To celebrate my completion of the program, I got weekend leave. I contacted Morris, hoping he could come with me. He did. I asked Lieutenant Perry if we could borrow his car, and we set off for Victoria, British Columbia, Canada.

***

Before Morris and I left, Perry said, "Be sure you go see those gardens I told you about. They're mostly in an old quarry."

"I'm not so sure it will be worth seeing a garden in December," I commented.

"It *will* be worth it. And be sure you get back in time tonight," he said as he handed me the keys. "My year is up, and I'm going home tomorrow."

A few miles up the road, I spotted a sign pointing to a lookout point. "Let's check it out," I said.

Morris parked the car at a wide spot in the road, and we clambered up the steep, wooded trail. We emerged onto a rocky ledge. Before us, the Sound glistened in the sun. Behind us rose snow-covered Mount Rainier, half-hidden by clouds. I snapped pictures in all directions with my Brownie. Then we bounded down the hill to the car. Morris stopped at a rocky beach covered with driftwood a little farther along. We collected twisted burls and smooth branches he could carve into gnomes, a hobby I did not know about till now. I joked with him about whether he had a "Gnomenclature," but he didn't get it.

The ferry captain was blowing the foghorn as we drove up. The ticket agent urged us to hurry. We pulled onto the ferry to Vancouver Island a minute before departure time, parked on the lower level as they pulled up the ramps behind us, then climbed the stairs to the upper deck. Morris quickly found a seat between a couple of beautiful girls. I took my camera and went in search of photographic subjects. A few minutes into the crossing, I spotted a large fin breaking through the water's surface.

"What's that?" I asked a passing crew member. He looked over the railing.

"It's a killer whale. Strange that it's still here. They usually spend the winter somewhere else. Is there only one? Usually, they swim in pods." The crew member went off on his business.

Other passengers gathered around me, and we watched the whale swim next to the ferry for the next fifteen minutes but didn't see any others.

"They usually swim as families," a young man wearing a Canadian army uniform told me, repeating the crew member's information. "And they're usually out to sea by now. There must be something wrong. It is very unusual to see a lone Orca."

"Orca?" I asked.

"Yes. The Latin name is *Orcinus orca*. It means 'belonging to Orcus,' the Roman god of the netherworld, what we would call Hell. We call Orcas 'Killer Whales,'"

"You seem to know a lot about the area," I said.

"I learned from my grandmother. My grandfather owned a cement company, and when they exhausted the quarry that provided the limestone, it was an eyesore right in their front yard, so grandmother began planting gardens. They gave the garden to me last year for my twenty-first birthday. I'm about to ship out for Europe but got leave to visit the family one more time before I go."

I probably looked astonished at the luck. The owner of the garden Morris and I were going to see stood right in front of me! Wow! "Goodness!" I exclaimed, "We're on our way to see your garden. A Washington National Guardsman told us about it. Is it worth the trip in December?"

"Oh yes!" The Japanese Garden and the Italian Garden will be beautiful. Don't expect too much from the Rose Garden, though. I'm heading straight out there when the ferry lands. Why don't you follow me?"

I reached out my hand to shake: "Gene Sinclair."

"Ian Ross,"

The ferry finally eased up to the dock, dropped its front gate, and cars began driving off.

Ian came up to me. "An employee of the garden is meeting me. See that Delahaye Coupes des Alpes over there?" He pointed at a car with a design I had never seen in the United States. "Grab your friend and follow us to the gardens."

"Will do," I said. "We'll be the last ones off, though. Can you wait, Ian?"

"Sure, I'll pull off to the right."

Morris drove us off the ferry about twenty minutes later, finding the Delahaye parked beside a fence about twenty yards off the right. We honked. The Delahaye took off, and we followed. The city and the woods passed in a blur as Morris concentrated on following him. Twenty minutes later, we parked in the driveway of a large house and went up a slight hill to some greenhouses. Morris and I wandered around a tiny picnic area while Ian spoke with his greenhouse employees. Christmas rose, winter jasmine, fragrant camellias, and heather all were flowering in glorious colors. Ian returned and led us down the hill.

"The Japanese Garden is the first one my grandmother planted," Ian told us as we walked toward the sea. "She worked with a famous Japanese landscaper, Isaburo Kishida from Yokohama. This entrance is known as a Torii gate." The gate was a massive structure, with huge posts with a curved, tiled top, almost like a roof.

"This garden wouldn't indicate that the Japs were as aggressive as they are these days," I said in awe as we followed a path winding among leather-leafed rhododendrons and Japanese maples with red leaves still clinging to them. Streams and waterfalls looped from one pond to another. Crossing a bridge, I thought I recognized the pool we walked beside.

I asked Ian, "Weren't we just on the other side of this pool?"

"Yes. This is the third time we have viewed this particular pool, all from different angles. Isaburo was a master at creating different views from every vantage point."

"This garden isn't so big as I thought when we entered," Morris said.

"It is about one acre," replied Ian, "But has over a quarter-mile of paths and stepping stones with different views on every stretch. I love how peaceful it is."

We emerged from the Japanese garden near a star-shaped pool, a frog sculpture spewing water in the center. The brightly colored ducks swimming in the pond came ashore, waddled to the lawn, and surrounded us. Clearly, they wanted food.

"My grandfather loves birds. He collected them from all over the world. These are his ornamental ducks." Ian explained, pouring some pellets he scooped from a nearby bucket into each of our hands. We tossed them to the ducks. They snapped up the food as we dropped it, a melee of ducks.

"I've never seen ducks like these before. Do you know their names and where they come from?" I asked

"Sorry, no. I've concentrated more on learning about the plants."

Tall cypress trees screened the next garden. A stepped lawn led to a large area planted with dormant rose bushes.

"My cousins were upset when Grandmother plowed up the tennis court to plant the Italian garden, but I prefer the garden to an expanse of concrete."

This area was as geometric as the Japanese garden had been natural. A paved walk formed the garden's center, divided by a cross-shaped shallow pool. Plants in huge pots, as well as several statues, dotted the garden. Gardeners were busy planting bulbs in beds set into the walkway. They would be gorgeous in spring.

Ian led us down some stairs into the heart of the former quarry, where a deeper, natural pond, surrounded by flowerbeds and shrubs, sparkled in the sunlight. A few rhododendrons bloomed in an immature sequoia grove.

"I'm particularly fond of this area because it's the first garden I helped plant. Although the gardens all belong to me now, I'm not sure how I'll maintain them. I'm off to war."

"People would pay to see this. You could open the gardens to the public and generate revenue to keep them up." I suggested.

"I'll keep that in mind," he said. I'm not sure if he liked the idea. "We have always had visitors but have never charged admission." He looked down at his feet for a few seconds, then checked his watch. "I have to get back to town before my family starts wondering what became of me, but you two can stay as long as you like," he offered.

"Thank you so much for showing us around," I said. "I would love to go through the entire garden again if you don't mind."

"No," Morris spoke up. "I'm starving. I need to get some food."

I'd enjoyed the garden so much I had lost track of time. It was almost lunchtime.

"Maybe we can come back after I feed him," I said. "Would you mind if we took a closer look at the greenhouses?"

"Not at all," said Ian.

Morris and I climbed back up to Perry's car and headed for Victoria, with me driving this time at a more sedate pace. Morris tuned the radio to NBC and turned it up. We drove, laughing as we attempted to sing along with "I am a Pirate King" from the *Pirates of Penzance*. The music stopped suddenly in the middle of the song, and an announcer came on.

"We interrupt this program for a special announcement. The Japanese have attacked Pearl Harbor, Hawaii, by air, President Roosevelt has just announced. We take you now to Washington." Morris and I let out an exclamation, and I had to pull over to the side of the road, my body trembling.

"The White House is now giving out a statement. The attack apparently was made on naval... on all naval and military activities on the principal island of Oahu. Hostilities of this kind would mean the President would ask Congress for a declaration of war. There is no doubt from the temper of Congress that such a request would be granted."

My pulse raced. "Damn, damn, damn!" I shouted, pounding the steering wheel, angrier than I could ever remember. How dare they attack the United States.

"We're in the war," said Morris dully. A vein pulsed in his neck.

We sat for a few minutes, breathing heavily, then I pulled back onto the road as the music resumed. Everything had changed in the blink of an eye. Both Morris and I were angry that the Japs had attacked us, and I was mad for personal reasons. We knew that this would frighten Americans everywhere. There was no doubt we were in the war now.

"We have to get back to the fort as quickly as possible," I said. Morris nodded in agreement. I drove us back to the dock without stopping for lunch.

"The next ferry won't be leaving until three o'clock," the ticket agent said.

"But the Japs attacked the United States. We need to get back to our post."

"What?"

We told her what we knew, but our pleas didn't get the ferry to the dock any faster. Morris and I walked back toward the car.

"How did the forces in Hawaii so completely miss the signs of an attack?" he asked.

"With so little information, it's impossible to know how they pulled it off," I said. "I don't understand it. They have coastal artillery there, too. And ships coming and going every day. You would think somebody would have seen something."

We went to a little diner near the pier and sat down. The employees stood around the radio. A waitress handed us menus, recommended the seafood chowder, and returned to listen for more news. She came back for our orders a couple of minutes later. We ordered the chowder.

Morris and I downed our food, barely tasting it, as we waited for another newsbreak on the radio. But nothing came on to provide anything newer than we had heard on the car radio.

We left what was probably an outrageous tip since neither of us had looked at the chowder's price nor accounted for the difference in value between Canadian and American dollars. When we asked for our bill at the cash register, the burly owner said, "No charge. You guys will have a real battle on your hands—best of luck. We didn't feel much like sightseeing anymore, so we sat on the dock for about an hour until we could get back on the ferry. Every few minutes, my anger would bubble to the surface.

"How could this happen?" I asked. "How could we not have detected enemy activity near Hawaii? How did the Japs do it?"

Morris sat beside me, red in the face, cracked his knuckles, muttering something I couldn't hear. Then he turned to me, answering my question without answering it. "This means we're at war." He said it so that I understood all of his statement's implications. We both had plans, but now they had been tossed out altogether.

Almost every US citizen on Victoria Island gathered at the dock, the news of the Japanese attack on American soil having been widely broadcast by now. They were trying to get back across the Sound. When the ferry finally arrived and had released its passengers onto Canadian soil, the crew flagged Morris and me on first because of our uniforms and then packed vehicles as tight as they dared behind us. I walked around the ferry talking to people but got so much conflicting information I wasn't sure what happened. Some said Manila had been bombed; others insisted the Japs were en route to Seattle. I knew less by the time we drove off the ferry than when we went on.

We had the radio on all the way back to the Fort, hoping for more news. All we got was music. Finally, on the evening news, Drew Pearson repeated what we had already heard, verifying that Manila had not been bombed. The Sunday evening visit with Eleanor Roosevelt came on.

"This is Leon Pearson speaking for the Pan-American Coffee Bureau. And now here's the Pan-American Coffee Bureau's Sunday-evening news reviewer and newsmaker, Mrs. Franklin D. Roosevelt."

"Good evening, ladies and gentlemen," said Mrs. Roosevelt. "I am speaking to you tonight at a very serious moment in our history. The cabinet is convening, and the leaders in Congress are meeting with the President. State Department and Army and Navy officials have been with the President all afternoon. In fact, the Japanese ambassador was talking to the President at the very time that Japan's airships were bombing our citizens in Hawaii and the Philippines and sinking one of our transports loaded with lumber on its way to Hawaii.

"By tomorrow morning, the members of Congress will have a full report and be ready for action. In the meantime, we, the people, are already prepared for action. For months now, the knowledge that something of this kind might happen has been hanging over our heads. And yet it seemed impossible to believe, impossible to drop the everyday things of life and feel that there was only one thing which was important: preparation to meet an enemy, no matter where he struck. That is all over now, and there is no more uncertainty. We know what we have to face, and we know that we are ready to face it.

"I should like to say just a word to the women in the country tonight. I have a boy at sea on a destroyer. For all I know, he may be on his way to the Pacific. Two of my children are in coast cities on the Pacific. Many of you all over this country have boys in the services who will now be called upon to go into action. You have friends and families in what has suddenly become a danger zone. You cannot escape anxiety. You cannot escape a clutch of fear at your heart. And yet, I hope that the certainty of what we have to meet will make you rise above these fears.

"We must go about our daily business more determined than ever to do the ordinary things as well as we can. And when we find a way to do anything more in our communities to help others build morale, we must do it to give a feeling of security. Whatever is asked of us, I am sure we can accomplish it. We are the free and unconquerable people of the United States of America.

"To the young people of the nation, I must speak a word tonight. You are going to have a great opportunity. There will be high moments in which your strength and your ability will be tested. I have faith in you! I feel as though I am standing upon a rock. And that rock is my faith in my fellow citizens."

Finally, back at the Fort, we returned the car to Perry.

"Thank you for the use of the car." I said. "Good luck in Seattle."

"I won't be returning to Seattle," he replied with bitterness in his voice. "Everyone is in for the duration. The whole area is on high alert, and reinforcements are coming tomorrow."

"In for the duration?" I repeated.

"That's right." He answered my question, which was not a question. "The duration."

CHAPTER 10
THE WORLD AT WAR

Blackout curtains covered the hospital windows as I made my way to my first pharmacy shift in the early morning. At the entrance to the hospital, I couldn't open the door. An orderly opened it in response to my pounding, urging me to enter quickly. He looked out behind me for the enemy as he promptly slammed the door shut and relocked it. Two days before, the Fort seemed like a vacation resort. Now a fortress on the front lines of the war, we anticipated the arrival of Japanese planes at any minute, or maybe Japanese parachutes landing softly, then their paratroopers charging us. If they could reach Hawaii, they could reach mainland America.

I rode the elevator to the basement. Something niggled at my brain. How low is a pharmacy in the army medical world that they tucked it away in the basement? The pharmacy, to my right, seemed abandoned.

"PFC Sinclair reporting for on-the-job training," I called out loudly.

After a few moments, a corporal emerged from the backroom. "Hello. Come on in. The door's around the corner." He pointed

I entered the pharmacy's back room. Floor to ceiling shelves overwhelmed with a jumble of medicine bottles crammed most of the space. A counter along one side held metal trays, pill bottles, scales, and other supplies. A single bare bulb hung from the ceiling, casting shadows across the concrete floor. I had wired barracks to be better lit than this, and they were for sleeping, not for accurately distributing drugs to everyone on base.

"I'm Corporal Heinz. I'm glad you're here. I've had no help for months" He sounded pained. "Here's the list of medications the nurses need at their stations. That's what you do first."

"Where do we get the list?" I asked.

"An orderly delivers it first thing every morning."

"How does he compile the list?"

"From the nurses!" Heinz said too emphatically. He seemed a bit out of sorts with my question. He turned away, saying under his breath, "Those damned nurses are so demanding!"

I think he meant me to hear his comment.

I searched out the medications on the messy shelves, counted out the pills and poured liquids into the appropriate glass bottles, brown, green, and clear, put those for each nurse's station on different trays, placed the trays on a metal cart, and pushed the cart to the elevator. On the first floor, the nurse at the desk told me to wait for the charge nurse.

"PFC Sinclair," I introduced myself to Nurse Carlisle. "I have six medications for you." Handing her the first tray.

Nurse Carlisle checked the medications against her copy of the list.

"Perfect," she said. "The pharmacy order has never been correct before in all the time I've been charge nurse."

I shrugged my shoulders. "Not hard," I responded. Curious, I asked, "How long since your last correct order?"

She smushed up her face to think. "Maybe about two years."

I cringed. Counting pills? Heinz? "What the hell?" I said out loud.

She raised her eyebrows and looked at me over her glasses. But she was smiling.

"I'll make sure things are correct every day," I promised.

I went on to the second floor, then surgery. The nurses in each department were amazed I got theirs right, too. I asked Heinz for my next assignment back in the pharmacy, saying nothing about my experience with the nurses.

"Now, you take the ones they need but weren't on the list," said Heinz. "Try to be back here before nine. That's when officers pick up prescriptions. Enlisted will come at ten."

As a teacher, I often encountered students who tried to make their failure the fault of someone else or establish some obfuscation about their performance. Heinz seemed that sort of person.

"I don't have to take any back," I said, undermining his excuses. I didn't think he realized it. "All the prescriptions were correct."

Surprised, I realized he did understand my accusations. He stood up taller and tried to deflect my insinuations: "Amazing! I bet Nurse Carlisle was surprised. She's quite critical. It's almost impossible to please her. What a nasty person. Well, check these for the officers."

The pharmacy dispensed medications for all three forts of the Triangle of Fire, the navy base, and the naval airbase, so there were some officers I did not know. I corrected two of the five prescriptions Heinz had filled, confirming my suspicions about his practice. He had messed up badly on the two prescriptions, one the wrong medicine and one the wrong dose. While I waited for the officers, I started filling orders for the enlisted men.

"Don't get the officers and enlisted men's mixed up," Heinz told me. His tone told me that he had a lot of experience doing so.

"I won't. I put the officer's prescriptions on a white tray, and I'm putting the enlisted men's on green trays."

Heinz looked dumbfounded at my organization of the medicines. He breathed hard and stood up straighter. "Very good. I'm sure it helps to have some training."

"They didn't train you?"

"No. I worked in a drug store before, so they put me here."

"You were a pharmacist?"

"No. A soda jerk," he said with a wry grin.

"And you didn't tell them?"

"And lose this cushy job?"

I felt sad. Heinz, I concluded, based on the fact that I had corrected some of his counting and many other mistakes, had caused the problems the nurses had told me about. His CO should have reassigned him immediately since he couldn't count accurately or read well. Worse, he didn't care, other than wanting to keep his "cushy job."

Three of the officers showed up right at nine. I gave them their prescriptions and recorded the date and time in the book

Heinz gave me. They each looked at the label, opened the bottle, looked at the pills, and left. The others did not come that day.

"Sometimes they don't come on Monday," Heinz said. "They say they don't have time to wait around."

I wondered if Heinz's comment meant that the officers didn't have time to wait for him to recount and reissue their prescriptions. What a mess.

The enlisted men began showing up around nine-thirty, jostling to get toward the front of the line. They didn't mind waiting for anything. Promptly at ten, I went to the window with three green trays, the pill bottles arranged alphabetically. As each man approached the window, I asked him his name and had him sign the book saying he had received his prescription. I then asked if he had any questions about when and how to take his medication. If so, I explained. If not, he went on his way. I dispensed all the meds in under an hour.

"Now, you fill in the medications and the amounts you gave them," Heinz said, appearing from wherever he had been holed up. I suspected he had gotten a lot of criticism at how he had filled prescriptions and disappeared to avoid it today. I noticed that most enlisted men settled down after reading their labels and looking inside the prescription bottles, nodded their thanks, and then took off.

"I did that while I filled the prescriptions. Then I had each man sign on the appropriate line and entered the time he picked up his medication."

He looked at the book. "Sure enough, it's all done. There's the report with how much of everything you dispensed. You need to fill it in so we can order new stuff."

After checking Heinz's totals for accuracy, I filled out that report. It took around twenty minutes.

"Now what?" I asked.

"I don't know." Heinz shrugged his shoulders. "I haven't gotten everything done this early before. We could eat. We close from twelve to one, but we could go a little early. Nobody ever comes down here."

Just as Heinz finished his sentence, the elevator door opened, and Dr. Reyes stalked out.

"How is the training going, Heinz?" he demanded of the Corporal.

"I think he knows everything already," Heinz responded, standing at attention and saluting. I followed suit.

"At ease!" Reyes barked at both of us.

Dr. Reyes shoved a manual on pharmacy operations at me.

"Why don't you spend some time reviewing this, Sinclair," he ordered. "Keep it down here for the other new guys. When you tire of reading, you can organize and clean." He peered at Heinz in a way I would not like to be peered at. "May I see your records from this morning?"

Heinz responded with confusion, like Reyes's request was the first of its kind. "Yes, sir," I said as I quickly cast an amused glance at Heinz. He was my superior officer, after all.

I handed Reyes the records he requested. "Everything seems to be in order," Reyes told me. "I don't believe you'll need any training beyond reading the manual. I'll put in the paperwork for your promotion to Corporal. I'm putting you in charge here, and you will have to have a higher rank than all the PFCs you supervise."

Turning his attention to Heinz, he said, "Heinz, your transfer to the kitchen is approved. You'll start tomorrow." I shook my head.

After Dr. Reyes left, Heinz explained. "I would have gone home this week, but I can't now, so I'm gonna be a mess sergeant. I put in for it yesterday. Isn't it amazing? A promotion. And Dr. Reyes got all the paperwork done so soon!"

"It's incredible how fast things can change in an emergency. I hope you enjoy the mess hall," I replied with a smile.

"Why not?" he asked. "I'm a professional soda jerk."

I didn't know what to say.

The CO of the Fort called General Assembly in the early afternoon. Heinz wrote out a "Pharmacy Closed" sign.

"You won't need to come back," he said. "Our shift will be over before the assembly is finished. Goodbye forever, Pharmacy. Upward and onward, to the kitchens!" I wouldn't have considered that a promotion. We shuttered the dispensary window and went to the assembly.

The auditorium, packed because reinforcements had arrived already, reverberated with a loud mumble of voices. I spotted Morris and pushed through the crowd to stand by him. We would learn more recruits were due daily in the next few weeks.

"In response to Japan's heinous act of aggression on the United States of America, Congress has declared war on Japan," announced General Cunningham. Cheers went up around the room.

"Great Britain declared war on Japan while it was still the middle of the night here. In return, Germany and Italy declared war on the United States, being allied with Japan. This is a war extending around the world."

More cheers. I felt sad that so many men seemed happy about going to battle and maybe dying far away from their homes and families. The cause, I knew, was good, but the death war entailed was never good.

"All personnel will consider themselves in for the duration. Paperwork has begun. You'll report to the Adjutant General's office to sign your papers when ordered. Whether you like it or not, some of you will be reassigned as needed for the war effort. Thank you for your service on behalf of the American people. We are the greatest nation on earth, and, as we all pull together, civilians and military, we will defeat the enemy, with the help of our allies," Pausing for breath, he ejaculated, "On all fronts." He took a deep breath. "Now, please return to your assigned duties. Dismissed!"

Morris and I strode away from the auditorium and across the parade ground, Morris swearing under his breath.

"Why did the Japanese have to attack us? Now I—all of us— are in the army for who knows how long," I complained.

"We should put in for Officer Candidate School," he said.

"I already applied to become a medical officer. I completed all the tests last week."

"What? A Medical Officer? That would be a waste of skill. With you in the battery, we never miss a shot. You should stay in

Triple-A."

"I've always had my heart set on a medical career. An acceptance letter from Washington School of Medicine arrived in the same mail as the draft notice. Since they ruined my chance at medical school, the army might as well pay for the education."

"The Japs attacked Pearl Harbor. The world will never be the same. You should use your skills to help defeat them. If you go to medical school, the war will probably be over by the time you finish, and you won't see any action."

"I still think medicine is for me."

Why did Morris always think he knew what was best for me? And I wondered why he thought he would be officer material. He certainly had charisma, but I did not see him as a leader of men in battle, more like a leader of men into trouble. *If only I had arranged my life better and gotten into medical school straight out of college! But why should I go over that again? My mood darkened.*

We continued until we reached my favorite hiking path, taking us over a crest and down to the beach. I walked on, muttering to myself. "I should have known this would happen, But I thought it would be all those ships sunk in the Atlantic. I never dreamed it would be the Japs that got us into the war."

As we began to work up a sweat, my tension slowly evaporated. A while later, ensconced on a driftwood log on the beach, Morris said, "The past six months haven't been all that bad, have they?"

"Maybe sixty percent bad," I replied. "Although I've seen places I would never have gone otherwise and learned things I would not have known. I can still get medical training through the army—I hope."

Pitched out of my funk, I realized the sun had dropped below the water's flat horizon, and the temperature approached Kansas-like winter temperatures.

Let's get some grub," I suggested

We sauntered back to the Fort, the foggy darkness reflecting my mood.

In the mess—the actual enlisted men's mess hall, in which I had strung lights as my last duty before pharmacy school, the bravado of men preparing for war amplified the usual loud talk, the clanging of metal trays, and the scraping of chairs.

***

Puckett stopped by the pharmacy the next day. "You won't never guess where I'm going. They're sending me to Mississippi to train dogs! The army's going to teach dogs to sniff out land mines and patrol beaches and things. And I'm going to train the dogs. Dogs are even better than mules. They ain't as stubborn."

"Congratulations," I said, clapping him on his back. "I knew they would find the perfect job for you eventually."

On Friday, nearly a week after the attack on Pearl Harbor, they called me in to sign the new enlistment papers, which committed me for the duration of the war.

"State your rank, name, and date of birth," ordered Captain Lynch, a uniquely appropriate name, I thought.

"PFC Eugene Sinclair, December twelfth, nineteen hundred fourteen."

"Happy birthday, Sinclair. You're assigned to serve as lead pharmacist, Fort Worden hospital. You are promoted to Corporal."

I shook my head. "I hadn't even realized it was my birthday." I signed the papers, accepted the stripes, and returned to the pharmacy to prepare the coming week's duty schedule.

Over the next several days, I reorganized drug storage as I filled prescriptions. I ordered the other pharmacists to do a general cleanup of the entire pharmacy. Within a week, the pharmacy operated according to the manual. I got some wire and bulbs and installed as much lighting in the pharmacy as the circuit would allow, though not enough. Some places still had shadows even with the improved light.

The pharmacy was busier, although I still spent most of my time alone, waiting for someone requiring a prescription. I had never been so bored in my life. After hours I went to the Fort library to get new books to read. I bought a newspaper every day to keep up with the war. The British advanced across Africa, and the Soviet army pushed the Germans back from Moscow. The Japanese invaded more and more Pacific islands. The paper alleged that the Germans recently killed Jews in Lithuania and Romania by the thousands. At that point in my life, to my knowledge, I had never met a Jew. I didn't know the arguments people had used to justify pogroms and expulsions. All I knew about Jews came from Bible stories I had learned as a child.

Christmas came and went without much notice. Mom sent a wreath-shaped Three Kings cake and other gifts in early January for Epiphany. I invited several friends to join me to eat the cake.

After stuffing his piece of cake into his piehole, Heinz complained. "There's something hard in my cake."

"That is the bean!" I exclaimed. "You'll have good luck all year. Usually, Mom bakes a tiny figure of the baby Jesus into the cake, and whoever gets it has good luck. She substituted an uncooked bean because she didn't have an extra baby Jesus figure, but it still works."

"I've been having so much luck already I can't hardly stand it," Heinz said. "I might have my own kitchen in another year."

***

Within six weeks after we finished cleaning and organizing the pharmacy, I had read the meager supply of books in the Fort library. I went into town to the public library to see what they had. After leaving the library with an armload of books, I decided to stop by to visit Yu-Ling. I found her crying.

"There's no business," she sniffled when I asked her what was wrong. "No one's coming in for alterations,"

"I don't know why. We're getting new men assigned to the base every day. Surely some of them need alterations."

I told her about my job and how little work I had to keep me busy.

"I'll teach you some games," she said, her mood improving.

She took out a deck and laid out seven columns of cards.

"Solitaire," she said.

"I know how to play solitaire, but I never started this way," She had laid out the cards in a way I had never seen before.

"There are hundreds of ways to play solitaire," she told me. She showed me this way, then had me try it. I didn't win, but I did well. She offered me the deck of cards.

"I have a deck I picked up on the train. You keep your cards. It seems that you need them as much as I do."

As I emerged from her shop, a soldier stopped me.

"Why are you visiting that Jap shop?" he asked. "Are you a spy?"

"What? Are you crazy? She's not Japanese; she's Chinese. And the Japs invaded China, murdering thousands of Chinese just because, and made China a puppet state." I had read about what had happened in Nanking.

"How do you tell a Jap from a Chinese?" he asked.

I hesitated. Then I said, "The name. Japanese first and last names have several syllables, like Yokohama, Tokyo," I suggested. "Chinese names, first and last, one at a time. Yu-Ling Wong" I wasn't sure that what I said was right, but I couldn't think of anything else.

"Humph!" He stalked off.

I walked back into the shop.

"You need to put a sign in your window," I said to Yu-Ling. "Write, 'Have Your Uniform Altered by a Chinese Ally.' They think you are Japanese."

"Japanese!" she said with disgust. She looked like she was going to spit. "Maybe I will find a Japanese and do to him what they have done to my people!"

I wasn't sure how to respond to her anger, so I said, "I'll do my best to send business your way."

When I walked into breakfast the following day, someone yelled, "There he is!" Men surged toward me. One of them socked me in the face, knocking me down.

"What the hell!?" I exclaimed from the floor as Morris, Stewart, and several others rushed to defend me

"You're the one with the Jap girlfriend, aren't you?"

My friends pulled me to my feet. "No. I don't even have a girlfriend."

"I saw you coming out of that Jap shop."

I shouted, "She's Chinese, you idiot. The Chinese have been fighting the Japanese a lot longer than we have! The Japs have massacred hundreds of thousands of Chinese. Look at the news, you numbskulls!"

Three MPs rushed into the mess. They hauled off three of the unruliest guys bringing me along behind to HQ.

"Can you explain yourself?" the MP captain asked me.

"I made friends with the Chinese tailor in town. I went to visit her yesterday. This morning, someone accused me of befriending a Jap, of being a spy. It seems some people don't know the difference between Chinese and Japanese. They attacked me this morning for no reason other than they thought I had been talking to a Jap."

He questioned me for forty-five minutes, then finally released me, admitting that I'd done nothing wrong. I rushed to the pharmacy, not stopping to get anything to eat. Gladstone, one of my successful remedial students in the pharmacy program whom I had assigned to the night shift, had taken the medications to the various nurse's stations and started the officer's prescriptions. I worked all morning with my stomach grumbling and my lip throbbing. I made my first mistake on a script that morning. A new man walked into the pharmacy mid-morning. "Corporal Ratliff reporting for duty. Doctor Reyes said you handle the duty schedule."

I wondered about having two corporals in this little pharmacy but shrugged it off. "I do. Let's start with an orientation today, and I'll put you on the schedule."

As I showed him the layout of our little pharmacy, I asked him, "Where did you get your training?"

"Letterman Hospital in San Francisco, It's huge compared to this. And what's with us sleeping in tents with all the empty barracks around?"

"Most of the barracks need critical repairs before anyone can sleep in them. Troops on the hill watch the sky and water, but more of them are busy refurbishing the barracks so you can move in. The Fort still isn't at full capacity, but I understand four more batteries will be arriving soon."

Stewart, my hiking companion, came in to relieve me that afternoon, all smiles.

"I am going to the San Francisco Army Hospital to train to be a male nurse," he said. "The Colonel said I'll probably go to a field hospital when I finish the training. I'm so excited. They want you to report to HQ, too. Maybe we will be going together." He handed me the order to report.

A long line of soldiers waited at HQ. I finally reached the door, entered, and saluted the captain. "Sinclair, we have new orders for you. Our army is ramping up the Antiaircraft Artillery to combat the Japanese Air Force. These new units need officers. We're sending you to Officer's Candidate School to become an Antiaircraft Artillery Officer."

"Antiaircraft? I applied for training as a doctor."

"There are enough doctors out there." The statement stunned me. How could that be? "We'll recruit doctors who've already gone through medical school and call up all the reserve doctors. There are not enough Triple-A officers. Your math scores are outstanding, and your ratings are excellent. You've also shown incredible initiative and leadership skills in your time here. You're the best candidate we have for antiaircraft artillery. Pack your kit. You'll be leaving at 0500 tomorrow morning."

I stood at attention, probably more stiffly than the captain considered proper, judging by how he raised his eyebrows, clenching my teeth and tightening my left fist, shoved hard down by my side until I regained control.

"Yes, sir," I said, turning and striding out of his office.

CHAPTER 11
RIDING THE RAILS

In my room, I threw my things into my duffel bag. The new corporal in the pharmacy made sense now. And Stewart! Stewart got nurse's training. All he really wanted was to be lazy. And I get to shoot guns into the sky. Where is justice in this world?

I went to the communications office to call the folks at home. The phone rang and rang as I stewed. Finally, Millie, the telephone operator back home, said, "Sorry, Gene. No one is answering."

"Thank—"

"Wait a minute. Your mom just walked by the window. Hold on while I run out and see if I can catch her."

Millie must have caught up with Mom because Mom's voice came on the line.

"Gene. How are things going? Are you OK?" She sounded a bit worried.

"Mom, the army's sending me to officer's training school. They're making me an antiaircraft artillery officer."

"Antiaircraft artillery? What happened with your application for medical training?"

"They said they would get all the additional doctors from the reserves and civilian doctors who I guess they'll draft. Many of those reserve doctors are too old for overseas duty, and civilian doctors will be needed in the United States. I think they need to train more doctors before the war is over, but they want me in antiaircraft artillery."

"But you had such a wonderful plan for your life. A safe plan, an orderly plan."

"Mom, the country is at war, and I'm stuck defending it against all enemies. My plan makes no sense to the army."

"Where will you go for training? Will they give you time to come home?"

"No, Mom. I leave tomorrow morning for North Carolina, but I won't be able to come through Kansas."

"How long is the training?"

"They take college-educated enlistees and turn them into officers in ninety days. They're calling us Ninety-Day Wonders."

"I'm so sorry things aren't going according to your plan. But you'll do well as an officer!" She hesitated, I sensed, wanting to say more. Instead, she said, "Be careful, son."

"Don't worry. I will, Mom. How are things there?"

The fort operator broke in. "Your three minutes are up." He disconnected the line.

Mom. She had always encouraged me to have a plan, to be careful. And now she said I would make a great officer. I allowed a bit of eagerness for officer's training to sneak in.

***

I shouldered my duffel bag and ran out of the barracks into the pitch dark winter morning. The private behind the wheel of the jeep stopped his insistent honking. He had awakened most of the other men in the barracks and would probably have hell to pay when he got back. I had packed my footlocker the night before and left it on the porch. The private had already thrown it into the back of the jeep. To my surprise, Tom Morris sat in the back atop my footlocker, and I assumed his

As I hopped into the jeep, the driver gunned the engine, jerking my head back, probably to get away from anyone he had awakened. Maybe he was more intelligent than I thought.

"Where are you off to?" I asked Morris. "You didn't tell me you got an appointment."

"Flight school in Georgia. I'm going to fly planes! You didn't tell me either. You off to Medical School? "

"No, damn it. Triple-A Officer's Training."

"I told you that's what you should do. You going to Chicago on the Empire Builder?"

"Yes, then on to Cincinnati, Ohio, south to Chattanooga,

Tennessee, then across North Carolina to Camp Davis."

"Great! We'll be traveling together to Chattanooga."

By exceeding the speed limit and pushing his way onto the ferry as it was pushing off, our driver got us to Seattle three hours before the Empire Builder arrived. Morris couldn't wait around. "Have you been to the Seattle Art Museum?" he asked.

I shook my head.

"Neither have I. Let's go. We can get there right when it opens at 1000 hours."

"Are you sure we'll make it back in time?"

"You be the timekeeper," he said.

We checked our luggage, and I went to pick up a trolley schedule from the stationmaster. As I turned from the counter, I spotted Morris jumping onto a trolley that had just left the station. I ran after the trolley and as I sprinted alongside, he pulled me on board.

On the way, I mentally calculated when we would have to catch the return trolley. We had about two hours available for the exhibits.

We quickly toured their extensive collection of Oriental art and furniture. A sign next to a small side room door read, "Photography Exhibit."

"Morris, let's check this out," I said, tapping him on his arm, pointing.

I strolled into the room, examining each photograph. One picture stopped me dead in my tracks.

"Morris, come over here." I pointed at the photo. "By someone named Ansel Adams. Look at the way he uses the light. How he manages to create the mood."

A docent walked by, overhearing my comment.

"We have two other pieces by Mr. Adams," she said. "Let me show you."

We followed her to two more stunning nature photographs.

Her badge said her name was Marge. She told us, true to her docent nature, "Adam's been commissioned to take photographs in all the national parks. They say he originally had his mind set on becoming a concert pianist. His family and friends told him he should be a photographer, but it took him several years to give up the piano and accept photography as a profession."

"Some people take time to discover their true calling," I said.

"Hey Sinclair, how are we doing for time?" Morris asked. Unusual for him to be so responsible.

I looked at my watch.

"Oh, no! We need to get out of here right now!" I told the docent. "Thank you very much, Marge."

Luckily, we made it. The train was boarding as we retrieved our duffel bags. We jumped on board. The train left Seattle through a tunnel, emerging into a light rain. I couldn't get Ansel Adams out of my mind. The idea that such a brilliant photographer had tried so long to be a pianist when it was apparent that he should be a photographer disturbed me.

Our stomachs reminded us that we had missed lunch, scheduled early because of the Empire builder's departure. I was glad to have gone to the museum: Adam's work was magnificent. However, we made sure we were among the first in line for supper. As Morris and I found seats in the dining car, the rain diffused light through the windows went dark.

"What's happening?" I asked a waiter.

"We're in the Cascade Tunnel, sir. It's nearly eight miles long. We'll exit it in about twenty minutes."

The dining car took on the ambiance of a glamorous restaurant in the dim, flickering illumination as the light from inside bounced off the uneven walls of the tunnel.

"Let's have the salmon," I suggested to Morris. "It might be our last chance to have fresh salmon in a long time."

A young civilian man approached our table and asked if he could join us.

We invited him to sit. "Mike Watson," he said.

After we introduced ourselves, I asked, "Where's home?"

"Whitefish, Montana."

"On your way home?" I asked. Morris seemed disinterested in Watson's story.

"Sure am. I've joined the navy, and I'm going home to say goodbye."

"What made a Montana man decide to join the navy? The state is landlocked."

"Just that. My sales job got me out of that little town, and I loved it. So now I want to see the world and what better way than on a ship?"

"You do know there is a war going on?" I asked, "The navy will not be a grand vacation. And how do you know you'll be stationed on a ship?"

"Of course, I joined up to defend our country," Watson said. "But I've learned any sort of travel can expand the mind. As for being stationed on a ship, the recruiter promised I would. He wrote it down." He pulled the paper out and showed us.

Watson reminded me a little of Herman Hazelton back in Burns, but maybe only because he was a traveling salesman. Herman went all over the Midwest, peddling toilets. His sample case contained an intricately detailed miniature model, wooden seat and all. When in Burns, he would regale people with his stories, somewhat exaggerated, about what he had observed and experienced. When he held court at the barbershop, crowds of men and women would jam in to hear his renditions of life in the heartland.

In fact, Watson reminded me a lot of Herman. He told great stories about fishing and hunting in Montana. Even Morris listened without interrupting. When we finished the meal, we wished Watson the best of luck and returned to our sleeper car.

***

By morning the rain had changed to snow. A blizzard obscured our views. Huge drifts on the tracks from central Montana through North Dakota slowed the train. As we traveled through the vast whiteness, I contemplated what might be next. The United States had been in the Great War for less than two years. No wonder they needed officers in ninety days. Within fifteen to eighteen months of becoming an officer, I might be back on track.

Somewhere in Minnesota, on our third day on the train, the snow stopped, and we began to move more quickly. As we sat down to luncheon after leaving Minneapolis, the train turned south. A river emerged from the mist to the east. After traveling for several miles along the St. Croix River, the border between Minnesota and Wisconsin, we cut straight east across northern Illinois to Chicago, which upheld its reputation as the windy city on this late February day. A thermometer at the train station said thirty-five degrees, but it seemed well below freezing in the biting wind as we ventured out. We had expected a long layover in Chicago, but because of the snow delay, we only had time to look at the skyline and have a cup of coffee at a café near the station. Finally, we found the train platform to Cincinnati and waited with a crowd of new recruits for the train.

***

The noise level was more typical of a military mess hall than a luxury streamliner. Soldiers packed the car. After a quick meal, we found our sleeper berth. As the steward made up my bed, I mentioned there seemed to be a lot of military men on this train.

"We're way overloaded," he said. "Mostly new recruits. Second class is bursting at the seams with buck privates. They have to sleep in their seats. You're lucky you got berths. Took them boys too long to get on; we had a late departure."

"I've tried to sleep in a train seat before," I said. "I sure am glad I got a space in the sleeper car."

A waiter stood at the door of the dining car the following morning.

"We're very sorry, corporal, private. We're all out of food. I can get you some coffee."

"We should've gotten up earlier," Morris complained.

My stomach growled.

"You would have had to be here around 5:30 this morning," the waiter told us. "Those boys were awake and hungry, standing in line before we opened."

To make myself feel better, I said, "I enjoyed sleeping in. We'll be in Cincinnati soon, and we can get some breakfast there."

The conductor came to apologize that we would arrive late. Our train to Chattanooga left about fifteen minutes before we arrived. We had to wait until evening for the next train.

"What can we do in Cincinnati?" asked Morris as we stepped off the train.

"I have no idea! This will probably mess up our whole itinerary. We might not even get to training on time."

"Nothing we can do about it," replied Morris. "There's a coffee shop there, and I'm famished."

We strode into the shop, outdistancing most men headed in that direction. But we still had to wait for a few minutes for a seat. As we waited, the two men behind us asked, "Where you two headed?"

"Douglas, Georgia for flight training," Morris said.

"I'm on the way to Camp Davis for officer training."

"Really?" they said. "We're going to Camp Davis, too. Ron Willis and Larry Duffy." We all shook hands. "Willis here hails from Oklahoma. My Dad's an army man, so I'm from everywhere. He's stationed at Fort Sam Houston now. Both of us graduated from Texas Tech and trained at Fort Riley."

"Glad to meet you," I said. "Morris here is from Kansas City, and I'm from a little town in northern Kansas. What do you know about Camp Davis?"

"Camp Davis is new," Duffy told us. "And huge—twenty thousand troops posted there. We'll start our training at the Camp proper, but they'll probably send us to one of the outlying training fields after the first week or two. I think they have five of them. They train antiaircraft, seacoast defense, and barrage balloon officers and troops. What are your orders, Sinclair?"

"Antiaircraft artillery officer," I replied.

"Me too," Duffy said. "Willis is training for balloons."

Willis bought a newspaper, and we shared the sections to pass the time.

"Anybody see anything interesting to do?" asked Morris.

We all shook our heads.

"We could at least walk down and see the river," I suggested. It had a pretty important role in the history of the nation."

"I suppose," said Duffy,

We hopped on a streetcar, where I struck up a conversation with a local man. He turned out to be a history professor at the University of Cincinnati. He proceeded to give us a tour of historical sites in Cincinnati. Willis and I were fascinated. Duffy and Morris grew increasingly bored until we stopped at a White Castle hamburger shop. We each ate several tiny sandwiches, and the bill came to over three dollars, but the professor insisted on paying. We thanked him profusely and headed back to the station, where the train to Chattanooga had just started boarding.

"We're in luck," Morris said. "It's a streamliner. It'll be fast and comfortable."

Morris and I did not have a sleeper berth and joined the rest of the sleeping men sprawled out on the seats. Few servicemen were on this train, and the kitchen seemed well supplied. At least we all got breakfast.

"Well, I guess this is it," Morris said as we got off the train in Chattanooga.

"We'll stay in touch," I said. "I'll write to you as soon as possible."

We shook hands, looking at each other sternly, like army men. Although I think Morris was kind of "full of it," such as when he tried to drown me on the sailboat back at the Fort, I still liked him. I hoped he would succeed and survive.

"Do well," I ordered him.

"Yeah, you too!"

"Sinclair, the train is about to leave," Duffy called.

Running, I left Morris on the platform and jumped on as the train moved out of the station.

***

Leaving Chattanooga, the passengers were nearly one hundred percent military, going to Camp Lejeune or Camp Davis. As the train descended toward North Carolina's coast the next day, the temperature got warmer and warmer. In Kansas, it would still be winter. Here in North Carolina, it felt more like mid-spring.

We parted ways with the Marines in a small town surrounded by piney woods, where they boarded a local train bound for Camp Lejeune. Duffy, sitting next to me, moved to an empty row so we would both have more space.

We picked up several civilians who worked in the camp at the next station. The last passenger on was a petite auburn-haired teenager. She stood by the door as the train started moving. Her slender waist and short stature made her appear fragile, but something about how she stood, perfectly still on the moving train, communicated physical strength. She looked up and down the aisles, her intense green eyes checking out the servicemen in the seats, then she moved up the aisle and stopped next to me, locking her bright green eyes onto mine.

"That seat taken?" she asked in a soft Southern drawl.

"No," I replied. "Please have a seat."

Duffy, who had been staring at the girl, glared at me.

She sat down. "Y'all on your way to Officer's Training School at Camp Davis?"

"Yes, how did you know that?"

"I heard that was startin next week. You're a corporal already, with pharmacy insignia, so you wouldn't be a recruit for basic AAA training."

"How do you know I wouldn't be coming in to be a pharmacist at the camp?"

"The hospital trains their own pharmacists. Just finished training a whole new batch." She looked at me sideways out of her bright green eyes. "I know that 'cause I pick up a little extra money sewin insignia on uniforms. I just finished sewin on a bunch of pharmacy insignia. Besides, y'all used to be in the coastal artillery. Y'alls uniform's faded 'cept for where the crossed cannons used to be."

"The Sherlock Holmes of Eastern North Carolina," I declared. I had to listen carefully to understand her, not being used to the southern accent.

"I read that book. My li'l brother Davie brought it home from school. I wouldn't say I'm anywhere near as good as him at figurin things out. But I'm friendlier than him."

"I can tell. What do you do when you are not sewing on insignia?"

"I work in the laundry. Daddy and my brothers helped build the camp. Most men 'round these parts did. They had twenty-six thousand people workin all together buildin the camp, and they built it in only five and a half months. My Daddy and brothers made better'n twenty-five dollars a week each."

"That's more than I make as a soldier," I said.

"More'n Daddy ever made before, too. They also brought home a bunch of extra stuff and put two new rooms on our house."

"Isn't that illegal?"

"They said the boss didn't care. The construction company had some kind of contract. They had to finish it fast, so if something got broke or wasn't cut right, the workers tossed whatever it was in a scrap pile and cut another from a new piece of lumber. If a nail keg broke, they just got a new one instead of picking up the nails. So, Daddy and the boys went through the scrap piles ever evenin and brought stuff home. I never had my own bedroom afore. I slept in the main room with Granny. My six brothers sleep in the loft, and Mama and Daddy in the bedroom. I have one older brother, one the same age as me, my twin, Jeb, and four younger. Daddy and my brothers brought home enough stuff to put on a bedroom for me and a new kitchen. Jeb teases me about my bedroom not bein regulation, 'cause the ceilin's seven feet five inches, but that don't bother me. I'm only five feet four inches, so it's plenty high for me."

"I suppose it is better to have a short bedroom than no bedroom at all," I said

"Sure is! And in the kitchen, we have all new appliances. We're too far out for the REA's 'lectric lines to reach us, but we got a propane icebox and stove. Daddy wanted to make life easier for Mama, so, 'cause o the high wages and all, he bought her the latest thing. I buy propane every weekend when I go home."

"That's nice," I said, wondering how many other homes had been brought into the twentieth century by the construction of Camp Davis.

"Y'all should see that laundry I work in. I bet it's bigger'n Daddy's farm. They have these new-fangled 'lectric washers and dryers and irons. I grew up doin laundry in a tub with a scrub board. We didn't even have a wringer like some of the neighbors did. But now I spend my days washin and ironin with modern 'lectric machines. Summer's comin. Boy, are we gonna be busy. Them cotton summer uniforms need washin more often than wool ones. And with these boys trainin in the swamps and on the beaches, they sure will get them uniforms dirty, that's for sure."

"I'm sure they all appreciate your work to keep their uniforms clean."

"Them boys is used to havin women do their laundry. They don't know the difference 'tween me doin it or their Mama."

"I suppose so. I had a local woman do my laundry when I taught school."

Her eyes widened a bit' "Y'all taught school? I loved school. Daddy didn't hold with women having too much schoolin, but Mama and Granny insisted I finish sixth grade. The boys all went through eighth grade, though."

"So you enjoyed school?"

"Sure did. But now I don't do much school stuff 'cept to read the newspaper to Granny when I'm home on weekends."

The conductor called, "Last stop, Camp Davis."

"It's been nice talking with you, Miss," I said.

"Oh, sorry, Sarah Gale Simmons. "Glad to meet y'all, Corporal Sinclair," she said, holding out her hand.

I shook it. "And I'm glad to meet you, Miss Simmons.

"I hope to see y'all around, Corporal."

I walked Sarah Gale to the bus that would take her to the laundry, then joined the mob of enlistees and officer's candidates milling around under a tall tree that never would have grown in Kansas. Sarah Gale was a fascinating girl. She sure talked a blue streak, but she was intelligent, and those big green eyes held something of substance.

CHAPTER 12
CAMP DAVIS

Uncomfortable on the wooden seats in the back of the cattle trucks designated for OCS, we gazed at our new home. The trucks drove between the brick pillars that held Camp Davis's gate and down the main street. Wood frame buildings gleamed under a fresh coat of white paint. Sparse tufts of grass pushed through the barren soil around the new structures. We rode through this brand-new city on paved streets laid out in square city blocks. A series of connected shed roofs covered one impressive building for an entire block—wide doors, protected by awnings, alternating with large windows along the front.

"What do you think that is?" I asked Duffy, who sat next to me on the cattle truck's hard bench.

"Read the sign," he said. "Camp Davis Laundry."

"Whoa!" I gasped. Sarah Gale was right. I had never seen a laundry this big. But I hoped her father's farm covered more than a city block if he fed ten people.

We rubbernecked our way through several more blocks, spotting theaters, service clubs, and hundreds of barracks. Every two or three barracks had one administration building, a storage building, and a mess hall. The logistics of feeding and supplying twenty thousand soldiers and their civilian support in this formerly remote part of the North Carolina coast must have been mindboggling. And expensive! No wonder Sarah Gale had been so happy, proud, even, of her father's and brother's wages.

A bump bounced us on the rough seats, the end of the surfaced roads.

"Good thing we're in the first truck," a fellow named Jackson said. "You never want to be second on a dirt road."

"Where you from?"

"Birmingham, Alabama."

Dust billowed toward the truck behind us. Like Jackson, I had been in trucks and pickups, following others down rural dirt roads. The men in the trucks behind us covered their mouths and noses with hands, handkerchiefs—even their hats.

The drivers pulled up in front of the OCS Headquarters, a modest little building with a service window facing us.

"Proceed to the building on the right to register and get your housing and platoon assignment," the training officer ordered. He stood stiffly on the bare earth near where we had to jump off the truck, legs spread like a sheriff in a western movie. "You'll receive a letter outlining the topics covered in training. Read the letter on your own time. If you don't have the new style summer uniforms, request them at this time. Rip any insignias off your uniforms and replace them with the AA Candidate patch you'll receive. In this program, your rank is Candidate. This is not a real rank. You will leave here either to return to your former rank or as a lieutenant. Keep that in mind. When you have registered, proceed to your barracks. Set up your cots and lockers. Keep them in order at all times. Like at boot camp."

The service window opened, and a woman with short salt and pepper hair stuck her head out and began calling out names. One by one, we stepped forward to receive a packet containing our assignments and patches. I picked up two of the redesigned summer uniforms at the next window.

When I ripped open my envelope and breathed easier—a barracks assignment, not one of the tents in the field beyond the OCS HQ building, which we had all noticed as we drove up to the structure. The truck drivers had tossed our duffel bags into a big pile on the ground at the barracks. I started checking bags and calling out names. Soon others were doing the same. A lucky few grabbed their bags and ran into the barracks. I heard my name shouted from the other side of the pile. I ran to get my bag and carried it into the two-story barracks. Each building housed two platoons. Aside from a light covering of dust, the place was clean and smelled of newly sawn wood. Bunk assignments were alphabetical, putting me closer to the door and the toilets than I would have liked. Not as close as Wilson, though. Across from me, a Negro candidate was sitting on his freshly made cot, ripping the corporal's stripes from his uniform.

"Gene Sinclair," I said, holding out my hand.

He looked at the hand, looked at my face, then grasped my hand and shook.

"Lucas Thomas," he said.

"So, Thomas, what's your specialty? I mean, before coming here?"

"Engineers. Building bridges and that sort of thing. They sent me there because I taught math before I got drafted."

"I was a science and math teacher. After being drafted, I became a pharmacist because I taught chemistry, but my math skills landed me here. What school did you go to?"

"Tuskegee Normal and Industrial School. How about you."

"Emporia State Teacher's College, Emporia, Kansas."

"Well, Tuskegee's in Tuskegee, Alabama. I guess we both graduated from colleges named after the town they are in."

"Indeed," I said.

Mess call sounded. Thomas and I headed for the mess hall together. We got a few stares from some of the guys. I didn't like that and thought they were inappropriate. I wanted to learn more about Thomas's experience.

"I graduated three years ago and began teaching in a small black high school in South Carolina," he said. "My family share-crops, so I worked my way through college as a busboy."

"Really? I worked as a house boy for the newspaper editor in Emporia."

"William Allen White?" he asked.

"Yes. What do you know about Mr. White?"

"He got the Ku Klux Klan outlawed in Kansas. The first state to do that."

"True," I said as we sat at one of the long tables.

"And he won the Pulitzer Prize," said the man on my left.

Before I could acknowledge the comment, Jackson interrupted.

"Are you sure you're in the right place?" Jackson, from across the table, asked Thomas.

"Quite sure. This is Antiaircraft Artillery Officers Candidate School, isn't it? That's what my orders say."

"How come you ain't in Negro Antiaircraft Artillery Officers Candidate School?" Jackson sneered his question.

"My understanding is AAA officers are sorely needed, and there isn't time to build two schools or enough knowledgeable officers to staff them." Thomas turned to me. "Man, this food is good."

"Best army mess I've ever eaten in," I said.

Jackson gave up, tossed his fork onto his tray, and moved to another table. He started talking to the man next to him, pointing at us. Luckily the listener appeared to shut Jackson down. Jackson picked at his food sullenly, turning every once in a while to glance our way.

I turned to the man on the left. "What did you do before coming here?"

"I came straight from college," he said. "Majored in English Lit. Took me five and a half years to get through college, and I barely scraped by on the officer qualification tests, but I studied my ass off. I didn't want to end up as cannon fodder in the infantry. Jim McKittrick's my name."

The man across the table concentrated on shoving food into his mouth. He didn't make eye contact with anyone.

"How about you, Reinhardt," I asked, reading his name off his uniform.

"Came here from the Philippines," he said. "I guess I did well enough while we was running from the Japs, so they wanted me to become an officer."

"Attention!" called out Lieutenant Hobbs, our platoon leader. "Clear your tables and return to your barracks."

We picked up our trays, shoved them through a hole in the wall to the dishwasher, and hurried back to our barracks. While we stood at attention, Hobbs inspected us and our bunks.

"One gig for failing to stand with proper military bearing!" he shouted.

"Poorly made bed!" he told the next Candidate. "One gig."

A corporal following him recorded the gigs.

"Candidate," he shouted, arriving at my bunk. "Your bunk is not even made up. Two gigs. One gig for not lining your shoes up straight. No more gabbing before your bunk is in order." I felt my face flushing. I should have known better.

When the lieutenant had completed his tour, a general walked in.

"At ease," he hollered. He continued in his thunderous voice, which I took as a condition of leadership. "Gentlemen, you are here because the army has determined you would make good officers. This is not a competition. There is a set of second lieutenant bars waiting for each and every one of you. All you have to do is earn them. Work together. Be diligent. In twelve weeks, your mothers or sweethearts will be proud to pin those bars on you. Attention!" We all stood up straighter. He saluted us. We saluted back. He strode out of the room.

Captain Cooper, our training officer, who had entered with the general, barked, "Your schedule, Candidates." He tacked a paper to the wall next to the door. "Now get this barracks in order. I don't want to see any dust! I want that latrine sparkling. Scrub it all down!"

We got soap, water, and scrub brushes from the supply closet off the latrine, scrubbed boards that weren't dirty, dusted the shelves and the open trusses overhead, and scoured the unused latrine. We all got two gigs for the whole barracks at inspection.

After I made up my bunk and lined up my shoes, I examined the schedule.

```
0500 Reveille
0527 Formation
0527 - 0645 Physical Training
0645 - 0715 Hygiene
0715 - 0730 Inspection
0735 - 0820 Breakfast Mess
0830 - 1220 Academics
1230 - 1320 Lunch Mess
```

```
1330 - 1420 LAP
1430 - 1820 Academics
1830 - 1915 Dinner Mess
1920 - 2230 Candidate Individual Leadership
Designs
2230 Call to Quarters
2245 - 0500 Lights Out
```

When Call to Quarters sounded over the loudspeakers, about half the guys were already asleep. I hadn't yet sewn the patches on my new uniforms. Too much talking again. I finished by flashlight under my blanket, feeling like a nine-year-old.

***

Morning came way too early. I stumbled out of bed, pulled on my trousers and undershirt, and put my bunk area in order. In the required twenty-seven minutes, I was in formation on the training grounds with the rest of the men from my barracks.

Cooper ordered, "Duffy, Sinclair, McKittrick, on the platform. Lead calisthenics this morning.

As we mounted the platform, McKittrick said under his breath, "I know how to do them but don't know in what order to do them."

"I've got that," said Duffy, "but I don't have much of a voice for giving orders. My Dad was always yelling at me to speak up."

"I can call out the exercises and count," I recalled some of Dad's auctioneer techniques. I'd watched and heard my Dad elevate his voice over many a noisy or unruly crowd of bidders. He could shut them down even with a gesture, but his voice was the key. He projected it beyond the edge of the gathering at any auction location. He even made me practice, which came in handy in my career as a teacher. Projecting the voice involved pushing air from the diaphragm and the throat as it turns from the esophagus into the mouth area. I found it relatively easy to project my voice. Maybe it was partly genetics, but my Dad's coaching helped.

McKittrick had the appearance of a perfect officer, at least six inches taller than Duffy and I, muscular, ideal form as he led the exercises. Duffy told me the activities we should be doing. I called them and kept count. Together the three of us made one reasonably good officer.

Our performance seemed satisfactory—at least the tactical officers, also called TACs or bird dogs, didn't stop us or give us any gigs. As we ran on the dirt paths back to the barracks to shower and dress, fine dust formed a cloud around us.

Our first class, math, heavy on trigonometry, with a bit of calculus thrown in, moved quickly, challenging even to those of us who got good grades in college trig based on the comments I heard at lunch.

The schedule called for fifty minutes of LAP after lunch, whatever that meant. Captain Cooper shouted, "Attention! Line up for the Leadership Application Program! Coombs, Thomas, you lead the platoons this week. Duffy and Wilson are your non-coms. Platoon A will be everyone with last names from A to N, Platoon B everyone else. Candidate Platoon Leaders, march your men to the parade field."

Captain Cooper shouted out instructions, and the platoon leaders ordered us to do them. Each platoon leader earned a few gigs for failure to perform their duties appropriately. I thought Thomas got a few more than he should have.

**

A heavy thunderstorm blew in while we were in the second math class of the day, turning the dust to boot-sucking mud. At the mess hall, we scraped our boots the best we could to the shouts of the Sergeant of the Mess about keeping that muck out of his bloody life.

TAC officers followed us wherever we went, watched us whatever we did, observed how we interacted. Their job was to instill the discipline and order that army officers had traditionally learned through four years at West Point. They gave gigs for walking too fast, walking too slow, any momentary lapse in military bearing. I got a gig for cutting myself while shaving—destroying government property. We lost weekend leave or other privileges if we got too many. The young corporal recording all the gigs seemed quite harried. I wondered if he had graduated high school, and here he recorded the performance of college men.

Individual Leadership Designs meant everyone worked on their weaknesses. Thomas, who, in my mind, was an excellent teacher, held math study sessions during this time. About fifteen men bowed out because they did not want to study under Thomas. I didn't see how they could be so stupid. The rest of us were happy to study under his patient and expert instruction. After the study session, we worked on getting our boots and pant legs clean. We didn't know why, but on the night after the first thunderstorm, Thomas left the barracks and did not return until Call to Quarters. He cleaned and polished his muddy boots, leaving the mud on his uniform pant legs to dry. He would brush off the dry dirt in the morning after reveille.

During the usual morning scramble to get out of the barracks for morning assembly, all the work we had done the previous night seemed futile. We clean our boots at night only to run out into that muck first thing in the morning. But this morning, wooden walkways led from our barracks to the mess hall, parade grounds, and sidewalk. A skinny civilian boy came in during breakfast and shouted, "Who took all our duckwalks? We had a stack of them ready to deliver to the barracks."

At first, no one answered. Finally, Duffy said, "Whoever did it sure saved you a lot of work, then, didn't they?"

After pondering a moment, the young man said, "Oh, thanks." and ran back out.

That afternoon it rained again. Several duckwalks disappeared from our barracks and appeared in front of other barracks. Thomas got up to leave that night. Suspecting where he was going, I called out, "Thomas, mind if I join you?" He waved me over. A couple of other guys came along, too.

It hadn't cooled off at all when the sun went down, the humid North Carolina air holding the heat of the unseasonably warm day. North Carolina winter seemed much like spring in Kansas. Unlike Kansas, frogs chirped in the swamps around camp, and insects buzzed in our ears. We walked carefully through the mud, avoiding the more pondlike puddles. McKittrick tripped over a board and fell flat on his face as we approached the carpentry shop. He would take some cleaning up!

"Watch where you're going, McKittrick," said Thomas. "This isn't a sightseeing trip. Keep your eyes on the ground. Take small steps and feel what's under your foot before putting it down."

Only a few duckwalks remained in the stack in front of the shop. We took those and headed around the building, looking for more. Thomas spotted a couple of TAC officers coming our way.

"Hurry, get behind that truck," he whispered. Awkward with the duckwalks, we hastened behind the truck. I peeked out to see how close the TAC officers were.

"Sinclair, get your shining white face down; they'll see us," Thomas said in a loud whisper. I ducked back down. The TAC officers glanced in our direction, but they kept walking.

We replaced about half the missing duckwalks with new ones, then retrieved some taken the previous night from other barracks. When Call to Quarters sounded, we rushed back to clean our boots and be ready for lights out. As I brushed my teeth, Candidate Piper, at the next sink, made several insulting comments about Thomas under his breath.

"What were you doing out there with him?" he finally asked. I wanted to ignore the comment but couldn't.

"Saving your ass from more gigs for tracking mud into the classroom," I replied.

***

Friday night, the Service Club held a dance. Mom and Doris would have been disappointed with the complete lack of decoration. There wasn't even a tablecloth on the refreshment table. Someone had pushed all the grey metal tables and chairs against the drab brown walls and set out punch and cookies on one of them. Sarah Gale brightened the room as she bounced toward us, laughing, and waving to the girls behind her. The full skirt of her bright green dress, which made her green eyes even greener, swirled and sparkled as she walked.

"I was hopin y'all would show," she said.

"Would you like to dance?" Duffy asked.

"Sorry, I already promised the first dance to Candidate Sinclair." She grabbed my hand and pulled me to the dance floor.

The band was a mashed-together group of servicemen who might have practiced together a couple of times before playing for the dance. They were a bit rough as they played an enthusiastic swing. Taking Sarah Gale's right hand with my left, I effortlessly found the rhythm of the music, as did she. Dancing together seemed to be the most natural thing in the world. We went from swing to foxtrot. Early in our third dance, McKittrick cut in on us.

"You can't keep the girls to yourself, Sinclair," he said. "Give someone else a turn."

As I looked around, I realized there were two to three men for every girl. I had been so focused on Sarah Gale that I had not realized that. I sat out the rest of that tune. I asked a tall, dark-haired girl named Sally to dance for the next dance.

"They bring a couple of busloads of us up from Wilmington every Tuesday and Friday for dances and socials," she said in response to my question about why there were so few women. "Some of my friends don't feel comfortable coming because they don't trust the soldiers. I come every chance I get. Sometimes I'm on Coastwatcher duty—a bunch of us work with the Navy to spot German U-boats off the coast—but tonight, I was lucky I could come"

Later we joined McKittrick and Sarah Gale by the punch bowl. I poured each of us a cup. McKittrick and Sally gulped their punch and headed back to the dance floor when the music started. They were as well-matched as Sarah Gale and I, both in height and personality, and danced swiftly across the floor. I took a sip of the punch. It was cloyingly sweet and fruity, devoid of alcohol, and did nothing to quench my thirst.

"Shall we walk around outside for a bit to cool off?" I asked Sarah Gale.

"That would be very nice,"

We strolled along sidewalks and duckwalks to the music of tree frogs. The sweet, seductive scent of pine and Carolina Jasmine floated in the air. It was much cooler outside, and a light breeze kept the mosquitoes from swarming.

"It's beautiful here," I said

"I'm sure y'all have beautiful nights in Kansas, too. I'd love to see those amber waves of grain. Right here's the furthest I've ever been from home. 'Bout seventy miles. I wish a woman could join the army. I'd join up and see the world."

"There is a bill under consideration for a Women's Auxiliary Army Corps. The Southern senators are blocking it, though."

"Sounds like typical Southern men. Think they know what's best for everyone."

"Even if you were in the army, they wouldn't send you to see the world. You would probably still be working in a laundry somewhere or sitting at a desk taking orders from some officers."

"I'd apply for a transfer, though. Maybe I could wash clothes in California. I could sit on the beach with movie stars when I had a day off."

"I doubt you'd get too close to movie stars, but California is beautiful," I agreed.

"My family came to North Carolina in 1740 somethin and ain't left since. I'd certainly like to see somethin new."

"Some of my ancestors came to Pennsylvania and Maryland about the same time. They didn't stay put, though. They kept moving west. First to Kentucky, then Ohio, Indiana, and finally Kansas."

"I wish my folks had been the movin kind," she mused.

We walked in silence for a bit longer until Return to Quarters sounded. I walked Sarah Gale back to the service club, where the MP's waited to escort the girls out of the camp. She was a delightful girl with an incredible eye for detail and a strong desire to learn and experience more. Also very attractive and easy on the eyes. I couldn't get her out of my mind.

***

"Candidate, Sinclair." Captain Cooper's pronouncement pulled me back from my mental picture of Sarah Gale in her green dress. "You'll lead Platoon B this week. Be sure your men are ready for all scheduled activities. Here is a list of the drills you need to complete."

That afternoon Candidate Piper came to me. "I got a sore throat and a headache."

I felt his forehead and realized he had a very high fever.

"Report to sick call."

Piper stayed in the infirmary for two days. He had been falling behind even before he got sick. After he was released, I told him, "See if Thomas can help you catch up with the coursework."

"I ain't gonna study with that coon!" he shouted.

A nearby TAC officer pounced, "Two gigs for inappropriate response to a command."

After the TAC officer left, Reinhardt said from his bunk nearby, "Thomas is one of the best teachers I ever had. You should work with him if you don't want to wash out."

Piper walked over and punched the reclining Reinhardt in the stomach. Three men jumped in to defend Reinhardt.

"Attention, men," I demanded of the five.

Two men who had jumped to defend Reinhardt stepped in to hold Piper, while the third helped Reinhardt up. They came to uneasy attention at my command.

Two TAC officers ran into the barracks. "Whose been fighting?" they demanded. "We heard it!"

"Ain't nothing you can do to get me to work with the likes of him!" Piper exclaimed.

"Stand down, Candidate," one of the TAC officers ordered.

"This SOB ordered me to study with *him!*" he pointed at Thomas a few bunks over. "You have no right to force us to eat and sleep with him, let alone pretend he can teach me anything."

"You won't have to worry about that anymore, soldier," the other TAC officer said as they dragged him out.

"You get to return to your old unit tomorrow," the first said on the way out the door.

Piper had caused trouble before, and most of us were not sad to see him wash out. I felt guilty about precipitating it, though, and started second-guessing every order I gave. The next day the Training Commander called me into his office.

He sat back in his chair and motioned for me to sit in the

straight-backed chair in front of the desk like Dad sometimes did when he wanted to teach me something. "You're not their friend, Sinclair. You're their leader. As a commissioned officer, you're responsible for taking care of your soldiers, but not for being their buddy. The most important thing is that they work as a team to accomplish the mission. They don't have to like your orders, but they have to follow them. Now return to your platoon and make sure they pass inspection tomorrow."

If I had to take care of them, I might as well see that we passed inspection and got some time away from the bird dogs. On my way back to the barracks, I stopped at the PX and bought a bottle of bleach. The men were already scrubbing the floor by the time I walked in. I ordered them to strip to their underwear to avoid bleach spots on their uniforms, poured a dollop into each scrub bucket, and set them to work.

"Now that's something new," Duffy exclaimed. "Bleaching the quarters in our underwear!" We had the barracks and latrine looking and smelling cleaner than ever in short order. I did a pre-inspection in the morning, before reveille. None of the men objected to a somewhat earlier wake-up call.

"There's shaving cream on this sink. Whoever did it, get in here and clean it up!" I ordered. Three men ran in to check. Duffy rinsed the shaving cream down the drain.

The TAC officer arrived for the inspection. He checked the latrine first, scowling at the smell. Maybe we had made a mistake. He looked under the sinks, making me glad I'd had the men wipe down the plumbing and wall. He checked the frame of every bunk for dust. Finally, he called Captain Cooper in and presented his clipboard.

"Zero gigs!" announced Cooper. "A first for this battery. Everyone gets a weekend pass. Sinclair, come with me to my office to collect the passes."

Duffy slapped my shoulder as I walked past, happy to have done the extra work to get out.

After school and drills, I walked into the Friday night dance and scanned the room for Sarah Gale. One of the laundry girls crossed the room to meet me. She seemed to know who I searched for. "Sarah Gale went home for the weekend. She asked me to tell y'all. Would y'all like to dance?"

"No, I don't believe so, sorry." I had a glass of sweet punch and watched the dancing for a bit, then returned to the barracks to read the March 5 issue of the Jacksonville Daily News. I learned that Leningrad's siege continued; the Japs captured the Dutch East Indies' capital and moved on to Burma. Lots of deaths. Lots of misery. Lots of concern.

Passes in hand, Duffy, Reinhardt, McKittrick, and I headed for Wilmington to taste local history and culture. A drizzle started as we boarded the train, growing to pouring rain by the time we arrived. We got directions to a couple of museums, but the most exciting part of the weekend turned out to be sampling the local eateries, where we stuffed ourselves with fried catfish, hushpuppies, shrimp, grits, and best of all, sweet potato pie. We returned stuffed to the gills with the fats and flavors of North Carolina.

***

Monday morning, before class, I hurried to the laundry to ask Sarah Gale if I could see her before she left for home on Friday.

"How 'bout I stay over this weekend?" she asked.

"That would be wonderful," I said, surprised at how my heart had jumped when she said she would stay. I felt especially pleased with her smile when I said, "Wonderful."

Classes shifted from math and engineering to memorizing parts, specifications, and operating information for the various guns we might use. Not everyone in the unit had come through coastal artillery. What was a review for me was new to some of the other candidates. I took over the lessons in the evening from Thomas, who had never aimed a rifle, let alone shot a cannon before his basic training. After the first lesson, I teased him, "You should have grown up in Kansas to learn how to shoot a gun."

He nodded his head and said something under his breath.

"What?"

"Black men in Alabama would never see the light of day with a rifle in their hands."

"You're in the army now. Maybe things will change for you."

He shrugged his shoulders.

I pondered his response. He's an American. What's wrong with him using a rifle or shotgun for hunting?

"Range finders, aiming circles, straight and circular slide rules, clinometers, and compasses. I don't get this indirect firing business," Wilson said later that morning on the way back from class. "I just want to sight the target and shoot it down."

"The planes are high in the air; they're moving fast. We can't hit them by sighting them," I said.

"But all this math to try to figure out where they are. I can't do it fast enough."

"You'll learn," I said. "Keep practicing. We'll work on it tonight," But Wilson never learned. He and a couple of others washed out because they couldn't wrap their minds around the math and its application.

Thirty of the one hundred fifty men washed out of our battery by the end of the classroom portion of our training. From a conversation with one of the TAC officers, I understood that twenty percent was better than average. A few men had come in with less than a high school education. There was almost no chance for them to complete the course successfully. Just learning the math necessary to shoot the big guns took more than twelve weeks. I had been told everyone in the class would be a college graduate, but that was not true. More college graduates were here than in the rest of the army, but some were eighteen-year-old high school graduates. Many of them were too young and immature to be officers. Some would get another chance, but most returned to their old units.

Meanwhile, I waited impatiently for the weekend when I could see Sarah Gale again.

CHAPTER 13
SNAFU

On Saturday, I sprinted to Sarah Gale's boarding house immediately after Captain Cooper dismissed us from inspection, again with no gigs for our platoon. Her landlady, Mrs. McCurdy, escorted me to the parlor, her plump arms bouncing as she marched in front of me.

"Have a seat, Candidate Sinclair," she ordered.

I immediately found the nearest chair. Given Mrs. McCurdy's demeanor, I sat at attention.

"What are y'all's plans, Candidate Sinclair?"

"At this point, Ma'am, I plan to help the allies win this war as quickly as possible, then go to medical school."

"I'm talking about plans with Sarah Gale," she said strenuously. She waved her right arm between us. "For this afternoon."

"Oh. I was thinking of taking a walk and talking for a while, and then we might go to a movie back at camp. After that, we'll get something to eat."

"Y'all better have her back before dark, Candidate Sinclair. I'm responsible for the young women who stay in my home. I won't have y'all compromising Sarah Gale's honor."

"I assure you, Ma'am, I have no intention of compromising Sarah Gale's honor. I'll have her back before dark."

I waited a few more uncomfortable minutes under Mrs. McCurdy's stern gaze for Sarah Gale to be ready. She finally came downstairs, wearing a sleeveless turquoise dress that beautifully set off her auburn hair, cinched at the waist by a sunshine yellow belt. She flung a yellow cardigan over her shoulder and held out her hand to me, smiling. We walked out the door hand in hand and strolled along the streets of Holly Ridge.

"Tell me more about your family," I said.

"Not much to tell. They've been farmin the same plot of land for two hundred years. My great-granddaddy fought in the War of Northern Aggression, but nobody else has left the state since they settled here, as far as I know."

"What war are you talking about?"

"Y'all probably call it the Civil War. That's what the history books at school called it."

"Oh yes. I just never heard it called the War of Northern Aggression before. Three of my great-granddads and my grand-dad fought in the Civil War."

"Y'all had Confederate soldiers in y'all's family too?"

"No. They were all Union. Except for Granny's family. Her father was Union, one of his brothers was Confederate, and a third spied for both sides. My Dad's father marched with General Sherman to Atlanta."

"What? Y'all's granddaddy helped out that scoundrel? Sherman?"

"Some people consider him a brilliant tactician and strategist."

"He was a vicious, insane murderer who burned half the South for the fun of it," she declared.

"He was sometimes overzealous, but not for fun. He was the one who first said 'war is hell.'"

"If that's what y'all think of that demon, I don't know if I should be seen with y'all," she exclaimed and flounced off to sit on a log under a nearby tree.

"The war ended almost eighty years ago. We're fighting a different war now and fighting together."

She sat on the log, scuffing her Mary Jane pumps in the dirt. "I'll have to think about it," she said. "It might have ended eighty years ago in the North, but our way of life ain't been the same since."

"I'm sorry. Forget I ever said that. Why don't we go to a movie? *Ziegfeld Girl* is showing at the big theater in camp."

She considered my offer, then followed me to the camp's gates with a frown on her face. Although she still wasn't talking to me, I bought tickets and popcorn, and we sat silently, side by side, through the movie.

"I can take you back to your rooms if you want," I said after the movie. "Or we could get something at the Knotty Pine Inn."

"Let's go eat."

At the Inn, we studied the menu once we were seated. She carefully and slowly said, "What will you be having," copying my accent.

"Ahm thinkin maybe the poke chops with taters and sweet tea," I said, trying to copy her accent to get a smile out of her.

"That sounds good. How do y'all say chitlins 'n greens in Yankee?"

"Yankees don't eat chitlins and greens."

"What? What do they eat?"

"Baked beans, clam chowdah, maple syrup, Boston Cream Pie," I said in a dreadful New England accent.

"No chitlins? Maybe I don't want to see the world," she said with a lilting, soprano laugh.

We talked and laughed until I noticed the sun going down.

"I need to get you back to your rooms, or Mrs. McCurdy will be fuming," I said.

"She's worse'n Mama and Daddy." Sarah Gale said. "I'll never hear the end of it if I don't get back."

Outside the boarding house, I leaned toward Sarah Gale to kiss her. Just then, Mrs. McCurdy opened the door. "See ya next Saturday." Sarah Gale laughed at my expression. "Have fun shootin them guns." She ducked inside.

***

"You aren't allowing for the movement of the target," I told the group at my gun on the first day on the firing range. "Raise it by eleven degrees."

"Eleven degrees?" asked Coombs from the elevation controls.

"That's right. Eleven degrees."

They raised it by eleven degrees, and on the next pass, we hit the target pulled behind the tow plane square in the middle.

We trained on a beach on the outer banks, living in tents on Topsail Island during the week, firing old guns from the Great

War mounted on wooden platforms placed on the sand above the high tide line. Tow planes flew over the ocean, pulling the targets behind them.

Minor accidents occurred among the other platoons every day—burns, bumps, and bruises. Our platoon did well the first week, following all the safety precautions, and ended the week without a single injury. The following Monday, Captain Cooper lectured us about picking up the speed. In the middle of the second week, we rushed to fire the gun when Jackson tripped over an oil can, spilling it across the wooden gun platform. Reinhardt, hustling to drop the ammo into the barrel, ran toward the steps of the stand. He slipped on the oil, falling behind and below the big gun when the gun fired. The recoil hit him hard in his ribs.

"Reinhardt, are you OK?!" I cried, jumping to his side.

"Can't breathe," he gasped.

"We need medics here," I called.

Captain Cooper yelled, "Who's responsible for this?"

"I spilled the can of oil, sir," Jackson admitted.

"Report to HQ!"

As Jackson walked off, the medics lifted Reinhardt onto a stretcher, bundled him into the ambulance, and rushed him to the hospital. We stood around watching the ambulance leave.

"Get that gun loaded and continue firing," Cooper yelled. "The war isn't going to stop just because you have a casualty!" We continued shooting, much more careful now.

Jackson rejoined the unit the next day, much chastened.

"Hey, Eleven Degrees, how should we aim this one?" he asked. I looked around, finally realizing he was talking to me. I had already calculated the coordinates and called out, "Forty-eight degrees elevation, Thirty-six azimuth."

"You fellows are getting the hang of it," Captain Cooper said as he walked by. "If there are no more mishaps and your kill rate stays the same, we will move on to the big guns next week."

***

"Listen up, men," Captain Cooper called out as we jumped off the cattle trucks at the beach on Monday. "These guns have a ninety millimeter bore and can be shot at a ninety-degree maximum elevation to 43,500 feet. Their range is almost twelve miles. They can bring down bombers." Coombs whistled.

"The shells have timed fuses. You'll use the appropriate fuse for the distance between the target and the gun, based on the target's elevation and flight path."

Behind me, McKittrick groaned and whispered, "More calculations."

"Cut the sound effects," Captain Cooper commanded. "You'll have charts showing fuse timing for different distances. Locate a target and determine the target's elevation and azimuth, set the fuse, load, and fire. A direct hit is unlikely, but the shells spread shrapnel as they explode. The shrapnel can bring down almost any plane it hits or flies into it. Try to aim in front of and slightly above the target."

I could see McKittrick's gears turning in the attempt to figure that out.

Captain Cooper drew a triangle in the sand, pointing to the tips of the angles as he spoke. "Your target is flying at eight thousand eight hundred forty feet. It is approaching your beach location at four hundred miles per hour and is currently twenty miles out. What fuse would you use, how long do you have to prepare, and at what elevation would you fire?"

I did some quick calculations, looked at the chart, and said, "In a minute and a half, you could fire a shell with a seven-second fuse at an elevation of seventy-eight degrees."

"You could," Captain Cooper said. "But it would be better to begin firing as soon as the target comes in range and not wait until it's right on top of you. If you miss, it will drop bombs on you. If you know a target is coming straight at you, begin firing as soon as possible."

"Would you fire at half that elevation and twice the time on the fuse?" McKittrick asked.

"No. Unfortunately, the formula is more complicated than that. Let's look at how you would calculate it."

We calculated times and elevations for potential targets at every possible speed. Finally, we were able to shoot the big, ninety-millimeter guns. No more old, broken guns. These were straight off the assembly line. The twenty-four-pound shells were difficult to load at first, but we learned. Our goal was to fire thirty rounds per minute. Each twelve-man crew mastered the task, passing the shells forward in two lines with the front men alternately tossing the shells into the gun. As soon as we achieved that goal, we stopped daily practice on those guns, going to once a week. The army didn't want us to waste ammunition that could be going overseas.

***

After my first week as a platoon leader, I hadn't gotten another leadership assignment. Some men had leadership assignments quite frequently. McKittrick was one of them. Standing still, he was the picture of the perfect officer, but let him move, and his long limbs became gangly. He was slow with calculations and often at a loss when interpreting the table. Maybe he was being given more practice. Maybe, I wondered, they didn't feel I needed it.

"There are so many numbers. How do you keep them all straight in your mind?" McKittrick asked me.

"There are only ten numbers," I said.

He stared at me, his mouth and eyes squinched like he might cry. Then he frowned in confusion.

"I mean ten digits. All numbers are combinations of ten digits."

His face lit up. "Really? Just ten numbers to make everything?" He whistled an aha and returned to studying the chart.

How could he not have known that? I wondered. *That's basic arithmetic.*

I worked with McKittrick a bit more on the nature of numbers, and he improved quickly. He never became the fastest, but he did learn to make field calculations well enough to pass the course.

Sarah Gale decided to stay in Holly Ridge again the following weekend.

"I feel real guilty," she said. "It's getting on to planting season, and I'm just too exhausted from workin' in the laundry. I should go home and help out, but they put me to work the minute I get off the train, and I don't stop 'till time to come back. I like having a weekend off.

"Planting time starts in March here?" I asked.

"Not much chance of frost after the first day of spring, so Daddy gets us into the fields right away."

"What's that?" she asked, looking at the box I carried

"A radio. You can listen to it in your room and try to speak like the announcers. Try to listen to national broadcasts rather than local ones. I also bought you a book on English grammar. We'll have you speaking correctly in no time. Here are some high school textbooks for you to study other subjects. You will have to pass some tests if you're going to be in the army."

"Am I just a project for y'all? Y'all want me to talk like y'all do so I can be good enough to be seen with y'all? Leave me alone if that is what y'all are trying to do!"

"No, Sarah Gale. You are much more than a project for me." I said, but she had already slammed the door in my face.

I slumped back to base, stopping by the hospital to visit Reinhardt. I'd visited a couple of times over the two weeks since his accident.

"Eleven Degrees! Glad to see you." He pointed to the one chair in his room, and I sat down.

"How are you, man?" I asked.

"My broken ribs seem to be healing up nicely, and Doc says the punctured lung is about back to normal," he responded. "Did you know they wanted to wash Jackson out, but they interviewed me, and I talked 'em out of it? It was an accident. It wouldn't have happened with the new guns based on my experience in the Philippines. They're set up differently."

"How are we ever going to manage overseas?" I asked. "Hopefully, we'll have new equipment. We don't have enough experience with any of it,"

"You'll get more practice on the new equipment. You'll spend at least six months with your battalion before you ship out. What's up? You aren't usually this grumpy."

"I think I made a mistake," I said. Then, I described Sarah Gale's reaction to the radio and textbooks.

"If you thought you were coming a-courting, you certainly did make a mistake. You're making that smart, lively girl think she is good for nothing just because of her accent. Haven't you noticed how much her grammar and enunciation have improved? She's constantly trying to do what she thinks will please you. You keep asking for more. Maybe if you gave her a little encouragement and relaxed a bit, things would go better."

I thought about it. Sarah Gale had spoken with a beautifully lyric southern accent, not sounding at all like a Yankee, yet her pronunciation was completely understandable. I realized her vocabulary was growing, too.

"Do you think she would let me try again?" I asked.

"I believe she might."

"I'll do it," I said.

The following Saturday, I went into town and bought a new Brownie camera and several rolls of film at the department store, then returned to Mrs. McCurdy's.

Sarah Gale pulled open the door and crossed her arms.

"I've been trying to learn photography," I said. "I was wondering if you'd like to join me." I held out the new camera to her. "We could go to the woods and see what we can find to photograph."

"Is everything about learning with y'all?" she asked.

I shrugged my shoulders. "I guess. Both my parents taught school before they got married. My mother's family were even involved in establishing both Harvard and Yale."

"Those are Yankee colleges, aren't they?"

"They both are about as Yankee as you can get," I admitted. After a pause, offering her the camera again, I asked," Would you like to take pictures with me?"

She glared at me for almost a minute, then smiled. "Yeah!" she said. She snatched a sweater off the coat tree and grabbed the camera on the way out the door. She seemed pleased with the idea of taking photographs.

We spent the afternoon in the woods. I reached across her shoulders to hold the camera and show her how to look through the viewfinder. She turned, her face disconcertingly close to me, and asked me, "How long have y'all been taking pictures?"

I took a step back.

"Almost six months," I said shakily, unnerved by her nearness.

She smiled, and we walked deeper into the woods, hiking along deer trails and beside streams, stopping to photograph anything we found interesting. We laughed and talked too much to see any wildlife, but the trees and flowers were beautiful. I watched her take pictures at odd angles, getting too close to the subject, shooting things like tree trunks or a pile of leaves. I refrained from correcting her. We stopped at the drugstore to drop off the film. After we had given the film to the clerk, I tentatively put my arm around her

"How about a milkshake at the soda fountain?" I asked

"Could we do that?" She smiled at me. "Here's y'all's camera back."

"I bought that for you," I said.

"Oh, it must have cost a fortune. I'm not sure I can accept it."

"It is a Brownie. Don't worry. They're not very expensive. The film and developing will cost more than the camera."

"I'm sorry! I used up three rolls of film today. Let me pay y'all back for those."

"No. It's my gift to you. And my apology for upsetting you last week."

She placed the camera on the counter with her sweater, grinning, and we ordered our milkshakes. "There's a soda fountain in my hometown, but we never had enough money to buy anything there when I was growing up."

I gazed at her as she slowly sipped the milkshake. The depression had been hard on my family, but we could always scrape together enough money for a Saturday night treat. And with Dad managing the creamery, I was no stranger to ice cream and milkshakes.

We finished our milkshake and walked arm in arm back to her boarding house.

I dropped her off just before dark. Mrs. McCurdy sat on the porch swing knitting, waiting for her girls to come home. Another missed opportunity for that good-bye kiss.

On Friday, Sarah Gale left a message that her uncle was driving her home, but she would be back Sunday evening. So, after Saturday morning inspection, I picked up the photos at the drugstore and bought a National Geographic magazine to help pass the time until Sarah Gale arrived back in her boarding house. As I looked through the pictures, I proudly told myself two of mine might be good enough to appear in the magazine. Then I looked at hers. Almost all were works of art, finely textured close-ups taken from unusual perspectives, beautiful and unique compositions. I laughed at myself for thinking I could instruct her in photography. I hadn't even known a Brownie camera could take pictures like these.

I stopped by to give the photos to Sarah Gale on Sunday evening. Mrs. McCurdy opened the door.

"Come in, young man. Sarah Gale is cleaning up for dinner. Won't y'all join us?"

"I suppose I can if I don't stay too late."

"Carol," Mrs. McCurdy called back behind her, "set an extra place at the table. Mr. Sinclair is joining us."

I sat at the foot of the table, Mrs. McCurdy at the head. The six girls staying at the house lined both sides of the table between us. Sarah Gale sat to my right, refilling my bowl with stew when I emptied it and piling more hush puppies on my plate.

"I'm stuffed," I said at her third ladle. "We'll be back in the classroom this week. All I do all day is sit."

"Nonsense, y'all need to eat to keep y'all's strength up," Sarah Gale said.

"Can y'all handle a slice of coconut cream pie?" asked Mrs. McCurdy when I finished my third stew bowl.

"I believe I could manage," I admitted.

After dinner, Sarah Gale and I walked out to the porch. For once, Mrs. McCurdy didn't follow us. "Here are your pictures," I told her.

She took them and examined each one. "This one is a little blurry," she said. "I think I need to be more still when I take pictures."

"Brownie cameras can't focus well at close range," I told her. "That is the best closeup I have ever seen with a Brownie."

"I bet I can do better," she declared.

We sat a while longer, enjoying a warm evening and cool breeze, then I managed to steal a quick kiss before I rushed back to the barracks.

***

We started our new class in aircraft identification on Monday. Reinhardt said he would rather be back in the hospital than memorizing specifications for U.S., British, German, and Japanese planes all week. When Captain Haley, the instructor, stopped for questions, Reinhardt raised his hand.

"Sir, based on those specifications, the Zero seems the best."

"As of now, it's the best carrier-based plane hands down in both range and maneuverability. That's why we're training and equipping so many new AAA units. If you end up in the Pacific, do everything you can to shoot these down. We don't have a fighter in the air that can hold a candle to them. And the Japs have pilots who can do unbelievable things with those planes. Never let your men know this, never admit it to the public, be careful how you talk about it even with your men or the air corps, but you are vital to winning the air war in the Pacific."

The army had convinced us the United States was superior in every possible way. Now here was an army officer saying we weren't. We dropped our eyes to our desks, too shocked to look at each other or the instructor.

McKittrick asked, "Are we developing better planes."

"Of course, we are," the Captain said. "Within a year or two, we'll have planes in the air that will easily outdo the Zeros and have men trained to fly them. Until then, you'll hold the line. On the defensive side, we're way ahead, and that is where you come in."

Even back in the barracks, we avoided discussing the officer's disclosure of Japan's air superiority. *Just like the army,* I thought. *Lying to us to make us think we were invincible. More like unprepared and outmanned.*

***

Sarah Gale took me further afield on our next photography expedition. We returned later than usual, and Mrs. McCurdy invited me to stay for dinner again.

"I was wondering, could y'all come home with me the first weekend in May to celebrate my twentieth birthday?" asked Sarah Gale as we sat on the porch swing after we ate.

"I'm honored! But I have to see if I can get leave," I told her.

"I bet y'all can," she replied.

Mrs. McCurdy poked her head out the door.

"Jack Benny's on. Would y'all like to listen with us?"

I looked at my watch. "Oh, no! I'm supposed to be in the barracks in five minutes. I'm going to be in so much trouble." I ran off, telling Sarah Gale I would see if I could get leave.

Captain Cooper was waiting for me with his clipboard when I arrived ten minutes after lights out.

"Confined to barracks for five days," he said. "And five gigs."

This was a disaster! What would Sarah Gale think when I didn't get back to her about her invitation?

***

"Sinclair, aren't you coming to the dance?" McKittrick called as he put on his dress uniform Tuesday evening.

"No. I'm confined to barracks. Came in after lights out. I got five gigs for it."

"Wow, that girl's doing something to you. Mr. Perfect got five gigs. You watch, first it's five gigs, then it's a diamond ring."

A little peeved, I told him, "Go on. You don't want to miss your black-haired beauty."

I wandered around the empty barracks for a while, then heard someone come in the door. Captain Cooper was checking the rifle rack near the entrance.

"Sir, my friend has invited me to go to her family farm to celebrate her birthday in two weeks."

"You got five gigs, are confined to barracks, and dared ask me for weekend leave?"

"Yes, sir."

He snorted and looked away. "Ask again when you're not confined to barracks," he mumbled as he walked toward the door, which I barely understood. I was too focused on Sarah Gale's invitation to be dismissed.

"But sir, we're required to request leave at least a week before the desired leave begins."

He looked back at me with stony eyes. "Yes, you are. You have ten hours between the end of your confinement and the last opportunity to request leave." His voice became ironlike, each word enunciated separately so I would understand without question. "Now. Get. Back. To. Your. Bunk. Before. I. Extend. Your. Punishment."

I hustled off in dismay.

CHAPTER 14
A BACKWOODS BIRTHDAY PARTY

Captain Cooper generously excused me from Friday afternoon classes, which were a review of the math I had already covered in Coastal Artillery training, and Sarah Gale got off early so we could catch the afternoon train to Elizabethtown.

"The boys are real happy y'all're coming," chattered Sarah Gale over the sound of the train. We had a hard time hearing each other, the wheels moving along the uneven track making more noise than most trains. "How come y'all took so long to tell me y'all could?"

"I was confined to barracks for staying at your boarding house too late. Captain Cooper wouldn't even let me ask for leave until after I had finished the punishment."

"How awful of him. I'll have to talk to him about that the next chance I get."

"You think you'll have a chance?"

"I just might." Her emerald eyes lit up with amusement as though she knew a secret. I wondered if I should be worried.

"I do have to warn y'all before we get home," she continued, "sixteen is marrying age in my family. No woman has ever stayed single until she turned twenty. The whole family will be checking y'all out to see if y'all'd be good husband material. The boys want to take y'all out hunting to see if y'all can provide for me."

A bit shocked, I said, "We've only known each other for ten weeks. Why would they expect us to get married?"

"They want me to marry somebody. I'm an old maid to them. And since I'm bringing y'all home with me, they think it's you."

"Marry somebody? You mean they don't care who you marry?"

"Well, they want me to be happy, of course. And for my husband to take care of me so as I don't be a burden on my Daddy and Mama. If I got married and moved out, Granny could move into my new room and free up the living room! That's not a bad thing, is it?

"I suppose not," I responded. "Though not the best of reasons to get married." *Folks around here had different expectations about courting and marriage than back home in Kansas!*

We paused our discussion for a minute, looking out the window at the passing foliage. I couldn't help asking, "Is it serious?"

"Might be." She smiled, batting her eyelashes to make me laugh. After a very slight pause, she added, "But mostly, I wanted to bring y'all so they wouldn't think there was something wrong with me. That I can't find a man who's interested in me." She was quiet for an additional moment, quite unusual for her. I wondered what pain was behind her statement.

Before I could ask her why she felt that way, she continued, "My older brother, Johnny, won't be there. He joined up about two months ago and got sent to Georgia. Surprised everybody. I told y'all that great-granddaddy was the last member of the family to leave the state."

I nodded.

"Don't tell my daddy y'all's family had anything to do with that scoundrel Sherman," Sarah Gale whispered.

"Don't worry. I won't mention it." I promised.

She sat up a bit taller. "Y'all'll graduate before Decoration Day. That's when we decorate great, great granddaddy's grave."

"In Kansas, we decorate just about any grave on Decoration Day. It used to be just Civil War veterans, but now we decorate all the graves."

"Y'all celebrate Decoration Day? I thought it was to decorate the graves of Confederate soldiers. Who started Decoration Day?"

"I'm not sure. It seems to have started after the Civil War in both the North and South."

"And here I thought it was a Southern holiday."

"Well, different states celebrated on different days, I think, until relatively recently. I remember when Congress set the official holiday on May 30. Of course, I was pretty young, but it was an important day for my mother and grandmother."

Soon the train pulled into Sarah Gale's hometown station, Elizabethtown.

Sarah Gale's brother Robby met us at the Elizabethtown station. We clambered into a buckboard hitched to a team of mules, crowding onto the seat. Robby slapped the mules with the reins the minute we were seated and pulled onto the highway. The mules plodded across a long bridge that spanned a slow-moving, murky river at the edge of town, then veered off the highway onto a narrow muddy road. Fragrant piney woods rose around us as we meandered alongside the muddy river. All the roads and rivers seemed muddy here. The mules sometimes strained to keep the wagon moving through the muck.

"What's the name of that river?" I asked after a while.

"Cape Fear," Sarah Gale replied.

Robby teased, "Y'all took up with a furriner who don't even know the Cape Fear River?"

She swatted him on the back of his head with her oversized purse. "He gives me presents and teaches me things," she cooed, snuggling up against me, much more familiar than she had been at Camp Davis. "He knows lots of other things even if he don't know about the Cape Fear River."

Robby snorted and nodded. "Shore 'nuff."

We plodded on for about an hour, filled with good-natured teasing between Robby and Sarah Gale, with me often the silent subject. I didn't mind. It was both fun and interesting to watch Sarah Gale and Robby interact. I could tell they loved each other very much and knew each other very well. I had that kind of attachment with my sister, but not with my brothers. Finally, we turned away from the river, climbing an even narrower road between tall, old trees. Grass covered the floor of the virgin forest with a bit of moss here and there. The mules strained to pull the wagon through the muck up a hill steeper than any before, the road still muddy. The babble of swift-flowing water overcame the creaking of the harnesses and the stomping of the mule's hooves. Around a bend, we came upon a small waterfall.

Sarah Gale tapped Robby's shoulder. "Stop, Robby. Let me take some pictures. I've been thinking of this spot ever since Gene gave me the camera." She pulled the camera from her purse. I wondered if that hard object had met with Robby's hard head when Sarah Gale had whacked him with her purse earlier. It had to have hurt!

She hopped down from the wagon onto the edge of the road, dry by comparison with the road itself. Slipping off her shoes, she turned her back to us, hiked up her skirt, and removed her stockings. She waded into the water, bending down to take photographs of the waterfall from different angles. Then she ran back to the wagon, still barefoot, the hem of her skirt damp. I held out my hand to help her climb up. Instead, she shoved her muddy shoes into my hand and boosted herself into the sear by the mud-caked wagon wheel. Robby turned, slapped the reins on the mules' rumps again, and they trotted forward, the narrow road bending away from the creek. Sarah Gale cleaned her hand on a cloth she fished from under the seat.

A short way up the track, we emerged from the woods. Robby pointed out small sweet potato, peanut, cucumber, and sweet corn fields and larger cotton and tobacco fields. The farm was much bigger than the Camp Davis Laundry but smaller than the average wheat field in Kansas. A chicken coop barely stood at the homestead, propped up by boards that matched the rafters in my barracks. A new tobacco barn stood next to a corn crib that leaned precariously, also propped up by sections of new wood. Thanks to Uncle Sam, the low, unpainted house had a new roof. Several chickens scratched around in the front yard, and an old woman sat on the front porch smoking a corncob pipe.

"Granny," yelled Sarah Gale, "We're home."

The old woman stood and squinted into the dusk. A younger but worn-looking woman stepped out of the front door.

"Welcome, welcome," she said. "Come on in and git some victuals."

Although Robby snickered behind us, I jumped down from the wagon and helped Sarah Gale down.

"This is Granny Vance and Ma," Sarah Gale introduced me.

"Mrs. Vance, Mrs. Simmons, glad to meet you." Both nodded

Inside, Sarah Gale went to work immediately, helping finish preparations for a feast of fried chicken, mashed potatoes, green beans, collard greens, fresh biscuits, and sweet potato pie. I could see how the new appliances helped Mrs. Simmons cook since they replaced a wood stove and an icebox. It must have been hard to get ice up the hill before it melted in the summer.

A short time later, Mr. Simmons arrived home in an old, green Chevy pickup. Mrs. Simmons rang the dinner bell, and boys came running from every direction. Mr. Simmons barked a sharp command, and they stopped. He was a small, wiry man with a stern expression, but the twinkle in his eye proved there was more to him than hard work and strict parenting. He shook my hand vigorously, then made all the boys introduce themselves.

Everybody washed up at a washstand on the porch and then crowded around the kitchen table in various mismatched chairs. Upon Mr. Simmons finishing grace, the boys instantly grabbed for whatever food they could reach. Sarah Gale took my plate and filled it.

"Could you please pass the gravy?" I asked Mrs. Simmons. Everyone stopped eating and stared at me

"See, I told y'all," Sarah Gale said to her brothers. She turned to me. "They make fun of my rooming house manners. They think passing is for prissy girls."

The image of my family passing all the dishes around the table, no one eating anything before everyone served themselves, popped into my mind. "Well," I said. "it's a Kansas custom, I guess, to ask someone to pass something." I stood up and reached for the gravy bowl.

The food disappeared quickly, but Sarah Gale and Mrs. Simmons made sure I had plenty. At long last, I sat back and breathed a sigh as I finished off my last bite of sweet potato pie.

"The meal was delicious, Mrs. Simmons. Thank you very much. Can I help clean up?"

The boys hooted.

"Y'all come out on the porch with me," said Granny Vance. "We needs to figger out y'all's relations."

I followed her out to the cane rockers on the porch. She handed me a corncob pipe and a bag of homegrown tobacco. I stuffed the pipe, lit it, pulling hard to get it going, then sat back, rocking, lulled by the frogs singing in the woods. We puffed our pipes, the tobacco excellent, until we had enough of a smokescreen to keep the mosquitoes away.

"So where do y'all hail from?" she asked.

"Kansas."

"And before that? Where y'all's people from?"

"My grandparents moved from Illinois and Indiana to Kansas. I think my great grandparents were born in Kentucky or southern Ohio, then went to Indiana."

She asked me several more questions I couldn't answer with any certainty. She knew a lot more about her family tree than I did mine. It turned out the Simmons family had a lot of men in the Confederate army even though they'd never owned slaves themselves. They fought for State's Rights, Granny Vance claimed.

"Afore y'all git too serious about Sarah Gale, y'all need to check y'all's history a little further back. Cain't be too careful."

"Yes, ma'am."

Sarah Gale had joined us on the porch, listening to her granny's questions, and explained, "Granny's making sure we aren't too closely related to get married. Most people around here don't pay too much attention to that, but Granny has a thing about close cousins marrying."

"I seen way too many invalids and idiots born outta cousins marryin," Granny declared.

"Granny, he hasn't had any relations around here in the last two hundred years, so I don't think there's much chance we're related."

Mr. Simmons came out on the porch.

"Time for bed. Y'all go on up in the loft with the boys," he told me. "They got more room up thar than they know what to do with since Johnny left."

I climbed the ladder. It looked like wall-to-wall bodies lying on featherbeds scattered on the floor, but they scrunched together to make room for me.

***

The whole family was up before dawn, spreading across the farmyard with kerosene lanterns to feed the animals and milk the two cows. I helped fourteen-year-old Davie milk. That had been Johnny's job before he joined the army. We were back in the house for breakfast before Sarah Gale and Mrs. Simmons were ready to feed us. Sarah Gale cracked several eggs into the butter melting in a cast iron skillet but had to run out to the well house to get some milk for her mother to make gravy. I stepped up to the stove and started flipping the eggs.

"Y'all can cook!" Mr. Simmons exclaimed as I put over-easy eggs on the plate,

"I can. It comes in handy sometimes."

After breakfast, Davie said, "So y'all can milk cows and fry eggs. Now let's see if y'all can shoot. We need to see if we can get something special for the party tomorrow."

Sarah Gale stood with her arms akimbo. "Of course he can shoot. He's an artillery officer. He's been doing nothin but shoot for the last month and a half."

"What will we be shooting?" I asked.

"We're gonna see if we can bag us a wild hog," declared young Davie. "I found scat yesterday, not two hundred yards up the crick."

"Can't y'all give him a day off from guns?" asked Sarah Gale.

I hadn't mentioned to her that I had failed to qualify in rifle. I did know how to shoot if I had a decent rifle with an accurate sight. But I appreciated her question.

"Come on, y'all don't want to marry a man can't put food on the table," Jeb said. The boys all grabbed their guns.

"I'd go," I said. "But I didn't bring a rifle."

Jeb went to the fireplace and took down a rifle hanging above it. "This is the piece great grandad used in the war," he said.

I examined the ancient rifle. "Which war?" I asked.

"The War Between the States."

"Has anyone fired it lately?"

"Granny takes it out and fires it ever so often."

"That there's a muzzleloader," Granny said. "Let me show y'all."

She lifted a leather satchel down from a hook on the wall, took the gun from my hands, and put the stock on the floor. Pulling a paper packet from the bag, she ripped off the top with her teeth and poured the gunpowder into the gun's barrel.

"Look at this here mini ball. It's cone-shaped. This end goes to the top, an' the round end goes down. Now y'all shove it into place with the ramrod like this. See this thang. It's the percussion cap. I'm not goin to put it in now, 'cause I don't want y'all blastin somebody to kingdom come cause y'all trip over a root. Put it right here and make sure it fits snug afore y'all try n shoot anything."

She handed me the loaded rifle.

I looked at Sarah Gale, wide-eyed. She shrugged, smiling. I did enjoy seeing her smile.

"I don't think they expect y'all to fire it," she whispered as we walked onto the porch.

"Y'all be careful," said Mrs. Simmons. "Them dang hogs is mean."

"Come on," the boys shouted. "The hog will be halfway to Cape Fear if we don't git out there."

Their four dogs bayed and strained at the leashes. I had second thoughts. I had never shot a gun this ancient. What if it came to that? But between the baying hounds and the boys crashing through the underbrush, I doubted we would find anything to shoot, much less a wild hog.

As we reached the creek on the farm's far side, Robbie signaled the dogs, who immediately quieted and sniffed the ground. The boys inched through the thick underbrush without making a sound. Thanks to Luke Thomas's instruction, as we retrieved duckwalks from around the camp, I was able to pass just as silently through the woods.

It didn't take long to find the wild hog. Davie had scattered corn on the ground the evening before, and it had come for the free meal. Before we saw it, we could smell it, the acrid smell of a hog wallow, swamp mud, feces, and urine. Jeb held up his hand

and whispered, "Hogs got real good hearing. Quiet now."

We carefully approached the clearing where Davie had scattered the corn. The hog was gigantic, at least four feet tall and well over six feet long, with dangerous-looking tusks. It lifted its head as we approached. We stopped dead in our tracks, thinking it may have heard us. Jeb nodded to Davie, who raised his gun and fired at the boar. His bullet hit the boar in the upper flank. The angry boar wheeled and charged. I moved back into the brush fumbling with the percussion cap as both Joe and Jeb fired. They hit it, but the boar kept coming. Sixteen-year-old Curt fired and missed. I finally got the percussion cap seated into the nipple as Robbie released the dogs. Their furious barking turned the boar toward them, and it crashed through the brush toward the dogs. They viciously attacked the boar. It ripped its tusks into the side of one of the dogs, barely slowing to shake it off. I cocked the Civil War rifle and stepped forward. The boar turned toward me as I raised the gun, aimed, and fired like Graham had told me and hit the boar between the eyes. It dropped at my feet.

"Whoa. Incredible," shouted Davie.

"I've been shooting every day for the last month," I said, gripping the gun tighter with my shaking hands, hoping to hide my fear. If the old rifle had misfired, the boar would have ripped us all to pieces

Robby knelt by the bleeding dog. The boar had torn through the skin and muscle of its shoulder. He took off his shirt, bound the dog's wound, and made a bed of leaves for the dog.

As Curt ran back toward the farm, Jeb pulled a knife from his belt and slit the boar's throat. Then he slit the belly. He and Joe had the pig gutted when Curt returned with his Dad. They brought some burlap bags and a longer, sharper butcher knife. Mr. Simmons cut off the belly meat and dropped it in the gunny sack for Mrs. Simmons to render. Then he quartered the hog, leaving the skin on, and cut off the backstrap, also with some skin attached. He loosened some of the skin on each piece and cut slits in it. Mr. Simmons handed me the bag with the hog belly. He grabbed the two backstraps. Davie and Curt hefted the shoulders, using the slits in the skin as handles, and began pulling them toward the farm, skin side down. Jeb and Joe pulled the hams the same way. Robbie picked up the injured dog, slung him over his shoulders with its feet hanging down in front, and we made our way back to the farm.

Robbie entered the farmyard ahead of us. His mother screamed at the sight of blood dripping down his chest. She sighed in relief when he lifted the whimpering dog from his shoulder, and the rest of us emerged with the various parts of the hog. We dropped the hog on a piece of plywood labeled "Property of the United States Government. The boys and Mr. Simmons began skinning the quarters.

Sarah Gale ran toward the dog. "This gash is so deep," she moaned.

"We're gonna have to put that animal down." Mr. Simmons nodded toward the hound Sarah Gale was comforting. Tears began to flow down her cheeks.

"Let me take a look," I said. "I have helped my Granny with doctoring all my life. Do you have any silk thread?"

"What makes you think we would have silk thread?" asked Sarah Gale.

Granny, however, hurried into the house and returned a moment later with several feet of white silk thread and a bottle of moonshine.

Sarah Gale stared at her.

"Savin it for your wedding dress," Granny said.

"That dog ain't gonna drink any 'shine no matter how bad it's gettin on," Robby said.

"It ain't for drinkin," Granny replied as she poured some of the alcohol into a small bowl and dropped a bent needle into it.

I poured moonshine onto my hands, took the needle out of the bowl, and threaded the silk thread.

Robbie held the tissue together as I instructed him, and I sewed the muscle, then the skin back together, and daubed on some iodine Mrs. Simmons brought me. The dog resisted vigorously, even with Sarah Gale, Robbie, and Mrs. Simmons holding it as steady as possible, which gave me great hope for his survival. The pain of the stitching must have been terrific. Finally, Sarah

Gale made a bed of straw on the porch, and Robby laid the dog on it.

"You saved his life. I don't know if we can ever thank you enough. He is our best hunting dog." Sarah Gale gushed with tears in her eyes.

"I hate putting an animal down if it can be avoided," I told her, thinking of an old plow horse my Dad had been forced to shoot, remembering the tears in the eyes of a man who never cried.

By the time we had cleaned up and Robby had changed clothes, Mr. Simmons and the boys had wrapped the hog meat in wet burlap, then chicken wire and dropped it in the roasting pit, covering it with leaves. Apparently, there hadn't been much doubt about whether we would get the hog, as Mr. Simmons had lit the fire in the hole right after we left for the woods.

Once the hog was in the pit and everyone washed up, Mrs. Simmons and Sarah Gale brought barbequed pork sandwiches, collard greens, and fried potatoes out onto the porch.

"Y'all wannna sprinkle a little more vinegar on that sandwich?" Granny asked me, holding out the vinegar bottle.

"I don't know. I've never had this kind of barbeque before."

"What other kind of barbeque is there?" Davie asked.

"We usually barbeque beef and use a different kind of sauce," I said. "Something from Kansas City."

"Aint nothin better than good old southern barbeque," Jeb declared.

I wasn't sure I agreed with him. This spicy, vinegary barbeque would take some getting used to. But by the time I had finished two sandwiches, it had grown on me.

After devouring lunch, Mr. Simmons brought his fiddle out onto the porch. The boys got a banjo, harmonica, washboard, jaw harp, and three sizes of jugs. After tuning the banjo and warming up the rest of the instruments, they began singing. I didn't know any of the songs. Finally, they started in on Wabash Cannonball. I knew that one. Although I didn't have quite the same twang as Mr. Simmons and the boys, I joined in.

"Y'all got a good voice," said Mr. Simmons. "Jist need to push it a little harder and sing it a little louder." I nodded to thank him for his advice.

Sarah Gale came out with an instrument like a small piano soundboard with double strings when she finished in the kitchen.

"What is that?" I asked.

"A dulcimer."

"It's much bigger than any dulcimer I've ever seen."

"Taint no mountain dulcimer," said Granny from her rocking chair. "That there's a hammer dulcimer brung from Ireland by my kin."

Sarah Gale propped the dulcimer on the porch floor with a couple of wood blocks, grabbed the two long wooden hammers poking out from her pocket, and began playing. The pure sparkling sound of the notes made the air shimmer around us. I sat mesmerized as Sarah Gale played, the sound refreshing my mind, body, and soul. Her father started a Celtic tune on his fiddle. Sarah Gale picked up the tune on her dulcimer, then everyone joined in. Mrs. Simmons began dancing, stomping on the porch floorboards, adding percussion to the song.

"Is that some sort of a jig?" I asked. "I've never seen anything like that before."

"It's a dance that started in the mountains called clogging," she said breathlessly. "We've only been doing it in the flatlands for about twenty years, but I like it." She pulled me up and gave me a clogging lesson. I was wearing my combat boots. Once I got the hang of it, they made a satisfying loud thump on the porch floorboards.

***

Sunday morning, we didn't get up as early. Even so, chores called, so I went milking with Davie. After breakfast, everyone put on their Sunday best. Sarah Gale appeared at the door of her room, her auburn hair carefully curled, wearing a white dotted Swiss dress trimmed in green velvet that matched her eyes.

"Mama made it for my birthday," she said. I offered her my arm, and we strolled around the tiny living room to the whistles of her brothers.

Jeb spread quilts in the bed of the truck. The boys, Sarah Gale, and I jumped in. Mr. Simmons helped Granny into the front, then Mr. and Mrs. Simmons took a seat on either side of her, and we were off. Sarah Gale sat against the truck's cab with me on one side and Jeb on the other, trying to keep her curls from blowing. Despite the warm spring morning, she snuggled against me.

We piled out in front of the little country church. Several people thought I was Johnny at first, but when Sarah Gale took my arm, they immediately assumed I was her fiancé. Several people asked about our wedding plans. We said we didn't have anything definite at this time. After all, I had not asked.

The sign on the front of the church said Methodist, but the preaching was much more fundamentalist than my church in Kansas. The scripture was Psalm 33:12, "Blessed the nation whose God is the Lord and the people whom He hath chosen for His own inheritance." The minister preached that Americans are those chosen people, and we will win the war because God is on our side. I thought it was quite a leap from David's army to the US Army as God's chosen people, but several members of the congregation seemed stirred by the powerful preaching.

After church, we scrambled back into the pickup and hurried home for Jeb and Sarah Gale's birthday party.

The yard was already abuzz. Neighbors and church members had already begun laying boards across sawhorses to make tables. People pulled blankets from the back of pickups and wagons to sit on. As we set up the last sawhorse tables, a sedan I recognized drove up. Captain Cooper climbed out and opened the passenger door for a beautiful woman, an older version of Sarah Gale.

"Hello, Aunt Lily! Uncle Ray, I need to talk to y'all!" Sarah Gale ran across the yard toward them. He shouted, "Happy Birthday!" laughed and hugged her, followed by Aunt Lily. I watched open-mouthed, maybe more than open-mouthed, because my jaw felt as though it had plummeted to the ground.

Captain Ray Cooper was Sarah Gale's Uncle Ray! No wonder she might be able to speak to him about my gigs. But I hoped she wouldn't. The first chance I got, I told Sarah Gale not to say anything.

"Don't worry, I won't," she laughed. "I know about them army rules. If I said anything, y'all'd get fifty gigs!" She laughed again. "I was just foolin y'all."

"Thank you," I said. I don't mind being fooled that way anytime!"

Everyone gathered around to watch the boys lift the hog sections from the pit. They placed them on another large piece of plywood stamped "Property of the United States Government" and carried it to the waiting sawhorses. The neighbors spread their dishes on the tables—about ten kinds of Jell-O, twelve potato salads, six green pea dishes, and eight of green beans. Besides the hog, fried chicken, catfish, deviled eggs, and potatoes au gratin loaded down the tables. There were five cakes and seven pies beside piles of bars and cookies on the dessert table.

I estimated about 60 people at the party, but we all finished the meal stuffed to the gills with plenty of food left over.

Before dessert, Mr. Simmons set up a soapbox podium on the porch where several people told stories about the twins, Sarah Gale and Jeb. Then a few made rousing speeches about bravery and victory in the current war. Sarah Gale's younger brothers pulled me toward the porch where the speakers stood. I wasn't prepared. I thought about all the platitudes I had been hearing for the past year, then started talking.

"I have known Sarah Gale for only a short time and met Jeb only yesterday, but I can tell from the number of people here to honor them and the joy of this celebration that they are loved and respected in this community. The Simmons family has welcomed me into their home and made me feel part of their family, half a country away from my own family. This will be a memory that will stay with me as I leave North Carolina for the next step of this unexpected adventure I find myself on.

"Sarah Gale is an exceptional and joyful young woman who has opened her heart and home to me. She has given me more reason than ever to perform the duty the army has set before me. To do what is morally right in any situation, to believe in my men, and lead them to do things they didn't know they could do. I promise to do my best to be worthy of that trust. I promise to fight to make the world safe for Sarah Gale and every one of you.

We have every intention of going over there and winning this war, bringing peace and freedom back to all nations on earth."

The crowd cheered and clapped even as I felt ashamed to stand there lying to them. I really wanted to get out of the army and get on with my life. Several young men fired guns into the air. Then Jeb and Sarah Gale approached the dessert table, cut two cakes, and invited everyone to the table to get dessert.

"That was a very good speech," Sarah Gale said beside me.

"I guess being in the Thespians in college paid off," I said. "Mostly, I wanted you to like it."

"I did. But what's a thespian?"

"Someone who gives speeches. We had a thespian's club at my college."

"A club just for givin speeches," she said. "Who woulda thought."

Things quieted down, and Sarah Gale and I sat on blankets under a tulip tree. "This tree was already growing when the family settled here almost two hundred years ago." Sarah Gale noted.

"That's amazing! Your family has lived under the same tree for the last two hundred years."

"I actually think it's rather boring. I'm ready to get out and get to know a few other trees."

***

Late in the afternoon, people began clearing the yard and taking the table apart.

"Is it time to go?" I asked.

"Oh no. They're getting ready for the dancing," Sarah Gale replied.

"But I have to report for roll call at 0500," I said.

"We have that all taken care of," she promised. "There are some things we can't talk to Uncle Ray about, but in this case, we could. So, it's arranged. We can dance till midnight, and then Uncle Ray will drive both of us back to Holy Ridge. We can sleep on the way."

I learned at least half a dozen local dances and taught Sarah Gale to waltz to some ballads.

As midnight approached, I told Sarah Gale, "Well, Cinderella, it looks like time to leave the ball."

"But I get to take my prince with me," she said with her dazzling smile.

We kissed, and I heard at least one brother snicker.

We woke Uncle Ray, who was sleeping on the sedan's seat. As friends and family said goodbye to Sarah Gale and pressed food into Aunt Lily's hands, there was an intermission in the music and dancing. Uncle Ray started the engine. Sarah Gale fell asleep against my shoulder almost immediately as we lounged in the spacious back seat, the car rocking and bouncing on the nearly dry roads. I didn't fall asleep quite so quickly. I contemplated how far I had come from my safe, well-thought-out plan. I had fallen deeply for Sarah Gale. Part of it was the war. Part of it was discovering I liked having a little excitement and uncertainty in my life. Mostly it was Sarah Gale. Everything about her was perfect. The way we could talk to each other and just spending time with her was such fun. We shared so many interests, a love of adventure, learning, and zest for life, which excited me. Sarah Gale in my arms, I fell asleep as we sped down the highway toward Camp Davis.

I woke as we stopped in front of her boarding house. I walked her up the dark walk to the door and kissed her goodbye.

"All right, Candidate Sinclair." The captain said as I returned to the car. "No more Uncle Ray. It's Captain Cooper now."

"Yes, sir!" I saluted and got into the back seat.

CHAPTER 15
NINETY DAY WONDER

As we walked to the mess the next morning, Reinhardt asked me, "Did you hear what really happened in Tokyo?"

"No, what?" I had heard that a raid had been attempted, but nine US planes had been shot down.

"The Air Corps flew right over Japan and dropped bombs on Tokyo without losses. They shot down three Jap planes and bombed some ships. Payback for Pearl Harbor. A Lieutenant Colonel in the Air Corps led the raid. His name is Doolittle, but he sure did a lot." He chuckled a bit at his own joke. "The tide is turning. We aren't running from those Japs anymore!"

"I hope you're right," I said. My hope lifted a bit—what a daring tactic.

We were back in the classroom for more lectures, the last thing I needed after staying up half the night. When Captain Hanley walked to the head of the lecture hall, I knew we would be getting a boring lecture on some technical issue. He always covered technical subjects and didn't know how to bring them to life. How would I possibly stay awake?

"Today, we are introducing Radio Detection and Ranging, RADAR for short. The RADAR transmitter sends out a high-frequency radio signal that will bounce off solid objects. The signal returns to the antenna. The time the signal takes to return tells us how far away the object is."

I perked up. Meanwhile, McKittrick complained, "Oh, no. Do we have to learn to calculate that, too?"

Hanley shot McKittrick a look that might have meant he did not appreciate McKittrick's attitude. His first word indicated so. "No! The machine analyzes the signals, and a blip appears on a screen. You line everything up correctly, read the numbers, and relay them to the searchlights."

"So, it locates the plane in microseconds and gives us an exact location?" I asked.

"You've got it. This RADAR will revolutionize antiaircraft."

"How do we tell what kind of plane we're detecting?" asked Reinhardt.

"We can't identify individual aircraft. However, RADAR can establish range and speed and provides other useful information through signal strength. With practice, you'll recognize single aircraft versus a squadron."

"But we don't want to shoot down friendly planes," Reinhardt said.

"What if our pilots sent out a secret radio signal that indicates they are allies. Can we receive that and know friendly planes are approaching?" I asked

"I believe that is in the works," Hanley said. "RADAR was installed on Oahu the day before the Pearl Harbor attack. The privates watching the screen detected the incoming planes, but when they reported it to their lieutenant, he thought it was a squadron of US planes scheduled to arrive that day. We don't want anything like that to happen again." Hanley sort of rose up higher and glared at us, braying, "Ignorance is not bliss!"

"At any rate," he said, sinking back down to his usual slump, "radio signals would probably be the best way to identify friendly aircraft."

"Could a signal be relayed to the lights and guns electronically, so they're automatically directed to the target?" Thomas asked.

"I recently saw an experimental version that could do just that. We hope it will be delivered to the army soon.

"The army is developing different types of RADAR." Hanley went on. "You will be using the SCR 268, which can locate planes within twenty-two miles and is better in the rain than our other RADAR types. Some can detect objects up to one hundred fifty miles away, but they get a lot of interference from rain, snow, or high humidity. The 268's reliable even when it's raining. Look at these photographs." Hanley distributed a stack of them among us trainees.

The objects identified by RADAR were fuzzy white dots on the picture. On some of the photographs, the entire screen was white. Hanley said they showed a rainstorm. On most images from the 268, we could make out the aircraft's blips even in a rainstorm. Hanley got into specifications and details, like in previous lectures, but I didn't have any trouble staying awake. This new equipment would definitely revolutionize antiaircraft!

"Imagine what we can do with this," I thought aloud to the class when Hanley stopped to erase the chalkboard. "Not only will we know where planes and ships are, we could probably even help predict the weather with RADAR that picks up rainstorms. See what direction the storm is traveling and how fast. This would be great back in Kansas to detect tornadoes before they hit. This RADAR thing is wonderful!"

Hanley smiled in response to my comment. He seemed please that finally, someone found one of his lectures exciting. Instead of replying to my conjectures, he said, "This afternoon, report to the airfield where we will set up the SCR 268 and begin learning to track actual aircraft."

I had three cups of coffee during lunch break, hoping the caffeine would keep me going all afternoon. Instead, the coffee hyped me up more than I already was, given my excitement about RADAR. I probably didn't need the joe.

As we hopped out of the cattle truck at a newly scraped field near the end of the camp's runway, another truck towing a large trailer pulled up. Three other trucks hauling trailers followed.

Hanley explained, "Truck number one is hauling the power source. The SCR 268 requires fifteen KVA of power." I whistled.

"How much is that?" whispered Reinhardt.

"Enough to power two or three houses," I whispered back.

Hanley overheard us, agreeing with my assessment: "That is a lot of power, and you'll have to make sure you have enough fuel wherever you go. The generator burns three to four gallons an hour.

"On the second truck, we have the equipment that provides

the power surges for transmitting the pulses. The peak power must be seventy-five kilowatts. This equipment produces that power spike for each pulse.

"The RADAR equipment is mounted on the pedestal on the trailer pulled by truck number three. The components for building the radar are in trucks three and four. Today the training team will demonstrate the assembly of the RADAR. Tomorrow, you'll assemble it yourselves. Take notes so you'll be able to do the assembly. The rest of the week, you'll learn to calibrate the RADAR, and finally, learn to detect targets with it."

The training team took two hours to assemble the RADAR. That was one of the disadvantages of this system. Artillery units usually move more slowly than infantry in the field. Still, if we had to set up and recalibrate this unit every time we moved, it wouldn't be reasonable to move forward every day. Maybe there wasn't too big a problem given the twenty-two-mile range of the SCR 268. It would take days for the infantry to move forward twenty-two miles in a combat situation.

Once they had it together, they disassembled it and repacked everything, ready for our trial in the morning.

I poured over the manual that evening to figure out what came next.

"What are you doing, Sinclair?" Thomas asked me.

"Figuring out how to calibrate the RADAR."

"Why? We can just ask tomorrow."

"Because this thing intrigues me. It's almost like magic. Do you realize the potential here?"

"I realize you seem a little bit crazy. Why don't you go to sleep?"

But I was too excited and caffeinated to fall asleep.

***

The following day at the training field, we unloaded RADAR parts and spread them out on the ground. First, we had to identify each piece. Next, we studied the manual, determining its purpose and proper location. Then we began assembly. It was one thing to see the picture in the manual and quite another to connect the parts and then sections to assemble the unit. For six hours, we struggled to build it correctly. We argued over the proper way to do it. The previous night, I figured out the manual was not precisely accurate, probably written in a hurry. But I didn't complain.

We made mistakes, ours and the manual's, and had to take things apart. Captain Cooper was no help at all. I assumed he had never put one of these things together—he certainly had not been part of our training—and Captain Hanley was back at the base lecturing to the next group. Meanwhile, the training team one field over demonstrated calibration to the group that was one step ahead of us, so they couldn't assist us.

Finally, Captain Cooper ordered, "Disassemble it and put everything back on the trucks."

We hadn't assembled it yet, but we were eager to get back for some hot chow, having missed lunch, so we took it apart and stowed the pieces on the truck.

We dragged ourselves into the mess hall at the end of service hours, feeling discouraged.

Day two was somewhat better. We did get it fully assembled before we had to take it apart.

By the third day, we had reduced our setup time to four hours and almost had it calibrated by the time we started taking it apart. I spent each night studying the manual, determining our errors, and correcting the manual's errors. We could set up, calibrate, and dismantle it in six hours by the end of the week.

***

I dashed to the boarding house to get Sarah Gale as soon as I was free on Saturday.

"Let's go to the beach and see if we can get any good pictures of gulls," she suggested.

"Sounds like fun," Anything with Sarah Gale sounded fun. We walked to the beach, where I tried to sneak up on the gulls as they pecked their way across the sand. Whenever I got close enough to lift my Brownie to take a picture, the gulls took off like they were camera shy. Behind me, Sarah Gale laughed at my frustration. The third time I turned quickly to see her flapping her arms.

I chased her down the beach. She was barefoot, and I wore my boots, which gave her an enormous advantage in the soft sand, so I didn't exactly catch her. Eventually, we both collapsed into the sand, totally out of breath. The sun glinted off her hair, showing ruby highlights in the burgundy waves.

After a minute, catching her breath, she asked, "Do y'all know y'all's eyes are the same color as the sky?"

I looked into her eyes. "And yours are... hmm... yours are the color of moss in the forest."

"Moss in the forest?"

"Yes, like when it is very shady, and the moss is deep green. Or like algae in the farm pond. They're not as dark as pine needles."

"Pond scum?" she said, I hoped in mock horror. "Y'all better quit while y'all're ahead."

"I don't think I'm ahead at this point. But your cheeks are like roses."

"Now y'all're talking like the silly romance novels the girls at the boarding house read, but I guess clichés are better than insults."

"Let me at those ruby lips, then."

I kissed her long and hard, then drew back, realizing I had better stop before things went too far. I felt a bit too flushed. She sat up and straightened her skirt, brushing off some sand.

"Y'all know I love y'all," she said.

"I know that. And I love you."

"What am I going to do when y'all leave? I'll miss y'all so much."

"I'll miss you, too. I promise to write every chance I get,"

"Carol is getting married to a man in y'all's class before he leaves," she said.

I paused for a second, unsure what she meant by bringing up her friend's upcoming marriage. I asked. I hoped my voice sounded cautious, "Are you saying you want to get married?"

"No, not really."

"Okay," I said slowly, unsure whether I felt relieved, embarrassed, or disappointed. "Because I'm not sure that would be very practical for us. We've only known each other for a couple of months. We really should get to know each other better before talking about marriage. And I was hoping you could meet my family so you can check them out. What if that doesn't work out? Besides, I'm going to be shipped off somewhere. We wouldn't be able to be together. I wouldn't want to leave you by yourself. Who knows what will happen? When I get married, I want to be able to take care of my wife."

"Don't worry, y'all know I can take care of myself. If that law about the Women's Army passes, I'm going to join up just as soon as possible. If they don't pass it, I guess I'll grow old as a laundrywoman."

"I'm sure they'll pass the bill. And I'm not going to let you grow old as a laundrywoman. This war won't last forever." I took her hands in mine. "I'll be back for you!" I said, a little more fiercely than I intended. I think I should not have assumed she was hinting at marriage in her comment about Carol. I teased, "I think I need to rescue you from your brothers."

She smiled broadly. She loved her brothers; they loved her. She didn't need any rescuing.

Changing the subject, I asked, "Do you want to take some more pictures tomorrow?"

"We have a girl's day planned. Wedding shopping for Carol in Wilmington."

My heart dropped. I would not be able to spend the day with Sarah Gale. With graduation coming up, we would have only a bit more time together.

***

"Hey, Sinclair," Reinhardt called to me as he and Johnson left the barracks Sunday morning, "where's your gal?"

"One of her friends is getting married, and they're doing wedding stuff."

"We're trying to hitch a ride into Wilmington. Wanna come?"

"I don't think so," I said. "I'll stay here and read."

"Are you going to marry that girl of yours? You better get hitched with her if you want to keep her. She might take up with another man when you leave, and you'll lose the best catch in the

Carolinas."

"I don't think she'll take up with another," I called back. Yet, I could not shake the ache in my chest about not seeing her today and the possibility of marriage. We both felt it was too soon to get married, but I didn't want to leave her. I dropped by the post office to pick up my mail and a newspaper, then returned to the dayroom.

First, I read the little note Robert had sent me.

Great news, brother. Laura and I are getting married! I decided to join the army and want to tie the knot before I take off.

Mom says you will have leave after your training. We are planning the date so you will be here to be my best man.

All my love,

Robert.

Everywhere I turned, someone was getting married. I dashed off a note to him agreeing to be his best man, including my leave date, to make sure they had that right. Then I picked up the newspaper.

The Japanese were bombing Manila and the allies were still retreating in the Philippines. Our total lack of progress in the Pacific discouraged me.

Then, inside the paper, a minor headline. "President Signs WAAC into Law." I read, "Women will be able to join the Women's Army Auxiliary Corps. They will be given jobs on the home front, releasing more men for overseas duty." Sarah Gale would be so happy! Suddenly my melancholy lifted. Such an intelligent, artistic woman deserved to get out of the laundry and see the country, if not the world. And I hoped she would be so intent on the adventure she wouldn't take up with anyone else. I could imagine her face when she read this. After carefully ripping the article out of the paper, I walked to the camp's gates and practically ran to Sarah Gale's boarding house. I knocked on Mrs. McCurdy's door.

"Do you know when Sarah Gale will be back?" I asked.

"They were planning on coming back on the four o'clock train," she responded, looking me up and down like I should have known better.

I went to the Knotty Pine Inn and ordered a burger and fries.

Unfortunately, I put too much ketchup on my fries in my exuberance. Reinhardt and Johnson came in soon after my food arrived. They helped themselves to the smothered fries.

"We couldn't get a ride," they said. "Want to join us at a movie this afternoon?"

"Sure!"

"What happened to the blues?" Johnson asked.

"This," I said, pulling the newspaper article out of my pocket.

"Women's Auxiliary Army Corps?" asked Johnson, frowning.

"Yes! I'll be leaving soon, and I couldn't imagine Sarah Gale stuck here forever. This is what she wants, to join up. She'll be able to develop some skills, use her talents."

"I wouldn't want my girl in the army," said Reinhardt. "No way."

"I would rather have her in the Women's Auxiliary Army Corps than spend the rest of the war washing dirty, sweaty clothes. You both stink too much. Anyway, she would get so worn down and discouraged washing clothes ten hours a day, five days a week. Would either of you do that instead of the duties you're training for?"

They looked a little sheepish.

After the movie, I rushed to the station to meet the four o'clock from Wilmington. I spotted Sarah Gale as she got off.

"I'm so glad to see y'all," she said. "Guess what I found out today?"

I pulled the newspaper article from my pocket.

"Y'all saw it, too? I'm going to try to get a little time off tomorrow to find out how to sign up."

"Good luck," I said. "I have to get back to camp. I don't want Uncle Ray to give me any more gigs. I just wanted to make sure you knew."

"Thank y'all, y'all're wonderful!" She pecked my cheek and twirled around, capering quickly after the other girls.

***

We hopped on a bus for the ride to the range at the beginning of the second week of RADAR training. Apparently, the camp had acquired a few new buses and was now carting Candidates around in style. Being in an enclosed bus seemed a luxury after riding through the rain and dust in cattle trucks.

We planned to beat our previous setup record. However, the RADAR was assembled and calibrated when we arrived.

"I want three of you watching the screen," Captain Hanley said, pointing to me, Reinhardt, and Coombs. "The rest of you line up behind them in equal length lines. When I say advance, move to the next screen."

I started on the range screen. When a blip appeared, I turned the crank that moved one antenna until the target blip aligned with a reference mark, then read the range from the wheel.

"Range correct. Sinclair advance. Elevation and azimuth are incorrect. Reinhardt and Coombs try again." I moved to the back of the azimuth line.

On his next try, Reinhardt was able to advance, and someone else sat in the elevation control seat, but Coombs had still not gotten the azimuth right. Another plane came in, and he finally called out a correct azimuth. The next person replaced him in the azimuth seat. The azimuth seemed to be the most difficult. I found out why when my turn came. To find the azimuth required turning two cranks and matching two signals. I turned both cranks until the blips were equally bright and read off the azimuth. It reminded me of adjusting my Dad's wheat drill to get the right amount of seed planted at the proper depth.

"Congratulations, Sinclair. You're the first one to get the azimuth right in one try. Advance."

I watched the elevation screen over Reinhardt's shoulder. "Look, there's a whole squadron coming in."

"You can't tell that from the RADAR," said Reinhardt.

"Just wait and see," I said. "That's a powerful signal at almost the limit of the range."

A few minutes later, several planes appeared in formation on the horizon.

"Eleven degrees is right again," Reinhardt said.

I shrugged. "Just logical. Strong signal, long-range; there must be something big out there."

We practiced until everyone accurately found the coordinates on all three scopes. On the bus back to the barracks, I sat next to Thomas.

"Do you realize how much more effective this will make the AAA?" I asked

"You're so good at calculating the location on the guns. I wouldn't have expected you to be so excited about a machine that does something at which you excel."

"But don't you see? I have to be able to sight the plane to calculate its location. This RADAR machine can do it even if it's cloudy or dark, or we can't see the plane."

"The RADAR isn't much good if the plane is on the other side of a mountain."

"Well, neither is visual sighting." I puffed out my cheeks and shook my head. I didn't see why he couldn't see how great RADAR could be.

"Hey, I was just playing with you. I can see how it'll be much more effective. It's just that you're like a child with a new bicycle."

Before we got off the bus on our return to the barracks, Captain Cooper gave us new orders. "Report at twenty-two hundred hours for searchlight training."

The buses took us in a different direction that night, pulling up at a beachfront range. The beach was pitch black with only a sliver of moon about to sink below the western horizon. The headlights of several trucks approached. They towed searchlights, power units, and RADAR trailers.

"You have studied this process in the classroom and on the training field. Now we will see how well you can perform on the battlefield. Sinclair, you'll be the RADAR officer. McKittrick, you are the searchlight officer. Get your men assigned."

I deployed the men: RADAR operators, power supply monitors, radioman, machine gunners. Setting up in the dark was a whole new challenge. Amazingly, we managed to beat our daytime record. Then we waited. A target appeared from the direction of the airfield about half an hour after we were operational. We followed it as it flew out over the ocean. Several minutes later, we detected it again, and we lit it as it returned to the airfield. Our goal was to locate and light three targets successfully. Our third target appeared before sunrise. Although we discovered it quickly on RADAR, the twilight conditions made it more difficult for the searchlight operators to find, but they did manage to light it. We dismantled and packed up the equipment and then climbed wearily onto the trucks to ride back to camp.

Captain Cooper stopped me as I exited the bus: "Good job, Sinclair. Are you aware that you have the top score in leadership for this class?"

"No, sir. I've only been in leadership positions a few times."

"You can get leadership points even when you're not assigned a leadership position." He glanced toward the men heading into the barracks, then said significantly, "The men look to you for direction."

"I just try to help out these guys, We're all in the same boat, and I don't want it to sink."

***

I knew Sarah Gale was going to HQ to ask about WAAC enlistment at the end of the day, so I decided to see if I could go with her. I waited under the awning of a laundry door, out of the light rain, until she came out.

"I'm free this afternoon. We're training at night. May I go to HQ with you?"

She smiled and slipped her hand into mine. We walked through the drizzle to camp headquarters. Sarah Gale asked the receptionist who she could talk to about signing up for the WAACs. She shrugged.

"Could you ask someone?" I suggested.

She picked up the telephone and asked to be connected to a recruiter.

"Go to the third office down the street," she said, pointing.

We walked back out into the rain, coming down hard now. Sarah Gale held her apron above her head as we ran to the recruiting office.

"We don't have the paperwork for that," the recruiter said. "Go back to HQ and check with Colonel Bryce's office."

Four offices later, we stood in front of a corporal in charge of filing regulations and reports. He went to the far end of his bank of filing cabinets, the drawer labeled with the large letters "W – Z," and pulled out a folder.

"It doesn't say when the applications will come out. It does say you have to put in your application in your home area. Talk to the draft board when you go home," he told Sarah Gale.

"I hoped I would find something out today," Sarah Gale moaned. "I guess I'd better go home this weekend to talk to the draft board. But I wanted to take some more wildlife photos this weekend."

"There's more wildlife around your house than there is here. You could take your camera."

"But it won't be with you," she lamented.

I met the train when she returned Sunday afternoon. "Did you apply?" I asked.

"The applications aren't available yet, but they said they would let me know as soon as they come," she replied. As I walked her to her boarding house, I could tell she was disappointed by the news.

***

Except for Johnny, Sarah Gale's entire family showed up for my graduation. All the candidates marched in formation to the rousing music of the band. We turned and faced banks of bleachers set up on the grass, the bleachers full of friends, family, and community supporters. The band played the Star-Spangled Banner, and the flag ceremony began. General Smith, the training center commander, gave a speech. Then he called several people forward. I was surprised to be among them.

"Presenting the awards for the first Officers Candidate Class of Camp Davis is Colonel Daniel Murphy," the general announced through the microphone, huge speakers set on each end of the platform broadcasting the announcement through the camp.

"The award for top academic score goes to Candidate Thomas." He stepped forward to scattered applause from the audience.

"For top leadership score, Candidate Sinclair." As I stepped forward, Jeb and Robbie led the younger boys in hooting and cheering, the rest of the crowd also cheering loudly. Thomas looked ruefully at me, and I shrugged a bit as I got back in line. He should have gotten as much applause, but the Simmons family made a lot of noise and had many relatives and friends in the crowd.

There were awards for top scores in gunnery, searchlight operations, then, "For top RADAR scores, Candidate Sinclair." I stepped forward again.

One by one, in separate presentations, we received our graduation certificate, orders, and, lastly, second lieutenant bars. Sarah Gale pinned mine. Then we marched off the field and were dismissed.

"Where are you stationed?" asked Sarah Gale as she ran over to me after dismissal.

"Let's see." I ripped open the envelope containing the orders.

"Fort Bliss, Texas," I read. "513th Coastal Artillery. I get two weeks' leave to visit my family, then report to Fort Bliss at the beginning of June."

Sarah Gale told me the pickup was parked near the gate as everyone dispersed.

"I can walk you there," I said.

"No. Look at the train tickets in your envelope."

I pulled out the tickets. "Elizabethtown, North Carolina, 1000 hours tomorrow. You certainly know how to pull strings, don't you?"

"We all wanted to say goodbye, so I talked to Uncle Ray."

"Thank you," I said. I now have two families waiting for me at home.

I packed my gear and went home with Sarah Gale's family for a night of goodbyes. After a fantastic meal of fried chicken, mashed potatoes and gravy, and greens, Sarah Gale and I sat on the porch most of the night talking. We avoided personal topics until the wee hours. Sarah Gale spent quite a bit of time explaining how she saw the photographs before taking them.

Finally, she asked, "What is it like, going away from your family and adjusting to army life?"

"It is a little tough at first, I have to admit," I said, grimacing a bit. "But you get used to it. You'll make friends in the WAACs, and they'll become like family."

"I'll miss you terribly, starting tomorrow."

"And I'll miss you," I replied, taking her in my arms. "I have something for you. Since I am such a dismal failure at telling you in my own words how I feel..."

"I don't know. Pond scum eyes are pretty original." She chuckled, a somewhat muted version of her brilliant laugh.

"I bought you a book, Sonnets from the Portuguese. Imagine I'm reading them to you when you read the poems."

"Oh, thank you. I have nothing for you except this picture of me by the waterfall. I had Jeb take it." She handed me a snapshot of herself in her white Swiss dotted dress, standing barefoot on the moss at the water's edge.

"You can't see the color of my eyes, but I stood on moss to remind you."

"I will keep this next to my heart," I promised fervently, slipping it into my shirt pocket. "Are we making a mistake?" I asked. "I know I love you. Should we have gotten married?"

"It isn't a mistake," she said. "The world is changing. I am changing. I need to find out where those changes take me. But it is awful to see you go. I love you, too." Tears skimmed down her cheeks, and I held her close.

She finally pulled away and said, "We had better get a little sleep before time to get you to the train station."

She went to her room. I climbed into the loft, where there seemed to be a lot more room for me than on my previous visit.

CHAPTER 16
BACK HOME AGAIN

Half the town, it seemed, greeted me at the station when I stepped off the train. We went directly to the Legion Hall, which Mom had rented for a combined welcome home and going away party for my brother Robert and me. The party, attended by about fifty friends and family, lasted until well after midnight.

As we helped clean up, I asked Robert, "Why are you marrying Laura and leaving her two days later? That isn't the way to begin a marriage."

"We think it's terribly romantic. We love each other. Besides, what business is it of yours anyway?"

"I'm your best man. Isn't it the duty of a best man to make sure the groom isn't making a mistake?"

"It is the best man's duty to support the groom!" he shouted. "If you don't want to do that, you don't have to be my best man!"

"Well, I didn't marry Sarah Gale because I didn't want to take the chance that she would be a widow before we even knew what it was really like to be married!" I shouted back.

"So that's what this is about? You didn't marry your sweetheart, so I can't marry mine?"

"Yes!" I shouted and stomped off.

I sat on the back steps of the hall. "*Be realistic,*" I told myself. Robert and Laura had been going together for a year and a half. Sarah Gale and I for ninety days. She wanted to join the WAACs. Following me around would only have made her bored and sulky. I had to support her to follow her dreams, her possibilities. I took the time to write her a long letter before going to bed.

***

My body was still on an East Coast army schedule despite the late night. I woke early enough for breakfast with Dad. I decided this was as good a time as any for the conversation I thought we needed.

"This war will last longer than I thought it would," I said. "I believe I'll have time to profit from investing in the stock market. When the bank opens, I'm going to take my money out and invest it in war bonds and stocks."

"You can't do that." He looked at me with a sharp gaze.

"What do you mean?"

"I already took it out of the bank and bought you a farm."

"A farm? I'm in the army. How do you expect me to farm?" What made Dad think I was at all interested in owning a farm? I hadn't had any interest or skill at it even when we lived on the farm.

"Land prices are still what they were in thirty-five. Wheat prices are more than double. Think of the profit you can make. It'll make you a lot of money while you're gone, then when you get back, you can farm it."

"I don't want to be a farmer! Why do you think I became a teacher? Can't you see I have my own way? Sell that farm and put the money back in the bank."

"I can't sell it. Nobody is buying farmland. All the young men are going overseas. It won't sell until the war is over. Say this war lasts four years. When you get back, you'll be over thirty years old. What medical school will accept you? I bought the farm, so you have something to return to."

"Nobody's buying farmland? Why did you? Owning land will not make it any more likely I'll come back."

"Look, son. I know you like teaching, but owning land gives a man something to hold onto. It will ground you in the history of the place. Make you somebody. Besides, it is a good investment. You won't be throwing your money away on worthless stock."

"You bought it because you thought it was a *good* investment?"

"Yes. I found one hundred twenty acres I could buy outright. There's no mortgage, and it's partly family land. It includes forty acres homesteaded by your Great Aunt Nelly."

I looked down, trying to compose myself. He was buying his past. Our family had come from Scotland six generations before he was born, before the Revolution, but he still thought being a landowner made you somebody. As a young child, I had loved running through the locust trees along the stream, where Queen Anne's lace and larkspur bloomed at Great Aunt Nelly's place, but it had never been a profitable farm.

I looked up at him. "I thought Mr. Clark bought Great Aunt Nelly's farm. Surely he's not selling."

"He bought all but the southeast corner. I bought that corner, plus forty acres across the road and another forty to the west of Clark's place."

"Clark didn't buy that forty because it's more creek than farmland," I complained. "The creek continues across the road, through that large pasture. Another branch of the creek flows through the west quarter section. It's not a farm. It's three small fields, two creeks, and two pastures spread over two townships."

"Forty-seven acres of pasture with running water and fifty-three acres of good dryland farming. You own it outright, and it's close enough to Keith's place that he can farm it for you until you get back."

"You can't use my savings to buy me a—" I looked down, swallowed, and looked back at him, "I have no intention of being a farmer, and you know that. Is this some trick to make me come back here rather than settling somewhere else after the war?"

He stared at me for a second. "You should be grateful I kept you from losing your fortune in the stock market." He set down his fork.

"I'm not going to live on that farm after the war," I said.

He became angry. "Now get in the car," he commanded like I was a ten-year-old. "We're going to see your farm."

What could I do? It was done, the money gone. I regretted signing my father onto my savings account. I sighed and climbed into my coupe with him.

Sorghum grew in the field above the creek on the western forty acres.

"Old Howard will harvest the crop this year, then Keith will take over," Dad informed me.

Keith's horses grazed in the pasture on the forty south of the road. The wheat on the hill waved in the breeze, Sarah Gale's perfect image of Kansas. My little sister's grave overlooked the field from the cemetery in the property's corner, doubtless one of Dad's reasons for buying this piece.

The home Great Aunt Nellie had built on her homestead in 1871 still stood across the road. Both house and pasture stood empty, the house weathered and grey, missing several shingles, the alfalfa in the field going to seed.

"After he harvests the seed, Keith will plow the field and plant wheat," Dad announced.

I followed Dad on a tour of the fields without further argument, chagrined. I had a hard time accepting that he had used my savings in this way. I was not sure I would ever trust him with anything important again.

I switched to the driver's side after Dad got out at the creamery, posted Laura's letter, and drove to Keith's farm.

"What is the idea?" I yelled when I found him repairing equipment in the barn. "You let Dad use my money to buy a bunch of hills and streams, all untillable."

Keith stood and turned toward me. "What did you want me to do? He made the deal before he told me anything about it. Just came out one day and showed me the deed." He kicked at the dirt and picked up a dropped bolt. "He was so pleased to get Aunt Nelly's home place back. So now I have to farm those hills. I can make a go of it, and you at least won't have to come up with a mortgage payment in bad years. As stubborn as you are, little brother, Dad is more stubborn."

"I know that. Why do you think I am yelling at you, not him?"

He gave me a look, then said, "Dad... you know Dad. Own a piece of land, and you're a Laird. Sure, teaching is a noble profession, but it is nothing compared with being a landowner."

I shook my head. Keith, I realized, had more of Dad's attitude than any of the rest of us. He was a sharecropper now, but he dreamed of owning his own place.

"Grab that axle and help me lift," he said. "You now own 120 acres of farmland, half of it not tillable. I'll make the most of it—thank me for that—and you'll have a bit of income. You aren't much of a farmer, though. Too lazy."

"I'm not lazy. I prefer to work smart rather than hard. Have you ever tried that?" I jabbed. I thought I had made it out from under Dad's thumb when I became a teacher, yet here I was, angry at him and, I was sorry to say, at Keith, who was not culpable.

Keith and I spent most of the day on the repairs, and then I drove to the schoolhouse to pick up Doris. I parked on the empty playground and went into her classroom.

"Do you know what Dad has done?" I asked.

"He bought you a farm. I don't know why. You're no farmer. We all know that. You need to go back to teaching after the war."

"Maybe," I said. "Or maybe I could get into the medical field in some way. I did get some pharmacy training in Washington."

"I don't see you counting pills for the rest of your life."

"No, I didn't enjoy that," I conceded.

We straightened up her classroom, then went to the drugstore for a root beer float. Before we left, I bought a couple of magazines for Doris. For myself, I chose an Agatha Christie mystery and a new book by F. Scott Fitzgerald, "The Love of the Last Tycoon," to read on the train to Fort Bliss. By the end of the week, I had finished both books and had to buy more for the train ride to Texas.

At home, I walked to the sleeping porch where Robert sorted his clothes, deciding what to take and what to leave.

"Look, little brother. I only felt sorry for myself and was too tired to think straight after the long train trip and the party. You have the right to live your life as you please."

"I know," Robert said. "You can still be the best man. That is if you are willing."

"Willing and eager," I said.

***

Saturday morning, the day of the wedding, the house was in an uproar. Doris couldn't find her gloves. Mom was still baking some extra treats for the reception.

"Hurry! The best man's supposed to be there early!" I called to them.

Finally, as Mom pulled the cake and tarts from the oven, Dad roared. "Everyone in the car."

We piled into Doris's new sedan and headed for Hutchinson and Robert's wedding.

Robert was pacing alone in the preacher's dim little office at the church. Dad came in and spoke with Robert, giving him some last-minute instructions on married life. Robert sat down. I took over the pacing until Mom came to get Dad, and finally, Robert and I were alone.

"I'm; mm here to support you, but I still don't know what you think you are doing getting married and then leaving two days later to go into the army."

"I love Laura! She loves me! We want to be married before I leave, so no matter what happens, we have each other."

"As a husband, shouldn't you be taking care of her? Isn't that what Dad taught us? How can you take care of her when you're in basic training? After basic, who knows where you'll go. What happens if you don't come back?"

"Yes, Dad took care of Mom. She was a teenager when he married her. And I'll be taking care of Laura. She'll be getting a separation allowance. But that's not why we're getting married. We love each other and can't imagine waiting any longer to get married. No matter what happens, we'll have had each other for a while."

"What did Dad say to you?"

"That I should come back and be a farmer. That would be the best way to take care of Laura. And owning land would secure my position in the community.

I shook my head. "I'm not sure that's the best advice for you." Then I grabbed his shoulders. "You do what you want to support Laura. Farming is not always the answer."

He nodded. "Don't you think I know that? I don't think I even want to be a teacher like everybody else in the family."

The preacher poked his head into the office and signaled us to join him on the dais. The four bridesmaids marched up the aisle in lockstep to the Wedding March. Laura's young niece toddled toward us, flinging flower petals out of sync with the March. Then Laura appeared, an image of splendor in lace and organdy. She glided up the aisle, her father presented her to Robert, and the preacher began the ceremony.

I thought of Sarah Gale. I loved her. Maybe I should have asked her to marry me. We could be having our ceremony today, and she would come to Fort Bliss with me. We could have time together while I helped train the new regiment. I visualized a little cottage where we would set up housekeeping, where she would greet me each night when I came home. Robert snapped his fingers. I realized the preacher was asking for the ring, and I was daydreaming about Sarah Gale. I pulled it from my pocket.

I threw myself into the celebration at the reception. I danced with every bridesmaid, gave a masterful best man speech, if I do say so myself, tasted all the delicious treats on the refreshment table, and drank way too much of the vodka spiked punch. Finally, it was time for Robert and Laura to begin their brief honeymoon.

"Wait," demanded Mom. "I want a picture of the whole family together."

We lined up in front of Doris's car, and Nancy snapped a picture, then waved Robert and Laura off, tin cans clattering behind Robert's jalopy.

As the families milled around, I said, "Time for me to go," I hugged Mom and Doris goodbye.

Dad drove me to the station. I couldn't think of anything to say that would not be accusatory about his purchase on my behalf, and he wasn't about to admit any guilt about squandering my savings, so we drove in silence. Then, as I prepared to climb out of the car, he grabbed me.

"Be careful, son," he whispered into my ear as he held me in a tight hug.

"I will, Dad," I promised. I knew he loved me, even though I did not always welcome his way of showing it.

I sat on the bench in front of the train station, waiting for the overdue train, going over everything wrong with my life. I could barely speak with my father. I loved a girl who was halfway across the country. The draft had stripped me of my lifelong dream. I sat in a small-town train station all by myself in the middle of the night, waiting and waiting on my way to one of the most isolated posts in the entire country.

By the time the train arrived at two a.m. I was about as miserable as I had ever been in my life. I climbed into my berth and, thankfully, was out cold the rest of the night.

***

The steward tapped on the partition by my head to wake me up. "Excuse me, sir. The diner will only be serving breakfast for another twenty minutes. If you want to eat, you should be on your way."

As I rolled out of the berth, I recognized the steward.

"Samuel? Remember me. We met last year when I was on my way to California."

"Ahh!" he said. "Yes. The white houseboy."

I looked at the book he had under his arm. It was a copy of The Love of the Last Tycoon.

"Do you like that book?" I asked

"It's a powerful book," he said. "So sad Fitzgerald died before he finished it.

"I noticed you always went around with a book under your arm. I thought you must be reading them."

"Yes, sir. I took up reading when I got this job. It's a job where you work long and hard, then wait for hours. The books help me get through the waiting. You'd be surprised how much reading material passengers leave behind. I also do drawings of the fantasies that play 'round in my head."

"I'd like to see some of your drawings if I could," I looked at my watch. "I had better get to breakfast."

"Yes, sir. I'll have your berth stowed and your seat ready after breakfast, sir."

"You don't have to call me, sir. You're not in the army."

"If I don't, people call me uppity, which can make trouble with the boss."

"That hardly seems fair," I said.

"Nobody said this world is fair."

Yes, Samuel said it right, and probably a lot more toward him than me.

At breakfast, I thought about Samuel. He was talented and intelligent, yet he couldn't get a job that didn't involve serving people. Maybe my life wasn't all that bad. I had so many choices about what I could do after the war. Samuel seemed to have only one—serving white people.

I found a small folder of fascinating line drawings on my seat when I returned. I looked through them. They were pencil drawings depicting scenes from his travels. Mostly people, but a few animals. People were drawn in strong, bold strokes, surrounded by abstract images representing trains, landscapes, or work environments. Some were painted in bright, bold colors, but most were simple pencil drawings. As I put them back in the folder, a flyer fell out. It announced a sit-in in Chicago sponsored by CORE, the Congress of Racial Equality.

When Samuel came by again, I asked him about the pictures.

"Those things pop into my head," he said. "Can't keep them out until I put them on paper."

"I think they're fantastic. I don't have any art training, but I love them. You should go to art school."

"I've been saving for that, but most of my wages go to the family."

"Was I meant to see this?" I asked, pulling the flyer out.

A panicked expression crossed his face.

"Don't worry. I don't know a thing about it." I said, slipping it back into the folder. "But I support the idea."

He looked at me with renewed interest.

I gave him a big tip when I got off the train in Albuquerque. I hoped to add to his art school savings. The El Capitan would continue to California, but I headed south on the El Pasoan.

I sat in the observation car, watching the desert and mountains go by until the sun went down. A full moon rose over the hills. As the train moved through a valley and crossed a short bridge, the moon disappeared, then rose again.

"Pretty amazing, two moonrises in one night," I said to the

young woman across the aisle

"It is," she said. "Are you on your way to Fort Bliss?"

"Yes, how about you?"

"Fort Bliss. My Dad works there. I just finished my freshman year at the University of New Mexico. He got me a summer job on the base. My name is Becky."

"I'm Gene Sinclair."

"Nice to meet you, Lieutenant Sinclair."

Before I had time to continue our conversation, the conductor strode through, calling, "Next stop El Paso, Texas,"

I stepped into the West Texas summer night. I expected a much more oppressive heat, but a slight breeze made it feel almost cool.

Down the platform, a major general stood waiting. Becky, who had deboarded before me because I waved her through, ran to him, calling out, "Daddy!".

"Lieutenant Sinclair?" asked a corporal who approached from the other direction.

"Yes?"

"Corporal Flynn. I'm here to drive you to Fort Bliss. I'll retrieve your gear. Two other officers are already in the jeep, under a light north of the station." He pointed in case I didn't know which way north was. "I'll be there ASAP."

CHAPTER 17
FORT BLISS

I found the jeep parked under a dim light on a short pole. Two other tired officers slumped in the vehicle.

"Gene Sinclair," I said.

"Ben Carson," said the newly minted second lieutenant in the front seat.

"Paul Marshall," said the chaplain, who had somehow managed to fold his lanky body into the jump seat in the back of the jeep.

"We've been waiting forever," said Carson. "What took you so long,"

"We came in from the east about half an hour ago," said Marshall. "Carson here doesn't adjust very well to losing sleep."

"You're in the wrong place, then," I said. "I've lost more sleep in the last year than in my entire life before the army. Anyway, who said war and sleep go together?" Carson snorted in derision.

I climbed into the back seat with Marshall.

Carson grumbled about sleeping and waiting as Corporal Flynn lifted my trunk and duffel bag into the trailer attached to the jeep. He tied them all down, and we were off.

We followed the General's car through the gates of Fort Bliss. His vehicle turned right toward the large houses where senior officers lived with their families. Corporal Flynn turned left toward the unmarried officer's quarters, soon parking in front of something akin to a barracks.

"Reverend Marshall, if you'll follow me, I'll show you to your room," Flynn said. "Lieutenant Carson, you'll be in room 204, up those stairs there." He pointed. "Lieutenant Sinclair, you'll be in here with Lieutenant Sessions." He nodded at a room on the ground floor near where he had parked the jeep.

The room was small and dark, with two beds, two desks, and two wall lockers. I dropped my gear and went looking for a restroom. As I returned, I tripped over my duffel bag.

"Just strip down and go to sleep," said a voice from the bed to my right. "You've only got a few hours to get whatever sleep you're gonna get."

I took Sessions' advice and fell asleep as soon as I stretched out. After what seemed only a few minutes, reveille sounded over the PA system. I rolled out of bed, pulled on my uniform, and followed Sessions outside and down the steps onto the crushed rock in front of the building. Carson and Marshall were already wandering in front of the steps, wondering which way to go.

"Sessions, we haven't had any orientation. Which way do we go?" I asked.

"I got here yesterday too. Just follow everyone else."

Other junior officers meandered one way or another in the early morning sunlight, bright and hot already. A light breeze picked up the dust caused by all our boots on the crusher fines and wafted the pungent scent of horses to our noses. We soon learned the First Cavalry had recently departed to train on tanks. Their horses stayed behind in stables a short way upwind from our barracks. Of course, it reminded me of home and made me miss Keith.

A well-timed passing captain shouted, "To the flagpole."

Sessions had seen a flagpole the day before—he'd arrived while it was still light—so we headed in that direction and found morning formation. We later learned that seventeen different units called Fort Bliss home and had their own morning formations. This seemed to be the 'incomplete unit' formation, mostly officers whose soldiers were not here yet. After the flag ceremony, the officer in charge dismissed companies one by one. About forty officers remained on the parade ground.

"AAA officers, report to the officer's mess for breakfast, then assemble at the HQ auditorium," another Captain ordered.

We located the officer's mess and had breakfast. It was okay.

Not like at Camp Davis, but better than Fort Leavenworth. I learned our mailboxes were in the same building as the mess, so I checked mine and found a letter from Sarah Gale. I read it as I walked to the auditorium.

> May 30, 1942
>
> Dearest Gene,
>
> I hope you had a good time with your family and a safe trip to Fort Bliss. I am so lonely at Camp Davis without you. I still look for you every day as I go to and from work. The Camp is getting more built up all the time. Places that were tent cities when you were here are now barracks, and swamps are filled in and full of new tent cities.
>
> Jeb signed up for the Marines last week. Mama was really upset. Daddy told her she should expect her sons to do their duty for the country. She's still upset, of course. They had a big celebration and sendoff for him, and Mama made him giant batches of his favorite foods.
>
> Daddy still doesn't like the idea that his daughter might sign up. He thought the only reason I was working at Camp Davis in the first place was to find someone to marry. Now he says I should move home and wait for you. Mama would like me to come back permanently, too, so she has help with her work. Granny encourages me to go through with my plans, though. Granny is so amazing.
>
> I will go home every weekend now and help as much as I can when I'm there. This weekend we'll decorate graves for Decoration Day. I know your mother and sister will be doing the same. It makes me feel close to them even though I have never met them.
>
> I look forward to hearing from you. Please write to me as soon as you can.
>
> Love,
>
> Sarah Gale

Had she not gotten the letter I had sent while on leave? With things happening so fast and the mail moving so slow, it would be challenging to keep up with each other by letter. I considered weekly telephone calls, but that would be too expensive. It would have to be letters.

I slipped into one of the worn leather seats halfway up the aisle of the HQ auditorium. It appeared to be one of the oldest buildings at the fort. It was possibly even built when the fort relocated to this site in 1868. The hall was less than half full. Soon a colonel and three lieutenant colonels walked onto the high stage at the front of the room. We all stood and snapped to attention.

"At ease, men. Take your seats. I am Colonel Willis Chapin, your regimental commanding officer," the Colonel barked. "You Battalion commanders are Lieutenant Colonels Myron Eddy, Richard Sheely, and John Squires. We are here to reactivate the 513th Coastal Artillery. When the regiment is combat-ready, we will ship out to the place that needs us most. You are here to ensure we are combat-ready ASAP. The remnant of the old unit is on the way from New York. More officers and enlisted replacements are leaving Camp Davis today. Materiel will be arriving this afternoon. Your Battery Commanders will give you your assignments."

The battery commanders marched onstage. One, a tall captain, caught my attention—military bearing, probing eyes, air of authority. He probably would not listen to anyone, not the kind of commander I wanted to work under. *Please don't let me get him*, I prayed.

One of the captains stepped forward, not the one who caught my attention.

"Captain Marcus Jennings, commanding Battery A. Lieutenants Flanner, West, and Murphy, follow me." Battery A officers filed out of the room. The next captain, short, muscular, and slightly older, stepped forward.

"Captain Paul Gill., Battery B." He called four officers. Then the Captains of Battery C. D, E, and F each called three or four lieutenants. The room was emptying, but I remained. So did the tall Captain. The Captain of Battery G stepped forward and called out the names of three officers. Then, the commander of Battery H called his lieutenants. The tall Captain stepped forward. "Captain Richard Henderson, Battery I. Lieutenants Carson, Sessions, and Sinclair, please follow me."

Oh, why did it have to be him? I thought as I rose and followed the others out of the auditorium. Once outside, Henderson said, "We are the searchlight battery for this regiment. We locate and identify the planes. The gun batteries shoot them down. There are record numbers of night bombings in this war. Searchlights will make the difference between success and failure.

"The Regiment arrives in two weeks. Until then, our Battalion Commander, Lieutenant Colonel Squires, will lecture every morning. We unload cargo in the afternoon. Report to the rail yards after mess."

Squires lectured on everything, much of it repeating lessons from boot camp and beyond; health and sanitation, the latest antiaircraft equipment, and his command philosophy. As new second lieutenants, we knew almost everything, but we didn't dare show any restlessness. Squires might send us out earlier to the backbreaking work of unloading freight cars and unpacking equipment.

At the rail yards, we worked hard under Captain Henderson's unyielding, unsympathetic command. He was every bit as stern and demanding as I had anticipated. We weren't working fast enough, we hadn't cleaned up well enough, we stacked boxes of supplies incorrectly. You would think we were buck privates the way he treated us. Henderson knew the exact procedure for every activity or process and specifications for every piece of equipment, the kind of mindless, by the book functioning that made me hate the army.

Some of the officers grumbled about doing private's work. But I did what Henderson told me without comment. I didn't intend to make things any harder on myself.

As we walked to mess one day, I asked Henderson, "Where did you train?"

He looked down his nose at me, eyebrows arched up, surprised at the question.

"West Point. I was army before this damned fight started.

Properly trained over four years of rigorous education, not a few weeks at camp, and magically you're an officer like you ninety-day wonders."

He gazed into the distance, then glanced at me again. "You need to stiffen that backbone of yours, Sinclair. You've got potential, but a man has to be brave, unyielding, and stand firm in the army. You're too flexible and submissive to be a good Army man."

"Yes, sir," I said, straitening up and marching faster.

I thought flexibility and submission were good qualities for a second lieutenant when dealing with a career Captain. I resolved to toughen up my approach a bit. I could take a lesson from Sessions. Before we were in Henderson's battery, he had seemed laid back and easygoing. As soon as he met Henderson, he subtly mimicked the captain's characteristics. Henderson and Sessions were the same height, although Henderson had more muscle. The bearing, the long stride, and the tendency to look down their noses worked for them both. However, I considered with some foreboding, being eight inches shorter and baby-faced, I would look silly, trying to match their imperious posture. Even so, I tried to emulate at least some of their approaches to leadership.

***

After Squires' incredibly dull lecture on searchlight operation and maintenance, we arrived at the rail yard to find carloads of ammunition for the big guns.

"All these cars have to be empty by dark," Henderson ordered. "Load the ammo onto the trucks and get it to the arsenal. Work carefully and quickly. Sometimes these babies blow up when jostled."

Carson complained. "I can do careful, or I can do quick, but I can't do both together, especially when things might blow up."

"Shut up and get to work, Carson." Sessions ordered in his face. "Captain says do it, we do it."

In the following silence, I suggested, "First, let's bring those trucks over here and back them up to the boxcars. There's no reason to carry twenty-five-pound shells across the yard." Carson and I each got a truck and backed it up to the open boxcar doors.

"If we pass the shells along a human chain, they'll get loaded faster, and no one will get in anyone else's way. We just have to be careful." I said.

The last trucks were on the way to the arsenal as the midsummer sun set. In El Paso, that meant it must be about 2000 hours.

"Now we're too late to get anything to eat on base," complained Carson.

Captain Henderson strode toward us. "Let's go, men. Good job, Sinclair, on the trucks and loading. It looks like other batteries will be here until midnight. Except for B," he added, "I'm starving. Captain Gill, how about you and your officers join us at Gordo's?"

"Sure, said Gill. "Padre, why don't you come along? A couple of the men can ride with you."

The captains got their jeeps, and we piled in. Henderson drove straight past the burger joints to a little Mexican restaurant.

The restaurant was nearly full, but most diners had finished their meals. As we walked toward a couple of empty tables covered with red-checkered tablecloths, Henderson shouted, "Hey, Gordo!" to the proprietor.

The smiling, rotund man shouted back, "Hey, Señor Capitan! You have brought your friends!"

"I wouldn't call them friends exactly, except Gill here, more like acolytes." He seemed pleased at that last word. "We've been working hard all day. Bring us Coronas all around and a huge basket of chips with salsa."

The waitress pulled two tables together to make one table for ten if we squeezed tight. She brought the beer and corn tortilla chips with spicy salsa a few minutes later. Gordo plopped sticky, stained menus down in front of us.

"How are the wife and that little man?" Gordo asked Henderson.

"Just fine," Henderson replied.

"What's good here?" I asked.

"Get number five," Henderson boomed at us. "It has a little bit of everything." He turned to the waitress. "Bring number five for everybody. They're all new here and have no idea what Mexican food is." Gordo quickly returned to the kitchen.

"I'm from Beaumont, Texas," Carson exclaimed. "Ate Mexican food all my life. We had a Mexican cook, and she made the best Spanish rice. Do you have any ceviche?"

"Sorry, no, sir," the waitress said softly.

"Dadgum it, what kinda restaurant is this?" he shouted. "No, ceviche? No fish on the menu at all?"

"No, sir. We are very far from the ocean," the poor girl said.

Henderson glared at Carson, his unspoken reprimand quite clear. Finally, Carson settled down a bit.

"We had Mexican food in southern Colorado, too," Marshal put in softly yet firmly to smooth over the situation. "But there are different styles of Mexican. I can hardly wait to find out how they make it here. Number five looks good to me."

"I'd like a number five, too, please," I added.

Carson pouted but agreed to get a number five. Gill and his men ordered number five as well. I wondered who was really in charge here.

"Say, did you play in that 'thirty-seven Army-Navy game?" Gill asked Captain Henderson.

"I did," Henderson replied.

Carson perked up. "You played for Army?"

Henderson nodded. "That was some game. It wasn't easy, but we held them. Six to zero."

His play-by-play commentary entertained us as we waited for our food. I didn't usually follow football, but Henderson's enthusiastic storytelling made it enjoyable. I sat munching on chips, not having anything to contribute. As the second baskets of chips dwindled to crumbs, the waitress brought a heavy tray filled with large plates piled high with food smothered in spicy red sauce. Gordo followed her with another tray of the same. We dove in as soon as the waitress set our plates down. The waitress returned shortly with tacos on smaller side plates and several little bowls of salsa. Henderson ordered another round of beer. Conversation ceased as we chowed down on the spicy food and pulled long on our beer bottles.

We ate every bite, then leaned back, groaning. We were the only party left in the restaurant.

Delicious," exclaimed Captain Gill, "I don't think I can eat another bite."

But Carson asked the waitress, "You got any flan?"

"No, sir." She said, "We have run out."

"Well, can you make me some?" he asked.

"Carson, flan takes hours to make," I told him. "I want to get back to base and get to sleep. We can't wait around for them to make flan."

"If you come back tomorrow, I'll have flan for you." the waitress promised.

Carson did not respond. Captain Henderson, looking at Carson, stood, picked up his hat, and walked to the cash register. The rest of us followed him, paid our bill, and jumped back into the jeeps.

"They had flan on the menu. I wanted some flan!" Carson whined on the way back to Fort Bliss.

I noticed the back of Henderson's neck turning red.

"Drop it, Carson," I said softly with a nod toward Henderson, who had launched into another football story.

***

More second lieutenants joined us the following week. Captain Henderson called out the names Brasseux and Wright. A stocky, dark-haired man with thick eyebrows, full lips, and a cheerful smile jumped up and trotted toward us. A tall, thin, handsome, and youthful second lieutenant with dark hair and blue eyes followed. We had a chance to get acquainted at lunch. Brasseux regaled us with hilarious tales about growing up in the bayous of Louisiana. Finally, I asked, "Wright, where are you from?"

"Ohio," he said.

"What did you do there?"

"Studied architecture. I just graduated from school."

We spent the hot June afternoon unloading radio and telephone equipment.

"I studied communications and electrical engineering at Loosiana State to work in radio, but dis wasn't what I had in mind." Brasseux laughed.

"Right-O," I said. "It's busywork because they don't have any men here for us to lead."

The topics of Squires' lectures followed a schedule, so we expected something on health and personal hygiene on Friday. He came onstage. "Gentlemen, thank you for the work you have done. You may have guessed we were testing you. We wanted to be sure you are willing to do whatever is necessary to lead your men, to lead by example. You are responsible for ensuring your men have the knowledge and skills to do their jobs. I now feel confident you'll contribute to the war effort in any way you can. Tomorrow both the remnant of the old regiment and the newly trained recruits will be arriving. The old guard, career enlisted men, knows army life and army ways. The recruits are young, well-educated, and trained on the new equipment. Both groups have things to teach each other. I expect you to merge them into one battalion that is both exemplary and modern. Spend today preparing for the arrival of the troops. I'll expect the officers of each battery to meet to finalize training plans. Dismissed!"

"He was treating officers like grunts to test what?" Carson asked.

"Our willingness to serve, or something like that," I told him. "Henderson made sure it was as challenging as possible."

"And, of course, we're all completely willing," Brasseux said, grinning at me.

At the Battery I meeting, Henderson told us, "Tomorrow morning, Battery COs are meeting. I'll get a list of the men attached to our battery. The recruits have general training on guns, radar, and searchlights. Old army men have only used sound to locate the planes and shot the old guns that are less powerful. We have to train them all to do the job the way it should be done. We may get radar, or we may use sound locators. We need to prepare for both. Sinclair, test everyone for sound location. You get the first pick of the men. Choose for both skill in sound location and scores on radar."

"Do you think they'll really send us overseas without radar?" I asked.

"They could. And the radar could fail. We need to be ready to do it the old 'tried and true' way."

I shook my head. It might have been tried, but it wouldn't be practical or successful with modern aircraft.

"Brasseux, train the radiomen. Wright, make sure the searchlight operators are up to snuff, and Carson work with the power plant operators. They need to know those plants inside and out. How to fix them and keep them going come hell or high water. Any questions?"

"How come Sinclair gets first pick?" asked Carson.

"I explained that," Henderson replied, staring at Carson. Henderson did not like Carson's complaints.

Wright raised his hand timidly.

"Yes, Wright."

"Don't we need men trained in more than one specialty in case... in case we lose some. In the field, I mean."

"Yes. We will test and train all the men in all the specialties. I want you to focus on the men you think would be best in each specialty. Good question!"

"I thought maybe assignments were all random at that level," Wright said.

"We are out to win a war. Random doesn't work in a specialized unit like searchlights."

"Yes, Sir."

"We're still short three officers. They'll come in tomorrow."

We adjourned to the common room in the junior officers' housing. Through his architectural program, Wright, trained in drawing, brought out a notebook and sketched our scene. I settled back, put my feet up and read Sarah Gale's latest letter.

June 14, 1942

Dearest Gene,

I'm so happy you made it to Fort Bliss safely. I enjoyed your descriptions of your fellow officers. Has Carson settled down and started doing his duty yet? It must be funny watching Sessions copy the captain.

I hope you don't get heatstroke spending the summer in the desert. It will probably be miserable. Take care of yourself.

Applications are out for Officers Training for the WAACS but not for the enlisted personnel. I'm not qualified to be an officer, so I'm waiting for the enlisted applications to be available. I have to apply in my home area, so I stop by every Friday when I get off the train. They are getting used to seeing me and have an answer for me as I walk in the door. Meanwhile, I keep washing, ironing, and waiting.

Johnny went to England. We haven't heard whether he made it yet. Mama is incredibly nervous about it, and Daddy acts angry, which means he is worried. There have been so many ships attacked in the North Atlantic that we will all be a bit on edge until we hear he made it. His job is to drive officers around, so I think he will be safe—unless WAACs take over that job and he has to go into combat.

Jeb said he was going to try to become a cook. I'm sure he would never have admitted he wanted to cook if you hadn't cooked eggs that first morning home. Mama is really grateful to you because she thinks there is no way a cook will get killed. I know he could be if a bomb falls on his kitchen, but he has less chance of dying than you. You are the one I worry about. PLEASE BE SAFE.

I have been using the camera you gave me to make a photo history of Camp Davis. I take pictures every chance I get. I have set up a darkroom in one of Mrs. McCurdy's closets and am learning to develop my photographs. It is the most fun I have ever had.

Meanwhile, the uniforms are coming in dirtier and sweatier than ever.

Take care. I love you.

Sarah Gale

I folded the letter and put it in my shirt pocket to read again. Sarah Gale was going so much farther with photography than I ever had. When the war was over, she would have things to teach me.

"Hey, Sinclair," Brasseux called. "How's your one and only doin?"

"She's doing great. You get any news from home?"

"Yeah. De raccoons stopped by for a taste test of de sweet corn, so it must be ripe.

"Dad's fixin to sell the old mule. My cousin Jackie got him to try out the tractor I bought him, and he decided plowin with a tractor was easier. Then t'other day, he started the tractor and decided to go inside for a drink of water. He sat down in his favorite chair and fell asleep. Slept a good hour. Mama said de tractor idles real good, and so does Dad."

A train whistle sounded in the near distance. We all rushed out the door to meet our troops.

CHAPTER 18
THE REGIMENT

New York regulars poured out of Pullman cars refitted to carry twenty-nine soldiers and one porter per car. They were still coming when the train from North Carolina pulled up, full of recruits trained at Camp Davis. Two thousand five hundred men wandered to and fro, searching for their battery. Officers shouted at and herded the arrivals, with much arm waving, toward headquarters, adding to the mass confusion. Two new lieutenants for our Battery arrived with them, Tilton and Douglas. Captain Henderson put them to work immediately.

Gradually, men appeared at battery headquarters. Henderson refused to hand out barracks assignments until we had tested all Battery I soldiers for their ability to locate aircraft by sound. Sessions sent them to the baseball field, where I waited for them.

I checked an old manual I had located for directions on how to perform the tests, then counted off the first twenty men who arrived at the baseball field, ordering them to form a circle. Walking to the center of the circle, I had them close their eyes, then I clapped. All of them pointed at me. I began moving around the ring's interior, calling out names and asking the men to locate me. In thirty minutes, I had eliminated only three men. I sent the three to Sessions, who was handing our barracks assignments. This process would take days at this rate.

No way did I want to waste so much time on a test for something so useless as sound location now that we had radar. Rather than test twenty at a time, I had men line up at arm's length around the baseball diamond. In this way, I could test a third of the battery at once. I repeated the test, calling out names, but almost half the men still passed this test. I told them all to get their barracks assignment and those who passed to return in the morning.

Early the next day, I set up the binaural testing system. The system consisted of an airhorn on a cable with a motorized pulley system to move it. A rod was mounted on a calibrated disc, and the soldiers would aim the rod at the horn while blindfolded. I had two rods, one on either side of the cable. I had almost completed the setup when suddenly sprinklers began spraying the baseball field—and me and my testing equipment. I ran off the field and searched for the groundskeeper who had turned them on. He was nowhere to be seen. When the men arrived, we spent thirty minutes standing around, waiting for the sprinklers to stop. Then we began the tests, two soldiers at a time. The tedious, repetitive process went on and on, but I had numerical scores for all the men by evening. That evening I combined each man's binaural scores and radar scores and selected the top half. When the men returned in the morning, I sent those with lower than average scores to Sessions for assignment to other duties. About ten of the men stood talking after I had told them to report to Sessions.

"What's the problem, men?" I asked.

"We was the best sound location men around. Why are you sending us away?" asked Nolan.

"The army is moving away from locating planes by sound and will be using radar. The men in the location units need to have radar skills. You'll get assignments as power plant operators or truck drivers. With you close by, we can use your skills if the new radar technology fails for some reason."

"You'll need us," the man said. "Them radar is too complicated. You can count on it. They'll fail."

"And we will need your support when they do. Talk to Lieutenant Sessions about an assignment that'll keep you close so you can step in when needed. I'll put in a good word for all of you."

More tedious testing of the remaining men followed. I had not expected to spend my days as an officer like this. No excitement, no variety, just testing and choosing who stayed and who left. Eventually, I was down to sixty men. We reviewed some practical skills that would be useful in sound location and radar. I now had two men for every position I had to fill. The training process would weed out the extras, and we would finish with the highest quality radar specialists possible.

***

Henderson took us Lieutenants back to Gordo's at the end of the week, the first chance for all the battery officers to interact socially outside of work. It made a huge difference in our ability to work together. Henderson knew how to form a team from men with different skills, different values, and backgrounds. I'll give him that.

"Gordo! Corona and number five all around!" he demanded as we pulled tables together to accommodate all eight of us.

"And you be sure you save me some flan," Carson said.

"I put it aside when I saw you coming," the waitress told him.

"First, there's a little business we need to take care of," Henderson said as soon as the waitress had the order. "The army has new fitness standards. We start testing and training tomorrow."

"How much testing and training is this damn unit going to go through before we get into this war?" said Tilton, who sat across the table from me.

"We will train and test until we have the numbers to be battle-ready,'" Henderson replied. "Did you see how chaotic the arrival was on Monday?"

"Damn right I did," Tilton said. "Those draftees don't know a thing about army discipline. That's what you get when you try to make an army from amateurs."

"We need manpower. We have to make an army of these amateurs. Continue skills training in the morning. I'll assign each of you to a testing station for physical fitness in the afternoon. Test yourself first. If you don't pass, work on it."

The waitress brought the beer, and business was over.

"Gene Sinclair," I said, extending my hand to Tilton.

"First Lieutenant Sam Tilton," he said, emphasizing the First. He and Sessions were the only First Lieutenants in the battery.

"Are you one of those ninety-day wonders?"

"I'm afraid I am," I said. "Yourself?"

"I graduated from West Point last year," he said. "Spent my plebe year under the thumb of Henderson himself. Now there's a man's man if I ever saw one. Wants to end this war as a general, and I bet he makes it."

I wasn't so sure. Henderson knew the army inside out but seemed too focused on himself to be a good general. He didn't have the vision or the political savvy to become a general.

"That big, quiet guy down there is Mac Douglas," continued Tilton. "He's a ninety-day wonder too. Owns a farm in Pennsylvania."

Brasseux's voice peremptorily drowned out all the conversation. "Anybody get a load a dat cute little hat check gal at da officer's club?"

"Now that one's a looker," said Tilton. "I've got my eyes on her."

"Not if I get to her first," Brasseux said. "Name's Becky, and she says she loves to dance."

"I would stay away from her if I were you," I said.

"Why? You laid claim to her already?"

"No, but she calls the General Daddy,"

"Whoa," Brasseux said, sitting back.

Tilton's eyes got big. "I'm forever in your debt, man," he said. "I came close to ruining my career before it even started."

Gordo and the waitress brought out the meals, and the conversation stopped for the shoveling.

***

"That's four fails, private. The test ends now," I said.

"I know I can do more. Let me try again, Lieutenant."

"No. Go on to the squat jumps."

I stood at the chin-up bar, recording the scores as the men completed as many chin-ups as possible. The test ended if the soldier dropped off the bar, could not pull himself up, or performed four incomplete chin-ups. A passing score was six chin-ups. After years of lifting hay bales to feed the animals we'd always kept, I passed with ease, but we had a long way to go before everyone in the unit passed.

Henderson came to check on the scores.

"Dismal," I told him.

"If they can't pass by the end of six weeks, they'll be discharged. We can't afford to lose that many men." He walked away, shaking his head. He turned back to me." Be sure to tell them." Inspiration via delegation.

Morning radar training, a review for Camp Davis's draftees, was new to the men who had been in the pre-war sound locator group, and the Camp Davis men had no training or experience in sound location. I split the group. Half trained on radar and half on the big sound amplification cones each day. I made sure there were old guards and recruits in each group.

At least within my group, the old hands and draftees worked well together, teaching each other skills and techniques. I just had to make sure the equipment was up and functioning. We used the SCR 286 radar and sound location horns from the 1920s. Planes were continually coming and going at the airfield, and we tracked them all morning with radar and sound locators.

I spent a little more time on radar theory than the training manual said I should. The way I saw it, if the men understood how the radar worked, they would be more prepared to deal with whatever came up. Henderson heard about my classes and came to talk with me.

"Sinclair," he asked as we were about to leave for lunch one day, "What do you mean to accomplish by talking to these men about electromagnetic waves, wavelength, and velocity? Teach by the book! All these men need to know is how to read those screens and find the planes. Give them more real-life experience and less of this mamby pamby about reflection and stuff. We need to prepare for war, not have some sort of physics class."

"Yes, sir," I replied, "but objects other than airplanes also reflect the waves, and they need to learn to interpret that."

"Sinclair, I will expect you to go by the book from now on!"

"Yes, sir," I replied. I wished he had not done that in front of the men.

Afternoon fitness training, on the other hand, was torture for everyone. The temperature reached into the nineties, sometimes above one hundred degrees. Within the week, summer arrived. June 21.

If the Japs hadn't attacked Pearl Harbor, I would be out of the army now, free to go to medical school, make up my own mind about things. It didn't help that Morris sent me a letter describing training to fly bombers. He was having a great time soaring and diving while I was stuck here, forcing men to exercise, then take salt pills to avoid heatstroke.

Looking back, it didn't seem like a year had passed. I had managed to come to terms with my situation by focusing on the men I worked with, making the ridiculous rules of the army less onerous whenever possible. However, I still chafed at losing my freedom and not being allowed to make my own decisions.

"Can't we switch fitness training to the morning?" asked Private Barkley, a particularly curious recruit. I totally agreed with him and thought it would be better all-around if we could do the fitness training in the morning, but I didn't want to buck Henderson on it.

"Orders say afternoon. The army wants us to be tough. I think the training is meant to acclimate us to the heat." I told him.

"So, we are going to North Africa?"

"I have no idea." I suspected that Barkley was correct, though.

***

A letter from my gal Sarah Gale, one from Mom, a box of cookies from my sister Doris and a postcard from my boot camp buddy Morris, who had just completed advance pilot training and was off to combat school. Not a bad haul for one mail delivery. I thanked the private who had located the cookies, probably crumbs by now from the looks of the box, and headed back to the unmarried officer's quarters, stirring up the ubiquitous dust of summer at Fort Bliss, Texas.

"Sinclair, we got ahold of a little Mary Jane. Wanna join us?" Brasseux called as I approached.

"I don't know. I have some letters here I'd like to read."

226

"Come on, Sinclair, don't be a drip. Come and take a puff," taunted Carson.

I sat down on the step and puffed on the hand-rolled cigarette Brasseux handed me. I sniffed the loose leaves in the bag next to me and recognized the distinctive aroma of marijuana. It grew wild on the ditch banks at home, and Granny used it for headaches and added it to her cough medicine.

The cigarette came around to me again.

"I really shouldn't," I said.

"Aw, come on, Sinclair. Don't be such a fuddy-duddy. Take another drag."

I did and passed it on to Carson, next to me.

My eyes dropped to the letters in my hand, the one from Morris sitting on top. I became mesmerized with the letter as it sat unopened in my hands, until Brasseux nudged me and handed me the cigarette stub.

I started to feel light-headed after drawing in the smoke. The porch lights faded, and I was transported into the all too real dream-like world of Arthur St. Clair and the Revolutionary War.

***

When I woke on the porch, St. Clair's words still reverberated in my mind. The letters I had been carrying lay beside me, along with the cookie box, empty. It must have been a dream. But why was I sleeping on the porch? I searched my mind—the marijuana we had smoked. I must have had a bizarre reaction to it. I stood, swaying a little, and walked carefully to my room. In the hallway, Carson spotted me

"So, you're up and at em. We couldn't rouse you last night. That stuff we smoked was pretty strong. I think somebody put something in it. Could have been opium. Brasseux said he got it in Mexico. All of us were woozy by the end of the evenin. Are you feeling up to snuff this mornin?"

"I'm fine," I said, mentally checking my body to make sure it was toned, fit, young, and alive. "What day is it?"

"It's Sunday. Don't worry! We wouldn't have left you out there all day. We were just a bit too off-balance last night to carry you in and everything."

"Sunday. I think I'm going to sleep a little longer."

"You look like you need it," Carson smirked.

He continued to the bathroom as I entered my bedroom. Sessions still slept, so I slipped out of my clothes and crawled into bed. But the experience had been too strange to allow my mind to rest. Had this really happened, or was it a hallucination or a dream? It felt real. Arthur St. Clair was me, but at the same time, wasn't me. While I was there, I could remember this existence but could only act as St. Clair. Here and now, I could remember that experience but could only act like myself.

I knew the treaty with the Indians wouldn't last. None of the original treaties had, but I had been unable to let St. Clair know. Had he been able to sense my presence at all? Thoughts went round and round in my mind getting me nowhere. I kept returning to the statement, "I hold that no man has a right to withhold his services when his country needs him. I'll serve if called."

I had to think of something else.

I switched on the bedside light and read the letter from Sarah Gale.

July 11, 1942

Dear Gene,

I'm accepted into the WAACs. I have to report on August 14. They sent me a list of things we are supposed to bring. It includes two pairs of slacks and two pairs of shorts. I have never worn anything but dresses in my entire life. The stores here don't even have pants or shorts for women. So I don't know where I'll get them. The army doesn't have enough uniforms because it is so early in the corps, so we will be doing some of the training in these slacks and shorts we are supposed to bring.

I resigned from the laundry as soon as I got the letter. They wanted two weeks' notice, so I'll be working until July 24. Then I'll be at home for three weeks before I have to report to the Elizabethtown recruitment station. Granny has turned the family around about my enlistment. I'm so happy about that. I would be so upset if I had to leave with my parents still angry at me. I have no idea how Granny did it.

I have waited for this for so long. Now that I have done it, I'm a little nervous. I'll have to travel to Des Moines, Iowa, for basic training. I have never been that far from home before. I get restless on the train rides to Camp Davis. I have no idea how I'll be able to stand the trip to Des Moines. Then I'll have to go through basic training. To hear you and my brothers talk about it, that will be tough. And I'll be away from my family for who knows how long. At least they won't have to worry about me getting killed. They say WAACs will be in safe positions far from the front.

I love you
Sarah Gale Simmons, WAAC

Why would her parents be angry with her? In England, female volunteers were already keeping the country and the military operating while the men fought. American women should have that opportunity, too. If we had to go off to combat, someone needed to take care of the work here.

My mind more settled now, I understood that no man, or woman, has a right to withhold his services when his country needs him—or her. On the contrary, it is a person's patriotic duty to serve when called.

CHAPTER 19
EXECUTIVE OFFICER

Monday morning, I still felt slightly disoriented. I couldn't say whether it was caused by the drugs and strange out of body experience or lack of sleep. Probably both.

A private knocked on my door. Captain Henderson wanted me to report to his office. I ambled to the long, low headquarters building, hoping I was not in trouble for the weekend incident. The sun's glare bouncing off the fresh white paint on the buildings and even more brightly off the windows hurt my eyes.

"Sessions got promoted—to CO of Battery G," Henderson announced as I walked in. "I'm making you my Executive Officer. That's your desk." He pointed to the metal desk, papers already stacked in the inbox. "This is Corporal Fitzgerald, your clerk, and PFC Perry, your radioman.

I cringed. But St. Clair's voice in my head declared, *'no man has a right to withhold his services when his country needs him.'* "Yes, sir." I hesitated. "May I ask why you chose me? We see things so differently."

"Squires says a CO and his a second in command should see things differently, and you're as different as I could find. Besides, you would never make a decent platoon officer in a combat situation. I can keep an eye on you and make sure you go by the book if you're here." After a pause, he said, "I requested an early promotion for you. An executive officer has to be at least a first lieutenant."

"Thank you, sir."

"I'm not sure it's something to thank me for. You'll be dealing with all the boring reports and supervising the staff. You'll have to talk with other units, liaison and deal with personnel and personal problems. Probably be the one to stay up all night once we get to the field. Keep me briefed on all issues regarding operations."

"Yes, sir, I understand."

I wrote to Sarah Gale, expressing my concerns about Henderson's attitude. Why didn't he think I could lead a platoon into combat—not that I really wanted to. And being a liaison with other troops seemed fun, although I didn't look forward to all the paperwork. I found paperwork to be the most frustrating thing about the army, and now it would be a huge part of my job.

***

The men did make good progress. By the end of the six-week training program, a week after my promotion, all of them had passed the fitness test.

"I'm so glad fitness training is over," I said after the final examination.

"We're not finished," said Tilton. "Next week, we start battle conditioning."

"Oh." I groaned. "What does that entail?"

"Marching, starting at five miles, working up to thirty, hand to hand combat, a fifteen-foot rope climb, and a rappel off a thirty-foot tower."

We marched until we could barely put one foot in front of the other. Then we had to go back to camp and fight. First, we learned judo, jiujitsu, and karate, battle techniques new to army training since we had started fighting the Japanese. We bayoneted dummies repeatedly and learned to wield a knife and machete, hacking our way through stands of tall cane sorghum planted for machete practice. Next, we moved on to stands of dense creosote, mesquite, and saltbush, the more difficult task. The training also involved confidence-building exercises so the soldiers would act as a team under pressure. We formed squads, crawled, climbed, swung, and jumped across the combat training course.

"Lieutenant Sinclair, we're a searchlight battalion. Why should we have to do all this?" asked Private Barkley.

"Because we will be a searchlight battalion in the middle of a war. We won't just be standing on a hill watching the sky. There's every chance the enemy will sneak up on our emplacement in the dark and attack us. We'll always be working, day and night, including in the dark when most of the army will be sleeping." Surprisingly that seemed not to have occurred to some of the men, based on their reaction to my response. Maybe they preferred not to think about it. I could think of little else, even in my dreams.

Finally, we went to the gun range, where targets bobbed and wove across the field. We shot them up pretty good with Tommy guns. Next, we lobbed grenades at the grenade range, where the targets moved more slowly, like tanks. The entire battery rated excellent on both Tommy guns and grenades.

Sarah Gale's reply to my letter finally arrived.

July 25, 1942

Dear Gene,

I got your letter yesterday. Congratulations on your promotion. I think you will be very good at the job despite the paperwork. My approach to things like that is to get the unpleasant tasks out of the way first, as quickly as possible, then move on to the more interesting things. That way, you are not tempted to avoid the unpleasant and let it build up until it becomes a huge barrier to getting anything done. Fortunately, with the variety of your duties, you won't have to spend all of your time with Henderson. Instead, you can go check on the platoons or visit another unit to liaise, or whatever you call it. I am sure you will enjoy that part.

I have left Camp Davis for good. I did enjoy that job at first, but after you left and I applied to the WAACs, it became a matter of just putting in the time. Of course, as soon as I came home, it was back to work, especially now that the three oldest boys are in the service. Robby left a week ago. He joined the Navy. He has always been the least aggressive one. I hope it was a good *choice for him.*

Mama refuses to talk at all about my enlistment. At least, thanks to Granny, she doesn't say anything negative about it anymore. I still have a little over two weeks before I leave. Hopefully, we can have a good conversation or two before I go. I would hate to go off to the WAACs feeling that I am letting my mother down. Yet I am determined to do it, no matter what.

I did find some shorts and pants in a store in Wilmington. I wore the shorts one day, just to see what it felt like. I enjoyed the feel of it, but Granny was appalled. I reassured her that they were only for exercise and that the army men would never see us dressed like that. I actually think they might see us, but I prefer that she doesn't know that. Anyway, the shorts were cool, and it is really easy to move around without worrying about skirts and stockings.

Have to go weed the garden. Take care and be safe.

Love,

Sarah Gale

***

"Today, we check the training levels of all the sections. This manual describes the tests." Henderson handed it to me. "I'll take radar, searchlights, and transportation. You take power plants, communications, and gunners. You have about an hour to prepare."

That day I found out every one of the power plant operators knew what they were doing. They got the plant operational and attached all the cables correctly in record time. So, I sabotaged the equipment. Almost immediately, men ran to the sabotage site and fixed the problem. They could troubleshoot anything I threw at them. To my amazement, their training officer had been Carson. I had always wondered why Henderson hadn't found cause to discipline him. Despite his off-duty whining and arguing, he performed very well on the job. Granny often said, "Don't judge a book by its cover."

The gunners were competent, for the most part. The gun batteries got the best gunners, so we got the men who could handle a machine gun by and large and eventually hit something.

Communication was another story.

"Brasseux, we have a problem with our radio operators," I informed him.

"Whasat?" he asked, sounding a bit skeptical.

"Radio operators have to pronounce things a certain way. They should exaggerate some sounds because the radio makes them more difficult to understand."

"I bin doin my best. Dey gave me a manual about it, and I gave it to de men. Dey know how to work de radio, and dey are good at fixin de tings. I taught em dat. It's just dat in de Bayou we have some problems sayin tings de way de book says."

I thought, *Good God, you think your men are from the bayou?*

"I understand," I said instead. "What skills do you have other than radio repair?"

"I'm good at anyt'ing electrical."

"I'll talk to the CO," I said. Brasseux nodded, knowing Henderson would reassign him.

Henderson and I met back at HQ.

"The radar operators passed with flying colors. You taught them well. I'll put Tilton there," Henderson said. "He's an engineer. He probably understands what those things do.

"I put the drivers on steep, uneven roads. They managed. Douglas got the career men to work with the recruits. I like that.

"Wright didn't teach the searchlight operators anything. We're a searchlight unit, for God's sake. They have to do it right. They did everything wrong. I don't know what Wright was thinking. How did it go on your end?"

"The radio men understand the technical aspects," I began, "but I can't understand them when they speak. They haven't worked on pronunciation at all. Brasseux speaks Cajun, so that's the problem. Wright seems to speak clearly. Why don't we assign him to teach the radio operators? Brasseux can deal with searchlight operators. He said he could handle anything electrical."

"How are the other units?" he asked.

"Power plant operators are highly skilled, quickly solving the sabotage I did on their plants. The gunners are the best we can get under the circumstances. They did okay."

"Seems we're ready to proceed to unit training. We'll form platoons tomorrow. You assign the enlisted men. Three platoons of searchlights and radar. Mechanics, cooks, radio operators, and supply in the HQ platoon."

Fortunately, a manual on equipment and personnel gave me more detail on making the assignments. If I was lucky, I could read manuals fast enough to keep up with Henderson's expectations.

Later I sought out Wright and asked him about his performance with the searchlight training.

"I got off on the wrong foot with them. They're mostly old army. I'm the newest and youngest lieutenant here. They performed poorly on purpose. They know how to do it. They wanted to get me in trouble."

"Mr. Wright, you may be the youngest lieutenant, but you *are* a lieutenant, and you know how to give an order. You'll soon be assigned to replace Brasseux as Communications Officer. Teach the radio operators how to enunciate over the radio in American Standard English. To be understood over the radio, they will have to speak some words more loudly and clearly than others. Take charge and believe in yourself."

"Who assigned Brasseux to teach them to talk properly?" asked Wright. "He has an incomprehensible accent."

"He did an excellent job teaching them to set up, operate, and repair the radios. Your emphasis will be language, pronunciation in particular while keeping up their technical skills."

"I should be able. Since I was ten years old, I've performed in the Little Theater at home. And my mother was a stickler for proper enunciation. And I did ham radio and got good grades in physics in high school."

I returned to my office to tackle the platoon assignments.

***

Early one morning, I stood outside HQ reading a letter I had received from Sarah Gale before starting work.

August 16, 1942

Dear Gene,

I have never been so tired in all my life. When I got on the train in Norfolk, a sailor sat down beside me and started flirting audaciously with me. (Don't you like my vocabulary?) He got off in Richmond, so I only had to put up with him for about an hour and a half. It seemed like forever at the time, but it wasn't much in light of the length of the whole trip. I just listened to his overtures, unhappy about them, wishing he would get the message from my silence.

Next, a businessman from Cincinnati sat next to me. He talked on and on about his business concerns. I dozed off. He didn't seem to notice. Just kept talking, I guess. I excused myself and went to lunch in the dining car when I woke up. The dining car people were very kind to me. The food was great! I had a hearty bean soup with cornbread. They gave me a free bowl of ice cream when I told them I was on my way to join the WAACs. I took your advice and gave them a generous tip. They let me stay in the dining car until we got to Charlottesville shortly after two in the afternoon.

I went back to my seat and listened to the man from Cincinnati talk about the baseball team. I know you like baseball, and I don't mind watching a game, but he listed statistics on players I sure didn't know for hours.

He complained a lot that the war had taken away the best baseball players. Doesn't he know that we will lose more than good baseball players if we don't fight this war? He got off in Charleston, and an old woman sat next to me. Once we got underway, she fell asleep and sagged toward me. She laid her head on my shoulder, almost pushing me off my seat. I couldn't sleep. So I pressed my legs against the base of the bench in front of me until the dining car opened. I figured it was something I could do for her. She was so sound asleep that I could push her in the other direction without waking her up so she could snooze on her own. I hope I helped her neck!

That early, the dining car was nearly empty. So I ordered myself a big breakfast, ate slowly, then sat there, sipping my coffee. When the dining car filled up and a line of people waited in the next car for their breakfast, I finally returned to the passenger car. Almost everyone was eating breakfast, including the old woman, so I got an hour's sound sleep.

The old woman got off at the next stop, and a woman about my age named Mary sat next to me. We started talking, and I found out that her husband had died somewhere in the Pacific. He was in the navy. I got really sad and started thinking about how I would feel if you got killed. I started crying, and she ended up comforting me. I was humiliated. I got so upset at the thought of what might happen to you that I couldn't be helpful to someone who had just lost her husband. She said it helped her to be talking to someone who could understand how it felt, even though I hadn't experienced it. She told me that AAA officers are less likely to get killed than airmen, infantry, or marines. Still, I don't think I could deal with losing you.

Mary's father met her in Chicago. After I said goodbye to her, I looked for the platform to catch the train to Des Moines, but I got turned around. Chicago's Union Station is huge, with trains coming and going everywhere. We had arrived in Chicago just after noon. My train didn't leave until after five, but I didn't know how to find the right platform. Finally, I decided if I ate something, I could think more clearly. I overheard a group of women talking about going to WAAC training in the sandwich shop, so I asked if I could join them. Before long, I had made friends and was much less worried about everything. One of my new friends was from Chicago and knew the station like I know the woods around our house. She got us all to the right platform at the right time.

Almost every woman on the train is a WAAC recruit. Most everybody is asleep now, but I wanted to get this letter written to you. I'll post it as soon as

I can. I'm going to sleep now, the first full night's sleep in a couple of days. I am sure I will dream of you!

Be safe until I see you again.

All my love,

Sarah Gale

Henderson arrived as I finished reading the letter. He looked at the envelope as I put the letter back into it. "A letter from Des Moines?"

"My girl is there. She's starting WAAC training."

"Oh yeah? My family is in Des Moines. My Dad commands the post there. I'll be sending my wife and son to stay with my folks when we go overseas,"

I wondered if Henderson would be willing to introduce his family to Sarah Gale. It would be nice for her to know someone there.

"Here are the officer's assignments," Henderson said, handing me the clipboard. "Get the orders typed up. Do you have the platoon assignments?"

"Yes, sir, here they are."

He looked at the lists.

"How did you decide on these assignments?" he asked. He sounded a bit amazed.

"I based them on scores and longevity," I said. "We need twelve searchlight squads, so I took the top twelve old army men and assigned them one per squad. Then I took the top twelve recruits and assigned them in the opposite order. We need six radar squads, so I did the same thing with radar scores. Then I assigned the next highest scores to each squad. Finally, I assigned drivers and gunners to each platoon."

He looked at me for a second, his mouth squinched, then smoothed as he nodded curtly. "You take paper-pushing to a whole new level." In what way? I worried. Had I done well or lousy? My new commitment to duty made it all the more critical. I handed the list to Fitzgerald.

"Assemble the battery." He walked toward his desk, shaking his head.

I picked up the officer assignments. Tilton remained radar officer and Douglas maintenance officer. Wright had been reassigned to be communications officer. Brasseux and Carson would lead platoons. The third platoon CO would be Sessions' replacement, scheduled to arrive soon.

Now that the men understood the necessary skills, our goal became to get them to work together as they would in the field. We began cross-training as well. Henderson or I would walk up and tap men on the shoulder to take them out. Other men from different assignments would step into that position. We would have loved to have been able to train under different atmospheric conditions, but summer in the Southwestern desert was hot and dry, with only brief thunderstorms. We set up searchlight layouts, power circuits, and telephone lines in different terrain, always under clear, hot skies.

Besides the training exercises, I met with officers in our battery and other batteries, getting to know all the battalion officers. These opportunities to talk with other people and share ideas energized me enough that I could get through the tedious work of reviewing and signing daily reports, orders, and requisitions.

One night, I came back from a late dinner to find my gear in the hallway and someone else's gear scattered all over my room.

"What's going on here?!" I shouted.

"Ron Edelstein," the man removing the equipment said. "I'm replacing Lieutenant Sessions in this room, but his stuff's still all over the place. What gives?"

"Sessions already moved his gear to the captain's quarters. This is *my* gear. *That* is your side of the room, and this is mine."

He stood silent for a moment. "You mean to say we have to share a room?"

"Yes! We do."

"Why didn't they tell me? I thought, as an officer, I'd get private quarters."

"You thought wrong, Edelstein. Private rooms go to Captains and higher. Now replace my gear and get your gear out of my side of the room. Now!"

"What's with you? Nobody told me," he said as he dragged his duffel bag across the room.

"What's with me is I am the Executive Officer of this battalion, so you will honor my requests without complaint. When I get back, I expect to see all my gear back where it was and in good order!"

Leaving Edelstein to repair his nonsense, I went down to my favorite overstuffed chair in the officer's lounge to read Sarah Gale's latest letter. She sure can write. I wished I had enough time to respond to her letters as soon as they came in.

August 27, 1942

Dear Gene,

We didn't get to the training center until after midnight. They unloaded us and told us to pick bunks and go to sleep. First, of course, we had to make our bed. Some of us hadn't had baths or showers for three days, so it took a while before we all got into bed and got settled. They woke us up at six to go to the mess for breakfast and then to the induction facility.

When we got to the induction facility, we had to go through some very embarrassing procedures. They said it was not as bad as what they make the men go through, but we did get physical exams and shots. After that, they made us put on our uniforms in front of everybody. A seamstress tailored them to look neat and hemmed them just below the knees. Of course, living in the barracks, we will have to get dressed in front of each other every day. That will take a little getting used to. We got one uniform for now. They are busy making more for us. We also got a pair of slacks and two T-shirts for exercise. We wear them quite often. I had never realized how comfortable pants could be. We don't have to worry at all about bending over or sitting like ladies.

Some of the girls have complained about the amount of exercise and march-

ing. I'm used to being active, and the marching is less than the distance I had to walk to school. So, I don't mind it, except that we had to do an obstacle course the other day. We had to crawl through the mud! Now I know why the boys got their uniforms so dirty when I washed them in the laundry.

The food is pretty good. The cake is right up at the beginning of the food line, then potatoes. They even have bread and butter ahead of the meat. Vegetables are last. We would never set up a potluck back home that way. It is always salad and Jell-O first, then main dishes, of course, always meat, then vegetables, bread and butter, and finally desserts. Not that I mind so much. I'm famished by the time I get there, and I can nibble on cake while I wait for the girls before me to fill their trays. The officers ordered us to take some of everything.

Some of the girls think they are going to gain weight, but I think we are so active we'll work it all off. The other day the menu said BBQ Chicken. I got so excited to have some home cooking. When I got there, I found a chicken smothered in some sort of tomato sauce and cooked until the skin and sauce were crispy. They didn't even have any vinegar to put on it, only more spicy tomato sauce. A girl from Kansas City told me that's what BBQ is in these parts.

We are learning about army procedures, office skills, mail sorting, and operating a telephone bank. I'm glad you showed me how to read maps and compasses. I was way ahead in that class. There are no landmarks out here, and we have to figure out which way to go to get to a place on a map. It is easier to get somewhere here than at home because there are no swamps in the way, but it is a little scary to be so exposed. There is nothing but miles and miles of cornfields around Des Moines.

Yesterday afternoon, I saw a gigantic storm coming across the fields from miles away. It was magnificent and frightening at the same time. You told me about those storms, I remember. When the storm finally arrived at camp, we *were at dinner. It turned out to be one of the most spectacular thunderstorms I have ever seen. Then it was gone, and the stars were out by dark. Back home, we would have hunkered down all night listening to the storm beat on the roof and worrying whether the creek would flood the tobacco field!*

I miss you so much. I hope we get stationed close to each other.

Love,

Sarah Gale

Reverend Marshall lounged in a nearby chair, allegedly reading a book.

"That must have been some letter," he said. "It was fascinating watching your face as you read it."

"It's from my gal at WAAC basic training in Iowa. She's never been out of North Carolina. She made the trip come alive for me in her letter. I miss her a lot."

"She must be quite some girl," Marshall said.

"Oh, she is," I assured him

A private ran into the common room. "Sir," he said to me, "Captain Henderson wants to see you right away. Do you know where Lieutenant Tilton is?"

"Check his room," I said as I stalked out. What now?

Tilton arrived at Headquarters right behind me.

"Thank you for coming at such a late hour. Tomorrow morning, both of you to report to Regiment HQ for training on a new kind of radar. I want both of you to get up to speed on it.

***

At Battalion HQ, a single truck carrying a power unit and a trailer sat in front of the building.

"Didn't they bring the antennae?" Tilton asked me.

"I don't know; let's see what they've got."

Other officers were gathering with us around the truck and trailer.

A captain walked out of HQ and climbed the steps of the trailer. "I am Captain Eddy! This is a demonstration of the new

SCR 584. First the setup. Level the trailer, then brace it to prevent movement," he ordered. Two privates emerged from the trailer. They placed four braces, turning cranks at each corner of the trailer to move it up or down until it was level according to the leveling bubbles built into the trailer frame.

"The antenna folds flat for transport," announced the captain. The privates unfolded and deployed a circular antenna on top of the trailer. We pushed and shoved to get a better view of the small antenna.

"Attach the cables to the power unit," ordered the captain. The soldiers ran with the cables to the truck and plugged them into the power unit.

The entire process took about fifteen minutes.

"Our radar is now operational, gentlemen." The captain glared at us, we not being gentlemen. "The detection range is thirty-nine point seven miles. Automatic tracking range is eighteen point two miles. It can control lights and guns within fifteen miles." Then, glaring at us again, he ordered rather than suggested, "If the first six of you could come inside, we will show you how it works."

Tilton and I had pushed our way to the front of the crowd, so we stepped inside. Desk chairs sat in front of the radar screens and equipment. Operators would be out of the rain and sun as they tracked targets. It almost made radar location a *desk* job.

The captain said, "This radial screen is slightly different from the scopes you have used before. See how these signals show up every time the antenna sweeps in this direction? The radar is now in helical scan mode. Once the target gets within range, the system will lock the radar onto the target. It will also relay the location to guns and lights, automatically aiming them at the target. The system can operate at four frequencies. The range error is twenty-five yards, with an elevation error of point six degrees."

I leaned over to get a better view of the screen. "Incredible," I said. "It can locate several targets at once. How do you lock on all of them?"

"A system should be developed within your battery, so each radar focuses on different parts of the sky as necessary. Depending on the distance and direction of the enemy aircraft, different units lock on different targets. Or redirect if only one or two targets are found."

"How long will it be before we get these in the field?" Tilton asked.

"It should be available in May of next year."

"Who manufactures it?" I asked

"It is a cooperative effort between Chrysler and General Electric."

And I owned a dryland farm in Kansas rather than stock in General Electric. My heart sank.

We continued examining the controls and screens.

"Gentlemen," proclaimed the captain, "Please move outside so others can get a look."

We left the trailer so the next group could come in.

"That's the most incredible thing I have ever seen," I exclaimed. "Radar always amazed me. Now it's so improved it's not even the same thing. We can track air traffic from all directions. I have to go tell Henderson," I gushed.

"Tell him, but he won't care," said Tilton. "It'll be many months before it's in the field. Until he has to use it, he won't be interested."

Tilton was right. Henderson barely listened to my explanation of what we had seen.

When I finished, he looked up from the papers he was reading and announced, "Tomorrow we go to encampment number four. We'll see how well we can work with other batteries under actual field conditions." He paused, then added, "With what we have now."

CHAPTER 20
THE ENCAMPMENT

Three medics burst through the door of HQ as the battery assembled outside.

"Oh, good. We're on time," the one in the lead blurted out.

Henderson glared at them.

"Sir, platoon medics reporting for duty," the taller one in back declared, all three saluting when Henderson acknowledged them, then motioned for me to deal with the medics.

"Follow me, men," I ordered. "What are your names?"

"I'm Corporal Volkerson," said the one who had first spoken up. "O'Neill and Robertson," he pointed. I quickly evaluated them as we headed outside. Volkerson, short, thin, freckled with a mop of red hair. He looked so Irish that for weeks I would call him O'Neill. O'Neill a bit taller with a tanned face, brown hair, and rugged features. Robertson tall, dark-haired, and well-built. O'Neill seemed to be Volkerson's sidekick. Robertson followed behind, silently amused by the two younger medics. I guessed that his response to the other two would bode well.

"OK," I said, writing their names in the little notebook I kept in my pocket. "I'll introduce you to your platoon leaders."

Brasseux's platoon was at ease outside the door.

"Brasseux, this is Corporal O'Neill. He's the medic who'll accompany your platoon.

Brasseux nodded a greeting, then, slapping O'Neill on the shoulder, said, "Good t' meet ya. Tek up your position in the platoon."

We walked a little farther to where Carson's platoon was forming up. "Carson, your medic, Corporal Volkerson."

"Welcome, Corporal Volkerson. Glad to have your services."

Continuing to where Edelstein stood yelling at his platoon, I interrupted him.

"I'm busy here. This had better be important," he said.

"Your medic, Corporal Robertson."

"What do I need a medic for?" he demanded, sounding exasperated. He looked suspiciously at Robertson.

"A medic accompanies every platoon to handle injuries or illnesses," I explained.

After snorting derisively, Edelstein said, "All right, medic, line up with these damned idiots."

A fleeting frown crossed Robertson's expressive face as he walked to the rear of the platoon. The men stood at attention, their eyes darting back and forth.

"Put your men at ease, Edelstein," I whispered.

Edelstein shot daggers at me and ignored the order.

I put my hand on his shoulder.

"What is this all about?" I hissed.

"Here's the deal. They need to learn to respect me. That platoon is slow to obey my orders. I was punishing them for not forming up quickly enough."

"I don't know that making them stand at attention for long periods will make them obey more quickly. They should be at ease now to show proper respect by coming to attention when Henderson arrives."

"If this doesn't work, I'll find something that will," he declared.

Henderson emerged from HQ. The other two platoon leaders called their men to attention.

"The full regiment is doing maneuvers in an encampment to the north. You have thirty minutes to pack your gear and be back here. Dismissed."

The men ran off to their barracks. Edelstein and I walked to our room without speaking to each other

With our gear loaded into our trucks and jeeps, we took off to the north. The drive to the encampment took three hours on bumpy trails through the desert. By the time we reached the campsite and got our tents set up, it was getting dark.

***

The wind blew continually, carrying fine sand with it. We woke to sand in our bedrolls, ate sand in our meals, dumped sand from our socks and boots, and brushed sand from our hair and every crack and fold of our bodies. We bathed with a towel dipped in a helmet full of water, sand rubbing our skin despite the water, and shook our clothes out but did not wash them.

The radar men on duty during the day came in with sunburned faces and sweat-soaked clothes.

"Get something from the medic for that sunburn," I told Private Nash. "It looks awful,"

"I'm afraid Lieutenant Edelstein will call me a baby and come up with some sort of punishment because I'm weak," he said. "Edelstein pretty much keeps Robertson isolated. Only lets him hand out ointments or salt pills to reward good behavior."

"I'll talk to Edelstein. You go get that taken care of."

I approached Edelstein. "Lieutenant, we need to keep our men healthy. They must be at peak fitness to win this war. I am aware you are withholding basic care. Please have Robertson check out all your men every day. He can give them whatever aid they need to stay in tip-top shape. It's imperative to the war effort, and they'll respect you for understanding that."

"Are you giving the other platoon leaders the same order, or is this just for me. I think you've got it in for me."

"I am giving you an order, and I expect you to follow it," I said. "I will check on the level of care the other platoons are receiving."

First, I went to Robertson and explained the order. I promised him some extra supplies so he could hand them out generously. Then I visited Brasseux's platoon.

"O'Neill mingles with de men all de time," Brasseux said. "He knows dem better dan I do." I t'ink de men are all band-aided up!"

I drove the jeep to Carson's platoon's campsite.

"Volkerson's a pain in the ass. He's always looking for the worst and nags the men constantly about salt pills and zinc oxide," complained Carson. "But he is keepin em hydrated and healthy. I don't see any issues besides Volkerson's ragging on the men."

I hoped my inroads about medical care worked out.

Those of us on duty at night were more comfortable. The temperature was around eighty degrees at sunset, but in the sixties, by the middle of the night. We didn't have to stand in direct sunlight. But we slept fitfully in sweltering tents with guns blasting sporadically nearby during the day. At least we were in the shade.

"You know, I bet you we ship out to Africa," said Douglas at the mess one evening. "I mean, Africa has deserts like this. So it's the most likely place."

"This isn't exactly the Sahara," I replied. "It's a lot hotter and drier there than it is here."

"Knowin the army, they'll ship us to some southeast Asia jungle after trainin us here," drawled Carson, more Texas in his voice than usual.

"I think they're training us here because there's lots of territory with no civilians who could get hurt," I said. "They'll send us where they want to send us."

"Damn right they will, and we had better be ready for hell on earth," said Edelstein.

The following day, I talked with Henderson. "Edelstein treats his men very poorly. He expects them to perform perfectly and gives them no slack at all, no chance to let down even when they're not on duty. Last night, he also said we should expect hell on earth when we ship out."

"And where do you think we are going? To a tea party?" Henderson rejoined. "Edelstein's men perform better than any other platoon. He's toughening them up, and they're responding. I don't think you need to worry about it. His command style differs from yours. He paused. "War *is* hell on earth," he said, confirming Edelstein's perspective.

I decided to take a different approach with Edelstein.

"Edelstein, your approaches have done the trick. Your men have the highest scores in the battery. You can relax and ease up a bit now." I told him.

"Are you crazy? We're fighting a war. We can't ease up until we've defeated the Krauts and the Japs. There is nothing easy about that".

My new approach sure hadn't worked. Edelstein's men were responding, but ruling by fear went against everything I believed. I worried that something terrible might happen because Henderson was no help.

At the executive officers' daily meetings, we talked about how to improve our performance. We all agreed that the regiment's current command structure of ten batteries made it unwieldy. As a result, we couldn't coordinate orders effectively.

The old army veterans and recruits were mildly at odds in several batteries. The men with experience could take and execute orders and complain much less, but they did not know the new guns or radar. The new men had worked with the ninety-millimeter guns, automatic weapons, and radar, but they tended to look down on the older men. We had less of that problem in our battery, which pleased Henderson to no end because he often spoke to the men about what we tried to do, the need to share the skills we had and teach each other. In our battery, a few of the old guard still didn't trust the recruits, but they worked well together for the most part.

Ammunition was scarce. Radar squads detected the targets, searchlights lit them, but the gunners had nothing with which to shoot them down. Then, in the second week at the encampment, a new shipment of ammo arrived, and the gun batteries began shooting at the targets.

Gradually, thanks to Henderson's and the rest of the officer's encouragement, the mistrust between the old army men and the recruits disappeared. We began to experience other challenges. Regiment HQ took away half our fuel. We switched to sound location and didn't fire up the searchlights' generators until we thought we heard a plane. That reduced the kill rate to practically zero. One night we tried using half the radar units and half the searchlights. That worked much better, with a kill rate of twenty percent.

"I don't think we need to take the sound locator equipment with us," I said at the next morning's debriefing. "Even one functioning radar is better than the old sound locators."

"But what if there is no gasoline at all. We can still use the sound equipment to get a little warning." Captain Henderson said.

"If we don't have any gasoline, the lights don't work, and we're stuck wherever we are until someone brings us some," I responded. "Leaving the sound locators behind means we have more room for gasoline barrels to provide power to the radar."

"This is exactly the problem we have been having among the men," said Captain Jennings. "The old army men don't trust the new equipment, and the recruits want to abandon all the tried-and-true ways."

"In the case of a searchlight battery, Sinclair is right, though. No power means no radar, no lights, no telephone, which ultimately puts the searchlight battery out of commission," said Captain Gill.

In the end, we abandoned the old sound locator equipment, not because of fuel but because it could not locate modern aircraft that flew much higher and faster than aircraft in the Great War.

As we returned to Fort Bliss at the end of our field training, Henderson said, "We don't get to sleep tonight. The Battery will report to the infiltration course immediately. Pass the orders to the other officers. Have the men change clothes and repack their knapsacks for the course."

"The infiltration course? What's that?" I asked.

"You'll see," replied Henderson.

Before I repacked my gear, I checked for a letter from Sarah Gale. I read it on the bus that took us to the infiltration course.

September 6, 1942

Dear Gene,

I'm so busy. Basic training is almost over. Everyone is talking about our stations after training. Most of the class will go to the east coast for coastal watch duty with the navy. Virtually all the Southern girls are hoping to go close to home. If they send me back to the coast of North Carolina, I'll be furious. I did not join up to go home and sit around the outer banks being eaten by mosquitoes while watching for enemy submarines or airplanes. If I have to do coastal watch, I hope it's at least a different coast. They also trained us to be secretaries, telephone operators, and mail sorters. I might get one of those jobs. I was hoping for something less boring than working in the laundry, but my hopes are not very high at this point.

Before I go to my post, I'll get a week at home. Even though I don't want to be stationed close to home, I do miss the family. Since Robby signed up, Mama has been trying hard to keep the younger boys at home. Of course, they are only fourteen and sixteen, but if the war lasts a long time, they may sign up too.

The folks are talking about getting a telephone. The neighbors up the road brought the lines to their house. With the money we are sending home, I think they could afford to bring the lines on out. That way, we could call home.

Living with all girls is so different. I like not getting teased by my brothers all the time, but some girls are not so nice. It took a while to learn not to get involved in all that. But now I have found a group of girls I love spending time with. Tonight, we are going to a movie, and then we'll stop at the soda fountain. It is still a real treat for me to go to a soda fountain.

The girls are calling. Have to go.

September 7, 1942
I didn't finish my letter last night, then this morning, I found out something fantastic. They are offering advanced photography training. They teach both how to take pictures and how to interpret aerial photos. I signed up right away. You know how much I enjoyed taking pictures with you. I could be taking pictures on the ground, but it also might involve taking aerial photographs. I'm so excited.

If I am accepted, I can't go home yet, but I can live with that.

I can't wait to hear from you.

Love

Sarah Gale

Sarah Gale had found the perfect specialty. Surely, they would accept her. I tucked the letter into my pack as the bus pulled up to a trailhead.

"Follow that path," the driver told us and drove off after we had offboarded. We marched up the mountain in the glow of a fiery desert sunset that turned the rocks blood red. It was pitch black by the time we arrived at the course laid out on the other side of the mountain.

"We'll be firing live ammunition over your heads," explained the training officer. "Keep your heads down, crawl around obstacles, and do not stand until the all-clear sounds," he ordered. "Your Captain will lead the way, and your EO will bring up the rear. Any questions?" Not waiting for any, he shouted, "Everyone down." He shot a flare into the sky to tell the gunners to start shooting.

Captain Henderson crawled through the coarse sand under the barbed wire layout. Live ammunition flew over his head, and artillery rounds exploded alongside the course. I waited until the last group began crawling through, then followed. My job was to encourage those who fell behind. I inched along, for a while, with a couple of privates moving very slowly. A shell exploded beside the course, showering us with sand. One of the soldiers curled up, shaking.

"You can't stay here, soldier!" I shouted. "On a real battlefield, you'll die. You need to keep moving."

"They're shooting at us," he sort of moaned and shouted at the same time.

"We need to experience this, so we'll know how it feels. Keep your head down. Now crawl. Hold your rifle up. I know from experience it doesn't do to get dirt in your rifle barrel."

I coaxed him to move along beside me, encouraging him. Finally, we made it to the end of the course at the very last minute of the qualifying time.

"See, you made it," I encouraged when we finally stood at the other end of the course.

Edelstein walked up, shouting. "What kind of soldier are you, Moore? You are a yellow-bellied coward. I could have you shot."

Private Moore trembled.

I turned on Edelstein. "You are out of order! Stand down!"

Edelstein looked like he wanted to murder me for the reprimand in front of Moore. He turned and stalked off; I could tell by his body language that I would hear more about this.

"You made it in the qualifying time," I told Moore. "You have nothing to worry about."

But we both knew he did. Edelstein would treat Moore harshly, and nothing I could say would change Edelstein's mind because Henderson's mind was the same. Even so, my rebuke would stand somehow. Edelstein could not be allowed to keep abusing his men.

CHAPTER 21
WARGAMES

After we returned from infiltration training, Captain Henderson gave us the morning to sleep between breakfast mess and lunch mess. One thing I learned in the army, I should sleep whenever I had the chance.

The entire regiment assembled on the parade ground that afternoon.

"I want to commend you on your rapid progress in training," Colonel Chapin shouted into a bullhorn. "Over the past twelve weeks, you have honed your skills. Many of you have gone from raw recruits to lean fighting men. Others of you have updated and upgraded your combat skills.

"Tomorrow, we will put that training to the test. This regiment will be engaged in field exercises for the next two weeks. You will be placed in either a red team or a blue team. Your officers have their orders. Report to your battery headquarters immediately, get your assignments and prepare to pull out.

"Dismissed!"

I hurried to our HQ. As Executive Officer, I should have seen the orders. Edelstein was there as I entered, his back to me.

"Captain Henderson." I overheard, "what about the court-martial for Private Moore."

"Who? What did he do?"

"He showed extreme cowardice on the infiltration course last night. He's not fit to be a soldier."

"I'll talk with Sinclair about it.," he responded, nodding at me. Edelstein turned and frowned, muttering something about pain in the neck.

"Send Moore here and get the rest of your platoon ready for

the war games," ordered Henderson

Edelstein pushed past me. I ignored his insult and instead asked, "Henderson, what are our orders? Why haven't I seen them?"

"They were delivered here while the colonel was talking. I had just opened them when Edelstein walked in. Part of the exercise—to see how quickly we can deploy." The other officers had arrived by then. He showed us the map on which he had marked the location of the exercise.

"It's in New Mexico," I said.

"Yup, right up against these mountains, south of this huge bunch of dunes. The Quartermaster Corps has tents and supplies up there. Brasseux, Carson, get your platoons into formation out front. Douglas, Wright, Tilton, see to the equipment." As they all rushed off, he turned to me and said, "Sinclair, what's this about Private Moore?"

"He froze during the infiltration. I got him through, and he made it in the qualifying time."

"We don't have time for a court-martial. Put Moore in Brasseux's platoon and transfer someone to Edelstein."

That was it. Henderson knew how Edelstein treated his men. His solution was to change the men, not change Edelstein.

I selected Kramer, a tough older private from Brasseux's platoon, to join Edelstein's platoon and sent Moore to Brasseux when he arrived. I intercepted Kramer as he left the barracks and said, "It'll be hard under Edelstein. Hang in there. Let me know how it goes." Then I grabbed the transfer paperwork to fill out on the way north, where I would deposit it with a private of the Quartermaster Corps to take back to HQ. The battery joined the convoy to the staging site. We moved out, eating the dust of all the batteries before ours.

***

The Regimental officers assembled at the staging site for a briefing on the game's premise and rules.

"Obsolete aircraft refitted with autopilot and towed models will be your targets," the Colonel said. "We're also introducing

RPV targets. Dummy bombs will be deployed."

"What are RPVs?" Wright whispered to me,

"Radio piloted vehicles."

"This exercise will simulate North Africa." The Colonel continued.

The mountains behind us did not look like the pictures I had seen of the Atlas Mountains in North Africa, which looked rougher and higher, but the rocky desert with dunes in the distance could have been the Sahara.

"Attacks will come from Italy, which is to the northeast. Previous exercises have included armored vehicles, but those units have moved out. None of the newly arrived armored vehicle units are prepared for joint exercises. So it will just be us and the infantry out there. You will be notified of the location of the infantry and should plan and aim accordingly.

"Proceed to your assigned locations and set up. Keep communication lines open. Dismissed!"

We were assigned to a range of hills north of Regimental HQ. Henderson checked out the lay of the land, then deployed the searchlights and radar along hills overlooking the artillery camp. These bluffs held some excellent radar and searchlight sites. We had already practiced at a few of them over the past few weeks.

Not long after we began setting up, a flight of planes marked with red enemy insignia appeared on the horizon. We had not yet calibrated the radar. I had Perry radio the gun batteries that aircraft approached from the north coordinates undetermined. Soon they were within range, but the gunners didn't fire at them. They had fired only at towed targets in training; they had tried not to shoot down tow planes. So, I assumed they were searching for the towed targets.

"Fire!" the gun battery Captain shouted in the distance. "Those are outdated planes on autopilot—shoot them down!"

The artillery began firing. Amazingly, they hit one of the planes. The surviving planes continued flying in a straight line off into the desert. Several minutes later, they crashed into the mountains. Not a good start for the artillery, I judged. They looked for the wrong target, one that didn't exist.

"How did those planes do that?" asked Private Barkley.

"The planes are equipped with gyroscopes that keep them level and pressure sensors that keep them at a specific altitude. The air base's personnel start the engine and launch the aircraft using a huge slingshot. The planes gain altitude until they reach the preset height, then keep going in a straight line until they run into the mountains or run out of fuel," I said.

The platoon had set up tents and equipment by nightfall, but those of us in the moonlight cavalry would not get to use them until the next day. That night, balloons and towed targets came in hot and heavy. Temperatures were in the low sixties, with a brisk breeze blowing, which felt cold after the day's extreme heat. Men warmed their hands in their armpits during the occasional lulls in the action. I spent the night driving from section to section, making sure everything ran smoothly. My radioman, Phil Perry, rode with me. As we were leaving Edelstein's platoon, Carson's man called.

"Our former sound locators heard some RPVs coming in low, under the radar. They're approaching rapidly from the north."

"Get the lights on them and notify our automatic weapons batteries. I'll notify the gun batteries."

"Yes, sir," the radioman said. "Over and out."

"Perry, wake up the artillery. Let them know what's happening." I ordered.

All the lights focused on the flight of radio-controlled aircraft approaching from the north. As I turned the jeep, I noticed lights approaching from the east.

"Tell Edelstein to focus on the planes coming from the north and Brasseux on the ones from the east," I altered my orders to Perry.

The sky lit up across the northern and eastern horizons. Tracer bullets and exploding shells spiked into the night sky, washing out the stars and moon. Dust and smoke obscured our view as we drove from platoon to platoon. The forty-millimeter guns took on the enemy approaching from the east. The bigger guns targeted those coming in from the north. Finally, we managed to turn them all back.

The action slowed over the next few hours, but we never had more than an hour without enemy aircraft approaching. By morning all the platoons felt exhausted. We bolted our breakfast and fell into our cots. The following two nights were much the same.

During the day, one radar squad from each platoon kept watch under the direction of Lieutenant Tilton. I rose early, about three in the afternoon, to work on the battery paperwork. One afternoon I walked up behind Tilton to get his report on the activity that day and startled him. He dropped the letter he had in his hand, and a picture of a little girl fluttered out,

"She's adorable. Who is she?"

"Oh, nobody," he said, snatching up and tucking the picture into his shirt pocket. We smiled slightly at each other.

"Twenty-three targets identified today. Here's the tally."

As I left, I noticed, out of my peripheral vision, that he pulled the picture out again and looked at it.

By the fourth night, the frenetic activity began to wear on us. Men started to snap at each other; a few fights and the reprimands that came with them had left many on edge.

"Another fight last night," I told Douglas at breakfast. "Over whether the radar should have picked up the RPVs. Those things are tiny and can slip in so low to the ground our chances of seeing them on the radar are extremely slim."

"Youse can't expect this many men to live together in one place and not get on each other's nerves, but we have a job to do and need to work together. Youse could talk to them about doin their jobs all you want, but I bet a little friendly competition would gain you more. Form up some baseball or maybe volleyball teams. Even a good old tug o' war."

I decided to make a flyer inviting the men to join baseball teams that afternoon.

We had barely fallen asleep when the engineer corps came back through after making a road to somewhere. They had driven past us with their equipment the first day.

"Break camp. We're moving forward fifty miles," Henderson ordered. "Follow the new road the engineers built. We're leapfrogging the artillery to protect their advance."

We disassembled the equipment and repacked it in the trucks. I urged the men to move quickly, summoning all the energy I could to assist them. With the equipment hitched behind the truck, I climbed in beside the first truck driver and fell asleep. Many men caught what sleep they could as the vehicles bounced along the rough road.

Three hours later, we were rapidly setting up again on a hill overlooking the site designated as the new infantry camp, which from our view, looked like the engineers had vaguely flattened out. They hadn't done anything to our hill to make our lives more comfortable.

"Be glad you aren't infantry," said Henderson, walking by some grumbling men. "They have to march all night to get here," I admitted; he made a good point.

Since we set up more quickly this time, the night shift got an hour's sleep before we had to be on duty. Another cold, busy night faced us. This time we were ready before the first enemy targets came through.

I left Carson's platoon and drove across the desert toward Brasseux's, traveling on the smoothest bit of dessert I had seen yet. Perry suddenly yelled, "Stop!" I slammed on the brakes, but the front wheels went over a cliff at the edge of a deep arroyo, the jeep high centered on the edge of the cliff, tilting at about a thirty-degree angle. Looking left and right, I decided the bottom of the arroyo must have been about thirty feet below—maybe more.

"Perry," I requested, "carefully climb out of the back of the jeep." As I shifted the jeep into neutral and turned off the engine, I continued, "Take your radio with you and call Brasseux. Ask him to send his gunners and drivers to help is get this jeep out of here." I hesitated, then said, "In fact, maybe you should stand on the rear bumper, adding your weight to the rear of the jeep, after you make your radio call. If the jeep starts to fall off, hop back." He nodded and stealthily crawled out of the jeep and stood on the rear bumper, making his call.

I sat very still.

"Perry here," he said. "Sinclair and I have a bit of a situation. I'm shining my flashlight at you. Can you see it?"

"No... Oh yes, there you are."

"Could you send any available men and a truck over this direction? Bring some ropes. Lieutenant Sinclair drove the jeep off a cliff"—I thought I heard Perry stifle laughter—"We could use some help pulling it back up."

"He what? Is everybody all right?"

"We're fine. Just a little stuck."

Fifteen minutes later, a truck pulled up behind the jeep. Brasseux and six of his men hopped out. "Goin down with de ship, Sinclair? Whan did you join de navy?"

"I thought too much movement might dislodge the jeep. Besides, if I die, I won't have to explain this to Henderson. You would."

"Probably won't die. You might get hurt bad if de jeep slips, though. De men have de rope tied on now. Come on outta dere."

I slowly climbed out, not fully trusting the ropes. Brasseux gave me a hand up, then signaled the men to start the truck. The jeep's undercarriage scraped on the hard dirt until the front wheels found purchase, and the jeep settled back onto the relatively flat desert. One of the truck drivers scooted under the vehicle with a flashlight.

"Man, they build these things sturdy," he said as he came out from under. "It's dented a bit, but nothing's leaking. Should be good to go."

"Please don't tell anyone about this," I said to Brasseux.

"Oh yeah? Dis is too good not to tell, Sinclair! We'll be laughin 'bout it for years and years."

I shook my head, climbed back in the jeep, and followed the truck to Brasseux's location. He'd apparently radioed ahead. His Sergeant shouted, "Sinclair, glad you made it. Did your crankshaft get bent out of shape, trying to enter that ditch?"

***

Early the following day, the infantry moved out to attack the enemy camp. We held our position on the hill, defending against incoming targets. As the sun rose, we turned the watch over to the day shift and fell asleep to the sound of the big guns doing their best to shoot down balloons and towed targets.

That afternoon I had some of our HQ staff lay out a rough baseball diamond. Sergeant Hammond, our supply sergeant, somehow came up with some balls and bats. I later found out he had them airlifted from Fort Bliss and dropped with the dummy bombs. I posted a signup sheet in the mess tent. We had enough men signed up to form eight teams by the next day. I drew names out of a helmet to assign the men to different teams. Six non-coms had signed up, so I made them captains. Wright and Carson agreed to captain the other two teams. Douglas was right. Morale improved as soon as practice started. When the games began, having mixed the men up by randomly drawing names made an enormous morale booster. The men jawed at each other about how great or awful their platoons were, careful not to mention officers or orders.

The nights in the high desert, at about 4.200 feet, were getting colder as the season moved toward mid-fall, and we felt the cold more. Although we had to keep the searchlights ready and monitor the radar, no planes came. Without any activity or excitement for three days and nights, the nights, in particular, seemed to drag on forever. All of us dozed off a time or two, only to jerk awake again whenever we heard a noise. About 0200 the first night, the radio blared.

Perry rushed over to me. "Sir, I think something's happening over at Brasseux's location.

I grabbed the radio. Some sort of wailing was coming through, but I could not understand a word of it.

"Brasseux, what's happening? What's the matter?"

"Aint nuttin da matter. Jus singin a Cajun song to keep us all awake."

"You certainly woke me up. What is that song?"

"It's called Jole Blon. 'Bout a girl dat broke a man's heart."

Without pausing, he started to sing again, his voice sounding like a jeep running on two cylinders:

Jolie blon quoi t'as fait?
Tu m'as quitté, ouais, pour t'en aller
T'en aller avec un autre
Ouais pour moi jolie blonde
Quelle espoir, quelle avenir moi je vas avoir

"You sounded like something was broke. This isn't broadcast radio. Keep it clear in case we need it."

"Aw, heck, back home day say my voice ken melt hearts. Will do about de radio."

The day shift had no action either, and we nighttimers slept soundly. Two more nights passed without action. The men were used to staying awake at night by now but were restless with no action. At the daily meeting of COs and XOs, I said, "Why don't we try rotating day and night assignments for additional cross training. The men are getting bored with no action, and a change of routine would help."

Two days later, Henderson said, "This rotation is one of the worst ideas you've come up with. The men are so exhausted by the change of sleep hours that they're totally ineffective on the first day. That could be disastrous in combat." He looked at me and shook his head. "Someday, you might come to believe the army knows what it's doing."

The fourth night also passed quietly until just before dawn. Edelstein radioed me. "Activity noted to the east,"

"Perry, notify all units. Activity in the east. Wake them up if they are sleeping."

I hurried to Edelstein's location as the entire squadron of tow planes appeared on the horizon. Dummy bombs dropped to the north of our location. The searchlights illuminated the bombs, and every one of the regiment's guns, from the ninety millimeter Long Toms to the fast little ack-acks, fired as rapidly as possible. They shot down targets and "exploded" fake bombs before hitting the ground. We cheered as the tow planes turned back toward the airfield.

We thought the attack was over, but the planes returned with another load of bombs sooner than I thought possible. We were under full attack at the time we usually changed from night to day crews. One by one, replacement gunners slipped into place and kept up the barrage. Radar operators switched out without losing track of the incoming planes. We had a fantastic twenty-five percent kill rate that night. The cross-training sure helped.

Toward the end of the second week of the wargames, the planes came regularly, about one plane every hour. We got used to the routine. Before sunrise on the last morning, they hit us with everything they had—first RVPs, then a flight of tow planes with dummy bombs. A flight of autopilot planes close behind the tow planes swarmed in. Then all was quiet. The radio blared, "This round of wargames has ended—all officers report to the field HQ to review the games."

We gathered on a hillside overlooking the HQ tent, sitting on the bare ground as Colonel Chapin addressed us.

"This was a close one, men. There were errors in all areas of the field. Antiaircraft artillery failed to begin shooting down planes until they were almost out of range. Early on, artillery didn't even recognize the enemy."

I dozed off while the colonel listed the many failures that had plagued the games. Douglas poked me in the ribs.

Colonel Chapin said, "The one thing that decided the games was the alertness of the men in Battery I. After three days without attack, we anticipated the regiment might be careless late in their night shift. The men in Battery I performed admirably. The points the radar men and searchlights earned by alerting the gunners turned the tide. The games go to the blue team."

The blue team officers cheered. "Sinclair, good work!" shouted the Lieutenant Colonel. "Battery I, three days leave."

"One more important announcement, gentlemen," interrupted Lieutenant Colonel Squires. "The army is reorganizing all AAA regiments. AAA needs to be more agile, flexible, and able to respond quickly wherever your services are required. For this reason, the regiment has been split into three independent battalions, a gun battalion, an automatic weapons battalion, and a searchlight battalion. These battalions may all work together, or they may be attached separately to different units. It is even possible individual platoons will be attached separately. It all depends on what is needed in the field. This war is unique in Europe; faster, more deadly, non-traditional battle plans. In the Pacific, it is even more non-traditional. In those jungles, the Japs are fighting a war where surrender is not an option. Jungles and caves provide cover so they can ambush our troops suddenly. Fighting goes on day and night. The Japs are sneaky, treacherous bastards, and our troops in the Pacific must be prepared for them.

"We are finally turning the tide on both fronts. The Commander in Chief and the other national leaders have chosen a policy of Europe first. The bulk of the men and materiel will be going to Europe until that front is secured. However, we are still fighting in the Pacific. We beat their navy at Midway. We are pushing them back on Guadalcanal. Our boys are fighting for freedom all over the globe and making progress. You are now trained and prepared to join in on any front in any battle."

Men clapped, whistled, and cheered as they were dismissed.

***

Before I left, I was excited to see a letter from Sarah Gale.

September 20, 1942

Dear Gene,

I have graduated!. They had more uniforms ready by graduation, so now we each have two sets of fatigues and one dress uniform. Most exciting of all, I started the photography program the next day.

We started right in learning about how to get information from the photos. You wouldn't believe how much I have learned about figuring out direction, distance, and location on the photographs just from the coordinates the aerial photographer gives us. I can even tell how big things are by comparing them to other things like vehicles, sports fields, or other objects. The photographer sends us the altitude and time, so that helps.

Yesterday I was trying to interpret a photo, but I had placed it so that the shadows were going away from me. That makes it look like tall things are holes, and holes are tall things. They told us a name for that. They call it a pseudoscopic illusion. I love learning those big words. It makes me feel really important when I can rattle off terms like that. You probably think it's so funny that I like big words because you know so many of them—all those chemicals and medicines and things. But I never had a chance to learn big, important-sounding words until now.

In one picture, I identified a spot where a stream flows through a forest by the differences in the trees. It helps that I already know about woods and swamps. Different trees grow in wet than in dry soil. Some of the girls are from places that have mostly fields or cities, and they are not as good at interpreting photos of woods and jungles. I'm pretty good with towns and farms, too, though. Things planted in geometric patterns usually mean people grew them, but they are natural if they are scattered randomly.

Next week we are starting on stereoscopic viewing. I think it will be lots of fun. You look at those images through a viewer that makes them look like they are 3D. I can hardly wait.

So far, we haven't learned anything you didn't already teach me in the photography lessons, but the week after next, we get to go up in planes and learn to do actual aerial photography. I'm so excited. I have never been on an airplane before. It seems like it will be so much fun, though some of the girls say they get airsick. I hope I don't! I'll let you know.

The girls are calling for me. We are going to the soda fountain to get root beer floats. I have discovered I love root beer floats. Will write again soon!

Love

Sarah Gale

P.S. Please let me know what comes next for you as soon as you find out. That is if you can tell me.

CHAPTER 22
OLD MEXICO

"Sinclair! We're visiting Old Mexico while we have the chance," Tilton shouted from across the mess at breakfast. "Shopping, dancing, drinking! Why don't you come with us? We need a break after NEW Mexico!"

After hesitating to consider it, I gave him thumbs up.

Brasseux had arranged for a taxi to pick the six of us up at the gate immediately after breakfast. I squeezed in with Carson, Tilton, Brasseux, Marshall, and Wright. People were pouring from Juarez, Mexico, into the United States at the border crossing.

"Who're all those people?" I asked a Mexican border guard.

"They come into the United States to harvest pecans. So many US farmworkers have joined the military services that your farmers need help. This year your country began to allow workers from Mexico to cross the border to harvest the crops. Some of them have traveled to Oregon, Washington, or Idaho, but now the only crop still growing, except in southern California, is pecans. Most of these workers will take a break after the pecan harvest. They have made more money in a season than they could all year in Mexico. They will start north again in the spring."

"Interesting," I said. Noticing the numerous children in the group, I asked, "Do the children work too? What about school?"

"If they're big enough, they work. Most of those children were not in school before, so they're not missing anything."

"Sinclair, do you have to strike up a conversation with everyone you meet? Come on," called Tilton, waving for me to catch up.

"What's your rush? There can't be too much happening yet." I called out to him as I trotted up the street to catch up.

"We want to be the first in the Mercado to get the best souvenirs," Carson replied.

We soon found ourselves on a street lined with tiny shops, the shopkeepers in the process of setting out their wares. They displayed pottery, paintings, jewelry, trinkets, and various foods. Brasseux immediately began bartering for pottery. He progressed slowly from stand to stand, sometimes reaching an agreement, buying something, and sometimes walking away. Either way, he seemed to be enjoying himself. The merchants took American money, making both bargaining and paying reasonable prices easier.

"What are you buying all that stuff for?" I asked him.

"I'll send it home fer Christmas presents," he said. "But mostly, I buy it for de fun o' g'ttin a good price."

I bought a painting of a bird sitting on a branch, the head and tail adorned with real feathers. I preferred it to the flowery pictures on velvet some of the other men bought.

"Look, a puppet show," cried Marshall, pointing. Carson translated the dialogue for us. It was like a Punch and Judy show, except they called the main characters Juan and Juanita. Even without Carson's translation, I would have laughed. Wright sketched them as we watched. We dropped some American coins into a sombrero on the ground and moved on.

We wandered for hours, venturing farther and farther from the border, bartering, enjoying the entertainment, and laughing and joking with the locals. Around noon, spotting a taco stand, Carson said, "I'm hungry. Let's get us some tacos."

Marshall scrutinized the stand and asked, "Are you sure you want to eat there?"

"I want to eat some authentic Mexican food, and these street stands serve the best there is. It'll be fine."

"Let's just make sure we get freshly made tacos rather than something that has been sitting there all morning," I warned.

Tilton approached the stand. "Hello, sweetheart," he said to the old woman making the tacos. "Could you make us two dozen fresh, hot tacos, please?"

A teenage girl, probably her granddaughter, translated the request, and the old woman got to work.

"And you, pretty señorita. Where did you learn to speak English so well?" asked Tilton.

"Working here. I've been helping Abuela since I was seven years old."

"How would you like to meet us for a drink after work?

"I can't," she said. "But I can tell you where to go. Stop by the Cerveceria Martín on Avenida Benito Juarez. It is very close to the border. My cousin works there."

Abuela lightly slapped the girl's hand, and she turned to serve another customer, selling the premade tacos sitting on the rough wooden counter. Abuela soon gave us our two dozen fresh tacos wrapped in newspaper. Marshall threw in a generous tip, and the old woman shooed us off down the street to make room for new customers and rescue her granddaughter from Tilton, who had continued to try to talk to the girl. We found a plaza and settled on the edge of its central fountain to eat our tacos. They were amazingly delicious, especially compared to the chow back at the fort. As we ate, a group came into the square wearing black pants with metal buttons sewn down the sides and black jackets and white shirts with red ascots. Several women in bright, full skirted dresses followed them into the plaza as they tuned their instruments.

"Mariachis," said Wright. "This should be fun."

They played a song that sounded like a polka, but it wasn't the German version I'd heard at dances back home. Brasseux started dancing the polka with a Mexican woman in a ruffled red skirt and white blouse. They stepped and turned across the plaza. It surprised me that Cajuns danced the polka, too.

After a couple of songs, he persuaded Carson and Tilton to join him. The rest of us stood and clapped. The Mexican women soon taught them the steps for the dance. A crowd gathered around, even some foreigners, based on their clothing styles. The women grabbed me, Wright, and Marshall, showing us the steps. Wright was outstanding. Soon he and his partner were in the middle of a circle of onlookers who clapped and cheered as they performed an intricate polka, something I'd never seen back home. Must have been something he learned in Ohio.

Another guitarist showed up with a woman in a long, split skirt with an elaborate ruffle on the bottom. Wright stepped forward and struck a pose with one arm in the air, the other across his chest, and the right knee bent. The man strummed his guitar, and Wright began to dance, snapping his fingers and stomping his feet. The woman joined him. They danced closely, observing each other, coordinating their movements, circling, stamping, and kicking.

"Boy, howdy, look at that," Carson said. "Wright's a flamenco master."

It was more like a dramatic, erotic performance than a dance, how they responded to one another. I was breathless when they finished, and I hadn't danced. The crowd applauded the performance and cheered, asking for more, but Wright shook his head. He was clearly spent. That dance used other muscles than those we conditioned for combat.

We had spent almost the entire afternoon dancing in the plaza, so we walked back toward the border, where we found the Cerveceria the girl had recommended. We settled into a worn red velvet-lined booth and ordered Mexican beer and chips. A band played Mariachi music, but when a group of teenage girls walked in from the plaza, they switched to music Carson said was salsa. I watched the dancers on the floor for a while but couldn't get the movement.

The girls stood in a group for a bit, casting glances our way, then invited us to dance. I refused at first, but the guys pushed me out of the booth. Then, a petite, sultry-eyed teenager began showing me the steps. Once I learned to get the feet going in one direction and the hips in another, I enjoyed it. Three beers and six dances later, I laughed, danced every dance, and sang along in the worst Spanish possible. It was the first time I had unwound so completely since racing with Sarah Gale on the beach in North Carolina.

Suddenly I felt incredibly guilty. I had promised Sarah I was hers, yet I was dancing with girls in a Mexican bar. I sat down and ordered a soft drink.

"Please dance, sir?" one of the girls asked me.

"No. Thank you. I need a rest now."

"You rest," she said. "I come back."

The music changed to a slower pace.

"That's bachata," Carson told me. "It's a bar dance from the islands."

"What islands?" I asked.

"Caribbean."

Tilton had consumed three beers to every one of mine, but he was still on the dance floor, getting loud and obnoxious. I heard him yell, "Hold on there, buddy. She's mine."

I peered across the dim, smoky room. Tilton held tightly to the arm of the girl who had first asked me to dance. An older Mexican man gripped the other arm.

"No, Papa! No, Papa," the girl kept crying.

Marshall, Carson, and I jumped up and ran to Tilton. "Let her go, Tilton," Marshall ordered. "The man is her father."

Tilton refused to loosen his grip on her arm. The father threatened him with a gun. I quickly pried Tilton's fingers open and told the girl, "Go." She ran out the door dragging her father with her, helped by two other girls. We pulled Tilton in the opposite direction, hoping to make it to the border before the Federales showed up. I stopped, realizing we hadn't paid. I had also forgotten my picture. A barmaid caught up with us and shoved the painting into my hand.

"How about their purchases?" I asked her, indicating the men running toward the border. Marshall and Carson continued on with Tilton.

"The short dark man got them," she said, pointing at Brasseux. "But my brother painted this. I'm pleased you liked his picture."

Brasseux and Wright caught up then, carrying all our bags and packages.

I reached for my wallet, but the girl said, "The *bailarín extraordinario* paid."

I thanked her and followed the others, who had already made it across the border.

"Anything to declare?" asked the US border agent.

I held up the picture.

"No import tax on that," he said and waved me on.

Marshall had already hailed a taxi. I jumped in, spotting a group of Mexican police running toward the border crossing.

"Fort Bliss," I said. "And hurry before this joker pukes all over your taxi."

That night the tacos exacted revenge on all of us.

CHAPTER 23
FLORIDA

I picked up insignia from our new battalion headquarters to distribute to the men and sauntered back to battery HQ, enjoying the sunlight and soft breeze. Locals had told me that autumn was the best season in West Texas. I agreed. It was delightful after the heat of the summer. Henderson strode quickly past me in the same direction. I picked up my speed to catch up with him.

"What's up?" I asked. I didn't anticipate any repercussions from our little adventure in Mexico since nothing had come up in the past couple of days. The Mexican authorities would have a tough time identifying us, and I suspected they had bigger fish to fry.

"Jennings and Gill got promotions with the reorganization of the regiment. They skipped right over me!"

"Don't they have seniority?" I asked. "I thought you said you graduated West Point in the class of '38. You're a captain after only four years. Besides, you've been a captain for just over four months. They wouldn't promote you to major so fast, would they?"

Henderson almost paused as he looked at me with bullets firing from his eyes. Instead, his voice mildly condescending, he explained, "They *may* have seniority, but I'm army from birth. I know the service inside and out. I've put everything into being the best I can be, and I've made sure Squires knows it. They need West Point men at the top." He started to rant. "Standard waiting periods don't mean anything in wartime! Look at you," he spit, barely turning his head toward me. "You've had your bars for what? Five months? And you're a first lieutenant! Thanks to me, I might say. One of my classmates was promoted to major! I intended to be the first!" Now on a massive roll, Henderson almost shouted. "The army sent *him* to Africa almost as soon as this war started, and *I* got sent to this *backwater* fort to train *old* men who should be ready for *retirement* and raw recruits who know *nothing* of army tradition or code of behavior. There's *no* way to get promoted early without going overseas." I refrained from pointing out that none of the men came close to retirement age except for Sergeant Hammond, our invaluable forty-four-year-old supply sergeant.

We arrived at battery HQ, where he threw an envelope on my desk. "Now they're sending us to Florida. They say we don't have enough hours of nighttime experience to be shipped overseas. When the *hell* am I going to get my chance?"

Henderson looked at me, clearly in a funk. "I'm going to go tell my wife to start packing." Now his voice sounded resigned.

Henderson stalked out. He probably needed a more sympathetic ear to listen to his complaints. I picked up the envelope. Inside I found orders for the entire battalion to report to the Orlando Air Base.

***

The battalion waited alongside the railroad tracks. A long train of boxcars followed by an even larger number of flatcars pulled to a stop in front of us. All three batteries of the battalion began moving toward the flatcars. Men jostled to get their equipment to the front of the mob. Trucks and jeeps bumped into each other, cut each other off, and a fight broke out in one instance. The railroad transportation officer approached Lieutenant Douglas, our battery's maintenance officer, one of the physically largest officers on the field, and talked with him. Douglas stepped onto the last flatcar, shouting through a bullhorn ordering everyone to stop.

"Battery A, load your tents, personal gear, and ordinance in the first two boxcars. Battery C, bring your radar forward!" Douglas bellowed. Men started sorting themselves out to follow his instructions. "Battery B, load your ordinance and gear into the third and fourth boxcars and prepare to follow Battery C with your radar." A sense of order slowly emerged on the field. "Battery A, after you pack your gear and ordinance into the boxcars, get back in your trucks! Get your radar ready! Radar goes on first. As soon as you get your radar on, Battery C load your ordinance and gear into the last two boxcars." Douglas stood on the flatcar shouting through his bullhorn until all the vehicles were lined up in the order the transportation officer apparently wanted them.

"Load up!" he bullhorned.

The maintenance officers of the other batteries directed traffic. The radar trucks pulled up behind the last car and moved up the loading ramps the transportation technicians had positioned there. The men drove the vehicles up the steep ramps onto the flatbeds. Transportation techs bridged the space between the cars with iron tracks that the men had to cross to move to the front of the train. Several drivers almost missed the bridges and had to back up and try again. Often they stopped the vehicles in the wrong place. One Battery B truck even drove off a flatcar. As the panicked driver climbed out the window, the transportation crew brought two tractors and righted the truck. Officers of Battery B opened the back to check the equipment, and the transportation crew carefully lifted the vehicle back onto the flatcar with their front loaders and ropes.

Meanwhile, other crew members forced several vehicles to back up. A couple at the back of the lineup even backed off the train so the tipped truck could resume its correct position. Their Captain gave the driver the reaming out of his life.

"Are these the best drivers we could find?" I asked Douglas.

"I thought they were pretty good until today." He squinched his eyes and shook his head like he had a headache.

A transportation officer climbed on the flatcar and spoke to Douglas again.

Through his bullhorn, Douglas ordered, "Power units next. Battery C leads the way!"

The trucks and trailers carrying the power units moved to the ramp. By far the heaviest of our equipment, the power units took all the torque the engines could muster, but they moved up the ramp and onto the flatcars. These drivers seemed better prepared, and no mishaps occurred while getting the power units positioned on the flatcars toward the middle of the train. Searchlights came next, followed by the lighter trucks and jeeps used by the support units and officers. The men worked frenetically to tie all the trucks and equipment down on the flatcars. I did not want to imagine the mess we would find when we opened the boxcars in Florida. All the equipment the men had tossed in there would be jostled for two thousand miles.

Standing tall on the last flatcar, Douglas shouted instructions provided by the transportation officer through it all.

When all the equipment was finally loaded and tied down, we marched the men to the troop train in front of the equipment train. The men took less time to load than the baggage and equipment, but regardless, the process was still disorganized. Finally, everyone on board, we got underway.

"Surely we'll go to the European Theater," Douglas insisted, his voice raspy from shouting so much in the last few hours. "They wouldn't send us east, then turn around and send us west again, would they?"

"You haven't been in this damn army long enough," Tilton countered. "Just because we are going to Florida doesn't mean we won't end up in the Pacific."

"It makes it more likely," Marshall put in. "They want us at least to have seen a swamp, some rain, and some snakes before they send us to the Pacific."

"It can't be worse than the sand at Fort Bliss," Carson said.

"Wanna make a bet?" Brasseux retorted. "Enyway," he said, "I'm of de mind dat we gonna fight dem Japs! Worst case scenario!"

"We don't have enough field hours for overseas service," I said. "They want us to have some hours in different atmospheric conditions. And since they're sending us to Florida, it probably does mean we'll go to the Pacific just like Brasseux and Marshall said."

This discussion reoccurred in one form or another throughout the long, tedious trip, three nights and four days, from El Paso to Orlando.

***

I had sent an airmail letter to Sarah Gale when I found out we were going to Florida. Her response was waiting for me when we arrived.

October 17, 1942

Dear Gene,

Flying is even more wonderful than I imagined it. We were so high above the treetops that the WAACS marching below us looked like ants. I was a little bit frightened when we took off the first time, but it turned out to be such a thrill that I immediately got over that. We flew so high that we saw nothing below us but fluffy white clouds for several minutes, then we came down again to take pictures.

Of course, the cameras are high speed since we have to keep moving while we take the pictures. I snapped photos while we were above the designated area as fast as I could. Another trainee wrote down the coordinates every time I pushed the button. Above central Iowa, that's very easy. It might be a bit more complicated over some places where we'll take reconnaissance photos later.

It's essential to keep accurate records of the numbers the navigator and co-pilot call out while we take the pictures. The instructor talked about new cameras that will automatically record the date, time, and elevation on the photos as they're taken, but we don't have those for training. It would just be a matter of riding along, pushing a button at the appropriate interval with them.

I don't think I have ever had as much fun in my life as on those training flights, except maybe with you.

Stereoscopic pictures are fascinating. They look blurry when you look at them without the viewer, but when you pick up the viewer and look through it, everything just seems to jump out of the picture toward you.

We had already learned to develop film and print pictures, but printing stereoscopic images is very different. It's actually two pictures printed on top of each other, but they have to be done just right. That makes the image look blurry when you are not using the stereoscopic viewer. In the viewer, you see one picture with one eye and the other picture with the other, and the images become three-dimensional.

Tomorrow is graduation. I can't wait to find out where I'll be stationed.

October 18, 1942

Graduation was wonderful. I got a certificate for being the best photographer in the program. That is the first time I have ever been best at anything. They said I got the certificate because I have such a good eye for detail. I think I did because you taught me how to take pictures before I even started the program. Thank you so much for teaching me how. I got a promotion because of my skill in photography and interpretation. I'm a second leader now. That's like a corporal.

We got our orders immediately after graduation. You'll never guess where I'm going to be stationed! Orlando Air Base! I'm joining a unit that is already there, so I will be traveling alone, first to visit my family, then down to Orlando. But I am not afraid of that anymore. I am so excited that we'll be together again! I saw a postcard of the base, and it has palm trees!!! I have heard that it is beautiful there.

I'll see you soon.
All my love,
Sarah Gale

I couldn't believe it! We would be stationed at the same base. What fantastic luck.

***

At the airbase, my responsibility as liaison with other units took on a new dimension that Henderson seemed disinclined to care about.

"Our pilots need to be able to land under any condition," a flight trainer told me. "We want you to light up the runway to simulate landing on a newly constructed airstrip without functioning runway lights. We'll turn off the runway lights as they approach, and you'll turn on your lights, illuminating the runway. Once they can do that, we'll ask you to light the planes as they fly overhead so they'll experience flying in the beam of a searchlight, which can be disconcerting."

"I imagine it can," I said. "You know the enemy has their guns on you if they have a searchlight on you."

"The Germans, yes, the Japs maybe not. We don't think they have much understanding of electronics."

"I wouldn't count on that," I said. "We should assume the Japs know everything the Germans do. If they don't have it now, they will soon. I understand those Zeros are rather good fighter planes, which I assume means they have excellent electronic systems."

"All the more reason for our boys to learn some evasive techniques when you put your searchlights on them." He looked away. He had probably also been told not to discuss the Zero. "Can you have your lights at the airport tomorrow night?"

Fortunately, he just wanted lights. We wouldn't have to move and recalibrate the radar every time the pilots needed some night practice. All we had to do was haul the lights to the air training field twice a week, aim them at the planes above so they could wiggle back and forth to avoid them, light up the landing strip when the aircraft landed, then head back to our assigned training area.

In Florida, we did get plenty of practice under different atmospheric conditions. There were clouds in the sky more often than not, and one night out of three, we worked in the rain. One night, I arrived to inspect Brasseux's platoon to find tarps draped over the oscilloscope units and their operators, held in place by clamps. The operators stayed dry, and the rain did not distort their view of the oscilloscopes.

"That's an excellent idea," I said to Brasseux. "I'll recommend it to the other platoons." Brasseux was a clever guy; I really liked his initiative.

Carson implemented tarps the next night. Edelstein, unfortunately, refused to let his men rig any protection.

As I strode toward Edelstein's camp, I ran into Robertson. "The lieutenant says if the army had wanted them to be out of the rain, they would have designed the radar differently," he said as he walked by, handing out oranges. "As you can see," he added, "I've been loading them up with vitamin C. Edelstein's men should be in good health."

"Edelstein," I said, walking into the tent where he had taken refuge out of the rain. "Why do you insist on exposing your men to these rain squalls when there is a way to protect them."

"They're soldiers. I keep telling you they need to be tough to survive warfare conditions. Why do you keep questioning my decisions? Why don't you butt out?"

"Because I'm the Executive Officer, it's my job to supervise the line officers. That means you!"

"Well, I think you are too full of yourself. Only the Commanding Officer can order me to do something." Spittle came out of his mouth as he spoke. "We need to toughen these men up so they'll be prepared for what we'll face in combat. My Dad fought in France in the Great War and came back shell-shocked and barely functioning. My uncle had to run the deli by himself most days, and my mom raised us on her own while Dad sat on the roof and fed pigeons. If I can make these men tough enough, they may be able to come back to be breadwinners and fathers. If not, many of them won't come back at all."

I tucked Edelstein's comments away. They explained a lot. Meanwhile, I responded. "I'm sorry you had such a miserable childhood. But the men need to be psychologically tough, not just physically tough. And they should be protected from conditions that cause disease—like rain."

"Don't worry. I'll see to that."

I wondered if I could trust his promise.

Peeved at another unfavorable exchange with Edelstein, I

headed back to HQ to let Henderson once again know my concerns. Henderson heard me out but waived me off. "Edelstein's platoon continues to perform above norms."

Over the next few weeks, we learned that the rain scattered the light from our searchlights when we lighted the runway, making a blinding glare that would have been quite effective at deterring an enemy but creating a hazard for our pilots. They had to learn to trust their instruments, which I expected the trainers wanted. The light reflected off the clouds on cloudy nights, lighting up the orchards surrounding the airstrip.

I had an idea. I approached the executive officer of an infantry unit. He agreed to work with us as we tried to light up the infantry's targets by bouncing light off the clouds, making them much easier to see.

"Men," I said the next night before we manned our stations, "we will try something different. There's an infantry unit training to the west of us. We will shine our lights on the clouds and try to bounce the beam back onto their targets as they do nighttime target practice. Get to your stations and let Perry know if any planes approach. I'll be working with light number one."

Perry and I followed light one's operator to their control station. I said to him, "It's hard to say exactly how high those clouds are. Probably somewhere around a mile. The infantry is two miles away. Start with a forty-five-degree elevation. Perry, call their man. Here is the information." I handed him the piece of paper on which the infantry officer had written their call letters.

"Power up, light one. Elevation forty-five, azimuth two hundred seventy." I said.

"They can see the light. It needs to be a little to the northeast," Perry, on the radio, reported.

"Did they say how far?"

"No."

"Okay. Slowly raise the elevation," I ordered. "Let me know when it is lined up with the target range, Perry."

"Now,"

"Slowly increase the azimuth,"

"Got it," said Perry, taking the headphones off.

We heard distant shots from the target range where the infantry unit practiced their marksmanship.

"Cut the light," Perry shouted, headphones back on. "Their CO is coming. They're supposed to be doing night vision firing."

The men cut the power; the light faded.

"There's not much chance that went undetected," I said

The radio squawked. "This is Colonel Milton Kincaid. Let me talk to your CO."

I took the radio. "First Lieutenant Eugene Sinclair, sir. XO of the unit. I'm responsible."

"Brilliant!" the Colonel said. "Report to my office in the morning. I want to know how you did that."

"Yes, sir."

The infantry radioman came back with instructions to find the Colonel's office.

When morning came, I shaved, showered, put on a clean uniform, and ate breakfast before going to the Colonel's office.

He still hadn't arrived. I sat in the outer office, nervously waiting for him. When Colonel Kincaid finally came, about half an hour later, he had me follow him into his office.

"How did you do that?" he asked.

"I noticed the searchlights reflected off the clouds and decided to find out if we could use them to light up a battlefield. I got the location of the practice range from the company XO, Lieutenant Barker. The distance was about two miles. Stratus clouds are around a mile above the earth, so I calculated the elevation from that estimate. Then the radioman guided us in. The clouds were a little more than a mile high, so we raised the lights slightly to correct the angle. I believe we may have been at the maximum distance for that to work. This was my first experiment with it."

"It worked very effectively. With the men standing in the dark, the glow on the targets made them perfectly clear. I think it could be done over a longer range with several lights. I'm going to recommend this technique to our men in the field. If you could use searchlights like that to light up a battlefield, that could turn the tide in our favor in a night battle."

"Yes, sir. But only if we can divert the lights from incoming aircraft."

"Priorities must always be determined based on actual field conditions," he said. "You may return to your unit now."

Henderson was irate when I walked into HQ. "You aren't here to play games. You're here to train soldiers."

"The radar was active, sir. No targets were approaching. I wanted to do a little experiment."

"Next time you want to experiment, run it by me first. I can't have you embarrassing me like this. Everyone was talking about it, and I had no idea what had happened. The army has a chain of command, and you are near the bottom. Next time you have an idea like this, you bring it to me. You DO NOT go off half-cocked experimenting with army equipment and men. We have regulations for a reason."

"I'm sorry, sir. I didn't anticipate anyone finding out until I had experimented a few more times."

"No? Well, those searchlight beams aren't exactly invisible. You can see them for miles. There will be a reprimand for this. If anything like this happens again, you will definitely be taken down a step!"

"Yes, sir."

I knew that Kincaid's XO, Barker, had not suffered such a tirade.

I flopped onto my cot back in the barracks, sure that Henderson was more upset that he could not take credit for the idea than whether I had followed the chain of command to get his approval. When I woke up that afternoon and returned to my desk, the first thing in the inbox was my own reprimand, typed up in triplicate, ready for me to sign.

After roll call the following day, Colonel Squires called to me.

"Sinclair, you're not qualified in rifle."

"That's correct, sir. Unfortunately, we moved on to the big guns in basic before I qualified, and I have never tested again."

"We can't send you overseas without a rifle qualification. Spend all your spare time on the rifle range until you qualify."

"Yes, sir. I'll start today."

How could I get in any time on the target range? I already

spent twelve hours supervising the troops' night training, attending an hour or two of liaison meetings with other units early mornings before dropping into bed and then rising again at 1500 to deal with the battery paperwork. I resolved to wake up at 1430 to go to the practice range.

I did wake up earlier that afternoon when a private entered my tent with a telegram from Sarah Gale saying she would be arriving in three days. I ran to HQ to request permission to pick her up at the train station.

"Sinclair, you're an officer. You can't fraternize with enlisted personnel. She is completely off-limits," Henderson said.

"But sir, we had a relationship before she enlisted. It isn't as though I'll be taking advantage of her. I don't supervise her and will not have any opportunity to influence her promotions or reviews."

"Sinclair," Henderson said. "A relationship with that WAAC is off limits. "

"What?"

"No fraternization." He smirked as he turned to go to his desk. "Now, get to the rifle range."

I bolted out the door and ran to the range, where I discovered that so much practice during basic training with the bent sight meant I tended to aim high. I had never been that good a shot, but I could bag a rabbit or pheasant for dinner with a shotgun, and I had killed a badly wounded boar with a muzzleloader. Now it seemed I could only shoot this new, high-powered carbine over the head of that giant Roosevelt elk in Washington.

Three days later, Sarah Gale arrived on base. I muttered under my breath all the way back to my quarters that morning.

"What's the matter," asked Douglas as I stomped up the steps.

"Everything," I said.

It was worse than living half a country apart. I knew she was just up the street all the time, but I couldn't see her. We managed to cross paths every once in a while but could only exchange a quick hello. Security was very tight around the WAACs. Their officers kept a close eye on them, and any minor breach of protocol was suspect. Having women in the army was new, and both male and female officers were cautious. Then one day, I had an idea. I knew the route she took from her barracks to her post. I walked past her, conspicuously dropping a wadded-up piece of paper. She picked it up, opened it, and read the note inside, inviting her to meet me at a department store in town. When I glanced back, she nodded slightly.

Now all I had to do was get permission to leave the base.

"You have no off-base privileges until you are qualified in rifle," Henderson told me.

As I arrived at the range that afternoon, I called the instructor over and asked to be tested.

I felt much more confident this time around. First of all, I had checked the site on the rifle and found it accurate. I also remembered the boar hunt. Sarah Gale's granny's words echoed in my mind. "*Hold it real steady and squeeze slow.*"

I fired from a standing position and hit the target. Not a bullseye, but close enough to pass. I dropped to a sitting position and fired a second round. I grazed the side of the target, but the paper was still intact. I tried again and once more missed while sitting. If I was going to pass, I needed to pick up my average. Picturing Graham in my mind checking the wind, pointing the rifle at the target, and making the slightest adjustments, I rammed another cartridge in place, hit the mark sitting, then kneeled for the next round. Six rounds and I was at four hits. I had to do better from 200 feet if I was going to pass. I did well on the two standing rounds but again missed once while sitting. I needed a perfect score on all the remaining rounds, which involved standing to kneeling twice and standing to a prone position twice. I concentrated and hit the target with the following six rounds. Twenty minutes until I had told Sarah Gale I would meet her and two more rounds to go. I shot, hit the target, dropped prostrate, and fired again. I was barely within the perimeter, but a bullet had pierced the paper. I had passed. To my surprise, knowing I could hit what I aimed the rifle at gave me new confidence in my ability as a soldier, even though I didn't believe I would be likely to shoot a rifle as XO of an AAA artillery unit.

"Congratulations, Lieutenant Sinclair. You passed. Just don't do much sitting when you get sent overseas. Come with me while I prepare your certificate."

I glanced at my watch.

"I have a meeting. I'll pick up the certificate tomorrow. Could you call my Captain and tell him I passed."

"Sure thing."

I sprinted back to HQ, grabbed the keys to the jeep I had requisitioned, and headed downtown.

CHAPTER 24
TOGETHER AGAIN

Sarah Gale stepped out from behind a rack of women's clothes and smiled at me when I entered the department store. I strolled toward the stationary department, where I stood examining some linen fiber paper. Soon Sarah Gale appeared at my side.

"You don't know how good it is to see you," she gushed. "I had a week at home on my way to Orlando, and it was the strangest experience. Of course, I've grown and matured quite a bit in the last several weeks, but it was just three months of the same old thing for my family. They treated me like the same young girl who left." She picked up a pen and examined it. "They did welcome me home with a big dinner, but I was back at my old chores the next day as though nothing was different. I tried to explain how I had changed, but they didn't understand. I was glad to leave. I feel like I'm doing something important when I'm working on photography. I was so busy cooking and cleaning, washing clothes, and slopping hogs when I was home that I didn't even have time to write to you." She carefully placed the pen back on the shelf and moved around to the other side of me, barely pausing for breath.

"It is really interesting how people treat me when I'm in uniform. Some people treat me just like a guy in uniform. I mean, they respect me and thank me for my service to my country. Others are very negative. One woman came up to me and shouted at me. She said it was not a woman's place to join the army. That we should be keeping the home fires burning for the men who have gone overseas to protect us. I tried not to take it personally." She picked up some onion skin paper, flipping it back and forth.

"The thing I did take personally was a group of new officers

(I could tell from their very shiny second lieutenant bars) who seemed to think the WAACs were created to provide relief of their personal needs. It was very embarrassing. I'm here to serve my country as much as they are." The onion skin slipped out of her grasp, and I bent to pick it up as she continued.

"Even though I said I wanted to see the world, I'm getting very tired of train travel. It was almost a week on the train to get home and three days more to get here. It can be very boring when you're traveling over territory you've seen before.

"I missed you so much. I know you have been busy with training the men and everything."

"Hello to you, too," I said.

"Oh, I'm sorry. I didn't let you get a word in, did I? How is searchlight training?"

"Enlightening," I said. "And it does keep me busy day and night."

"How is your family doing? Is your Granny still going strong?"

"I just got word that she has pneumonia. I am worried about her. At eighty-six, pneumonia can be serious. Otherwise, things are going well. Doris has a boyfriend. It's a guy who has been helping Dad out at the creamery, but he will soon be going into the service. I'm a little worried about Dad running the place all by himself, but he's worked hard all his life. How are you enjoying Orlando?"

"I love the palm trees, but there aren't any beaches. I thought Florida was surrounded by beaches."

"It is, but we are pretty far inland here. Maybe we can figure a way to escape the beach one of these days."

A soldier walked by and eyed us closely.

"I'm not sure we can get away with this too often," Sarah Gale said. "What if that had been one of our superior officers rather than a private? We really need to be careful."

"We do." I pulled her behind a display and quickly kissed her. "This is agony. I never anticipated anything like this."

"It won't last forever," she promised, "and we can keep finding ways to sneak in a little time together."

I kissed her goodbye, and she left the store. I bought some

stationery, drove back to base, and returned the jeep to the motor pool. I had thought it would be so much better to have spent a little time with her, but not knowing when I would see her again or even if I could spend time with her was torture.

***

It rained all night, and I came in wet, soggy, and exhausted. But before I could go to sleep, I had to talk with the AAF pilots.

"Those lights didn't help at all," the squad leader complained. "In fact, they blinded us as we were about to land. I'm surprised the men all made safe landings."

"I'm sorry. We were given the wrong coordinates. We thought you would be landing from the opposite direction."

"The ground level winds switched directions in that storm. Don't you know anything about landing an airplane?"

"Actually, no."

"We land into the wind. When the wind switches, you should turn the lights around."

"The lights don't move as quickly as your airplanes. We would have to haul them to the other end of the runway. We can't move them while burning, so we would have doused the lights, and your first men would have landed in complete darkness. While we relit and adjusted them, the light would be directly in your pilot's eyes for a time, and they would be blinded much longer. We kept them as low as we could under the circumstances. If we'd tried to move the lights, things would have been much worse. However, the fact that you land into the wind is handy information for us. Maybe we could put lights at either end of the runway and use those that will allow you to land into the wind without being blinded."

"I have no idea why you were never told that we land into the wind," the wing commander grumbled, shaking his head.

"Army communications, I guess," I responded, shrugging my shoulders. "At least we know now. We'll watch the windsocks and try not to blind the trainees again.

I went back to battery HQ to sign a few more reports and check in with the staff before going to sleep.

***

Christmas came, my second away from home. I worked all day, then left an unsigned gift for Sarah Gale at her barracks on the way to Christmas service. Marshall presided. Because Christmas fell on a Friday, we had to be out of the Chapel before the Jewish services started, so it was rushed, and because Marshall was a Presbyterian, it wasn't much of a celebration anyway. I missed the caroling and parties back home. I left the chapel wholly demoralized and headed quickly for my barracks.

"Gene," I heard, "you were leaving so fast I almost didn't catch you."

I turned to see Sarah Gale.

"Please, I don't want either of us to get into trouble," I said, frowning at her. "We can't be seen together."

"Oh, Gene, what's wrong?" Sarah Gale asked, sensing my mood.

"Sarah Gale, I'm sorry. I had a tough day—or rather night."

"I have good news that might cheer you up. We don't have to worry about fraternization anymore," she said.

"But my CO is adamant I can't associate with you because you're enlisted."

"No. I'm not enlisted anymore. I'm a second officer." She tapped the new insignia on her uniform. "That's like a second lieutenant. They assigned me some new duties that only officers can do, so they promoted me. Something to do with security clearance only officers can get. I thought that was a little backward, promoting me rather than training an officer to do the job, but they said there aren't enough WAAC officers yet. It's only a temporary promotion. I'll have to go back to Des Moines for OTS to make it permanent, but they want me to start the work ASAP. I don't know when I'll be trained to be an officer, but I already have the rank. The work I'll be doing is top secret. I can't tell you anything about it. Only twenty-four WAACS, scattered around the country, do what I'll be doing.

"It's a good feeling to work hard and be appreciated for what you do. There's something different about this group compared to the friends I've always had before. I think it's because we respect ourselves and our work, and the men around here do too. That helps us all be more confident, which leads to doing a better job and earning more respect."

Before I could reply, she scurried off. Why could I never get a word in with her? I could talk about almost anything with anyone else, but Sarah Gale somehow left me tongue tied.

Strict rules in the officer's mess prohibited male and female officers from sitting together. Still, I managed to talk with Sarah Gale in the mess line, where we "happened" to get in line together. We made plans to go to dinner and a movie on Saturday. I could hardly wait after the weeks of her being so close and yet so far away—until her promotion.

I filled out a pass and took it to Henderson to sign.

"Is this some sneaky way to meet up with that enlisted WAAC?" he asked. "I know you've been seen talking with her."

"Sir, she is an officer now. There are no rules preventing officers from meeting off base."

"New rules need to be established for those women. Do you know the kind of women who enlist in the WAACs? You don't want t get yourself involved with that sort of woman."

"I was involved with Sarah Gale before the WAACs existed, and she is the sweetest, most ladylike girl you can imagine. She just wants to do her duty for her country."

"You are certain she has not been tainted by those other women?"

"Sir, I don't believe those rumors are true. However, I have not been allowed to speak with her until today. I thought your father oversaw their training. Would he allow that sort of thing?"

Henderson seemed shocked that I would make this personal. He turned away from me slightly, seeming to consider his answer.

"The old man and I don't always see eye to eye, but you have a point. If an innocent girl did manage to get into the force, I can't see him allowing her to be defiled. So, I'll give you your pass provided you give me a complete report on any change in her character."

I met her at the gate just in time to catch a streetcar.

***

We went to see *The Man Who Came to Dinner*. I thought it was hilarious, satirically, and wickedly funny. Unfortunately, Sarah Gale didn't find it as amusing as I did.

As we walked to a nearby restaurant talking about the movie, she said, "That man, Sherry Whiteside, was really mean to his secretary, to that family he was staying with, then he was so nice to that actress and other famous people."

"The movie is a satire on uppity people from New York."

"I thought they made fun of the people from small towns in the Midwest."

"That too. It was all exaggerated."

"Well," she sighed, "I suppose it was funny. I guess it was a good movie."

People waited in line at the restaurant. Nevertheless, the maître d' found us a good seat near the window.

"I love shrimp," Sarah Gale said. "Dad would bring back buckets of shrimp and crabs from a job he used to have on the outer banks, and we would boil them up and eat them on the porch so we could throw the shells on the ground. The chickens loved them, too. The next morning all the shells and leftover bits of shrimp were gone."

I ordered fillet of sole for me and shrimp scampi for Sarah Gale. As we sat talking after giving our order, a matronly woman rushed up to our table and started yelling at Sarah Gale.

"It's all your fault! You and *hussies* like you. If you had not taken his nice safe desk job and made them send him off to combat, my son would still be alive!" The interruption startled both Sarah Gale and me.

The woman started sobbing. Then suddenly, she stood straight up, seemingly preparing to hit Sarah Gale with her purse. I bolted out of my seat and stood in front of the woman.

"I'm so sorry about your son, ma'am. Can you tell me what happened?" I said in the calmest voice I could muster. Behind me, I heard Sarah Gale begin to cry.

"He was sorting mail here at the base before these, these *hus-*

sies came. They took his job, and he was sent to North Africa, and the Dagos killed him!"

"Now Margaret, you know our son requested that transfer. He wanted to fight the enemy," said her husband, having followed her. From behind, he put his hands on her shoulders.

"Before the war, they said he was not *fit* for the infantry. Then when these *loose* women signed up so they could waylay nice young officers like *this* one," She gestured toward me with her purse. "*They*," she spat at Sarah Gale, "sent him off to be *killed.*"

I said, "I'm very sorry, Ma'am. You've experienced one of the greatest tragedies of war. But I will not have you accusing my date of something she didn't do."

"I'm sorry for disturbing your dinner," her husband said. "Margaret, let's go. People are staring at us."

He pulled on her shoulders to make her come with him and led her out the door as Sarah Gale sat crying. Other diners continued staring.

"It's over, folks. You can go back to your dinner," I said.

"I'm not hungry anymore," Sarah Gale whispered through her hands as she covered her face, her tears beginning to subside.

"I know you're upset. But we're not going to let that woman ruin our first evening together in months," I said. "You know she's wrong about you and about all WAACs. The initial campaign to encourage women to sign up for the WAACs was unfortunate since it claimed WAACs would free men up for combat. Although that's true to some extent, it didn't emphasize the army needed more people to do jobs that there just aren't enough army men to do. We're fighting a war on two fronts, something we've never done since the Union fought the Confederacy."

"But there are more and more people against us."

"Yes, but like I sometimes do when my CO dumps on me, you can show a brave face, stay here, and enjoy your meal as best you can. You'll show all these people in the restaurant that you're strong, that you're army. Whatever you're doing that you can't tell me about, you're dedicated to it. Remember, you'd be doing laundry back at Camp Davis or slopping hogs at home if you weren't here. In your own way, you are a pioneer, and pioneers put up with a lot of hardship."

Sarah Gale mused a bit, then said, "Oh, Gene, I never dreamt I could have a life like this. I thought I was bold staying single to my twentieth birthday. I was right to do that because I met you, and I found the WAACs. And my parents got electricity and a telephone because of the money my brothers and I can send home. My family would be living in the nineteenth century if my brothers and I hadn't joined the services, helping out the rest of our family. But why does our success have to be at the expense of young men like that woman's son?"

"Sarah Gale, your brothers and I may also become part of that expense. We could all be killed, depending on our orders, our missions. That woman's grief occurred earlier than the grief that may occur to you, your parents, or my parents.

"The war against the Axis is a form of progress, a way to make the world a better place," I added. "But I wish we could make progress without war."

As we strolled down the street after our meal, Sarah Gale said, "I didn't want to talk about it there, but my brothers have been writing to me about things enlisted men are saying about WAACs. The soldiers think the job of WAACs is to keep up morale and keep the men happy. That we are mostly prostitutes, women of questionable morals. They are even saying we all have venereal disease or are getting pregnant. There is a rumor we are issued condoms at the end of basic training. Why would they say that?"

"I can't say for sure. Maybe soldiers who are overseas desperately want to assume everything at home will be just as they left it, especially no women in the army. They're fighting this war to protect our way of life, and if things change while they're gone, that way of life they are fighting to protect may be in danger. Women serving in the army is definitely a change. They probably like to think they're protecting you, and if you're in the military, too, they aren't really saving you from much.

"Of course, they don't know what you, and all the other WAACs, are really doing. Being in the army, to many, means being in combat, or at least being combat ready. That's not what the WAACs are all about, but soldiers in Africa or the Pacific theater might not be thinking clearly about the stateside jobs that keep the army going. So, they fall back on knee-jerk reactions. It's unfortunate."

Sarah Gale put her hand on my cheek, smiling then shaking her head, which I took to mean she understood my support and understanding.

I took the long way back to base detouring through the shopping district downtown, hoping this would distract Sarah Gale.

"The buildings are so tall. What is that really tall one?"

"It is the Angebilt Hotel. It is ten stories tall."

"I've never seen a building so big before."

"You've been to Chicago. They have several that are taller."

"I didn't leave the train station."

"Well, they have several more than four times as tall as that hotel. And in New York, the Empire State Building is one hundred two stories tall.

"Right, but have you ever seen the Empire State Building?"

"No, but I ventured out of the train station in Chicago and looked around a bit."

By that time, we were at the airbase. The guards saluted, asked Sarah Gale for her identification card, and I drove her to the WAAC housing.

I kissed her good night outside the WAAC officers' quarters, then walked to my own quarters. I had held my temper while I was with her, trying to calm and reassure her. But, once I was alone, the rage overcame me. I grabbed a handful of rocks next to the path and furiously threw them against the nearest tree. How dare they defame good women like Sarah Gale, who were simply trying to serve their country.

***

Rumors about WAACs spread throughout the communities around the base. Some local women resented the crowds of WAACs shopping in their favorite stores and eating in restaurants. Some became impatient when they had to wait longer for an appointment at their favorite salon. So, Sarah Gale and I began having our dates on base rather than in Orlando to avoid trouble.

We knew we wouldn't have much more time together. We both kept count of the field hours for my battalion, which was nearing the number we needed to ship out.

Then, the first week in February, when we should still have had three weeks of field training, Henderson returned from a meeting at HQ with new orders.

"Assemble the men," he ordered.

With the battery at attention before him, Henderson announced, "Men, we are shipping out in two days. Prepare the equipment and yourselves for deployment. We board the train at 1200 hours on Friday.

After dismissing the men, he turned to me.

"Notify the air corps units that we won't be working with them any longer, prepare HQ for departure, then begin checking on the platoons to make sure they are ready,"

"Yes, sir," I replied, wondering what he would be doing. I soon learned when he gave me a handful of requisitions to get typed up before Fitzgerald packed away the records and typewriter. Fitzgerald scrambled to get the required paperwork done while I ran around the base carrying out Henderson's orders. I then helped pack the documents and equipment we would take into shipping boxes.

Thursday morning, I made the rounds of the air corps units, then visited each of the platoons once more. Preparations were going smoothly. I was glad we had moved the battalion at least once before.

How would I get word to Sarah Gale? We had planned a weekend together. Unfortunately, I would be gone by then. I slipped a note to her at the mess.

"We are shipping out. Meet me by the PX at 2000 hours."

She met me there, carrying something wrapped in brown paper.

I hugged her, holding her tight for several minutes. Finally, she said, "I got this so you could always write to me no matter where you are."

I opened the box to find a neat little lap desk with paper, pen, and ink. It would fit nicely in the tray at the top of my footlocker.

"Ok. I'll try to write more often. But, I'm not sure what combat conditions will allow or how long mail might take to get to you." I kissed her lips lightly.

"I got you something, too." Tucking the lap desk under my arm, I pulled a small box out of my pocket. I opened it and showed her the pearl ring inside. She squealed and threw her arms around me.

"It's a promise ring. It means I promise to be faithful to you to the end of the war. Can you agree to be faithful to me until the end of the war? Then we can decide if we should marry."

"I know what a promise ring is," she said. "And I promise. You mean everything to me. I'll wait for you forever."

"And I you!" I pulled her close and kissed her to seal the promise.

We walked silently for a time, neither knowing where to start.

Finally, I said, "You know how much I love you, don't you?"

"Of course I do. I just wish I could go, too."

"What? WAACs can't go into combat. That would be going too far, putting women in combat."

"I don't want to go to combat. I want to be with you."

"I couldn't live with myself if I put you in danger. So no, I want you to stay here where you're safe."

She leaned against me. "I am proud of you and very scared."

I wrapped my arms around her. She was trembling. "Sweetheart, I will come back to you."

She looked up at me with tears in her eyes. Peering into their green, watery depths, almost too much for me, I kissed her and held her tighter.

"I'll be waiting for you to come back," she whispered. "If you can take back the Pacific as quickly as the Japanese took it away, that should be about a year from now."

"The Japs did have the advantage of surprise. I hope you'll give us a bit more than a year."

"Not much more. You'd better come back to me soon."

"I promise I will come back as soon as humanly possible," I took her in my arms and kissed her long and hard.

CHAPTER 25
SWAYING ACROSS THE PACIFIC

O nce Douglas gave the thumbs up, we were ready to move out. Loading the equipment had gone much more smoothly this time.

"Fall in!" Colonel Squires ordered. In parade formation, we watched the train move out with our equipment. "Right face! Forward march!" The battalion marched to the passenger train to the music of the base's marching band.

Squires had assigned Battery A cars two through twelve of the forty car train, a dubious honor, particularly for the men in the first four troop sleeper cars behind the two loud locomotive engines that would spew coal smoke and cinders the whole trip. The troop sleepers were split, four in front and five behind a kitchen car where our personnel prepared enlisted men's meals and an officers' car for the lieutenants. The other batteries had similar setups with an officers' kitchen, dining car, and lounge between Batteries B and C. Cars for the captains and majors plus one for Colonel Squires brought up the rear. I had never seen a train anywhere near this long, but I'd heard that even longer troop transport trains had been put together.

The train pulled out very slowly. Loaded with an entire battalion, a train this size had tremendous inertia. When we got rolling, however, we kept rolling. A porter told me that troop trains had precedence over all other traffic on the rails, including our equipment. We would cross the entire country in just two and a half days.

Demand for troop trains was so high the railroad companies used any car that was not falling apart. Douglas and I shared a compartment in an old first-class car. Over our door a plaque with the numbers eighteen eighty-nine.

"Do you suppose that's when this car was built?" I asked Douglas.

"Why look at this upholstery," he said. "And that carved wood door? It has to have been built in the last century. Nobody takes the time to do things like that anymore."

We settled on the worn brown upholstery. Douglas was soon asleep, having been preparing and loading equipment almost around the clock for the past two days. So I left the compartment, searching for something more interesting than Douglas's snore, walking through the sleeper cars. The men greeted me as I checked on their welfare and thanked the porters for looking after them.

The doorway to the very first car of the train stood open, so I decided to investigate. I stumbled upon a barbershop open for business.

"Shave and a haircut," I told the barber over the engine noise. I was his only customer.

"Are things usually this slow around here?" I asked as he worked.

"Only in the first few hours when nobody knows we're here. Two hours or even less after you walk out of here, it'll be standing room only. I'll work until ten tonight, and LeRoy will have a line waiting when he opens at eight in the morning."

"What else is in this car?" I asked.

"A little tailor shop," he replied. "And a mini commissary. They don't stock much, but the men can pick up whatever essentials they need during the trip."

"I hadn't expected anything like this. Do all troop trains have them?"

"Only the long-haul trains. Gives the men a chance to catch up on haircuts and uniform repairs and gets them to their destination looking good and ready to go."

As soon as I walked out of the car and the men got a look at me, they started lining up at the doorway.

"You certainly look spiffy," Carson said as I walked into the officers' dining car.

"Thank you. Just had a shave and a haircut at the barbershop at the front of the train."

Carson rubbed his hand over his head. "I could use one, too." He jumped up and hurried out. Tilton followed him, racing to try to be first at the barbershop.

"There's already a line," I called out, but they had reached the next car and didn't hear.

The barber was right. The line was almost back to my compartment when I returned.

Douglas was awake and staring out the window as the farms of Georgia flashed past.

"Are you missing your farm?" I guessed.

"My pigs. I'm missing my pigs."

"Pigs?"

"My brother-in-law is actually the farmer. I breed pigs. Got an MS in swine genetics from Penn State. I've been developing an American landrace pig, different from the original Danish stock. I have two boars and thirty-five sows at home, and nobody's really taking care of them. I mean, they feed them and all, but the breeding program is on hold until I get back. I miss my pigs."

"Are you afraid you won't come back?"

"I don't think about that. We're well trained. We won't be on the front lines. It's not like we're in the infantry. Or Marines. We'll come back. Is that what's got you down?"

"Not the thought of dying so much as the thought of killing. Philosophically I understand we have to defend our country and our honor, but war in general seems brutal. We'll be killing other human beings." Then I added, "And I miss my girl."

"Seems to me our part in the killing is pretty indirect."

"It may be less indirect than we expect. I'm just torn."

"Sinclair, we know what we have to do and how to do it. Try not to analyze it too much. You'll drive yourself crazy,"

I guessed missing pigs didn't count as crazy.

***

The train was halfway across the country before stopping for more than a few minutes. After a prolonged slowing down period, we pulled to a stop on a siding somewhere in West Texas.

The conductor came to the lounge car, turned into the officer's club. "This is the only siding along this section of track long enough for two troop trains to pass. We're waiting until the eastbound train comes along. In the meantime, you might as well get your men off and give them a little exercise." I thought the conductor might have taken over from Henderson, given his "order," but then I noticed several porters behind him, cleaning equipment at the ready.

We ordered everyone off the train and had them run five miles up and five miles back along the tracks. When they returned, they continued running to a water tank we had passed. Someone pulled the chain, and men ran through by the score for a refreshing, albeit cold, shower. About then, the other troop train rumbled by, and we headed back to our train, drying off as we ran.

After that long break, we changed engineers four times, all brief stops. Our train kept chugging across New Mexico and Arizona, then Central California. At last, we slowed, finally entering a little town not too far from the coast. A jumble of taverns, photo booths, small shops, clubs, jewelry stores, theaters, and other establishments crowded the streets. The men pointed out the places they intended to visit.

We disembarked onto a broad dirt road lined with a double row of trucks. A colonel rode up on a motorcycle and spoke briefly with Squires.

Squires turned and shouted, "Enlisted men, into the trucks. Stay with your platoon!"

Officers passed the order forward from Squire's car, and the enlisted men piled into the trucks, banging on the tailgate when the truck was full. A small convoy of jeeps for the officers replaced the trucks when they had moved out. The corporals driving the jeeps dropped us at our temporary HQ and officers' quarters. Across a narrow dirt road, the enlisted men hopped out of the trucks and bounded into the barracks.

Once the vehicles moved out, we could hear the bay's soft lapping against the dock behind the enlisted men's barracks, nothing like the constant roar of the ocean that assailed us during basic training at Camp Callan or the serenade of gentler waves of Peugeot Sound. Instead, it smelled of rotting fish and seaweed mixed with diesel exhaust fumes; the lapping water sounded thick and oily.

We spent our first day unloading equipment, which arrived a few hours behind us. The second morning Colonel Squires addressed the officers. "Gentlemen, the battalion must pass final inspection before we ship out. All equipment will be retested. Every soldier's uniform and field pack must be certified complete. Examine everything from shoestrings to helmet lining for wear or damage. Replace anything unlikely to last for the next year. Experts here at the camp will certify all arms and equipment. Then everything must be re-packed for transport. Finally, every individual must undergo a medical and dental check. Additional training will cover things we may encounter overseas. All of this must be completed within two weeks. Battery A will start with medical checks, Battery B at the mock airfield checking out equipment, and Battery C assure that your men and their personal equipment are ready, then report for First Aid training. Keep the men moving. There's a lot to do in the next two weeks."

As soon as we were dismissed, Henderson ordered me to get the men from the HQ sections to the infirmary for exams, then get onto the paperwork. The HQ battery's administrative section consisted of Henderson, me, five enlisted clerks, and two radiomen, but HQ also included the mess section, supply section, and repair section. As Henderson continued giving orders to other lieutenants, I found the staff sergeants of those sections and ordered them to get the men to the infirmary. As we entered, we were handed a pre-deployment health survey form, which the men filled out as they waited in line. The officers' line was much shorter. I barely finished my own record before my exam began.

"How many men go through here per week," I asked the doctor who checked my form and body.

"It varies," he replied. "The post can house twenty thousand. Two thousand are permanently stationed here—medical personnel, training officers, mess staff, security, everything we need to run the place. So, we can house eighteen thousand in-transit personnel. I'm not sure we can process that many in a week." He thumped my chest a couple of times. "You're good to go. Immunizations up to date, heart and lungs sound healthy."

I returned to our temporary HQ and began to sort the schedules, announcements, instructions, and forms that messengers continued to drop on the desk.

I told Sergeant Martin, our mess sergeant, "Camp staff will provide mess so all your men can participate in training. First aid class at 0900, followed by abandon ship training. 1400 report to the infiltration course—1900 to 2100 a lecture on troop conduct aboard ship. Have your men there."

Henderson returned from his physical.

"Sir, there's quite a schedule of classes and activities set out for us," I told him.

"Notify the platoon commanders. They need to have all uniforms inspected by 0900 tomorrow."

Fitzgerald typed up a schedule, which I posted in HQ, and sent a carbon copy to each platoon by messenger.

Messengers came and went all day:

"The mock airfield will be available for your radar and searchlight equipment tests between 0100 and 0500 on Friday."

"The following eight men in Platoon A received additional immunizations as they passed through the medical exam."

"The following three men in Platoon B. Assigned times are listed below."

"Anyone who wears glasses must have two pairs. Additional pairs of glasses will be available at fourteen hundred on Wednesday."

"Officers report to the firing range for the experts to fire your sidearms at eleven hundred the day after tomorrow."

"Lectures on mail censorship and security, Monday evening."

I passed on the orders and sent memos to the personnel involved.

"Platoon C needs five new uniform shirts, ten complete sets of underwear, thirty pairs of socks, three belts...." I signed the requisition form and passed it to the private sitting behind me.

"Get this to Sergeant Hammond," I said.

"The following eight men in the maintenance section and one man in Platoon C need additional dental work."

"Why would the maintenance section have so many men who need dental work?" I asked.

"Maybe they like their desserts a little too much," Perry said. "Or the mechanics have been tightening screws with their teeth."

"Probably because it's made up of blue-collar workers who had less dental work done as civilians," said Martin, who was hanging around without anything to do since he didn't have to fix our meals.

***

Henderson gave the men leave the first night. "I'll let them get it out of their systems," he told me. "Then we can get down to business."

Four men were missing at roll call in the morning—more paperwork.

Carson and Brasseux gave me their uniform replacement list on the way to first aid training. I scanned them. Twenty sets of underwear, ten helmet linings, five new shirts, fourteen belts, five hundred sets of shoestrings—did I read that right?

"Carson, what is this all about? Five hundred shoestrings?"

"No shoestring is gonna last a year in the jungle. So to have enough to last a year, I figured we need five hundred."

"I'll make sure Sergeant Hammond has plenty of shoestrings, but I won't have him order five hundred for your platoon."

First aid class reviewed the usual information. I fidgeted and squirmed, knowing that a mountain of paperwork was piling up on my desk. Several men, including Captain Henderson, slept through the film on foot care. The training spent an inordinate amount of time emphasizing keeping our feet dry and dealing with toenail fungus. Why was athlete's foot such a big deal?

Class finally over, we proceeded to the twenty-foot-high platform of polished decking from which we would practice abandoning ship. It looked like a section had been cut out of a vessel and plopped into the sand. Above the platform, a scaffold held two lifeboats. Four men in navy uniforms manned the station. The lead 'sailor' lectured us as we stood in the fine sand surrounding the platform.

"Seven short and one long blast on the ship's whistle means abandon ship," he explained. "When you hear the whistle, grab a life jacket and report to your lifeboat station. That will be assigned after you board. Life jackets can be found in cabins or boxes in enlisted men's bunk areas and on deck. When the lifeboats are lowered for boarding, climb in only on orders of the ship's officer at the station. When ordered, move quickly."

He ordered, "HQ and maintenance sections mount the platform."

Seven short blasts and one long blast sounded on the ship's horn as the last man stepped off the ladder.

"Retrieve life vests from the boxes," ordered the lead sailor, pointing at the boxes at the rear of the platform. "Put them on and prepare to board the lifeboats." We rushed to the boxes, pulled out life preservers, and put them on. The lifeboats were lowered.

"Board the lifeboats."

Henderson stepped forward.

"Officers last," the lead sailor said. "Make sure all your men are off the ship before you board a lifeboat."

The rest of the battery, waiting below, laughed loudly. Unfortunately, Henderson didn't appreciate their laughter.

"No leave for the rest of our stay here," he ordered. I didn't look forward to issuing that memo!

The laughter stopped, and attitudes became serious and focused as the drill proceeded. Starting with privates, we threw ourselves over the rail into the boats. As soon as everyone was on board, the lifeboats were lowered.

"Grab the oars and row away from the ship as quickly as possible."

We awkwardly got the worn oars into their slips and put them over the side, rowing in the sand.

"Ok. Out of the boats. Platoon A climb the ladder."

The sailors cranked the boats back up to the top of the scaffolding, and the drill continued platoon by platoon.

Over the next few days, a sense of urgency and gravity banished the schoolboy attitudes of the recruits as training sessions continued. Old hands tried to look confident, but they had not been to war before and were also on edge. Tempers flared, and terse jokes betrayed their nervousness.

Our equipment tested out well. Training in close combat, field sanitation, security, and intelligence flew by. Finally, on our last afternoon, we packed up our remaining gear and drove it onto the ferry, which would take it to a cargo ship that would arrive at our destination after we did. That destination would be unknown until we were out at sea.

Before we left the dock, Henderson ordered, "Everyone report to Building 345 at 1900. Dismissed."

We ate our last meal stateside.

"My men are well redaay, "Brasseux boasted at mess. "We can take on da world."

"We'll just be takin on the Japs, but that's enemy enough." Carson put in.

The volume of the conversation increased as more officers offered opinions on the superiority of their men. I noticed Edelstein sitting quietly, a little apart. I didn't approach him because it seemed each time we spoke, he resented me more, but I did point him out to Marshall.

"I can't talk to him," Marshall said. "He's against religion of any kind. It would provoke another argument, and I don't think this is the time. I'll pray for him, though."

Douglas finally went over and convinced him to join the group.

***

I had a few more loose ends to tie up, so I reported to Building 345 late. When I walked in, I realized Henderson had ordered us to a USO show.

Francis Langford came on stage, and the men went wild. She sang Moonglow and a couple of other songs.

"You really weren't upset, were you," I whispered to Henderson.

"Just wanted everyone to pay attention. And I needed them

all to be here tomorrow, so I kept them here tonight."

Red Skelton, the headliner, came out.

"Howdy, folks. You know I came up here on a train from Hollywood. Have you ever noticed how they call over the PA system when it is time to board a train? Now boarding on track (scratchy sound effect), Train number (silence) northbound for Scmmmto Pssdna, Snabara, and points north," he mumbled, just like we had experienced as we crossed the country during our travels since the beginning of the war. The whole place roared with laughter. When he finished his monologue, he said, "Patty Thomas is going to dance for us,"

She stutter-stepped to the microphone and pulled it out of its stand. "I would love to have one of you boys dance with me," she cooed into the microphone, stroking it with one hand.

"Wright!" shouted Brasseux, Tilton, and Carson in unison. The rest of the battery took up the cry.

"Who is Wright?" Thomas cooed some more. "Come on up here, Mr. Right."

After Wright sprinted up the steps to her, she said, "Those bars mean you are an officer, right?"

"First lieutenant," he said into her microphone, which she held out for him.

"Those bars look awfully shiny. Have you been a first lieutenant for long?"

"Six days now."

"Ooh, I have a newborn lieutenant here," she said, facing back to the audience and nodding toward Wright. The men laughed. She turned back to Wright. "Let me show you the steps to this dance. Just follow me." She put the microphone back on the stand.

She demonstrated a simple side step and a little kick. Wright copied her.

"Now we do the same thing back the other way," she shouted.

She cued the band, which began to play. Thomas and Wright did the step a couple of times. She changed it, so they moved away, then toward each other, and bumped hips. He took her hand and spun her around. Shouts and whistles from the crowd encouraged him. He started leading her, doing increasingly complex steps. The crowd roared as he turned and spun her. At the tune's end, she came back to the microphone, clearly breathless.

"He may be a baby lieutenant, but he certainly knows how to dance."

The crowd clapped and cheered.

Red Skelton came back and did another routine, then the whole cast came on stage and sang, "Always in My Heart."

The men left the show repeating parts of Skelton's routine, laughing loudly and singing bits of the songs. The tension of training for imminent combat had broken.

***

All executive officers reported to the embarkation center immediately after reveille—no breakfast. In the long, low building along the docks, a Sergeant handed us stacks of shipping cards to distribute to the men. These were essentially boarding cards and meant to make sure all the right people and none of the wrong people were on board when we left the embarkation center.

"The cargo ships are blocking access to the pier in San Francisco." The sergeant said. "You'll be required to climb from the ferry to the transport ship in the harbor using cargo nets. The procedure will be described while in route."

I sat on the long concrete dock and sorted the cards by section. As the men marched through the departure gate and up the wharf, I handed stacks of cards to the non-coms. "Each man must have the correct card to be issued food and board the ship," I told them. "Distribute them as quickly as possible so we can begin boarding."

I stood by in case there were problems. One private was missing from Sargent Johnson's section. As I picked up the radio to report him AWOL, he came running.

"Sorry, sir, I hadn't received my second pair of glasses. I had to stop by the infirmary to pick them up."

I made a note to follow up on his tardiness and told him, "Join your section and be sure to get your shipping card from Sergeant Johnson."

"Fall in! Attention!" I ordered.

Marshall stood in front of the battalion.

"Lord," he intoned in his booming prayer voice, "these men are going into the unknown. They go to protect our freedom and preserve our way of life. Go with them, guide them, protect them, and bring them back safely. We beseech thee. Amen." He backed away and stood behind the other officers.

"Forward march!" ordered Squires, and the battalion marched a short way down the wharf to board the harbor ferry. As the men boarded, they exchanged their card for two sandwiches to eat during the four-hour ferry ride and an envelope in which they could place up to three letters to be mailed before we sailed. While the men boarded, I explored and got acquainted with the ferry.

"Go to the third deck," I told the men of Battery A as we left the dock. "The berths at the dock in San Francisco are full, and we have to climb cargo nets to board the ship. The ferry pilot told me we will be climbing from deck three."

"Sometimes your chattiness does help out," Carson said.

In San Francisco Bay, we approached the USS Mount Vernon. It towered over the three-deck ferry. A ferry in front of us finished unloading a medical detachment, including several nurses. The nurses climbed the ropes, their baggage brought on board in massive nets.

"Look at that, won't you," smiled Tilton. "We'll have some female companionship as we cross."

"They're not on board for your personal pleasure," barked Captain Henderson, who had overheard him.

Tilton nodded to Henderson to acknowledge the correction.

The medical detachment's ferry moved out, and we pulled into place beside the ship.

"Four abreast, hands on the verticals," called the navy men from the deck of the Mount Vernon.

Most of the men scrambled up quickly, but a few hesitated. The officers encouraged them with a mighty yell to get their asses up the net. Henderson and I were the last of our battalion to climb up to the transport ship. I grabbed the rope as the ferry dropped from under me in the harbor's swales. I hung from the line for a few seconds, trying to find a foothold. The ferry buoyed up again and would have crushed my foot between it and the Mount Vernon had my foot not found the rope. I climbed as fast as I could, pulling myself over the rail, my gasping more from fear than from exertion. It took me a moment to get oriented.

Henderson seemed similarly engaged.

"Gather your baggage, Lieutenant, and move on," an ensign said.

I found my duffel bag and climbed the red-carpeted staircase, following signs that said "Officer's Quarters." I found my way down the walnut-paneled hallway to the cabin I would share with Lieutenants Wright, Tilton, and Douglas. The Mount Vernon, a converted luxury liner, the upper decks still showing the luxury from when they had paying passengers on board.

We dropped our gear in our room and went to the deck. Men still climbed the nets. Another ferry waited nearby with more men.

"How many men do you think they're puttin on this ship? Douglas asked.

"About six thousand," answered an ensign standing nearby.

"How many passengers did it take when it was a cruise ship?" I asked

"Maybe twelve to fourteen hundred."

"Is it safe?" Wright asked.

"Depends on whether we meet up with a U-boat."

"Are we going in convoy?"

"Can't say."

Can't say because he knows but can't share the information or because he doesn't have a clue? I shook my head, then thought of Sarah Gale and her assignment, cheering up a bit. The ensign was probably in the same boat as Sarah Gale. Couldn't tell me a thing. I felt proud of her for being so important to the war effort.

My cabin mates and I watched men climb for a while, then watched the sunset behind the Golden Gate. Wright pulled out a diagram of the ship the crew had left in the cabin, and we used it to find the officer's mess on the deck above us. The carpet, chandeliers, tables, linen, and tableware were unchanged from when it had been the VIP dining room on the luxury liner. The food we were served was not. It was typical army food, plentiful and well prepared but not gourmet.

The ship crawled with men—barely room on the decks to catch a breath of air. I went below to check on the enlisted men. The lower decks had been stripped of luxury and converted for troop transport. Hammocks were slung five deep from floor to ceiling; men packed in like sardines had barely any room between them. Narrow walkways between the bunks allowed the men to scuttle sideways between the hammocks.

"Sir, thank you for being so efficient with the cards and all," Perry said. "We all got hammocks because we got here early. Guys in other batteries have to sleep on the floor."

"You're welcome. Just came down to tell you the officers are planning an inspection at 0900 tomorrow. Pass the word and be ready."

I went back to our stateroom. Douglas complained of feeling queasy.

"This boat isn't even moving yet," Tilton told him. "Wait until we're out of the harbor."

***

We passed under the Golden Gate at 0200 Sunday morning into a stormy sea. A few hours later, a sailor awakened me.

"Sir," he said. "Your Captain is too seasick to deal with the men. You have about twenty men who have reported to sickbay."

Thanks to the heavy seas, I wobbled back and forth on my legs as I followed the sailor through the passageways, but my stomach felt fine. I checked on the men in sickbay.

"Lieutenant, please, Lieutenant, I need to go back. I'm not going to survive this." moaned Private Moore.

"You're all going to survive this," I said to all the men in sickbay in my best officer voice. "Eat soda crackers, limit the liquid you drink and get out in the fresh air as soon as you can."

The men moaned, but a few reached for the soda crackers placed in easy reach between the swinging hammocks. They had to time their grabs when the hammock swung close to the small tables anchored to the floor between hammocks.

Next, I got a plate of soda crackers from the officer's mess and went to the cabin shared by Captains Widmeyer and Henderson. Both moaned in deep distress.

"Crackers, gentlemen?"

"I couldn't hold a thing down," said Captain Widmeyer.

Captain Henderson couldn't take his head out of the toilet long enough to say anything. Maybe that's why they call it a head on a ship?

"Well, I recommend crackers, and I hope to see you on deck soon," I said cheerily, leaving the crackers on the table and hurrying out of the smelly cabin. Henderson barfing uncontrollably seemed a bit amusing.

After a hearty breakfast with the twenty or so other officers who could eat, I went below to inform the men we wouldn't have an inspection that morning. Someone had called it off because of the rampant seasickness. The stench in the enlisted men's bunks was horrible. About eighty-five percent of the men were sick. They were not allowed to go on deck because of the storm. I jumped aside as one man lurched out of his hammock and vomited on the two hammocks slung below him. They, in turn, vomited on the floor. Obviously, seasickness and the response to seasickness went hand in hand. I made my announcement about the inspection loudly and quickly and left. No one cheered.

Rather than returning to the cabin, I walked around the enclosed promenade deck a few times. The wind was blowing hard, and occasionally the waves splashed against the windows. I realized no other ships were in sight. No convoy. Colonel Squires sat in a deck chair, reading a book.

"Ah, at least one other seasick resistant soldier on this ship."

"Yes, sir," I replied. "Excuse me, are there other books available?"

"The library is one deck down at the rear of the ship," he told me. I found a book and settled into a chair.

Over the next day or so, almost everyone found their sea legs. Colonel Squires gathered officers for lectures each morning, several of the same lessons some of us had heard in the first days at

Fort Bliss, so I tried to sit in the back and hid a Reader's Digest or small book behind the pamphlet of the day.

The navy led a lifeboat drill the third day out when the sea had calmed slightly. We held a few classes for the men those first three or four days out, but most often, the enlisted men, after morning calisthenics, sprawled on the many decks playing cards, craps, or smoking. I spent as much time as I could walking the deck and visiting with them.

***

On our fifth morning on board, we were awakened by loud banging on our cabin.

"King Neptune requests the presence of all polliwogs immediately," the sailors shouted. "Report to Promenade deck immediately."

We grabbed our life jackets and rushed to the Promenade deck, still in our skivvies. It turned out we didn't need the life jackets. At the top of the stairs, we were handed a subpoena to appear at the court of King Neptune. As we walked onto the deck, sailors holding tritons slapped us with dead fish and forced us to crawl through a tunnel filled with rotting garbage. I came out gagging as salt spray from the fire hose hit me full force, knocking me face-first into the garbage. I crawled to the chair where a Navy officer dressed as King Neptune sat. Beside him sat another dressed as his Queen.

"Swear your fealty to the King," the Queen ordered in a falsetto voice.

An ensign beside me recited the oath, and I followed along. Another ensign pulled me up and walked me to the other end of the deck, where a gentler saltwater spray washed the garbage off. I received a certificate of initiation into the Royal and Very Ancient Order of Shellbacks and a beer. I had it easy, I realized, as I watched some other officers being ordered to eat raw, dead fish or to kiss the feet of the Queen only to get kicked in the face.

I could see a similar ceremony for the noncommissioned officers on the open deck below, except their beer came in a keg. Every once in a while, a partially dressed enlisted man would wander onto that deck holding a mug of beer, indicating that similar ceremonies must be occurring all over the ship. I assumed that we only got one bottle of beer rather than free access to a keg because we might be expected to sort things out and restore discipline by the end of the day.

"How did I get off so easy," I asked a Navy lieutenant.

"You were the first pollywog to walk straight on the decks after we left port," he said. "You were also one of the first to report to the promenade deck this morning. So we've got a lot of respect for you."

"What's a pollywog?"

"Besides frog spawn, someone who has never crossed the equator."

I returned to my cabin to shower and dress. Wright showed up before I left, but I didn't see Tilton or Douglas anywhere.

The beer flowed freely, and the party lasted all day. Steak and lobster were on the menu in the officers' mess at dinner, and the enlisted men got steaks. In combination with the rich meal, the beer led to even more barfing. The barfers had to clean up their own messes.

Almost a week later, we crossed the international dateline in the middle of the night and lost a day. I recalled my attempts to explain different time zones to the boys on the train on the way to basic. The loss of a day would have really confused them.

Three days and five lectures later, we disembarked in Sydney, Australia. I stepped off the gangway and swayed. The earth felt unsteady under my feet.

CHAPTER 26
SMARTER, FITTER, HUNGRIER

A short train ride brought us to a quaint station outside Sydney. When we disembarked into a light rain shower, we spotted hand-painted signs pointing the way to Camp Warwick. So we marched in that direction. As we approached the camp, a white picket fence surrounding a grassy field emerged out of the rain. The stripped trunk of a sapling had been balanced on forked branches across a wide opening in the fence, guarded by a crude tin shack. A lone Australian soldier stepped from the shack to a nearby pole on which a telephone had been fastened. He placed a call. By the time we got there, an officer had arrived.

"Let's get you blokes settled," the Australian captain said. We started toward the barracks we could see from the entry to the camp.

"That's the bailiwick of the Royal Australian Navy. They call it the HMS Golden Hind, and we have to be piped on board if we want to go there. You'll bivouac on the racetrack. Officers next to the bleachers. Officer's mess in the clubhouse, enlisted under the bleachers."

"We're camping on a racetrack?" I asked as the men moved out. "Who was Warwick that you named the camp after him?"

"Warwick is the cockie what owned the farm before it was a racetrack. At least, this used to be a racetrack. It'll be a racetrack again as soon as this damn war is over. The Australian Jockey Club still owns it. Their president shows up every few weeks to complain about damage to the place."

"And what's a cockie?"

He looked at me with a slight frown. "A farmer," he replied.

I sat next to an Australian Royal Navy Lieutenant Commander

in the officer's mess that evening.

"Gene Sinclair," I said. "Just arrived here from the US."

"George Taylor," he replied. "Royal Navy since '39. Just got a promo to Lieutenant Commander, and I'm waiting on my new ship."

"What service have you seen?" I asked him.

"Pretty much seen it all," he said. "When the war in Europe started, we went to the Mediterranean. Had a few engagements off North Africa, several close to Italy. Then I helped bring a load of Italian POWs back here. There's an Italian POW camp across the railroad tracks.

"When the Pacific attacks started, I was on a cruiser protecting shipping lanes between Australia and the US. Then the Battle of Coral Sea. A terrifying few days. Mostly an air battle. We never saw the Jap ships, just the planes from all the carriers. Guns blasting constantly, ships sinking, men dying, bombs all around. Nobody can say yet who won. Those flyboys dropped a lot of Jap ships, but the Japs did considerable damage to the American vessels first. I think the Japs sank more ships than we did, but we busted their morale. They thought they were invincible until then. I was wounded on the third day and came back here to recover for a time.

"Most recently, it's been troop transport. We brought a load of injured home from the Kokoda Track campaign up in Papua, New Guinea. Poor blokes. The map showed Kokoda as a road, but it was more like a deer trail straight up one side to the central mountain ridge then straight down the other side. Jap pillboxes every few hundred feet as I understand it. Supply issues for ground troops—that still hasn't been worked out. When they ran out of food, our guys lived off the land. Got soaked to the skin every day by torrential rain. If the men didn't fall to the Japs they got jungle rot, dengue fever, or malaria.

"I've been helping train the Americans in amphibious landing since I came back from New Guinea. Our coral reefs and volcanic islands are much more challenging than the sandy beaches in Europe and Africa. Next week I'll ship out on HMSA *Warramunga*. She's a destroyer, and we'll be supporting amphibious landings."

"You have seen it all," I said. "Where's home?"

"Inglewood, Victoria."

I must have looked confused.

"I know," he responded to my look. "You haven't heard of it. Even Australians don't know where it is. In 1869 it was a gold rush town. Now there's a eucalyptus oil distillery there. The whole town smells like cough medicine."

"I love the smell of eucalyptus oil."

"It gets old after a while. Where you from?"

"Kansas, Smack dab in the middle of the country. Home's about forty-five miles from the geographic center of the US.

"Oh, you grew up in the Outback?"

"I think it is a little different from the Outback. Lots of wheat is grown there."

"Oh, so more like Victoria, but far from civilization."

"We like to think we're civilized in Kansas," I said.

"Crickey. I didn't mean it like that, bloke. I meant far from the big cities."

"We are that," I said. "Very, very far."

***

Two days later, we got word our equipment had arrived in Sydney. Apparently, our gear had warranted a convoy. The harbor was crawling with ships.

When the ship carrying our equipment had maneuvered to the pier and docked, I stood on the concrete marking the check-list as the material came off the ship. Brasseux and Carson directed traffic.

"We should get the smaller equipment at the front," Carson said. "If we line everything up by size, everybody can see where they're going."

"Naw, "Brasseux replied. "We should lead off with de search-lights since we're a searchlight battalion."

"It's safer with the smaller vehicles first," said Carson looking distressed at Brasseux's contrary opinion.

"Everbody just follows de vehicle in front of dem anyway. It doesn't matter if dey can't see down de highway."

"You don't know what you are talking about!" Carson shouted, fully upset.

I intervened. "What makes either of you think you have anything to do with the order of the convoy?" I asked. "Carson, tell Henderson we can go as soon as we get these last two power units on the dock." Sending Carson off immediately defused the situation.

After Carson left, I challenged Brasseux, "Why do you do that? No matter what he says, you disagree."

"It's so much fun. I time how long it takes to get him shouting."

"He sure doesn't enjoy it as much as you do."

"Nope. He doesn't. But I've been hopin he'll learn not to say dumb stuff like dat."

"You should stop baiting him. In a combat situation, it could get someone killed. Don't forget that."

Brasseux looked inward like he'd never considered that outcome. I hoped he would back off. If not, I might have to make Henderson discipline him.

I drove the lead jeep of the convoy with Colonel Squires beside me like the bell mare. The slow-moving, heavy trucks carrying the generators followed us, setting the pace. Squires looked back and grabbed the radio as we turned onto the main road.

"Tell those idiots to stay on the left side of the road!" I don't know who he radioed, but it seemed to work. All the trucks and jeeps moved over to the left-hand lane, the Aussie way.

The convoy followed us religiously, afraid of driving in the wrong lane. We headed south to Camp Warwick. When we got back to camp in the early evening, the guard lifted the pole over the entrance, vaguely indicated a field where we should park the equipment, and went back into his shack. We pulled in, parked the vehicles, then headed for the mess. A disgruntled American colonel marched into the mess halfway through the meal shouting.

"Who parked their goddamned equipment on our campsite?"

Colonel Squires rose to talk with him.

"Should have known," the colonel shouted. "Always one step ahead of me, Squires."

The colonels clapped each other on the back and strode out

shoulder to shoulder to get things straightened out. It didn't take long because they came back into the mess, enjoying their dinners together before I finished eating.

For the next several days, Fitzgerald and I shuffled papers as each platoon checked their lights, power units, and radar, the repair section did maintenance on the trucks, and Douglas and the drivers checked jeeps. Everything appeared to have made the crossing in good shape.

"We're short one jeep," Douglas announced as he came into our HQ tent.

"How did that happen?" I asked, perplexed. "Everything was accounted for when it came off the ship."

"Who stole our jeep?" demanded Henderson, who strode from the back of the HQ tent. "Sinclair, call the MPs."

"Let me ask around first. I'll see if I can find it." Henderson nodded.

No one had an extra jeep. The a jeep loaded down with six GIs roared past me as I strode toward the MP HQ. I recognized them as part of Brasseux's platoon. And Brasseux was with them.

Running after the jeep, which almost ran into Brasseux's tent as it swerved to a stop, I shouted to the men, "What the hell?"

Brasseux momentarily looked at me with a blank stare, then said, "I needed a little somethin, so I took de boys to look for it."

"What did you need so badly?" I asked. "And why did you pull five enlisted men to look for it?"

"I wanted de best beer in Australia and wanted dem to try all of dem, an' tell me which one is da best."

"You didn't have permission to take a jeep."

"I signed de paper. Dey's fifty jeeps sittin over dere doin nothin'. Who's got a problem with it?"

"Douglas and now Henderson."

"What did he have to tell Henderson for?"

"I sometimes think, as bright as you are, you're an idiot. You took government property without permission and went AWOL for beer. Could be trouble. Now, I'll take the jeep."

"By the way, what is the best beer in Australia?" I asked the men.

One of the soldiers said, "It's a tossup between Victoria Bitter and Tooheys."

By the time I got back to HQ, Douglas had found a requisition form for the jeep at the bottom of the stack of paperwork waiting for processing. We took it to Henderson and explained the situation.

"Did they choose Victorian Bitters?" asked Henderson as he signed the requisition.

"That or Toohey's," I replied, amazed at his lackadaisical response.

***

Our orders instructed us to report to the Queensland Jungle Training Centre near Townsville. Once again, we loaded all the equipment on flatcars, blocked the wheels, and tied everything down. This was getting to be routine. The battalion departed on its first Australian troop train. It seemed, on average, about the same as an American, berths comfortable enough, food okay. However, it did not have porters. The men soon realized that they would have to make their own beds and police their cars on this two day trip. Squires ordered inspections to make sure.

At Townsville, a local constable boarded the train.

"The speed limit for all vehicles within the city limits is twenty-five miles per hour. Do not move any vehicle faster than that. Keep your men in the camp and limit their activity in town," he told the officers.

The ordinance the constable upheld was intended to create a safe environment for the townspeople. Instead, slow moving convoys of American equipment blocked the streets. As we sat in the traffic jam on the main road, I stepped into a nearby shop to buy pipe tobacco and learned that many of the townspeople had evacuated inland and farther south, fearing a potential attack by the Japanese. Not many townspeople remained who needed protection from our presence.

Well past noon, we left our equipment at the staging area at Armstrong Paddock, apparently cockie Armstrong's former horse pasture, and boarded several troop landing ships at the

Townsville wharves. As the sun set, we cruised along the coast. We slept on the deck of the troop transport, awakening to find the boats moored at the mouth of a river. An instructor joined us and ordered us to march up a narrow road that followed the river. A wall of green surrounded us as we trailed the instructor into the jungle. I knew some of the plants well, primarily as houseplants—ferns, philodendron, and palms. Others were new and strange, trees with fruit on their trunks but not their branches, plants with no roots, and plants whose roots started above ground. We walked past a stand of tall trees with flaking bark. The fallen bark formed huge piles around the six-foot diameter trunks. The top of the tree was invisible, obscured by the forest's dense understory. Thick vines wound around some of the trees and seemed to reach out to trip us as we walked. Orchids, lichens, staghorn ferns, and mosses grew on the trunks of trees and fallen logs.

"Stay away from this tree," the instructor said, pointing. "It is called the stinging tree. The leaves are covered with little hairs like fine shards of glass. Get them in your skin, and you'll be sorry."

Few of us had traveled outside our home state. None of us had been out of the country before, so finding ourselves in the middle of the jungle on a sweltering late summer day in March felt unreal.

As the ground rose more steeply, we passed a sign, half-hidden in the plants growing alongside the road, that said Jungle Warfare Training School. We didn't see a school. The instructor ordered us to halt. "This jungle is much like what you'll find on the islands of New Guinea, Indonesia, and most of the Pacific, except the slope is gentler here. Battery A, we'll drop you mates off here. Your objective is two miles north northwest of this point." He handed each officer a map and compass. "In the jungle, you'll almost always move by platoon. Platoons A, B, and C will chop individual trails. Captain, divide your HQ men and have them follow the platoons."

"We can't see more than ten feet into the jungle. So how do we know where we're going to?" asked Wright.

"You won't see more than a few feet or yards in any Pacific

jungle. Use your compass to find your direction. If you encounter an impassable obstacle, skirt it, and return to the most direct route to your objective. You'd better rattle your dags. You've only got the arvo to do it."

We looked at each other and shrugged. The instructor moved out with Batteries B and C still following him.

Several men started hacking at the underbrush in front of us.

"Halt," yelled Henderson. "We need a path, not a boulevard. Each platoon will select two men to cut a path. After fifteen minutes, the next two men will take over. Sergeants, keep an eye on the compass. Cut the paths."

Carson started walking toward Henderson. "Get your platoon moving, Carson." Carson nodded, turned, and selected two men to chop the trail, then led his men into the jungle. Brasseux and Edelstein had already led platoons B and C into the forest.

Fifteen minutes later, the paths were long enough that the last man of each platoon had entered the jungle. Edelstein's platoon chopped fastest.

"Cookie, get the mess staff behind Platoon C. Tilton, Wright, bring up the rear. Make sure they keep moving." Henderson ordered.

"Hammond, have your supply guys follow Brasseux. Sinclair and Douglas bring up the rear there. Sergeant Jennings, bring your techs, and let's follow Carson."

The paths had started out within six feet of each other, but we could not see the platoons on either side of us. We inched forward through a moist green twilight, pushing branches and vines out of our way. Underfoot the slashed undergrowth, trampled by the sixty men in front of us, made a spongy walking surface. Warnings were passed through the line about hidden vines and low hanging branches. Those who did not heed them tripped or were slapped in the face. Sweet and spicy scents rose from the cut plants. The faint sound of the other platoons slashing through the underbrush told us they were there.

About an hour into the march, we heard a scream, then calls of "Medic" over the radio.

Robertson shouted, "I'm coming." He crashed through the

brush, trying to reach the head of the column on our right. On the radio, I heard Edelstein cursing loudly.

"What happened?" I asked.

"The idiot slashed his partner," Edelstein yelled back.

"How bad?"

"Into the thigh muscle," Robertson replied. "I can stitch it up, but we'll need to evacuate him. The aid station can make sure it doesn't get infected."

"Have two men carry him out," I said.

"We'll take him," another voice said.

"Who are you," I asked.

"Stretcher-bearers from the aid station."

"How did you get here so fast?" I asked.

"You're only about three hundred yards from the aid station. We heard the call for a medic."

"Oh, this is going to be a long day," I said.

Platoon B continued slashing as the medics cared for the fallen private, then hauled him off. A short while, we passed Edelstein's platoon. They had started chopping again but were moving more slowly and carefully now. I could no longer hear Carson's platoon on the other side of us.

After another six machete crew changes, our column came upon a stream that flowed in the direction we were going. Brasseux had his men wade into the stream, walking along the banks as much as possible, but men frequently slipped into the muddy water. We climbed over the rocks of three small waterfalls before the stream turned away from the direction we wanted to go. The men cut a path up the stream bank through more jungle until we emerged into a clearing where a giant tree had fallen, taking five smaller ones with it. The brush and vines were dense, but we could see sunshine. The men lifted their faces to the light.

"Take your boots off, get dem as dry as you can, and put dem in de sun while you eat," Brasseux ordered. "Den put dry socks on and hang de wet ones on de side of your packs."

"We're still on course," I said to Brasseux as we ate the rations from our backpacks.

"Sergeant Johnson comes from de Great Dismal Swamp country, and I know de bayous. We ken keep on course in any jungle."

"I'm glad," I said. "Where do you think the others are?"

"Carson veered off early. Dey was already out of earshot by de time Edelstein's man got cut. I bet he's off at least half a mile by now. De Ausies're gonna have to find him and bring him in. Edelstein's movin slow now. His men're afraid," he said.

After about half an hour's lunch, Brasseux ordered his men to move out.

Our boots were still damp. I began to realize the difficulty of us keeping our feet dry in the jungle.

We were climbing now, and the going was even more difficult. An hour and a half later, we emerged into another clearing. Sixteen men dressed in Japanese uniforms jumped out of the bushes as we crossed the clearing. Douglas and I reflexively shot at them with the blanks we had loaded in our sidearms. Several men fired their rifles. The "survivors" surged forward to engage us hand to hand. We "lost" three men before we subdued them, but we did manage to overcome all of them. A training officer stepped out of the forest.

"Good on, ya," he said." Not only did ya make it this far, but ya also made excellent time. And ya fought off the Jap patrol. Remember, there is no front. The Japs can infiltrate through the jungle to attack the flank or from the rear. Every man—artillery, officers, support personnel—gotta be able and ready to fight as infantry with little or no supporting fire. Ya can't provide supporting fire to the men in front of ya as ya'll not know where they are. Minor skirmishes will take place all the time instead of one big battle. Move on now."

There was a trail leading in the right direction ahead.

"Let's take the trail that's already cut," the next man up on the machete said, relief in his voice.

"If we were in de Guinea forest, it mos certainly would be a Jap trail. We can move along dat trail, but we go slow. Prepare to fight," said Brasseux.

The men moved forward silently. We were climbing more steeply than ever now. I walked behind Brasseux as Sergeant Johnson, Brasseux's staff sergeant, moved ahead with the machine gunners. About fifty feet along the trail Sergeant Johnson gave the signal to drop. We all fell to our stomachs. As I lay prone, my weapon ready, a thin, bright green snake slowly crawled out of the leaves and across my arm. I tensed and scrutinized it. The snake flicked its tongue in and out, then suddenly darted forward, snatching a tree frog off the trunk of the nearest tree, and disappeared.

When I took my eyes off the snake, the men still lay staring at the pillbox. I crawled to Brasseux, who seemed to have frozen. "We need to send some me forward to check it out," I whispered.

"Don't want to lose any more men," Brasseux whispered.

"It looks like there is an animal trail over there," I whispered, pointing. "We can crawl along it and get around to the side where they can't see us. Then we can approach the blind side of the pillbox."

Brasseux nodded. I selected five men and motioned for them to follow me. We crawled to the trail. The trail was narrow, and we could not have stood up if we tried; there were so many vines overhead. We reached the blind side of the iron structure and wriggled under a vine into the cleared area around the pillbox. When we had all emerged, I stood and led the men to the open viewing slits. We stuck our rifles through the slit but didn't shoot, fearing even blanks could harm the Jap stand-ins as they ricocheted around the inside of the metal box. One of the men lobbed a rock into the pillbox, shouting, "That's a grenade!" Five Australians in Japanese uniforms came out with their hands up.

The other men stood and moved forward. We motioned for our "prisoners" to walk in front of us and moved on up the trail.

We did not see any more evidence of the enemy in the next hour as we slowly crept forward. Then we heard talking in front of us. Brasseux sent a patrol ahead to the camp that had been chopped out of the wilderness."

"Hello," called the men of the patrol. "US Forces."

"Enter," came the call from the Australian group.

"You blokes made it!" they exclaimed as we entered the campsite. "You're the first platoon to make it since we started training Yanks."

"It weren't the Yanks that got us here," said Sergeant Johnson. The Australian lieutenant looked confused.

"Yankees are from the northeastern part of the United States," I told him. "The Platoon leader and Staff Sergeant are from the swamps and bayous of the southern United States. They don't consider themselves Yankees, but they did get us here."

"Now, men," said the lieutenant, looking at the soldiers stretched out on the ground. "All that's left for you today is set up your swag, string your mossie nets, dig your dunny and hunt down your tucker."

"We have to do what?" I asked.

"Set up your bedrolls, string your mosquito nets, dig a latrine and find food."

"We have to find our own food?" Brasseux asked.

"Supplies are a problem. There haven't been enough shipments of anything to supply your troops. The pasteboard boxes get rained on and disintegrate within days when they do get through. Then the cans rust. Wooden crates are too heavy, especially for the soft earth of the jungle, so neither men nor equipment can carry them. You'll always have to bring supplies with you or eat off the land because returning to a central mess is out.

"This pamphlet lists seventy fruits and vegetables found in the jungles of New Guinea. Also tells you how to identify and prepare them. Go find your dinner." He shoved the pamphlet into my hands.

We wandered into the jungle, barely able to move, thanks to our strenuous hacking, then the steepness of our march to the camp. We strained our eyes in the jungle's dim light and soundless late afternoon canopy. Eventually, I spotted a tree with large oval fruit hanging on it.

"Breadfruit," I said, peering at the manual. "Can be wrapped in leaves and baked or sliced and fried. Both the fruit and seeds are edible."

Our best marksman pulled out his rifle and shot down several breadfruits from the tall tree. We found some large leaves and wrapped them around the breadfruit as we walked back to camp. We managed to build a rock oven surrounded by a roaring fire in a short time. Our breadfruit was baking when the training officer walked out of the jungle.

"Next time, don't waste your ammunition to harvest breadfruit. First, you might need it to save your life. Second, you probably will give away your position by making so much noise and building a huge bonfire. Keep your fire low, just hot enough for cooking. And those leaves you wrapped the breadfruit in are taro leaves. Properly prepared taro roots make a pretty nutritious meal but don't eat the leaves." He looked like he wanted to spit.

"Tomorrow, watch for food as you go through the exercises."

We nodded. The manual said it could take an hour and a half to bake the breadfruit. As we sat around the eventually much reduced campfire and waited, I missed Zook and his harmonica. When the breadfruit was finally ready, we let it cool a bit and sliced it.

"This doesn't taste like bread," O'Neill declared. "Doesn't taste like much of anything."

"Maybe like something in between bread and potatoes," Johnson put in.

"Not like my gran's potato bread," said O'Neill.

"Tastes more like potatoes to me," said Brasseux. "Next time, I'm gonna fry it in butter."

"Ain't going to be a next time for me," O'Neill retorted. "And what butter?"

The Australians led the rest of the battery into the campsite as we finished setting up our tents. We told them how to find the breadfruit tree and let them use our fire's coals to roast their harvest.

***

All battery commanders and executive officers were called to a meeting at training HQ that evening. I decided to take the opportunity to talk with Henderson one more time about Edelstein's behavior as we walked down the jungle trail.

"Edelstein is still tyrannizing his men and pushing them too hard. Today, that accident resulted from Edelstein's insistence that his platoon stays ahead of the others. Did you see his expression when he discovered Brasseux got his men to the clearing without guidance from the Aussies?"

"You supervise the line officers," Henderson replied. "You need to correct him. Man up, Sinclair. Be forceful."

"The more forceful I get, the crueler he gets. He's sneaky and conniving. He tortures his men to the very limit of military law but hasn't stepped over the edge yet. He does nothing to win their respect or cooperation but demands perfect performance. I've been on him since the day he joined the unit. He has gone so far as to refuse direct orders from me. I think we will see more accidents in his platoon as the pressure increases."

"He disobeys orders from you? Charge him with insubordination."

"I'm not his commanding officer; you are," I said firmly. "If he disobeys your orders, it's insubordination. I am just one lieutenant telling another lieutenant what to do because you have not."

He stopped walking; I stopped as well. Henderson peered at me. I thought he was going to charge me with insubordination. Instead, he said. "I'll see to it."

"And another thing. Brasseux froze today. Wasn't able to issue the order to attack the pillbox. He said he didn't want to lose any more men after the hand-to-hand combat."

"That's the problem with trying to make men into officers within ninety days. They aren't fully prepared." Henderson replied. "He does seem to have snapped out of it, though. This training should show him the need for decisive action."

"I hope so," I said. "I'll keep an eye on him."

At the meeting, the Australian training leader looked like a caricature of a British officer as he strutted back and forth in front of us, talking about jungle warfare, occasionally slapping a riding crop on his hand.

"You have seen some of the difficulties of Jungle Warfare today. Fighting in the bloody jungle is always iffy. Men can be separated from their platoons. Platoons can be separated from their batteries. Be certain your junior officers are up to snuff on strategic decision making and combat tactics." He turned quickly and took three short steps toward Colonel Squires. "Senior officers should move their headquarters forward to avoid being cut off from the men they command. HQ itself may be attacked." He turned toward me. "Officers at any level must be prepared to make independent decisions. The survival of platoons separated from the rest of the army has hinged on their lieutenants' quick and accurate thinking." He turned again. "Make full use of your non-coms. They know their men and can offer valuable advice."

Despite his strutting and pompous voice, I thought the training officer did make sense.

"Everyone, down to the newest private, must prepare to make decisions that will save their own or mates' lives. This includes close order hand-to-hand combat and taking routine disease prevention measures."

He paused, looking at us all for a few seconds, clearly for emphasis.

"Disease claims more lives in the jungle than combat, starting with your feet. All soldiers must understand jungle terrain and how to live off the land. These are the things we will teach you here, to the best of our ability in the time allotted." He was in great form now. The strutting picked up speed, and the turns were almost pirouettes. Most of the American officers were silently chuckling at his movements rather than listening to what he said.

"There have been and continue to be supply problems. Senior officers will be occupied with assuring their men have ammunition to fire and food to eat. Other supplies are often unavailable at any price.

"The weather will work against success. Expect torrential rains that will make a quagmire of roads you have helped construct and a swamp of areas you may have selected as a base camp. Heat and insects will be your constant companions. Every movement will be measured in hours, not miles. Sometimes a single mile will take hours. We hope to prepare you for what you'll find. Now, return to your troops and be prepared to begin hand-to-hand combat training at 0600 tomorrow."

An Australian soldier waited to take Henderson and me back

to our camp in a jeep.

"How'd you blokes like Banty's talk?" he asked

"Banty?" Henderson asked.

"Colonel MacDonald's nickname," our driver said.

I chuckled at how well it fit. However, I wished he weren't so much like a banty rooster so we could all appreciate his message more. Henderson and Squires had looked unimpressed at Banty's regale when I looked at them a couple of times during the lecture.

"One of the more entertaining army lectures I've heard," Henderson said. The driver chuckled.

"We think there might be a few 'roos loose in the top attic, but he does know the jungle and the Japs."

The driver dropped us off a short walk from camp. As we approached, dozens of snoring men almost drowned out the jungle's many noises.

***

The high level of fitness we had achieved in the States had deteriorated on the ship to Australia, and the first day of jungle warfare training had pushed us to our limits.

The second day was more demanding. As the men dragged in from their forced march at the end of a long day of hand-to-hand combat training, our meal was in the mess tent. For the rest of our jungle training, the mess only had food every other day. We learned to forage as we marched and generally cobbled together something for an evening meal with what we collected.

I learned the snake that had crawled across my arm was the non-poisonous green tree snake, one of over 80 species of snakes in the rainforests of the Pacific. Many of them were poisonous, including one called the death adder. That didn't even include the sea snakes in the water surrounding the islands.

Very few days passed without rain. The temperature hovered in the high eighties, and the humidity at least ninety percent when it wasn't raining. We slogged through swamps rife with parasites. Our feet never dried out during the entire training. I was beginning to understand the toenail fungus issue. We took atabrine to control malaria and learned to sleep under mosquito nets.

"Lieutenant Sinclair, what good are mosquito nets if we're on night duty?" asked Private Barkley.

"Just be sure to take your atabrine," I told the private, but I knew the night shift had a higher risk of malaria than the daytime warriors.

We gradually regained the fitness level we attained at Fort Bliss. Ninety degrees in the jungle seemed hotter than ninety degrees in the desert, but we became acclimated. We could at least make it through the day without collapsing. Generous distribution of salt tablets helped.

Months and years of army training evolved as we grew accustomed to making decisions independently rather than always waiting for top-down commands. Colonel Squires seemed particularly adept at making his wishes and philosophy known in ways the younger officers could carry out even without a direct order. Henderson had more difficulty adjusting. He became angry whenever one of his lieutenants did anything differently than he would. I kept an eye on Brasseux, who seemed to be managing. He didn't freeze again and led his men safely through several more mock Jap attacks.

The Aussies had already been through hell, and they imparted their great learning about Japanese tactics and beliefs. Some baffled me, like the sense of honor that required officers to kill themselves if they lost a battle. It went against everything I believed in as an American—that you should try and try until you succeed. Others, like the willingness of the average Japanese soldier to die in a futile attack rather than surrender, instilled fear in me and the men. Even their most futile attack against the worst odds would kill some of our soldiers. Which was, of course, why the Japanese hierarchy insisted on it.

After going hungry a few times, most men could identify most of the manual's plants. However, only a few plants produced fruit as we headed into the tropical dry season.

We left the jungle smarter, fitter, and much hungrier than we had entered.

CHAPTER 27
MALARIA SCHOOL

As soon as I got back from jungle training school, I hurried to the Armstrong Paddock exchange to check for letters from Sarah Gale. There were two.

> February 28, 1943
> Dear Gene,
> I hope your trip was calm and unexciting. I worry about all the dangers of an ocean crossing these days. I know you aren't there as I write, but you will be when you get this letter. The war seems to be going much better for us. We watched a newsreel about the victory at Guadalcanal the other day. Those Marines are real heroes. If you see any of them, tell them thanks for me.
> You would not believe what people are saying about the WAACs. We are doing our best to help the army win this war, but enlisted men say any woman joining the WAACs has questionable morals. It is even worse than before.
> Our CO passed around a newspaper report the other day that said all WAACs are given medicines to prevent syphilis before they send us overseas and that Director Hobby, who oversees the WAACs, is in complete agreement with that policy. That is not true. It is the worst kind of slander. I know Director Hobby is putting pressure on the columnist to print a retraction, but it was a syndicated column that appears in papers all over the United States. The damage is done, no matter what little retraction that columnist prints.
> As a result of that, we all had to be tested for venereal disease, so the

numbers could be reported to officials in Washington. I was so angry and humiliated. We talked about refusing to be tested, but that would look bad. People might think we declined because we were infected. Our results were so minor compared to army enlisted men that Major Hobby got a commendation from Congress. I think we should all get commendations for being decent, God-fearing women.

Work is continuing as usual. I do a lot of sightseeing and go to movies and things like that with the girls, but it is not the same as going with you. Please do your best to get this **[redacted]** *war over with, so we can be together again.*

I wish I could be with you. I know you would comfort me. You are always so rational.

Love,

Sarah Gale

That letter angered me so much that, for a time, I was not rational. Then I wondered how she got it past the censors with only one black mark. I thought perhaps the censors were WAACs. Her other short note sounded a bit more encouraging.

March 1, 1943

Dear Gene,

I'm sorry about my last letter. I really should not disturb you when you have such important work to do. After the tests proved we were not infected, things calmed down slightly. There is even talk about making the WAACs part of the regular army instead of an auxiliary unit. I don't know if the pay will be equal, but the rank would be equivalent to the regular army.

With a lighter workload, we are actually able to enjoy Florida. Some of the girls from up north were amazed at the mild winter. It is even warmer than winter at home. I haven't worn a coat at all. How was winter in El Paso? It can't be too cold. The latitude in El Paso is closer to that here than at home. I don't imagine you even have winter where you are now.

Last Sunday afternoon, we went out to an orange grove and picked some oranges. I still can't get over how good fresh-picked oranges taste. And, of course, the mess has been serving that wonderful lemonade again, too.

Love

Sarah Gale

I would have to explain to Sarah Gale that winter in the southern hemisphere is in June, July, and August and that it would be like a Florida winter, at least in Queensland.

As I wandered into HQ re-reading my letter, Henderson said, "You're going to be battalion malaria officer. Training's in Darwin. Starts Monday."

"Why can't the medics take care of that?" I asked

"Has to be an officer. You leave in forty-five minutes."

I shoved Sarah Gale's letters into a pocket, hoping to reply to them on the train trip to Darwin.

***

Darwin was even hotter and more humid than Townsville. However, the hotel where I stayed was paradise compared to a soggy tent in the jungle. I had a tiny room, but all mine. I showered, lay down on the bed, and was immediately sound asleep. I woke to the sound of boots in the hallway and realized I had fifteen minutes to get to the training. I put on my cleanest uniform, which meant it didn't have mud up to the knees, and put the other uniform in the laundry bag I found in the closet, which I hung on the door as I left. My stomach growled loudly as I slipped into the last chair in the red-flocked ballroom. Most of the officers in the room were captains and majors.

After introductions of officers and sponsors, the instructor started his lecture. "In recent campaigns, up to 80% of the men have contracted malaria. General MacArthur has made it a priority to get malaria under control. He stated that he could not run a war with one battalion in the field, one battalion hospitalized with malaria, and one battalion weakened and recovering from the disease. You are the solution. You'll each be responsible for assuring the men in your unit use anti-malarial medication properly.

"The most effective malaria preventative drug is quinine. Unfortunately, the Germans now hold the Netherlands and, through them, Indonesia, where most quinine originates. The brilliant medical scientists in the United States developed Atabrine as a solution."

"It was actually developed in Germany," whispered the medical officer sitting beside me.

"This drug comes with a few side effects."

The medical officer snickered.

"First, it turns the skin yellow. This is useful in determining whether the troops are taking the drug. Heavy doses also cause nausea, vomiting, diarrhea, and skin irritations. The skin can itch, become scaly, or develop sores. None of these side effects are anywhere near as bad as getting malaria. Emphasize that! The worst side effect includes nightmares or unusual behavior in the soldiers as they begin taking the drug. These last two side effects have proven extremely rare, but any soldier affected should report to the nearest medic."

"Also known as drug induce psychosis," the medical officer whispered. "You don't want soldiers running around with guns with those side effects."

"There are rumors that the drug can cause infertility. These rumors are not true, and you'll do your best to dispel them.

"For the first ten days, each soldier will receive a priming dose." I realized that we had not received the priming dose, starting with just the daily dose on our second day of jungle training. How many of us had been bitten by infected mosquitoes before getting medicated? "Following that, the daily dose will be reduced to limit side effects that can take men out of the field. Oversee dosage. The medication should be given in chow line— they should be taken with food—and you'll observe each soldier swallowing the medication."

I raised my hand.

"Yes, lieutenant."

"I just returned from Jungle Warfare school. Apparently, chow, as we know, it is not always practiced in the jungle. How will the medication be administered when units are divided and not together for chow?"

"Each sergeant should be given a three-day supply for their men before going into battle. Within those three days, you'll be responsible for assuring an appropriate distribution procedure is established."

"Fat chance," whispered the medical officer. He raised his hand. "Is there enough Atabrine available for all the soldiers,"

"We currently have a three-day supply for all the soldiers in the field. Increased shipments have left the States and should arrive tomorrow or the next day. We are determined to resolve the supply issues."

The medical officer raised his hand again and was ignored.

We continued with lessons on dosages, side effects, and medication administration.

***

When lunch finally rolled around, I sat next to the medical officer.

"Gene Sinclair," I said.

"Dr. Byron Cantrell," he said.

"It sounds like you have some field experience,"

"Yes, I was at Bataan. Evacuated a group of injured and sick just before the surrender. But, of course, that surrender never would've happened if a third of the soldiers hadn't been in the field hospital with malaria. Have you heard what happened to the men who surrendered?"

"No."

"Well, that's a story for another time," he said, disgusted.

"If they have a three-day supply now and are expecting more tomorrow, how will they get it to troops throughout the Pacific in time to do any good?"

"They aren't. You're obviously new around here. I assume

they mentioned the supply problems in Jungle Warfare School?"

"I've been in the Pacific for four weeks, most of it in Jungle Warfare training. Everybody talks about supply problems, but nobody has explained the particulars."

"You know, of course, that the war in Europe takes precedent."

"Yes."

"That means we have about one-third the transport ships we need. The quartermaster corps is about a quarter of the strength we should have. We get supplies packed for Europe. The boxes disintegrate, and the cans rust before the food can be delivered. Ammo sits at the airfields in the rain and gets soaked, so it's useless, or even worse, dangerous. The camouflage nets they send are the wrong color and make things more obvious rather than less."

"I understand there's a real push to improve that."

"There is a strong push from this end. Washington seems to be rather slow at getting the message."

"The policy is Europe first."

"But just sending boys over here to die in the meantime is inhumane."

"Were you under the impression war was humane in the first place?"

"You said you haven't been in the field?" he asked me. "Where did you get such a jaded opinion of war?"

"My grandfather fought in the Civil War with General Sherman's army. Started working with the quartermasters at sixteen; at seventeen, he enlisted. He witnessed some pretty inhumane things. He told me all sorts of stories when I was growing up."

"This isn't Sherman's army, but there are atrocities. They're calling us back. Care to join me for a beer after class?"

After learning more about how malaria spreads, the different types of mosquitoes that carry different types of malaria, and the new, improved insect repellents "on the way," we were dismissed for the day. I located Cantrell lounging in a rattan chair under a slowly turning ceiling fan in the hotel bar.

"Bring me a Tooheys," I told the waitress as I settled into a chair across the table from him. I turned to Cantrell. "Tell me about Bataan."

"We were in the Philippines when the Japs first attacked," he told me. "They bombed the airfields and destroyed just about all the planes we had there. Then they invaded and drove the combined armies back to the little peninsula of Bataan. In the field hospital, we saw firsthand what the Japanese are capable of. They did not back down and did not accept defeat. The Jap soldiers were perfectly willing to fight to the death. They also had some very sneaky tactics that could inflict grave damage on our boys. To die in war is honorable for them. To surrender is dishonorable.

"MacArthur was on Corregidor, an island just off the Bataan peninsula. In March, he withdrew to Australia. I was assigned to accompany a group of our most seriously ill and injured soldiers at the same time. General King surrendered on April ninth. Immediately after the surrender, the Japs outright murdered hundreds of soldiers. They didn't feed the survivors and gave them almost no water. They marched them across the Bataan Peninsula and at least fifty miles north up the island of Luzon, maybe more. Along the way, they forced them to sit in the sun without a hat or helmet, beat and kicked them, and ran their trucks over the ones who fell down. A few of the Philippine soldiers escaped along the way and told shocking stories.

"It seems the camp they were taken to is almost as bad as the forced march to get there. A few reports have come back that they barely have any food. There is no medical care other than what prisoners can provide for each other. The Japs have refused the Philippine Red Cross access. Men are dying like flies in the camp."

"Dreadful. They told us about the Japanese way of thinking in Jungle Warfare School. The Japanese would never have surrendered. They would have killed themselves, so they probably had no respect for soldiers who surrendered. Regardless, it's unfathomable they could place so little value on life."

Cantrell shook his head. "Yes," he said, "though that unfathomable idea may apply to all of humanity when dealing with a human different from themselves,"

I nodded sadly and pulled on my beer.

***

In the morning, Dr. Cantrell stood in front of the class. As he described the symptoms of malaria, it became apparent he was speaking from personal experience.

"Symptoms start with a feeling of uneasiness that progresses rapidly to extreme fatigue, headaches, or body aches. These are followed by alternating high fever and bone-shaking chills. In some cases, particularly with people in their late twenties, for some reason, it can progress to loss of consciousness and hallucinations. Many of the soldiers in whom it goes this far have other issues, particularly respiratory problems or allergies.

"Symptoms generally develop within seven to fifteen days of exposure, although the symptoms can be suppressed by the medication and appear only after the drug is withdrawn.

The officer in charge stood up. "Atabrine prevents malaria," he thundered.

"The Surgeon General calls it a prophylactic. There have been many cases in the field where the disease appeared after its use was discontinued. Please encourage your men to continue using the medication for several weeks even after leaving infested areas."

"Soldiers will be provided with the medication only as long as they are in the field," the officer in charge said. "There is not enough of the drug to continue distribution when it is not needed."

Captain Cantrell shrugged, said, "Too bad," and went on to ways to treat symptoms in the field. We should increase the dose and keep the patient in bed until the attack passed. We were dismissed for lunch. I caught up with Cantrell as we proceeded to the dining room.

"Why are they so adamant about the drug preventing malaria?"

"Typical reasons. The goal of the generals is to keep the men in the field fighting. The pills work for that. They aren't too concerned about what happens to them afterward. Generals are supposed to win the war. If they start becoming too worried about individual soldiers' lives, they lose track of the big picture and find it psychologically difficult to do their jobs. Supply issues also come into play. There really aren't enough pills to distribute to people not in the field."

After lunch, a new instructor, Major Green, went over procedures for dealing with malaria cases. "Usually, malaria will be treated by medics in the field. Soldiers who don't improve within a week in camp or at the front-line aid station can be sent to field hospitals. Only if the infection spreads to the brain will they be evacuated to the rear base hospital. Evacuation is the last resort, only for the most severely affected."

The training lasted two weeks, by which time I was utterly convinced that effective malaria prevention treatment was both essential and impossible. However, I was rested and refreshed, having slept all night in a comfortable bed, in a private room, showered with hot water every day, rising no earlier than 0600, and eating three complete, hot meals every day.

I packed up my bags and went down to the coffee shop on the first floor to have breakfast before catching the train back to Armstrong Paddock. Captain Cantrell invited me to join him at his table.

"Are you confident about your ability to control malaria in your men after that training?" he asked me.

"Not at all. And that bothers me. I'm responsible for them whatever they do. There are so many dangers I can't protect them from."

"Careful. You'll not make it through the war if you feel personally responsible for the behavior of every eighteen-year-old soldier in the battery. You're accountable for the success of the battery, not the behavior of individual soldiers."

"Just like those generals you talked about?"

"A bit, yes. You can't afford to be too compassionate if you are an army officer."

"But if the individual soldiers don't perform their duty, the battery fails."

A waitress approached our table. "Hi, I'm Maggie. What can I get—?"

She stopped and raised her head. In the distance, an air raid siren sounded. Another, closer, took up the wail. A third joined it, then a siren right outside the building began to wail.

"Air raid!"

CHAPTER 28
THE WAR COMES TO ME

I grabbed Maggie's arm and ran toward the door behind Cantrell. "Where's the shelter?"

"We don't have a shelter in the hotel, so we have to go to the city building across the street."

About twenty Japanese G4M bombers and Zeros were bearing down on us as we ran out the door. Guests of the hotel were milling around, uncertain where to go. As Australian planes rose from a nearby airbase, bombs began dropping on the city.

"This way!" I shouted at them, waving frantically.

Then I turned and followed Maggie as she ran across the street to the exterior stairwell that led to the basement. The civilians continued to mill around in front of the hotel, trying to get a better look at the planes.

"Go on," I told her as I turned back, my heart beating rapidly.

"To the city building," I shouted to the guests, pointing across the street. "Over there. It has a basement. Hurry, the planes are getting closer."

Still, no one moved toward the city building. They would all be killed.

"YOU HAVE TO GO NOW!" I shouted.

Three bombs dropped on the other side of the hotel, and the planes strafed a business area to the south. Several of the civilians finally realized the danger and ran across the street. Others panicked and stood where they were, screaming. Finally, three women ran toward me. I grabbed the arms of the two most panicked and ordered everyone to follow us.

By this time, several Australian Spitfires were in the air. They climbed high, turned, and began firing down on the Japanese, an effective tactic in a sea battle but not so good above a city where the enemy planes flew low above civilians and their homes. Another bomb dropped close enough that gravel sprayed my back.

Finally, everyone ran toward the shelter. As I ran, two of the Spitfires dropped into the sea. I lunged for the stairwell, pulling the women with me. A third bomb knocked chunks of concrete off a wall in the front of the building. I felt something hit the back of my head as I ducked through the door into the basement.

About fifty people wandered around in the basement meeting room, some calm, others quite agitated. It had the black and white floor tile and cream-colored walls common in utilitarian spaces built in the last decade. The bright lights and festive music coming from a phonograph in one corner seemed incongruous with the destruction outside. Maggie and another woman dressed in a hotel uniform walked among the hotel guests, calming them. Captain Cantrell tended to some minor injuries. One woman had twisted her ankle coming down the stairs, and an older man had trouble breathing. But, all in all, it appeared to be more of a community gathering than a city under attack.

"You're bleeding from the back of your head," Maggie said as she approached me.

I rubbed my neck, and my hand came back bloody.

"Cantrell," I asked. "Do you have a bandage?"

"Let me look at that."

"It isn't anything, just a little flying debris. I'll—"

I crumpled to the floor. I woke to the sting of smelling salts in my nose. All was quiet; the people who had been visiting around the room earlier were all gone. I lay on a cot. Maggie sat next to me, holding my hand.

"What happened?" I asked. "Last thing I knew, there was a little cut on my head and a bombing raid going on."

"Dr. Cantrell said you must have gotten hit by a rock or something. He bandaged you up and wants to keep an eye on you. The raid is over. He said he would send some medics for you."

"I'm all right," I said. "I need to get to the train station. I'm due back at my unit." I tried to stand up, but the room swam. I fell back, dizzy and disoriented.

"You stay here! Doctor's orders." Maggie said

Two medics trotted down the stairs a few minutes later, put me on a stretcher, and carried me to their ambulance.

"Was anyone hurt in the raid?" I asked.

"You were," one medic pointed out.

"I mean, was anyone seriously injured."

"The Air Corps lost fifteen Spitfires. Rumor is at least two of them ran out of fuel. I heard they shot down eleven Jap planes."

"On the ground, you were the only casualty worth mentioning," the other medic told me, smiling inscrutably.

"There's hardly any military presence here. Why would they raid Darwin?" I asked

"At the beginning of the war, half the bloody navy was hereabouts. The Japs sank eleven ships in the first raid." Medic One informed me.

"It weren't half the navy," Medic Two said. "But they did kill more than two hundred people and wounded about twice that."

"This is not the first raid on Darwin?"

"Oh no. This is the fifty-fourth raid, ain't it?" Medic One asked Medic Two.

"I think the fifty-third," Medic Two replied. "They mostly don't do much damage no more, but they keep coming. The Australian Air Corps needs to figure out what they're doing, though. Their pilots ain't got much experience, and the ground crew ain't so bonzer either if they let the planes run out of fuel today."

They carried me into the military hospital where Cantrell met us. I tried to convince him I should return to my unit, but he insisted on keeping me overnight for observation. I fell asleep.

When I woke again, I marched at the head of a column of men in a mix of ragged homespun or deerskin clothing, blue and red uniform coats with buff-colored trousers, and a few in green hunting shirts and brown trousers. They carried a variety of muskets and flintlock rifles. I wore the blue coat of the Continental army with red trim, indicating Pennsylvania. My head swam, and I felt disoriented and confused. Was this a reaction to the drugs they gave me, or maybe the head injury?

I looked around to get my bearings. Sycamore and sweet gum trees surrounded us, trees commonly found where the soil is wet. A few aspens twisted their leave in the distance. I wore a blue uniform coat and tight white breeches. Based on the trees, I was St. Clair again, probably somewhere north of Pennsylvania this time.

General Thompson called, "Colonel St. Clair, I want you to take your Pennsylvanians and head toward Three Rivers. Surprise McClean if it can be done. We believe there are three hundred troops there. You'll outnumber them two to one."

"Yes, sir!" I replied. I signaled my column to follow and turned to the east along the Nicolette Road. The route played through my memory. I had been here during the French and Indian War. I proudly led the six hundred men I had recruited in Pennsylvania only two months before. They were shaping up into a skilled force, particularly the sixty sharpshooters with long Pennsylvania rifles, dressed in green and brown to make it easier to hide in the forest. Many units weren't interested in those rifles because they were slow and complicated to load, but they could shoot accurately at three times the distance of the British Brown Bess. The Pennsylvania sharpshooters would hide behind trees at a safe distance, cutting down a British soldier with every shot, making this a formidable force.

We reached the St. Francis River by late afternoon. The June days were long this far north. Still, I decided we should camp here and make the river crossing when all of us could cross in full light. The men spread out to set up campsites but could not seem to get settled for the night. I hadn't been in combat for twenty years. I decided a little encouragement was in order.

"Anthony," I ordered the drummer, "Assemble the men." He played the cadence, and the men came running from the woods where they had set up their campsites.

"Men, tomorrow you will be facing your first combat experience. I want to reassure you that our intelligence says the unit stationed at Trois Rivieres is small. They have only their Brown Bess muzzleloaders, bayonet, and pistols to defend themselves. However, we have sixty men with Pennsylvania rifles among us.

They will be able to decimate the British defenses. We will then be able to rout the British and be on our way to Deschambault to support the Northern Army there. If our intelligence proves correct, it will be an easy fight."

The men cheered.

"Return to your camps, post your sentries, and get a good night's sleep. Dismissed!"

The men settled down, but I couldn't seem to go to sleep. Memories of my time in Trois Rivieres played through my mind. If things hadn't changed, it would be best to land our boats a little way downriver, where the road came close to the shore, and march into Trois Rivieres from the south. The riflemen should be sent ahead to take up posts in the woods and would shield our advance. I finally fell asleep when I was confident of my strategy.

We marched all the next day, reaching the small town of Nicolette on the south side of the river about ten miles from Trois Rivieres. The village was friendly to patriots. While the men rested, I spoke with the local patriots and arranged for batteaux and boatmen to take us across the river in the early morning hours, then settled down to get what sleep I could.

At about an hour after midnight, a sentry awakened me.

"Colonel, General Thompson is here. He arrived by batteaux with about sixteen hundred men."

"General Thompson? Why is that?"

I rose from my bed and went to talk with Thompson.

"General Sullivan arrived. He is in command now and does not want to take any chance of failure in this enterprise. We are to attack at dawn. It is too late to prepare for this many men to cross tonight, so we will stay here overnight and proceed with the attack tomorrow night."

"The attack needs to be a surprise. If we spend the day here, the British will know we are coming. And the local patriots believe British reinforcements are coming. We outnumber the troops there now, but tomorrow their forces may be significantly stronger."

"We can't attack with exhausted men and wet powder. In the morning we should make a pretense of throwing up defenses here, then cross over tomorrow night." Thompson declared.

General Thompson supervised the erection of the defenses while I took several men who were fluent in French to gather intelligence. We learned that British ships were indeed anchored in the St. Lawrence. They had likely brought additional infantry, and each warship would have enough cannon to decimate our Continental troops.

Thompson decided to cross to Pointe du Lac, farther upriver, march inland a short way, then take a branch road to Trois Rivieres. We would have to march about seven miles before we engaged the British. We would have to start the crossing at midnight to get all two thousand men across and into Trois Rivieres by dawn.

Across the river, Thompson set two hundred fifty men to guard the boats, and the rest of us marched toward Trois Rivieres. Not far up the road, the column halted. A short time later, we were marching again. Apparently, the problem had been solved.

About half a mile farther along, I realized that we were marching right past the branch road the Nicolette patriots had advised us to take. I hurried forward to talk with Thompson.

"Why did we not take the branch road?" I asked.

"This Frenchman says there is a British outpost in a white house not too far up this road."

"What is your name?" I asked in French.

"Antoine Gautier," he replied.

"Antoine, how far up the road is this outpost?"

"We are near," he said. Something about the way he spoke aroused suspicion, but I assumed it was the natural antipathy of the French for the British.

We soon came upon the white house, but it was empty.

"We should return to the branch road," I insisted.

"That would take so much time. You speak French. Ask Antoine if there is any other alternative," ordered Thompson.

"We could go through the woods to the road. I know the way," Antoine told me. "It will not be difficult and will take much less time than backtracking along the road."

I relayed the suggestion to Thompson. "I really think we

should turn around and march on the road. It is much easier to keep the men together. We could easily be bogged down if we go through the woods in the dark," I suggested. "I recall several bogs and marshes in this area."

"We need to be in Trois Rivieres by sunrise," Thompson said. "We go through the woods."

Before long, we were mired down in the most horrible bog. We pushed our way through rushes, thickets, greasy roots, and decaying logs. We groped through the dark, slipping on the sticky muck. Some men lost shoes, and the gluelike mud even pulled boots off of their feet. I stepped on a sharp snag that pierced my foot, penetrating my boot, but I trudged onward.

Thompson rose up in a fearful rage and demanded to be taken back to the river road.

"But sir, we know there are British ships on the river. We may not have passed them yet. It will soon be sunrise, and they will fire on us." I told him

"First, you want to march on the road, then to stay in the bog! Antoine, lead us to the road.

Antoine quickly complied. The lead regiment regained the road, and Thompson led us on a brisk march toward the city, but dawn broke before we could get past the ships. They opened fire and peppered us with grapeshot. We plunged back into the woods, where we were soon mired in the morass. For two or three hours more, we struggled on through the slimy brooks, bushes, and muck, hoping at any time to come out onto solid ground. The men scattered throughout the woods, and we all know there was no longer any chance to surprise Trois Rivieres. We hadn't seen Anthony Wayne and his men for some time.

In the distance, we heard gunshots, then we broke through a thicket. Before us stood Trois Rivieres, and to our astonishment, it was surrounded by newly dug earthworks manned by two regiments of British regulars.

Thompson ordered a charge as soon as we got there. The fire of the ships at our back and the two regiments in front of us pinned us down. We crept back into the woods. I stationed the riflemen behind trees as we withdrew. They prevented the

Redcoats from leaving their entrenchments for a time, but it soon became evident that our only option was to retreat.

I led my men as best I could toward the Pont du Lac landing where we had left our boats, gathering men along the way. My inured foot throbbed. As we continued, men from other units joined us, bringing news that Colonel Wayne was making a stand but was outnumbered three to one.

"Where is Thompson now?" I asked Captain Chester from the regiment Thompson led.

"Nobody knows. You seem to be the ranking officer on the field now. What do we do?"

Should I take command? Thompson had disagreed with me at every turn, and he was the superior officer. If I countermanded orders Thompson had given, that could lead to a court-martial. To wait for Thompson to show up would only get us captured or killed, eliminating the Army of the North. The British had a much larger force in the area than we believed. There was only a slim chance of Thompson rejoining us. I took command and ordered the men to form up.

"Obviously, our intelligence was wrong," I said. "We need to regroup on the other side of the river. Fan out, pass the order to any other Continentals you see and follow me."

We gathered at least twelve hundred men as we limped and slogged toward the road. I realized that redcoats occupied the landing and guarded the boats as we drew near. A gunship and two sloops sat in the water between us and Nicolette. Again, we were outmanned, their highly trained troops and warships against our farmers and tradesmen. What now? How could we avoid total annihilation? If nothing had changed in the last twenty years, a village upriver, across from Sorrell, would provide shelter, and we might be able to commandeer boats to cross the river. Dare I risk the men's lives based on nothing more than hope and old memories? At least we might have a chance upriver.

I stationed the riflemen behind trees on the right side of the road, then formed the troops up and made as though we were about to charge. The Redcoats, rather than charging, also got into battle formation, confident they could easily defeat us. I darted to the right as we began moving forward, leading the men into the woods. The British followed, but the riflemen soon discouraged them.

"Move out! Head upriver!" I ordered, running through the woods, my men close behind me. Several yards into the woods, I fell, my injured foot too swollen and painful to continue.

"Colonel St. Clair, we need to keep moving," said Captain Chester.

"Yes, you do. I can no longer walk, and I don't want to slow anyone down. Cross the bridge at Riviere du Loup if you can. Gather at Berthier if you can't and cross to Sorrel from there." I drew a crude map in the mud. Several men examined the map then took off, leading small groups toward escape.

Two of my officers, pleading fatigue, said they would stay with me. The British were swarming the woods by now. Nearby a large tree had fallen, leaving a hollow under its roots. My men helped me into the hollow and piled leaves and branches on top of me before climbing in themselves. I fell into a feverish sleep.

***

When I woke, this time in the hospital, a nurse was making the rounds.

"You decided to join us again," she said. "You have been asleep for two solid days."

"Two days? You don't know how glad I am to be back. But, I need to get to my unit." I stood quickly and swayed on my feet.

"Dr. C says you can't go back until your sleep cycle regulates itself and you can walk a straight line."

I fell asleep again, and when I woke, it was pitch dark.

"Nurse! Nurse!" I called.

A grey-haired nurse came quickly. Her nametag, Doris, swam into view as she leaned over me.

"Doris, that's my sister's name."

"That's nice," she said as she fluffed my pillow. "Do you think you could go back to sleep?"

"No. I think I have had plenty of sleep. Can I return to my unit?"

"Orders are that you cannot return to your unit until your sleep cycle regulates itself. Being wide awake at 0200 is not a regular sleep cycle,"

"It is in a searchlight unit," I countered.

Doris came back about every two hours to check my vital signs.

"Isn't this a bit excessive?" I asked.

"Standard procedure with injuries like yours," she retorted as she wrote another set of numbers on her clipboard. She seemed a little exasperated that her usually quiet nights were interrupted by the frequent need to check on me.

Try as I might, I was wide awake the rest of the night. Cantrell came by for rounds just after the sun came up.

"Sinclair, glad to see you awake. That nasty bump on your head did some damage to the occipital lobe and brainstem. The occipital lobe injury affected your vision, and the brainstem injury has made your breathing a bit unstable. We want to keep an eye on you until everything is back to normal."

"How long will that take?"

"We can't really say. But, based on your recovery so far, I would guess you will be back at it in a week or two."

"A week or two? I need to return to my unit."

"We've notified them."

I started sleeping more regularly, and the nurses got me up several times a day to see if I could walk that straight line Cantrell had insisted upon. I was amazed at how weak I felt. Each afternoon an oxygen technician came by to visit me.

"What does an oxygen technician do?" I asked him.

"I help you breathe. Now blow as hard as you can into this tube."

I blew.

"What is that?" I asked as soon as I had regained my breath.

"It's a spirogram," he said, offering no further information.

Whatever he was measuring, I wasn't doing it well enough. He started coming twice a day with his tubes and tanks. Gradually I began to feel better.

After a week of this, Cantrell came by on his usual rounds. "If you sleep well tonight, wake at a reasonable hour, and perform well on the spirogram, you can catch the train back to Townsville. I think the injury has healed enough for you to function."

***

Cantrell gave me a ride to the train station, where we said goodbye, promising to stay in touch. I presented my original ticket back to Armstrong Paddock at the ticket counter and explained the situation.

"I'm very sorry, sir. Unfortunately, we cannot honor that ticket. You should have gotten it replaced before the date of the original trip if you were not going to be on the train."

"I was unconscious in the hospital. How was I supposed to replace it?"

"I am not allowed to accept that ticket."

"May I talk to your supervisor?"

"Actually, sir, my supervisor is in Adelaide, at the other end of the line."

"Do you have a military liaison of any sort?" I asked

"No, sir, he was killed in the first attack, and we haven't had one since. The navy left then, too, so there hasn't been as much need."

In the end, I bought a ticket out of my own pocket on a train that left the next day. Since the agent refused to accept a check from my American bank, it took all the cash I had for a second-class ticket. So I slept in the station rather than call Cantrell back.

When I got on the train, the conductor saw my uniform and lieutenants' bars and asked me why I traveled second class. I explained the situation to him, showing him the ticket the agent had not honored.

"You come with me. We have one berth empty in a sleeper car. You know, it's interesting how the people of Darwin are reacting to the repeated air raids. The majority of them left town. Some who stayed have become more generous and altruistic, while others are more difficult to get along with. We'll get you fixed up, and I want to apologize for that agent. I know the bloke you're talking about. I'll tell the company about him."

"No need to do that, really," I replied. "I am sure it is incredibly stressful to be expecting another attack at any time."

We had barely gotten underway when the train stopped.

"Tracks were bombed in the latest air raid," the conductor told me. "There will be a short delay while the crew finishes the repairs."

I wondered about that 'short' delay, but we were underway again within two hours. A short time later, another damaged section of track slowed the train to a crawl. I thanked the conductor repeatedly for the berth since it took thirty-five hours to make the trip to Townsville.

***

When I finally reached Armstrong Paddock, the area my battery had occupied was empty. I searched the surrounding area and could not find them anywhere. Finally, I checked with camp HQ.

"Where did the 227th AAA Searchlight Battalion go?"

The corporal at the front desk shrugged. He called a major who said the battalion had moved out to Camp Bluewater. "But that was over two weeks ago. Nobody stays at Camp Bluewater for more than two weeks. So they've probably shipped out by now."

"How could they leave me behind?"

"Oh, are you Lieutenant Eugene Sinclair?"

I showed him the name on my uniform.

"Let me check on something. In the meantime, there's a letter here for you. Your Captain said those letters were pretty important to you."

I sat in the office with a big ceiling fan whirring over my head and read Sarah Gale's letter.

April 11, 1943

Dear Gene,

Tomorrow, I leave for Officer's Training School. I'll officially be a leader by the middle of July. After that, I expect I'll be stationed overseas. I'll be doing work I won't be able to mention. It is work you prepared me for, though. I certainly hope I end up in the Pacific Theater and we can see each other.

The government has started a new program for getting a high school diploma. They have a test you take, and if you pass, they give you a diploma. I took the test the other day and am now just waiting to see if I passed.

Because of the bad publicity, there was a big drop in the number of women volunteering, but that is starting to turn around now, I think. More and more women see this as an opportunity to serve their country and learn new skills. I'm glad other women are seeing it that way. With all the difference it has made in my life, I can't see why women wouldn't want to join the WAACs.

At the hearings on making WAACs part of the regular army, they said our officers would have the same rank and get the same pay as male army officers. We would be entitled to all the benefits of the regular army. All the lies and rumors have not helped at all, but I think they are moving toward passing a bill that would make me regular army.

I thought about it really hard and couldn't understand why the seasons are the opposite. Then one of the girls held up an orange to the sun and showed me how the earth tilts to make the seasons. That made perfect sense. Both the top and the bottom of the planet cannot lean toward the sun at the same time, but I couldn't see that until she showed me. I guess I am just a visual person. Seeing is believing.

I had forgotten you were not at Fort Bliss during the winter. It seemed like we were separated for a whole year at least, not just six months. Now there is no telling how long we will be separated.

The photographs you sent of the jungle flowers are beautiful. I would love to be there with you in that tropical paradise. Send whatever pictures you like but be careful about the background. I was almost able to determine your location *from that one of the big tree. But, of course, you know I am better at that than most people, but the Axis has spies too.*

Love,

Sarah Gale

The Axis has spies too? I wondered about that comment. I laughed at the tropical paradise comment as I wiped the perspiration off my face and folded the damp letter, placing it back in its envelope. They said this was the beginning of the dry season, but it still seemed plenty wet to me.

A little while later, a Major Lloyd approached me.

"We seem to have a bit of a SNAFU here. You were supposed to have returned ten days ago!"

"The air raid in Darwin delayed my return. I was slightly injured."

"Your Battalion is leaving as we speak for Goodenough Island. There is no way we can get you to the ship on time. They'll be well on their way by the time we could get you to their dock," he said. "Are you by any chance at all familiar with the SCR 584?"

"The new radar? Yes sir. I would love to have the opportunity to work with that equipment. What does that have to do with my rejoining my unit?"

"There might be one way I could eventually get you back with your unit, but it will mean you'll have to hightail it to Sydney immediately. The Aussies are sending a radar station early to monitor the activity on the island your unit will eventually occupy. The General agreed to send the 584 prototype and a platoon of our men to the island. They will help watch for enemy activity and train the Aussies on the new equipment. But the platoon CO, Lieutenant Ratliff, is down with jungle fever. That's where you come in. You've just become their platoon commander. We'll send Ratliff to the island when he's better, and you can go back to your unit. They should be there by that time."

"My first experience in the field is to command a platoon I have never met on a brand new machine nobody has used in the field before, hundreds of miles from any mechanics or engineers who know how to fix it? And we will be the only Americans on the island?"

"That's right. They did tell you in jungle warfare training that you had to be ready for anything, didn't they? Grab your gear. There's a ship for Sydney boarding now, and I want you on it."

As I gathered my gear, I felt somewhat bemused. My first taste of real warfare, the air raid on Darwin, had undone everything I expected to happen. Since life and war mixed like water and oil, I suspected I would experience other upsets and undoings along the way. C'est la Guerre.

Acknowledgments

I would like to thank my family for sticking with me through the long process of creating this book, especially my husband, Robert Habiger, for his support and encouragement. I am also indebted to Geoff Gentillini of Golden Arrow Research for research assistance and to John Cornish, Elissa Dente and other readers, Kirt Hickman and Geoff Habiger for their guidance and assistance in editing my writing.

About the Author

Like many of her generation, Lynn Doxon knew her father had served in World War II, but he seldom talked about it. As she began researching genealogy and family stories, she wanted to know more. What she learned led her to write this novel. Although it is a work of fiction it generally follows her father's experience in the early years of the war. This and the two books to follow tell the story of many of that generation, now known as the Greatest Generation.

After years of non-fiction writing, this is Lynn's first full-length novel, although she has many works planned to follow this one.

Lynn lives in the midst of an Urban Food Forest in Uptown Albuquerque with her husband, 97-year-old mother, the three youngest of her six children, and a large collection of animals.